ALSO BY GLORIANNA SERBIN

Wheatlander: the Secret
One Small Angel

Wheatlander
the Revelations

the unraveling of the Wheatlander Secret

This is the continuing story about Mathilda Barlow Millering,
still sassy, bold, and brassy, but always a lady.

Her love for others stretched further than she ever imagined;
going to places she never intended.

That was her destiny.

Her legacy continues…

Glorianna Serbin

Published by
Inki-Link Press
Inkilinkpress@gmail.com

ISBN-10: 0-9895389-5-8
ISBN-13: 978-0-9895389-5-4
Printed in the United States of America

First Edition: September 2016

Cover Design ©   Glorianna Serbin
Cover Photo ©   Glorianna Serbin

This is a fictitious work.
All characters in this book have no existence outside the imagination of the author and have no relation whatsoever to anyone bearing the same name or names. They are not even distantly inspired by any individual known or unknown to the author, and all incidents are pure invention. Although the setting is mid-nineteen hundreds, it was not the intention of the author to write an historical book, except in mentioning certain places known to the author in Chicago, Illinois. All towns and names of places mentioned in Indiana are absolutely fictitious places.

Dedicated to my husband, Andy,
my forever love

Wheatlander

the Revelations

Glorianna Serbin

PROLOGUE

Yellow fear and panic gripped Henry's belly as he ran like a crazy man; knees shaking, weak and washy, all the while crying "no," over and over as he examined the kernels—pinching the grain in his fingers and dredging at the once healthy stalks of wheat. Aunt Mattie's golden crops were turning sickly black right before his eyes.

Henry drove to Mayette as a man possessed. He had to tell the owner, Mathilda Millering, his great sin and he had to tell her immediately. His heart dropped, because losing her crops was not the first time he failed this lady, this grand lady he now called Aunt Mattie—the very first time was as her late husband's illegitimate son.

The agony was unbearable as the incessant "if-only" thoughts flew through his head one after another tormenting him, striking at his manhood and pride. The grim reaper was having its way, eating, and ravishing every single healthy grain of wheat with stem rust fungus—consuming every penny of his yearly wages and breaking the promise for Auntie's purse! And if all that were not enough, he couldn't even pray.

Henry would never forget that day. It was Thursday, the eighteenth day of July, 1957

Glorianna Serbin

CHAPTER ONE

Mathilda climbed the ten concrete stairs to the Saint Gregory's Orphanage door. She hit the brass knocker two times and waited for someone to answer. It was only a moment before the heavy wooden door opened and she was greeted by the soft but cheerful voice of Sister Marie.

"Good Morning, Mrs. Millering, please come in. Father John is already meeting with someone, but you're welcome to wait."

"Thank you, Sister Marie, I guess I am a little early. The others should be here soon—at eight-thirty sharp."

"I just came down, so I don't know with whom he's meeting—it must be important though…it's so early."

The two women walked down the long hall together. Sister Marie in a floor-length black habit, veil, and silent black oxford shoes, and Mathilda, in a knee-length gray tweed suit, white blouse, perky matching hat, and white gloves. She had on much higher heels than Sister Marie, and they clicked loudly with every step against the highly polished marble floor. Prepared to wait for the others to arrive—two school board members and her fiance, Attorney Thomas Bealer, the priest's brother, she sat down on the cold bench next to Father John's office while the little nun graciously excused herself and went about her duties.

While sitting there, Mathilda couldn't help but recall that first time she entered this hall—this magnificent entryway into an unknown Catholic sanctuary where the priests wore long dresses and the women called nuns, wore them too. It was hard to believe it was almost four years ago that Henry prayed and laid his fiery hands on her painful ankle and leg, healing them and her deep despondency. The very next day was the first time in many months that Mathilda felt completely well, physically, and mentally, and that was the day she decided to visit this orphan home looking for a ten-year old boy named, Dudley Best. The boy had shared the green park bench, directly across the street from her house all the while she was too ill to do anything else. He intently listened to Miss Sally practice before her students arrived, while Mathilda just sat in the calming sunshine, resting. But suddenly, the boy didn't come to the bench anymore and she thought that he might be ill or maybe something had happened to him. Worried about this little fellow, and since she felt wonderfully well, she decided to walk the two blocks to inquire about him. She remembered it well, including her first meeting with the Reverend John Bealer, the same man she was meeting with this morning.

The church, school, and orphanage were unfamiliar places for her, since she knew nothing at all about Catholics. Friends warned her to stay away because they believed in all sorts of things, such as praying to statues of dead saints and telling one's sins to a priest. *I'd never tell my sins to anyone,* she thought as she sat there, and she set Father John straight on that when they first met. And now, just as that first time she entered this building, the lifelike man hanging on that crucifix at the end of the corridor caught her attention and struck her tender heart again. Soft light from the window was falling on the figure of Jesus, revealing the horrible criminal's death he had endured.

Sinking into the absolute silence, she began rehearsing the exact words and ideas she had been thinking about even before her unfortunate crop loss—until she suddenly heard men's voices sounding like a dispute or an argument, muted, but soon becoming quite loud.

4

Because the door to the office was slightly ajar, she could hear their words distinctly, echoing against the impenetrable stone floor, forcing their way into her hearing and understanding.

"What's the problem anyway? You've kept Mathilda—Mattie dangling for such a long time, I thought you were getting married last year?"

"I know, but what if she finds out that I'm not the great person she believes me to be?"

"Nobody is the person someone else perceives them to be, because they can only judge from the outside. However, Tom, we know the truth about ourselves, don't we?" Father John was very pointed—almost rude.

"Yes, and I'm afraid that once she marries me…she'd be disappointed. After all, my dead wife wasn't that crazy about me while she was alive. As you know, I have a lot of shortcomings."

"How well I know." Father John answered his brother—again sarcastically. "So, how long can you keep her in the state of limbo? She loves you…you know that, don't you?"

"I'm not too sure, Mattie's a secure lady and I'm thinking that she likes her life exactly the way it is, but why should you care? It's none of your business. Why not keep your nose on your own church work, and leave me—us alone?"

"She deserves better, Tom, she's had her life intertwined with our family for some time now. First, with our nephew Dudley…ever since he was eight years old, our parents, our sister and us. And you know she's always giving."

"I know…and we're always taking…right?"

"Even now she has an idea about the orphanage and wants to present something in the line of a donation. I'm not exactly sure what it is, but it's important enough that she would want to meet with us and the church board. That should mean something to you!"

It was as though Father John was begging for some sort of explanation.

"So what can I do—or say to her? I'm not ready to get married at this point of my life, and that's all there is to it."

"That's what I thought—so you should tell her and tell her soon. She's probably waiting for you, and all you do is lead her on."

"Hey, you sound like you care!" Tommy shouted in anger, forgetting where he was and that he might be overheard.

"I do care. I see a caring woman being taken advantage of—by my own brother, and I don't like it one bit." Father John's voice was rather subdued compared to his brother's childish temper tantrum.

"What else, Johnny? What else are you feeling? Are you maybe a little jealous? Is that what's eating at you? Maybe you want Mattie for yourself? Is that it?" Tommy was shouting again.

CHAPTER TWO

A blood-red hot-flush slowly spread up from Mathilda's spine to her shocked and dismayed face—with each word reverberating into her ears. Glancing up at the wounded Jesus on that cross, all the broken memories about her dead husband, Henry, came flooding back as though a dam had burst. She stifled the unexpected cry when she thought—*Jesus was betrayed for all humanity, but my Henry betrayed our marriage vows for black dirt and a promise! And now I've been ready and waiting for Tommy's proposal and...and...there has to be something terribly wrong with me to have Henry turn to another woman and for Tommy to change his mind about me too, saying I'm a secure lady, liking my life exactly as it is!*

Quickly, she removed her heeled shoes, picked up her purse and half-ran down the hall taking care not to fall on the highly polished floor. Flinging open the wooden door, she found herself at the top of the concrete stairs. Slipping her feet into one shoe first and then the other, she hurriedly brushed past the two gentlemen ready to climb the stairs. They were dressed in dark suits, ties and black shiny shoes, each holding fat briefcases.

"Pardon me," they each said as they stepped aside to let the distraught women by.

They're probably going to the meeting, she thought, *but I can't do anything about that now—I'll have to deal with it later.*

Every step Mathilda took toward home, she became more and more upset. Angry and hurt at Tommy for playing her along all those years, saying he loved her, and at Father John for putting him on the spot.

She opened the back porch door quietly and entered the kitchen, glad no one was there. Dropping her purse on the table and walking directly into the pantry, she picked up the everyday white dinner plates off the lower shelf. Grasping and holding them in her left arm, she threw them one by one against the floor with all her might—smashing her deep disappointment about marriage to Tommy, into thousands of pieces. The cups and saucers were next, and then the large platters, and every other breakable dish she could find. She was crying loudly and her eyes were stinging, as though she had been attacked by some plant sucking aphids.

The turmoil brought Sadie to the pantry door, watching, waiting, not knowing what to do, and then Booker T. came running up from the basement, his fourteen year old black face fast turning ashen when he saw shards of white glass covering the entire pantry floor.

"What's wrong, Aunt Mattie? Somethin' I did? I'm sorry if I did somethin' bad. Please don't throw any more dishes, ma'am."

Booker T. was crying almost as hard as Mathilda. When she heard the boy's sobs and saw Sadie wringing her apron, she stopped before throwing the last round bowl. She could hardly believe that it was she who displayed such outrageous behavior.

"Oh, my, I am feeling just a little woozy."

"A little woozy?" Booker T. said. "Here, let's go in the kitchen so you kin sit down at the table and have some hot tea." He put out his arm for her to hold as he guided her to one of the kitchen chairs.

"Miss Sadie has the kettle boiling…it's all ready."

"Thank you, Booker T. You're very kind to an old lady."

"Old—who say you old?"

"Now Booker T., please speak properly. I've told you time and time again to…"

"Yes ma'am, I'm sorry, ma'am." He poured the boiling water over the tea bag he placed into Aunt Mattie's lone cup that escaped the convulsion because it was still sitting next to the sink, on the drainboard.

The stunned Sadie finally got her voice, "What's the matter, Mrs. Mathilda, are you ill?"

"Yes, that's right. I'm feeling a little afflicted. After I drink my tea, I think I'll go up and rest for a while."

"What about your meeting with Father John and the board?" Sadie asked hesitantly, not knowing whether she should ask because it might stir something up—again.

"If Aunt Mattie is sick, I kin run over and tell them," Booker T. offered.

"Oh—Booker T., could you please do that for me? I would appreciate it so much. Just tell them that I'm not up to meeting with them today."

To make the point perfectly clear Mathilda repeated her words. "You don't have to tell them any more than that...do you understand?"

"Yes ma'am, I'll do it right now. I'll ride my bike over so I kin get there faster, but should I change my clothes, ma'am? I'm work-ing in the basement in these," he said, pointing to his dusty old shirt and pants that had more than a few patches.

"No, just go. And remember, don't tell them anything more. Say that I'm just a little under the weather."

"Yes ma'am, I will."

After Booker T. left, Sadie seeing all Mathilda's normal rosy color drained right out, used a cold damp cloth to bathe her forehead and face.

"That must have been some meeting you went to early this morning," Sadie muttered to herself not wanting Mathilda to actual-ly hear. Now Sadie was a trusted friend as well as this lady's housekeeper and cook, and she knew her well enough to know that this was unusual behavior. Something was very wrong!

CHAPTER THREE

Booker T. jumped on his bike and peddled as fast as he could the two and a half blocks to the school. He knew the way all too well since at ten years of age, he attended St. Gregory's Grade School when he first moved in with Mathilda. Booker T. even got in the habit of calling Mathilda his Aunt Mattie, just as his friend Dudley Best did. However, she wasn't Dudley's real aunt either. Usually, Booker T. rode around the block and down another street so he wouldn't be harassed by the three white boys who lived close to the school and church. Those boys now attended the same high school as Booker T. and they usually threw whatever they could find in the gutter at him, and warned him repeatedly about using their street or their sidewalk. But today, he didn't have time for that kind of safety, so he just sped to the red brick building, dropping his bike at the bottom of the concrete stairs and running up all ten. Then he pounded hard on the front door. It took a few minutes before someone answered.

"Why, Booker, is there something wrong?" Thomas Bealer asked, noticing right away that the boy was breathing heavily and wearing grungy clothes. Bealer repeated his question again but still had a hard time understanding exactly what the youngster was saying.

"Aunt Mattie can't come. She be sick, sir. She wants me ta tell ya, so now I gotta go," he shouted, and then quickly turned to leave.

Booker T. didn't want to be asked any more questions, since he knew he already messed up on how he was speaking. He said everything wrong, and Aunt Mattie would have been mortified if she heard him speak that way. Thomas was surprised too but didn't say anything except he would tell Father John and the two board members. He didn't mention that they were impatiently waiting for her.

As Booker T. was running down the stairs, Thomas called down to him …

"Tell her I'm sorry she doesn't feel well and I'll look in on her later today, okay?"

"Yes sir, I'll tell her." He jumped on his bike and rode off down the same route, forgetting the danger.

A two minute bike ride was all Booker T. needed to get safely home, but the three white boys he worried about spotted him as he left the orphanage. They were on the other side of the street, waiting—probably for a ride, but not to go to school because today was Saturday.

As usual, they decided to have some fun teasing Booker T. by throwing small stones at him and his bike tires. They did it quick before he would be out of range. One sharp blow hit Booker on the side of his left eye, then another hit the spokes of his front wheel. Down he went, hitting his head against the curb and twisting his side while trying to catch his fall. He was a little stunned. One of the boys, Nathanial Marsh, started walking across the street to where Booker T. had fallen.

"Hey, guys," he yelled as he neared Booker T. "Here's somebody on our turf. I think he needs his mama."

CHAPTER FOUR

Booker T. could hear the other two voices screeching with laughter. Who knows what would have happened if a man in the four-door Chevrolet hadn't stopped. Marsh ran back to the other side as a green sedan pulled over and picked up all three boys. They were gone in a flash, but Booker T. still sat where he had fallen, first rubbing his head, and then picking small peaces of dirt out of the palms of his hands. He held his side with his left hand as he pushed himself up.

The tall Negro man wearing sharply creased beige trousers, with a matching vest over a white long sleeved shirt and loosened tie, hurried out of his car to where Booker T. was trying to get his balance.

"You boy, are you okay?" he asked with a worried smile. He had a little black leather bag in his left hand as he approached the boy.

"Yeah, I guess so. I don't know—my forehead stings."

"Here young man, let me help you. I'm a doctor," he said as he began to help brush the dirt off the sleeves of Booker's torn shirt and then his pants. "Do you live around here?"

"Yes sir, I live a couple of blocks over that way." He pointed toward his house across from the little park.

"Well, lets put your bike in my trunk and I'll drive you home. I can fix that cut over your eye at your house, okay?"

"Well...I guess so." Booker T. pulled the dust cloth out of his back pocket to catch the blood that was now oozing down his face, but before he was able to touch the wound, the doctor spoke.

"Here, use my handkerchief for that...you don't want to put that dirty rag on an open wound."

"Thank you, sir." Booker took the white handkerchief, folded it into a square and held it on the stinging area to catch the blood.

Opening his trunk, the doctor slid the bike in and then opened the passenger side for Booker T. He noticed that the boy was poorly dressed and thought that he probably lived in one of the older homes a couple of blocks away, but definitely not where the boy was pointing in this more affluent neighborhood.

Booker T. walked slowly to the car holding his side. As he got in the man quickly scooped his suit jacket off the front seat and threw it to the back. Then he put his hand out and introduced himself.

"I'm Doctor James and I was just passing after a house call."

Booker T. took his hand and shook it with the greeting the doctor was expecting. "My name is Booker T. Fraze."

"Good to meet you, Booker T. Fraze. Now tell me, which house do you live in?" He began driving slowly in the direction that was pointed out.

"Right there, sir. I live there...you can drive around the back and I'll put my bike in the carriage house...and you don't have to treat me, because I'll be okay now that I'm home."

"I don't know Booker T. That's a mighty fancy house. Are you sure you aren't joshing me?" he asked. "Come on, tell me, where do you really live?"

The house Booker T. was pointing out was the little mansion Mathilda bought and opened as a refuge for widows the year after her Henry died.

The likes of this boy wouldn't be living here.

Anyway that's what Doctor James believed, but he was very kind, and didn't want to say anymore about it and hurt the boy's feelings.

"Why don't we drive over to my office, I can fix your eye, look at that bump on your head, and then I'll drive you home."

"I don't know. I was supposed to come right home after stopping at the orphanage. I'm cleaning the basement today and I don't think I should bother my Aunt Mattie, 'cause she isn't feeling very well."

Booker T. felt very uncomfortable trying to make that kind of decision.

"You live here with your Aunt Mattie?"

"Yes, sir, I do…I mean I do live here."

"I'm sure she would want you to be looked at, after that nasty fall. Don't you think so?"

"Maybe, but I just don't know. Nothin' like this ever happened before, except when me and my friend Dudley had our fingers broken while we played the piano at a music conservatory. Then we had to have x-rays, but we were okay after that."

"What hospital were you in?"

"It was long time ago when I was just a kid. It was in Chicago. Please, I have to go in." Booker T. opened the door and jumped out still holding the handkerchief on the cut over his eye.

He half-ran, half-walked as fast as he could across the street and up the front steps. Upon opening the front door, he bumped into Sadie who was about to open it for him. Meanwhile, Doctor James followed the boy, leaving his car parked directly across the street at the park.

"Hello, ma'am," he said when he saw Sadie. But he was still thinking, *that boy's going to get in a heap o'trouble for sure from this woman!*

"Yes, hello…I see that you brought Booker T. home. What happened?"

"Oh, Miss Sadie," Booker T. interrupted, "those guys were after me again, and look, I got a bump on my head and a cut above my eye. Look, can you see it?" He kept pointing as if she couldn't see the wound with oozing blood on the handkerchief. "And this Doctor James helped me. I gotta go up and wash." And off he went, through the front hall, kind of limping up the stairs, and not taking his usual two steps at a time.

"Doctor James…well thank you for your help."

"I'm glad I was there when the boy fell. I heard him call you Miss Sadie. Then you're not Aunt Mattie, are you?" he asked, grinning at his mistake in sizing things up.

"No I'm not. Mrs. Mathilda—Mattie isn't feeling well today."

"That's what the boy said. Where can I put his bike, Miss Sadie? It's in the trunk of my car."

"Oh, if you could just put it out back, Booker T. will take care of it as soon as he comes down."

Doctor James drove to the back of the house, removed the bike from his trunk, and leaned it against the building that Booker T. called the carriage house. *Some carriage house,* he thought. *And I thought the boy didn't live here!* But before he could get back in his car, Sadie called to him from the back porch.

"Would you like to come in for a cup of tea? I want to thank you for helping Booker T. and I know Mrs. Mathilda will be very pleased to hear about it. "

"Why yes, ma'am, I would be delighted. I had an early morning call today and I skipped my usual cup of coffee."

"Well, my goodness, I'll just make a pot of coffee instead of tea, it's no trouble at all. Please have a seat and make yourself comfortable."

Setting a place for the man, Sadie put out their last two Danish and found a fancy cup and saucer from the good china buffet. Since Mathilda destroyed the everyday white dishes earlier in the day, there weren't any others to use. The doctor was mildly flattered when he saw the fancy way she set the table for him. Of course, he didn't know the circumstances that prompted Miss Sadie in doing so.

Booker T. took a quick shower and then dressed in his good jeans, a solid blue shirt and a button-down, dark blue sweater. On the side of his eye, he put a clean piece of gauze to catch the blood and covered it with adhesive tape. Then he tried to hurry down the stairs to see how Aunt Mattie was doing, but he had to hold the rail with one hand and his hurting hip with the other. Doctor James was sitting at the table chatting with Miss Sadie.

"Oh, I didn't know you were still here, Doctor James," Booker T. said pleased to see him. "Thank you again for helping me. I guess I was pretty upset." Booker T. spoke more fluently now that he had calmed down, and was able to imitate how Aunt Mattie would speak to the doctor.

"Come sit, Booker T," Sadie said, "and I'll fix you some hot cocoa. Were you able to give the message to Father John?"

"Mr. Tommy answered the door, so I just told him. He said he would stop and see Aunt Mattie later today. I didn't say anything more. I didn't say yes, and I didn't say no."

"Thank you for going so promptly, We could have called over on the phone, but I guess we were too rattled to think of it."

"How's the bump on your head?" Doctor James asked.

"It's okay, kind of big, but okay. Only, the cut over my eye keeps oozing under my bandage." Booker T. continued to dab at it with the same handkerchief the doctor had given him. "I think I twisted my side too 'cause it hurts when I walk or do the stairs."

"By the looks of that cut, you may need a couple of stitches to stop the bleeding. I can do that for you, Booker T."

"Oh, it'll stop by itself, no need for that." He was deathly afraid of needles and the mention of sewing his skin together was something he wanted to avoid at all costs.

"Where do you go to school?"

"I go to the Mayette High School, sir."

"Any problems there?"

"Sometimes…like today. There's this one guy—they call him Nate—Nathanial Marsh. He calls me names and does other stuff just about every day. Aunt Mattie says not to pay him any mind…but… it's hard not to punch him up real good."

"I know exactly what you mean, Booker. I do know that feeling. But don't give up. One of these days, things are bound to change." Dr. James took his last gulp of coffee while wiping his chin from that second delicious Danish.

"Thank you, Miss Sadie. I must get going. I have some calls that must be attended to, and as long as this youngster is okay, I'll say goodbye."

"Thanks again, Doctor. But please write down your address and phone number for us. Just in case Mrs. Mathilda will ask where you live."

CHAPTER FIVE

A whole week had passed but nothing changed for Henry. He couldn't sleep and was constantly tormented by his failure. When Henry first started working the Wheatlander farm, he had counted on Andrew Crowper, called Crow by the townsfolk, for advice and training. Crow knew everything about the land and Henry believed with certainty that this blight would not have happened if Crow were still alive. Now, Henry needed bold courage to carry forward but couldn't find it within himself because he was as a child again, crying and chastising himself for not catching the blight sooner, and even for changing Crow's corn acres into wheat—only to die.

He and Catherine sat at the breakfast table that morning with their three-and-one-half-year-old twins, Henry and Andrew.

"Daddy?" little Henry asked. "Can we go to town with you to see Aunt Mattie today?"

"Yeah, we wanna to play with Booker T. and Dudley. They always tease us, and we have fun with them," Andrew chimed in.

"Well, I don't think I'm going today, boys. Booker T. has a few chores that Aunt Mattie wants him to finish so he won't be able to play with you, and Dudley is at his mother's house."

"But you never take us any more," Andrew whined.

"And you're always too tired, or busy or…sad, Daddy," little Henry added.

"Are you going to spend another day in your study?" Catherine wanted to know. "It's already Saturday and you've been locked in there every day this week."

"I know. I know. But I'm trying to pray again. I can't seem to do it as I used to—not for others or even for our own problems. I can't hear God no matter how hard I try. Yesterday, I was remembering the Christmas Party before Crow died, over four years ago. Remember Catherine? That day it was warm and balmy and misting rain. I believed the crops were ruined but Crow, seeing how worried I was, assured me all would be well, and it was. I wish now, with all my might, that I could have Crow's thoughts on what happened this year. What I could have done better, or if I did something terribly wrong. I know I worked the land exactly as I was taught—rotating and resting the fields. It should have brought in a very fine harvest."

"He might have been able to tell you, but maybe not, maybe it just happened and it would have happened even if he were here," Catherine said, trying to soften his shame and raging guilt.

"Catherine, when I saw how the wheat took on that golden glow of ripeness, I was already patting myself on the back because I did so well this year with the crop. Even waiting for that week long rain to stop didn't worry me, nor that hot peppered sun that followed. The night before the harvest as I checked the kernels, a balmy wind was blowing that wheat as though it was a huge sea—swells of golden grain waved and crested clear to the back of Auntie's acres. Catherine, it was so beautiful!"

"Henry, no one was able to do anything, don't you know that? Why won't you listen. Other farms in our area lost their crops too!"

"I was prideful. Full of pride about how well I did. And how it would be a lavish crop for Aunt Mattie's purse. She would be so proud of me...and then...it was all gone. I couldn't do anything...to save any of it." Henry's hands went up and out, showing how it all disappeared into the air.

"But you need to talk to Aunt Mattie again, and I mean *really* talk. She needs to know how you're feeling…that you're so depressed."

"Were we at the Christmas party, Daddy?" little Henry wanted to know. "I don't remember it very well."

"I don't remember it either. Did we really have a crow bird, Daddy?" Andrew asked with wide eyes.

"Well, Crow was really Mr. Andrew Crowper and we named you after that fine gentleman who used to own this very house that we live in," Catherine explained to the boys.

"How come you didn't name me after a fine gentleman?" Henry asked.

"Henry Millering! You were named after a fine gentleman. You're named after your father!" Catherine reminded him.

"Oh, yeah, I forgot," little Henry said.

Henry wasn't even listening to the boys, and proceeded to answer Catherine's question.

"Soon, I'll talk to her…soon. You know, when I told her about the ruined wheat she wasn't very upset, which makes me feel even worse. She should have been angry at me—at God—at the weather! I think her only concern was for the others who also lost their crops."

"And why should she have been angry? Think, Henry. Nothing could have been done to prevent it. As I told you…it just happened."

"Just give me some time. Why don't you take the boys, pick up your mother and go shopping or something. I need the house to be quiet for a couple of hours. What do you say, Kats. Do you think you could do that for me?"

Whenever Henry used his pet name for Catherine, she knew he was serious. She also knew for certain that if he could pray, he would be his old self again.

"Okay, boys. Let's get ready to see grandma. We'll have a nice, fun day."

"Can we take Donny with us too?" little Henry asked.

"Yes, but we'll have to stop and ask Mrs. Mary Beth."

Little Henry and Andrew's mood brightened. A day of games with Donny and Grandma seemed better than waiting for their daddy to play with them. Lately, he didn't have much time and they missed the funny faces he made at them because now, he looked sad all the time.

Donny was a year older than the twins and they played together almost everyday. Jesse, Donny's father, was one of the first hired hands on Wheatlander farm. He worked there as a youngster while Mathilda's husband, Henry Senior, still farmed all the acres. Now the three of them, Donny and his parents lived in Mathilda's farmhouse after she moved to a new home in Mayette, just about seven miles north of Mayetteville. Everyone called her new home the little mansion. It was large with Victorian architecture and a windowed four-sided cupola crowning the roof. Without delay, it had been turned into a rooming house for ladies without means.

Jesse bought a chestnut filly, that all three boys thought to be the most wonderful horse in the world. He named her, Lil Peaches—the same name Mathilda called her own horse, bought as a birthday present by her late husband. Jesse remembered how much Mathilda loved her. She sewed pretty bonnets for that horse and gave the children rides whenever she went to town. But Jesse's most treasured memories were the lunches and fresh lemonade Mathilda had prepared from the cold deep well and brought to the fields where he and the men were working and sweating in the intense heat. He was always glad to see her coming down the lane, Lil Peaches pulling that little cart with two large baskets tucked snugly beside ice-cold water swishing within large shiny milk cans. There was always plenty of water for the men to pour over their steaming heads, bringing relief from the red-hot, poker sun.

Mary Beth didn't sew bonnets for the new Lil Peaches, but when she went to town with Donny and the twins, she gave rides to the other children crowding around when they saw that high stepping little filly trotting down the road.

* * *

During Henry's prayer time, after Catherine and the children left, he felt the pressure of being a father to his two little ones, and husband to his beautiful wife, Catherine. They were all counting on him but he was only a man, a man completely defeated by wind, rain and disease. As far as he knew, all his prayers fell on God's deaf ears. Why? Why couldn't he pray the way he used to—with fire and assurance? Even the healing spark was gone from his hands. Everything vanished, stolen so quickly. It was as though it never existed, nothing more than some vain unreality he believed in for a time.

CHAPTER SIX

After hearing the private conversation of Father John and Tommy Bealer, and after the turmoil of breaking her everyday dishes, Mathilda was resting on her bed trying to put everything that happened in some kind of perspective. Sometimes she felt consumed by how unjust her life had been after Henry's death. She was strong, but how long could she continue to turn the other cheek to constant disappointments? Now, Tommy was reneging on all the shared plans they made together over the last few years.

Why would he suddenly think I was so independent? she asked herself again. *Do I put on airs, or is there something inside me that is overbearing toward others? Maybe he felt it and is reluctant to live that way.*

But then she remembered Crow, who had truly wanted to marry her. He didn't think she was overbearing—at least, he never said so. Poor, dear Crow, who died so suddenly on that Christmas night. His burial was only a few days later, during a fierce winter storm—the worst Mathilda had ever seen. Not even twenty-four hours had passed since she decided to marry, and he was taken from her and laid to rest in the church cemetery—beside his first wife. The headstone read: Andrew Crowper, 1902-1954, beloved husband of Margie. Crow was the beloved of Mathilda too, but her name couldn't be mentioned!

Still lying on her bed, her memories galloped and she could see Crow's whole funeral scene again. She was standing there, in the cemetery facing the casket and feeling guilty about the gift—the love-necklace Crow gave to her, and their passionate embraces on that last Christmas night, only hours before he died. Because Margie was Mathilda's close friend ever since childhood, she couldn't help that her aroused feelings for Crow had seemed almost like cheating and adulterous. And now, so many years later, Mathilda could still feel that old twinge of guilt even while she heard, as clear as day, young Henry's voice bellow over the short blasts of raging wind, as he read the comforting Scriptures.

"I am the Resurrection and the Life. He that believeth in me, yea, though he were dead, yet he shall live."

A shiver went through her as she felt those same piercing winds stinging at her legs and uncovered head. Instinctively she pulled the end of the bedspread over her head and shoulders, trying to warm herself.

The memory continued. Bessie, who believed she and Crow would have been married in early Spring, was standing between Mathilda and Sadie. They held her tight, thinking she could faint and fall into one of the snow drifts or worse, onto the coffin. Catherine stood next to Henry and Miss Sally along with the others from the rooming house. Maxine, her Mister and Father John were there too—all huddled together, because only a small area of snow had been cleared for the burial. After the scriptures, Father John blessed the casket and the earth. Before they lowered Crow into the ground Henry gave a very short talk mentioning how he personally would miss his beloved mentor and friend whom he loved. Everyone was crying as Henry spoke of this love and then it was time to go.

Bessie began wailing—that it was dreadful to leave her beloved Crow there all alone in the cold with huge snow drifts mounding over the gravestones. Mathilda, Henry and Father John had to coax her and then practically drag her from the grave site because she refused to leave.

Right from the beginning, when Bessie first moved into the rooming house, she was jealous of Mathilda's long friendship with Crow and his deep regard for her. Sometimes Bessie thought that Crow loved Mathilda, but Crow assured her that it wasn't true, at least not the kind of love Bessie was talking about, because Mathilda called it a brother-sister-love—only better. However, Mathilda felt sorry for Bessie and the pain she endured by her deep lost love—the same grief she herself bore. It was then that she decided to never…not ever…tell Bessie about the necklace, the letter, or the last evening she and Crow spent together. What good would it do?

Mathilda's late husband Henry, was buried just a few feet away, but she didn't look in that direction—not even once, because he had deceived her. He loved his land more than his faithful wife.

"Are you awake?" Sadie asked as she knocked lightly on the door, breaking the spell Mathilda was under.

"Yes, I'm awake. Did you need me for something?"

"Well, yes…I thought I should tell you about Booker T. Are you coming down soon?"

"I'll be down directly, Sadie."

That knock on the door had shaken Mathilda awake and fully alert. *Enough of this,* she thought as she got up from the bed where she had been brooding and looked at herself in the dresser mirror.

I'm not going to think about this nonsense any longer. I'm tired of living in the past. It's time to go forward and not worry about the motives of others.

She looked even closer and began combing her hair and straightening her clothes so she would look presentable.

I have Booker T. to look after and also Dudley. So what if someone is having doubts. I've had enough of my own, and Crow said he felt every bit as confused with my indecision as I do now, so…Tom-

my will have to work through his own problems. I'll do what I have to do, and he'll have to do what he has to do.

As Mathilda entered the kitchen, she began by apologizing. "I'm sorry, Sadie, and you too, Booker T. I'm sorry for acting like a child and breaking all our dishes."

"Are you okay, ma'am?" Booker T. asked a little hesitantly, not knowing just what to expect.

"Yes. I'm not going to dwell on anything more than getting you through school and on your way to a better life. I promise you that we're going to make it. You will be somebody in this world, and we'll do it together."

Mathilda said this while looking closely at Booker's face. He was almost a man, a little taller now, and older than the ten-year old that she came to love, but still the same Booker T.

"You have a bandage on your forehead?"

"That's what I wanted to tell you about," Sadie said. "Booker T. had a little happening this morning after he left the orphanage."

"I see…is it painful?" Mathilda noticed the adhesive tape with the gauze underneath. Dried blood had seeped through and now stuck to the outside of the tape.

"Not any more, ma'am. What do you mean, 'we're going to make it?'"

"She means that she's going to help you all she can so you can get a good education and make something of yourself," Sadie explained. "You should be able to understand that."

"That's right. That's exactly what I mean. Now tell me, how did you get hurt?"

"Well, those three guys were after me again and threw stones. I fell, but then a doctor stopped and drove me home. It was Doctor James and he was real nice…but, he didn't believe that I lived here!"

"I made him some coffee and he ate all our Danish rolls, all two of them," Sadie said with a broad grin, and then she told Mathilda the whole story.

"I would've liked to have met that man. Where does he live?"

"I knew you would ask and here's his name and address." Sadie handed Mathilda the paper on which Dr. James had written the information.

"I told Mr. Tommy that you weren't feeling very well," Booker T. added. "And he said he would stop to see you later today."

"That's fine, Booker T. Thank you for going so promptly. And you certainly look nice! Are you going somewhere?"

"No, ma'am. I changed my clothes when the doctor brought me home. I was pretty dirty from cleaning the basement and then falling, and I wanted to see whether I had any bruises, so I took a shower."

"And...do you have any bruises?"

"Just a few besides the bump on my head; I have one on my hip where I hit the pavement and one on my elbow...see?" Booker said as he pulled up his sweater and shirt sleeve.

Just then, Dudley walked into the kitchen where all the conversation was going on. "Hi everyone."

"Why Dudley Best, how good to see you," Mathilda said, surprised by his appearance.

"I let myself in. The front door was unlocked."

"Hi, man," Booker T. said as they punched each other on their arms. They'd been friends—it seemed forever but now, as they got older, it became increasingly difficult because Dudley's new friends couldn't see why he would want to associate with *that* kid. All Dudley ever wanted was to be accepted, but he wasn't strong enough to go against the guys, so now he made it a point to keep his distance from Booker T., except at Aunt Mattie's house, because there, he could be himself and no one else would have to know that Booker T. was his very best friend.

"Hi, man," Dudley answered, looking Booker T. up and down. "What are ya up ta? Ya look like your all dressed up and going somewhere."

"Nope, not going anywhere, just had to clean up."

"Hey, ya got a cut or somethin' on your eye." Dudley was looking at the bandage and tape. "Who did you in, man?"

"Just what we were talking about when you walked in, Dudley," Mathilda said.

"It's nothing," Booker T. replied, picturing the doctor stitching in such a sensitive area.

"Yeah, well, I need to talk to you, Aunt Mattie. I mean alone and I'm in kind of a hurry."

"Sounds serious, man," Booker teased.

"Do you mind, Aunt Mattie? Could we go up in your little room, you know, upstairs?"

"Oh, sure we can. You're having a problem, Dudley?" she asked, as she quickly turned and left the room with him trailing behind.

"Kind of." Dudley was rolling his eyes to the ceiling and then looking back at Booker T. to see whether he caught his nonchalant gesture. Sadie read his flippant behavior and just pursed her lips.

CHAPTER SEVEN

"Are you sick, Dudley?" Mathilda asked, noticing the way Dudley clutched his jacket close. "I mean you act as though you're cold. Maybe you're coming down with something?" She sat down on one of the comfortable wing chairs, waiting for him to begin.

"No, I'm not sick, but you're the only one I can tell, Aunt Mattie." He sat down on the edge of the other chair in that sunny room—a cupola it was called. His voice was shaking now and he didn't sound so self assured and flippant as he did in front of Sadie and Booker T.

"Well, you know you can tell me anything." Mathilda tried to reassure Dudley. "And you know I can keep a confidence."

"I know that, and that's why I came. But I don't know where to start." His fingers were running up and down his jacket's zipper and then through his hair.

"Come on, Dudley, I can't help you if you don't trust me."

"Well, I do trust you, Aunt Mattie, but this is different. I'm in so much trouble that you won't believe it."

"Try me—that's all you can do—or go to your mother. Wouldn't that be a better thing to do if it's that serious?" Aunt Mattie cautioned, becoming a little frightened at what she might hear.

"Ya don't understand. My mom can't help me. She's not as strong as you, Aunt Mattie. She is nothing like you—nothing at all!"

"I'm sure you're wrong. Your mother loves you and would do anything for you. And so would your two uncles, Tommy and Father John."

"Okay...here it is...I think I'll be going to jail, just as soon as the police find me, and my mother won't know how to deal with it. She probably doesn't care anyway 'cause she says I'm a bad influence on my brother and sister, Paddy and Annie."

The blood drained from Mathilda's face. She turned a deathly pale as she inched forward in her chair, making sure she wouldn't miss a word Dudley was mumbling.

"Tell me Dudley, why would you go to jail? Speak up so I can hear you plainly."

Dudley started to cry. He ran over to Aunt Mattie, knelt down next to where she was sitting and put his head against her lap. Suddenly, his fifteen years melted away and he was a small child again. He felt helpless, but thought she could save him, if she wanted to.

"I'm sorry, so very sorry I got involved with those guys." Now, he was looking up at her with tearful eyes. "They said that if I tell the police anything, they'd get me...and they will, too."

"Get you...what do you mean, get you?"

"You know, rub me out. They've done it before to other guys."

Now, Mathilda pushed his head away from her so she could look into his eyes.

"What did you do, Dudley Best? Tell me this instant and stop all the crying so I can understand everything you're saying."

Dudley wiped his eyes with the back of his hand.

"Well, our guys had a fight with some other guys. They live on the other side of town. Well, things got all mixed up and one of our guys pulled a knife and then he was...dead...Rudy was dead! He was all bloody, and now the police are looking for all of us that were there during the fight." Dudley wiped his nose and eyes again, this time with a napkin he had grabbed from the little table. He then took another and put them both in his pants pocket.

"Do you have a knife?" Mattie asked very calmly.

"Yeah, we all have knives."

"And were you the one who stabbed this boy, Rudy?" she asked, hoping with all her heart he wasn't, but knowing that she had to ask.

"No, but I know who did it."

"And they don't want you to tell, or they'll rub you out? Did I get that right?"

"Yeah, I'm a dead man if I say a word to anyone."

"But, I think the police can help you."

Dudley was now overly excited and began shouting at Mathilda.

"No, I can't go to the police you crazy lady! You're acting just like my mother and you don't know what you're talking about! Those guys will kill me…I know it for sure." He stood up and started to pace, looking out one window of the cupola and then another until he checked all four sides, as though looking for someone down below on the street.

Dudley's words were thrust outrageously right into Aunt Mattie's heart—a strange pain, like smarting from a blow or being struck with blunt brass knuckles—right where her love for the boy resided.

"But they could protect you from those boys," she whispered. "Why were you with them, anyway? What have you been doing?"

Dudley sat down again. He knew he had to tell the truth, at least to Aunt Mattie.

"We started by being friends, and then one of the guys had an idea to take some stuff from the five and dime store. It wasn't anything much, maybe matchsticks that we needed or something from the grocery store—like a Twinkie 'cause we were so hungry. Anyway, those stores have plenty money, so what did we care? But then it got to be a game about who could take the most stuff without getting caught. Then who could get the most expensive stuff. And then, some of the guys beat up a n…I mean a colored guy whenever they saw one alone. They thought it was fun to watch him beg for mercy."

"But, why didn't you..."

"Once ya started with those guys, ya couldn't stop, and you couldn't say anything either. Now I'm afraid of what they'll do to me. And I'm afraid of what the police will do to me."

"I can understand that, but how can kids get away with all that stuff without their parents knowing about it?"

"Aw, Aunt Mattie...how can you be so dumb? I can't go home. My mother would go crazy!"

Mathilda suddenly became suspicious of Dudley grasping at his jacket zipper while he talked.

"Here, let's see what you're hiding," she said, as she pulled his hands down, and his jacket fell open. Large dark blood stains were all over his shirt and now that she really looked, she could see that his hands were not just dirty but had dried blood on them too.

"Oh my, what have you gotten yourself into?"

Mathilda leaned back in her chair and tried to think.

"This is serious. It's not a game or something that can be brushed under the rug. We have to do something right away and your mother has to know...surely you know that!" Mathilda's voice was now raised and scolding.

"No, Aunt Mattie...she can't know about this. She just can't!"

"Dudley! This is beyond anything that I can help you with. This is your whole life. Your Uncle Tommy will know what to do. He's a good lawyer. He needs to know about this and I mean right now. I'll call him to come over."

"No, don't...I thought I could trust you. I thought you would hide me, and now you..."

"You can trust me. I'll help you all I can, but this is very serious, and I don't have a clue as to what should be done first." Mathilda's eyes were quickly filling with tears that were rolling down her cheeks as she realized her inability to convince Dudley to seek help.

Dudley stopped pacing around the small room, opened the door and ran down the two flights of stairs, slamming the door behind. Then he raced through the kitchen, past Booker T. and Sadie and out the back door.

"Man—where ya goin', Duds?" Booker T. asked. He had never seen Dudley in such a hurry, and he didn't get an answer.

Mathilda was right behind him, but stopped short in the kitchen.

"Sadie, we have to call Dudley's uncle Tommy right away. Please find me his number."

Sadie picked up her little address book and found the one for Thomas Bealer, Attorney at Law. She had his office number and the one for his home. She tried both.

"Here it is, ma'am. I thought you didn't want to talk to him," Sadie whispered as she handed her the phone.

"Mr. Tommy said he would stop," Booker T. said. "Remember, I told you what he said when I went there this morning."

"Yes, but I can't wait for him to stop later. I have to talk to him right now. Dudley is in serious trouble and he needs a good lawyer. He needs his uncle now more than ever before, and before anything more happens."

CHAPTER EIGHT

When Thomas heard Mathilda's voice, he thought at first that she might be ill, because she didn't come to the meeting earlier. And now, she sounded hysterical.

"Mattie, please speak slowly so I can understand you."

"Thomas, you have to come here right away. Dudley is in serious trouble. This time I can't help him."

"Do you want me to come to your house, Mattie?"

"Yes, please come here as fast as you possibly can. There isn't any time to talk on the phone. Hurry."

All types of scenarios ran through his head as he was driving to Mathilda's house. *One thing was for sure, Dudley wasn't dead because she mentioned helping him.*

* * *

Thomas Bealer sat down at the table with Sadie, Booker T. and Mathilda—who had no idea where to begin. Booker T. was silent, only watching for what would happen next. Then, she finally blurted out…

"Dudley had blood all over his shirt and hands when he was here earlier.

"Was he hurt? Why was he bleeding?"

"He said that he and some other boys had a fight. They all had knives."

"Knives? Did he get cut?" Thomas could hardly wait for her to tell him what happened.

"One of those boys…his name was Rudy, is dead. He was stabbed by a gang member and they warned Dudley not to tell, or they would rub him out. He ran from here just before I called you. I don't know where he went, but he didn't want his mother to know, and he didn't want you to know either. We have to look for him, maybe right around here first, don't you think? He hasn't been gone very long, so he couldn't have gone too far."

"Okay, I agree, let's go. Do you want to ride with me?"

"Yes, and Sadie, if he should call, try to get him to tell you where he is, or better yet, tell him to come back here."

"I will, and Booker T. and me will get some dinner started. He'll be scared silly and be needing something to eat."

Booker's mind could hardly grasp what had happened. He had to do something—anything.

"While you're gone, I'm going back down in the basement. I gotta finish moving those boxes and finish sweeping," Booker T. said.

"But, you're in your good…"

Mathilda didn't even have to finish her sentence, when Booker T. interrupted. "I know, I'll change first. I hope you find him real soon, Aunt Mattie. I'll be praying."

"Thank you Booker T. Pray hard, 'cause Dudley needs as many prayers as he can get."

Booker T. knew very well what those guys did when they got someone they were after, because of what they did to him. He lived with that fear every time he left the house. He could only imagine what they would do to a squealer even if he was white.

CHAPTER NINE

Mathilda and Thomas drove up and down the streets in Mayette, looking wherever they remembered seeing boys loitering.

"He wouldn't go home either, I know that because that's where those guys are, and they said they'd kill him," Mathilda said.

"I think you're right, but maybe he has some friends here? Who knows what a kid thinks of doing when he's that scared?"

They looked everywhere, driving up and down the streets. Finally Thomas pulled in front of one of the downtown department stores.

They sat quietly, each in their own deep thoughts about what was happening while watching the people going in and out, as well keeping their eyes on some teenaged boys who were fooling around near the alley. They acted like hoodlums, pushing and tugging at each other, being loud and obnoxious toward others who were passing. Their language was the worst that Mathilda had ever heard.

Thomas broke the silence. "I'm sorry you suddenly had to leave this morning and couldn't stay for the meeting. We cancelled it until you're able to meet with us again."

When Thomas spoke, Mathilda remembered the conversation she overheard that morning, but it no longer bothered her. *She would live and live well without marriage. She had been right years ago when she told Bruno Baggs that she would probably never marry Baggs nor anyone else—ever.*

"It was nothing that serious…nothing for you to be concerned about."

"I'm glad to hear that, Mattie. I was a little worried about you." As he turned, looking intently into her cool blue eyes, he realized that something was gone—a certain spark, or a certain something that had been shining for him during the last four years. It wasn't what Mattie said, but the way she said it, and it was at that moment that Thomas understood, that what he had hoped didn't happen that morning, actually did.

"Sister Marie told us that you were waiting earlier. Mattie, did you happen to overhear Johnny's and my conversation this morning?"

Even as he asked, he already knew the answer. Mattie's eyes were cold—not even a little regret or sorrow that their romance didn't blossom. The love he saw there, even yesterday was gone—washed away. Mattie seemed distant now. *But, maybe it's because of Dudley?* Thomas thought. It was hard for him to tell, everything was getting confusing.

Mathilda was not one to ever purposely lie or tell an untruth just to save face, so she said, "Yes, I did overhear you, but I do understand. You see, I acted the same way towards Crow. Not that I wanted to hurt him or anything like that, I just wasn't ready to begin again with all that marriage entails. We have a nice friendship, Thomas, so why not leave things just the way they are?"

"Are you sure, Mattie? You wouldn't mind just being good friends? And it's true, I would never want to hurt you on purpose and I'm sorry you heard me grouching. I don't know why I acted that way, except that Johnny was interfering in something that wasn't any of his business. It made me angry."

"I have to confess that I was angry too. In fact, I was so very angry and hurt that when I got home, I broke all my everyday white dishes."

"You didn't!"

"Yes, I did. I went into the pantry and threw them all at the floor. Well, actually I didn't throw them all…I smashed each one, individually—one at a time. It was a terrible fright for Sadie and Booker T."

"Every dish? You broke every white dish?" Thomas questioned. "The ones on which I've had breakfast, lunch and dinner?"

"Yes, every last one." And then she started to laugh, because she had acted so childishly and now felt embarrassed in the telling.

"Oh Mattie, it is funny, isn't it? And I caused you to do this?"

"Yes, you did, Thomas Bealer," she answered, still laughing.

Thomas joined her in laughing so hard it made his stomach hurt. Suddenly, he jumped out of the car and ran to the front door of the department store with Mathilda following.

"Where are you going?" Mathilda asked, following Thomas as he opened the glass door.

"To buy you some new dishes," he replied as he walked briskly to housewares department hardly waiting for her to catch up.

"Stop…we can't take the time, now," she begged.

"It'll only take a couple of minutes. Here's the clerk, she can help us get what you need and then we'll be on our way."

"But, we have to find Dudley—not buy dishes!" she pleaded again.

"May I help you," the lady asked, with a high falutin air about her. She wore a dark blue dress with tight-fitting, long sleeves, a white starched collar and matching cuffs. Mathilda thought the outfit made her look much too matronly for her years, like an old stuffed cabbage. And she was shrill and abrupt—her face taut—almost a scowl, just because it was five o'clock, and she had been interrupted while closing out her drawer.

"Yes, I need some dishes. Do you have some plain white, everyday ones?"

"Yes, we do. They're not in sets, so you may get any number of each. Shall I put a set of six or eight together for you, ma'am?"

"I need twelve: twelve plates, twelve cups, twelve saucers and twelve salad bowls. I need twelve of everything to make a whole set." The clerk's eyes widened with surprise.

"Mattie, you need twelve of everything?" Thomas asked.

"Yes, twelve of everything." They looked at each other and giggled a little. The salesclerk began to think they were acting a little silly, which they were. *But who cares? I'll make an extra bonus on my commissions today!*

After the clerk boxed up the dishes, she set them on the counter and began totaling the bill.

"Excuse me, do you have the gravy boat and butter dish for this set?" Mathilda asked, sweet as honey.

"We have them stored in back, do you mind waiting while I get them?"

"Ma'am, please see whether the salt and pepper shakers are there too," Mathilda added, grinning at Thomas.

The clerk smiled to herself as she hurried to the back room, forgiving all the extra inconvenience when she silently began calculating the extra cash in her paycheck.

"A gravy boat and a butter dish…and…and salt and pepper shakers too?" Thomas asked Mattie.

"Yes, a gravy boat, a butter dish, and the salt and pepper shakers, too." Mathilda chose the nicest ones they had, and Thomas paid the bill and carried them out to his car.

"Let's just concentrate on Dudley now, Thomas. He needs us now, more than any other time and we shouldn't waste precious time buying dishes."

"Okay, Mattie. I don't think he stayed here in Mayette."

"And he wouldn't have gone back to his home…but where else could he go?" Mathilda said.

"I'm wondering if he had any money?"

"That, I don't know. And I don't know how he got to my house…maybe he rode his bike."

"If he rode his bike, then he might ride out to the farm?"

"But that's another eight miles away," Mathilda reminded him.

"He's scared. Eight miles isn't far when you're scared. Just to get here from Blenning, he would've already ridden seventeen miles."

CHAPTER TEN

Dudley had been pedaling faster and faster. To get up more steam, he stood on the pedals and pushed with every ounce of strength he had.

"I didn't do it!" he screamed at the top of his voice, tasting familiar salty tears snowballing into his mouth. *They'll never believe me—even Aunt Mattie. Those guys are gonna get me if I don't get away from here! Henry could hide me...there's no one else!*

And then, the front tire hit a rut or something sharp and Dudley suddenly found himself in the dirt with the bicycle wheel straight up. Dazed, and unsteady, he got up, picked out the gravel stuck in his hands and pants and righted the bike. He could see that he wouldn't be riding it anywhere—the front wheel was bent. Wiping his nose and tears with the back of his jacket sleeve, he heard the motor of a truck coming.

Sheriff Bordon was on his way to Mayetteville, to see Maxine Bauer and her Mister. They had invited him to dinner on his day off, and it had been on his mind to cheer them up since their huge crop loss, so he made an extra effort to accept Maxine's kind invitation. As he was nearing Mayetteville, he saw up in the distance someone standing next to a bike on the side of the road, so he sped up a little to see whether he could help.

"Hey, boy, are you okay?" he shouted as he pulled up next to Dudley.

"Yeah, I'm okay," Dudley said as he looked up to see Sheriff Bordon. "I'm alright, but I think my tire has a flat and the wheel is bent."

"It's probably a blowout, the way it looks. Why you're, Dudley Best, aren't you?" the sheriff asked, surprised at seeing the boy.

"Yes, yes I am. I'm going to the farm to see Mr. Henry and the boys. I guess I hit something sharp," Dudley said, as he pushed together the two sides of his jacket.

"Well, here let me give you a lift. I'm on my way to Mrs. Maxine and the Mister's for dinner. I could swing by Henry's drive and drop you off. I'm sure Henry has what you need to fix it right there, don't you think? "

"Yes, thank you, Sheriff Bordon, he always has some spare tires in the barn." Dudley threw his bike on the back of the truck and climbed into the cab, trembling all the while.

"You got a little scratched, but it doesn't seem to be anything too bad. Do you hurt anywhere?" Sheriff Bordon questioned.

"No, sir. Thanks for stopping."

"You're looking so grown-up, Dudley. How old are you now?" he asked as he took off down the dusty road.

"I'm fifteen…almost sixteen."

"That's a good age, Dudley. I remember it well. That's when I made the decision to get into law enforcement. Have you thought about what you want to do with your life, you know, what you want to study?"

"No, sir. I haven't given it a lot of thought," Dudley said. But even as he said it, he remembered his dream of playing in an orchestra on a sleek black Steinway—exactly like the piano at the conservatory he attended in Chicago. But that was when he was ten and now he was almost a grown-up, and in big trouble.

"Well, here we are. I'll let you off right here at the gate and you can walk the rest of the way."

"Okay. Thank you, sir."

"Did you ever see such a beauty? The sign, I mean. Wheatlander is one of the prettiest farms around. You know they lost their wheat crops along with the others this year. Did you know that, Dudley?"

"No, sir, I didn't." He jumped out of the cab and ran to the back to get his bike. He knew he had to keep his jacket closed while trying to maneuver it out of the truck bed. It was awkward.

"Here, I can help you with that. Why do you have that jacket on when it's so hot this afternoon?" Sheriff Bordon asked, as he could see Dudley's nervousness with shaking lips. "Do you have a fever or something?"

"Oh, I guess I didn't want to carry it, so I put it on." Dudley was trying hard to hold the front closed.

"Hey, you got what looks like dried blood on your hands. It couldn't have been from your fall. Here let me take a look. And take off that jacket," he ordered.

Dudley could only obey. There wasn't anything else he could do so he removed his jacket. The sheriff could see the dried spattered blood stains all over the front of his shirt, already very dark.

"It's blood! Do you want to tell me about this, son?" Sheriff Bordon asked pointedly.

"No, sir. I came to talk to Mr. Henry and Catherine."

"Well, maybe I just better come with you. Let's put that bike back in the bed and drive over there."

Just then, Thomas Bealer and Mathilda pulled up behind Bordon's truck. They both jumped out and ran over to Dudley hardly nodding to the sheriff.

"Are you okay, Dudley?" Uncle Tommy asked the boy. He put his hand on his shoulder to reassure him and said, "I'm here to act as your lawyer. We'll go back to Mattie's house and talk…is that all right with you, Sheriff Bordon?" The law officer was an old friend and he knew that Thomas Bealer would honor his word.

"Yes, I can be there as soon as I tell Maxine that I can't stay for dinner. I'll meet you there."

CHAPTER ELEVEN

Thomas, Sheriff Bordon, Dudley, Sadie, and Mattie had just sat down around the kitchen table when Thomas suddenly stood and walked over to the telephone.

"Before we start, I'll have to call your mother and let her know what's happening. She has a right and a duty to know, Dudley, and it's not open to discussion." He spoke sternly to Dudley as he dialed the number.

Dudley didn't say another word. He made up his mind at that very moment not to tell what really happened—to his uncle, the Sheriff, or even his mother. He just couldn't chance it.

While they waited, Sadie made tea and sandwiches for everyone since the roast beef dinner she was preparing wasn't ready.

* * *

When Louise walked into the kitchen and saw Dudley and the others sitting at the table looking glum, she stepped directly behind Dudley's chair, grabbed his shoulders and squeezed as she bent to place a light kiss on the side of his face. Dudley stared forward, never moving nor acknowledging his mother's presence.

Finished with his work in the basement, Booker T. came up while everyone was talking about what to do first. He couldn't believe what was happening. It was so unreal, as unreal as the beatings he took from boys just like the ones Dudley was friends with. But he couldn't and wouldn't tell anyone about those humiliations. It would cause Aunt Mattie too much shame.

After some time went by without Dudley answering any questions or speaking at all, Sheriff Bordon had no other option than to call the Blenning Police Station to get information about the boy, Rudy. When he hung up, he was downcast. He blew his nose and dabbed at his tears as he put the handcuffs on Dudley, led him out of the house and into the front seat of his truck. Thomas followed them out and climbed in too, pushing Dudley into the center. He would ride with them to the station but felt helpless as Dudley's lawyer because the boy wouldn't open up and tell him exactly what happened.

Mathilda, Louise and Sadie remained at the table in stunned silence. Booker T. was watching it play out. The arrest, the tears, the disbelief—Dudley's uneaten sandwich—suddenly, he broke that frozen moment and ran like a streak of lightening after the truck, shouting as loud as he could…

"DUDLEY WOULD NEVER KILL ANYONE. THERE MUST BE A MISTAKE. WHY DON'T YOU EXPLAIN IT TO THEM, DUDS… PLEASE?"

And then Booker T. fell to his knees, his body humped over, head down. Dudley looked back from where he was sitting in the truck but couldn't say a thing. His own face was now cast in stone, hardened against everyone as they drove away.

Mathilda, seeing Booker's anguish, one that mirrored her own, quickly followed him out to the drive. It broke her heart to see him slumped over and crying. She gently put her hand under his arm to help him up, saying, "Come on, Booker T., there's nothing more we can do."

* * *

When Dudley entered that little, barred jail cell—the home he would now share with murderers and surly drunken men—the odor of urine hit him, sliding into his nostrils. He could taste it. The stench made him so sick that three times he had to puke into the sink beside the thin cot that would be his bed. Then he washed his hands with water—there was no soap—and made a cup with his hands, catching the tap water and slurping it into his mouth. It was warm and tasted putrid as though it came from a stagnant pond. He dried his hands, rubbing them on his pants.

Men were yelling about all sorts of things, but Dudley couldn't make out what they were saying because the sound was garbled as it bounced off the walls. Except the man in the next cell was clear. He kept swearing at Dudley through the concrete wall, as though it was Dudley's fault that the man was there. Then that same man took his metal cup and grated it back and forth against the bars. Others were yelling profane words at the man to stop, but he wouldn't.

Dudley put his fingers in his ears and fell on the cot, face-down. He could bury his face against the thin blanket but it couldn't block out the incessant noise. He began crying softly to himself. *What does it matter! Who cares if I'm crying,* he thought as he sank into exhaustion.

* * *

He was playing that black nine-foot concert grand piano for the little ballerinas. They were frolicking and twirling in glittering tutus to the Dance of the Sugar Plum Fairies. The conductor was telling the overflowing audience that, "This boy—this ten-year old boy, Dudley Best, may become one of our outstanding virtuoso pianists."

There was a standing ovation, all clapping for him. Aunt Mattie smiled from the front row. He could see tears of joy wet on her cheeks.

Auntie's arm was around him, holding him tight during that two-hour ride home. The sound of the train—the clickitty clack clack, clickitty clack—of the steel wheels against the rails—lulled him to sleep, making him feel snug and secure.

Little by little, the slow, soothing clacking became the harsh beating on the bars of the cell next to him and he woke with a start.

This must be what hell is like! was his only thought.

CHAPTER TWELVE

Ever since Dudley was incarcerated, a fear overtook Mathilda about Booker T. She understood about gangs now, and how dangerous it was for him to be out on the street alone. Booker too, became reluctant to go anywhere, even to school functions in the evening. Aunt Mattie or her sister, Angela, would drive him and pick him up. Sometimes Sadie or Henry would volunteer. Sundays, the ladies usually took Booker T. with them when they went to the Methodist Church in Mayetteville. There, he always felt welcome, mostly because of Aunt Mattie, Miss Angela, and the family. Catherine, too, joined the congregation right after the old minister Dailey was indicted and sent to prison for the demise of young Henry's mother. That minister was in the habit of dishing out God's heavy vengeance liberally on all who trespassed Dailey's ten commandments.

The people in Mayetteville couldn't get over the fact that the old minister was the culprit. They kept talking about the things he did to those he was supposed to be helping. They also spoke of how much he hated Mr. Henry because Henry's soul was black with sin. The reason it was so black was because he was conceived and born out of wedlock.

A new minister by the name of Harlan Hollester was hired after a thorough evaluation including the previous churches he pastored, his personal references, and the theological schools he attended. The Reverend Hollester was a very different sort of man than Dailey. He had a charismatic personality that drew people to hear him speak about the power of God, and the things prophesied to come upon the world.

On one particular Sunday, when many new people came from long distances to hear this minister's spirited sermon, Booker T. was outside, minding and playing with Mr. Henry's boys. It was then that Booker T. overheard a white man standing with other men and women, not far from him, mention that a Negro boy was out there in the yard playing with two little white boys, and he didn't like to see it because it was dangerous. But another man, Maxine's Mister, whom Booker T. didn't know very well, said as plain as day and fairly loud too, so the others would hear, "Oh, that's Booker T. He's Mathilda Millering's boy, and you best not say a word about that boy being colored, black or any other name."

The man who had made the remark was taken aback by that kind of answer from a white gentleman, and everything was okay at the church after that. Booker T. even began singing with the small choir, and sometimes he played the jazzy piano for entertainment, just like when he lived in Chicago or when he played in the basement of the Calvary Church in Mayette.

* * *

Booker T. was overcome with the same worry that Mathilda had, especially when he thought about how easily Dudley was accused and sent to prison for something he didn't do, and Booker T. was positively sure he didn't do it. If these horrible things could happen to his white friend, what hope did he have to escape the ravages of life in his own school? It was only a matter of time when it would catch up with him.

After Dudley was arrested, Booker's gut was constantly knotted and his appetite disappeared. Many nights he struggled to fall asleep, until he remembered another time he was so frightened, right after his daddy's death. He remembered the comfort he found sitting quietly in the church and ached to find that same solace again. A few days later, he took a chance and rode his bike the long way around— an extra two blocks, over to Saint Gregory's. It was the same church and orphanage he and Dudley attended and where Dudley's uncle was the principal director.

The very first time he entered the interior of that church was when he was eleven years old. It was when Father John explained to him about his papa having been killed in an automobile accident. Father John was gentle, and even hugged him for a long time, but he pushed free to get away. He had to run from the prying eyes of the boys and teachers, not wanting to play or even be with them. He felt alone and needed to be alone. On that day, it was late afternoon when he first thought to open the huge wooden door to the church— *a good place to hide*, he thought. As he looked into that spacious place where no eyes could see him, he entered walking slowly over the highly polished floor, almost tiptoeing, while looking wide-eyed at the huge floor-to-ceiling stained glass windows. As the light of the sun filtered through the stained glass, it created a multicolored softness that touched the pews, the altar, the floor—everything— with bouncing rays. He chose the center pew, pushed the kneeler back and sat down. Careening his neck to look slowly around at the immensity of the cathedral, he was filled with awe. Almost immediately, the tears that he had withheld since that morning broke free along with wracking sobs he could no longer choke down. No one could see him or hear him—except God.

"Oh, papa, why?" he sobbed into his hands covering his face. "Why did you send me away? I should have stayed with you, Papa. I waited for you to call. I was there, Papa, every week, just like you said. Papa…I need you. Why did you go away, Papa?"

At that exact moment he became aware of one bright ray of iridescent light falling on him—encircling him. He felt warmth, as though he was being caressed or held, maybe by his mama, or maybe by…God.

Now, almost four years had passed, but he still remembered the comfort he received, and was looking for it again because this new pain, in the pit of his stomach for Dudley and also for himself felt the same as when he was eleven. While sitting there, in the immense stillness he could almost imagine he was in another world, one where a boy like himself could be loved and not hated just because of the color of his skin.

Booker T. didn't know how long he'd been there, maybe an hour, just sitting and drinking in the quiet as it wove small bits of peace into his being. He didn't understand it or even try, he only knew his friend Dudley was in serious trouble, and only God could help him.

As he was leaving, Booker T. looked down the long isle and saw the pastor sitting alone in the last pew—the only other person in the whole church. It was Father John who would wait with the boy for George Fraze, his papa to call on Sundays. Fraze allowed ten-year old Booker to go home with Dudley and Mathilda to recover from having his fingers broken. He promised to call often while the boy healed, but called only one time—the first week Booker was there. On that day, Papa told Booker T. that he loved him and for him to go to a good black church, like the one he attended in Chicago, and to do what he was told. During those long afternoon hours, waiting for the phone to ring, Sunday after Sunday with Father John, Booker T. learned to play a mean game of chess and could actually beat the old priest when he placed his whole concentration on the game.

When Booker T. was walking past the very last pew where Father John was sitting, he could hear his sneakers making an embarrassing screeching sound against the waxed floor with every step. The priest motioned for Booker to sit down beside him.

"How are you doing?" Father John whispered.

"Okay, I guess." He didn't want to say that something was hurting inside his belly all the time, and that it made him feel sick. But Father John already knew this because it was hurting him too.

"It's hard, isn't it Booker T?"

"Yes, but I can't talk now, because Aunt Mattie will be worried and she'll come looking for me. I gotta go." The boy was more than a little uncomfortable with his feelings and didn't want to talk about them, not to anyone.

"Do you tell her when you come here…I mean, so she doesn't worry?"

"I guess she just kinda figures it out. But if I'm a little late, she always walks over and finds me here."

"Keep praying, Booker T. Everything comes through prayer." Now, the church was completely empty and a sudden uncontrollable gush of tears washed down Father John's face without warning. *What could I have done differently for Dudley, Lord? Everything I did for the boy, was all wrong!*

* * *

"Hey, you aren't supposed to be here–you know that!" Nathanial Marsh yelled. The three troublemakers were waiting on the sidewalk for Booker T. as he left the church.

"Yeah, did you forget so soon? This is our sidewalk," the other boy said, articulating each word.

"I'll bet you can run faster than all three of us. Why not start and if you can't, then we'll get you," Marsh taunted.

"Come on, run. It'll be fun," the third boy said excitedly.

"Yeah, let's have some action here. Get going, nigger boy."

Just then, they caught sight of someone walking up the sidewalk. It was a woman. The boys fell silent as they watched, waiting for her to pass so they could resume their game with Booker T. But it was Mathilda, walking fast toward the boys. As she neared she could see what was happening by the devilish looks on their faces.

"Are the boys giving you a hard time, Booker T.," she asked as she approached them. They were now acting as though they were only chatting with Booker T. saying, "see you later," and bouncing a ball against the pavement in a casual manner.

"No, ma'am. No problem here!" Booker T. said, as he picked up his bike and fell in step with Aunt Mattie as though nothing at all was wrong.

CHAPTER THIRTEEN

It was early Sunday morning—only seven-thirty by the clock on the kitchen wall—when a light knock at the back door startled Mathilda. She was the only one still sitting at the table after breakfast. Walking out to the back porch area, she slowly opened the outside screen door. It made a low grinding sound like a bow being pulled slowly across a string on a cello. She made a mental note to put a little oil on the hinges.

A pleasant looking colored man and woman with broad smiles stood there. The lady wore a blue two-piece suit, a pillbox hat, and white gloves, and the man, a gray suit, white shirt, and a paisley tie. To Mathilda, they looked like church people, and wondered what they might be selling or giving away. *Maybe Bibles,* she thought, but she already had a good one, although it was getting a little worn.

Booker T. was curious when he heard the screen door squeak and followed to see who would be visiting so early in the morning.

"Oh, Dr. James!" Booker T. exclaimed when he saw the doctor on the step. Then turning to Mathilda he said, "Aunt Mattie, this is the doctor that helped me when I fell off my bicycle. It's Dr. James. Could they please come in?"

"Hello, Booker. And you must be the Aunt Mattie I've heard so much about."

"I am, and I'm so glad to meet you. You were so kind to our Booker T. Please, come in. I thought at first you might be selling Bibles or something."

"Do people do that on Sunday mornings?" the lady asked, still smiling.

"No, not in the past, but everything is changing so fast, you never know what new things people are doing. Please come in and have some tea," Mathilda said as she led them into the kitchen."

Sadie had been upstairs, but heard voices. As she entered the kitchen, she was pleasantly surprised to see the couple.

"Well hello, Doctor. It's so good to see you, but I'm so sorry we're fresh out of Danish." Sadie teased. They both laughed, enjoying the moment. And then, the doctor looked at his wife and introduced her before they sat down.

"This is my wife, Ethel, the love of my life, my forever companion, and the mother of my babies."

"Hello, Ethel. It's so good to meet such an important person," Mathilda said, a little envious that her Henry never once introduced her in that wonderful way. Of course, she never had any babies to be proud about, but now she did have Booker T. and also Dudley who was in that ugly prison.

"Hello, Mrs. Millering. It's good to meet you too. Jimmy—Doctor James has spoken about Booker T. many times, and I actually had to force him to finally come and do the thing he's been contemplating since they met."

"Please have a seat, Mrs. James—ma'am," Booker T. offered as he held the chair for her and then sat down beside her. Sadie was already busy setting out the cups, saucers, and a second batch of cinnamon rolls that she had just removed from the oven. After pouring hot water over Mathilda's tea bag, she filled the decanter with fresh-brewed, hot coffee and placed it on the table before the guests. Doctor James piled two rolls on his plate while Booker T. watched to see if Aunt Mattie would tell him not to take that many at one time, same as she would tell him. She didn't, but she did look as though she would. Doctor James buttered the rolls and cut them into smaller pieces while sweet cinnamon filled the room.

After several bites, Doctor James began. "I hope it's not an inconvenience to have us drop in this morning. We were on our way to church but decided to take the time to meet with you since I had no calls."

"Oh, what church do you go to?" Mathilda asked.

"We go to the Faith Pentecostal Church on fifth street."

"We—Sadie, Booker T. and I—go to the Methodist church in Mayetteville. My sister, Angela, goes there too, with her daughter Catherine's family who live near the church. Her husband, Henry used to preach in that little church quite often."

"I used to go to a Baptist Church in Chicago," Booker T. added. "My papa wanted me to go to a good black church here too, so sometimes Aunt Mattie will drive me to Calvary Baptist—'cause Father John said I should go there, like my papa said."

"Oh, Father John said that, did he?" Doctor James raised his eyebrows, as though a little confused, then he looked down at his plate, he immediately realized how greedy it may have looked to everyone, and said, "sorry, my wife didn't make breakfast this morning." He winked at Ethel. Booker T. thought she would be embarrassed by his telling something that private, but Ethel acted as though she didn't mind one bit.

"I'm glad you came, and it must be something very important for you to do so," Mathilda said, now completely ignoring the Doctor's plate, and extremely curious about his explanation.

Booker T. was most attentive to Mrs. James, since he sat next to her. He poured coffee into her cup and then quickly got up to get the milk when she mentioned it. He acted very gentlemanly, and Mathilda felt proud, but then Booker T. placed the quart bottle squarely on the white tablecloth instead of putting it into the small creamer. He glanced at Aunt Mattie, and immediately felt embarrassed knowing he shouldn't have done that. Mathilda ignored the error and Booker T. hoped Mrs. James hadn't noticed.

"Yes," Doctor James said. "You see, for most black folks, it's hard to climb the ladder of success. In fact, it's just about impossible." The doctor hesitated. He looked at Booker T. and then at Ethel. She nodded her head encouraging him to continue. "Booker T., I want to propose something to you. It concerns your future...have you thought about it at all?"

"Well, sir, I'm only a sophomore, but I get good grades—'cause Aunt Mattie helped me so much when I first came here from Chicago. And I speak better, at least, I think I do most of the time. You speak good too, Doctor James," Booker T. added. He was paying attention to everything the doctor said and did and noticed that his fingernails were filed and clean. The man was very different from Booker's papa who didn't value the white man's education or the way words were used in speaking.

"I have to say that you do speak very well," Doctor James commented.

"Yes, sir, we used to go to the library almost every day, but now Auntie—Aunt Mattie brings me books to study at home. She says it's not too good for me to go there alone."

"Yes, she's concerned about you, boy. You understand that, don't you?" Ethel James asked.

"Yes, ma'am, and she used to read to me about my namesake, and she helped me understand that my mother wanted something more for me than just digging ditches like my papa does—did. But papa didn't care much about the things my mama said. He thought she was stupid, wanting things she couldn't possibly have. They would argue all the time."

"Then you may want something more for yourself than what your daddy wanted?" Doctor James asked.

"Like what, sir?"

"Do you want to be a person that can help people, you know, like your namesake. He was quite a man."

"Yes, sir, if I can. But I don't know how or what that could be. I help Aunt Mattie all the time."

"Would you like to help our people, you know, like I do?"

"Yes, sir, you mean like a doctor? Could I do that?" Booker asked, surprised.

Sadie and Mathilda were amazed when Booker T. began to speak and answer in such a thoughtful way. And Mathilda was proud of the progress he made during the past four years—from a little waif to a fifteen year-old scholar. But she couldn't take the credit for it. It was, after all, Booker T. who decided to do it. She only showed him the way.

"If you think you would like to try to become a doctor, like me, I'll help you. It'll take a lot of hard work but I can see that you wouldn't have any trouble in the study department, now would you?" Doctor James asked.

"No, sir. I like to study…but …"

"Booker T.—when I was just a little older than you, another doctor mentored me. His name was Doctor Arnold A. Higgs. I studied and went on calls with him almost every day and I learned enough so that after high school I was able to pass the pre-med undergraduate entrance exams in one of the few colleges that offered pre-med majors. I then went on to do well in medical school."

"But, how did you know—you wanted to become a doctor?" Booker T. asked.

"I didn't but I admired Doctor Higgs and believed that he saw something in me that made him think I could do it."

"Then you kind of—just believed he was right?"

"Yes, that's about it. I didn't have any other aspirations—not many sixteen-year olds do—especially black sixteen-year olds."

"Oh, because I never thought about becoming a doctor, either. You think I could do it?" Booker T. was very unsure about the whole idea.

"Yes, or I wouldn't have asked you. You know Booker, Doctor Higgs said that the day was coming when we would need many excellent doctors, not just for our race but for everyone. I had to promise him, and it was a solemn promise that compels me to pass that opportunity forward. Doctor Higgs believed that one day I would meet the right boy. Do you understand me so far?"

"Yes, sir. You're saying things will get better for us."

"That's correct. Do you think you could be ready for the future, Booker T.? Are you that boy?"

Mathilda couldn't keep still any longer.

"Doctor James, are you proposing Booker T. work with you and go on calls with you? And am I to understand that you think he could become a doctor like yourself?" Even as she spoke those words, she was hoping against all hope that this was the opportunity Booker T. needed and she had been praying and striving for.

"That's exactly what I'm proposing." Doctor James looked intently at Booker, then continued, so there wouldn't be any question about what would be required. "Going on house calls with me will be your after school job and you will be expected to study the medical terms I give you in addition to your regular studies. You'll get paid, just as though you were working in a grocery store or doing other work after school. Do you have any questions so far?"

"No, sir, I understand," Booker replied, but inside he was unsure. It sounded very hard.

Me, a doctor? he questioned in his mind. He never had such an idea and he only studied hard to please Aunt Mattie. That was the only reason his grades were good.

Dr. James continued, "extracurricular activities at school will be out of the question and you won't have time for any type of sports."

"But I'm not interested in sports sir, and I don't have any other hobbies."

The doctor and his wife seemed very happy with Booker's answers, and so was Mathilda, but Booker T. didn't say that was what he wanted for his life. How could he know anything about his future when it was so far away and he only worried about getting though each day alive?

CHAPTER FOURTEEN

Dudley's uncles, Father John Bealer and his brother Thomas, both tried to prove Dudley's innocence, with all the means within their power. Father John wanted the charges dismissed since there wasn't enough evidence, but the public and the mother of Rudy demanded justice immediately and made sure that all the newspapers called for it.

The five other boys, when questioned separately, were adamant that Dudley had planned and then stabbed the boy, Rudy. They claimed he did it for no apparent reason. He did it just to have fun! The case was closed and the records sealed. Exactly what those records contained, no one knew except the District Attorney, a man by the name of Baxter Marlow, who sought the harshest treatment that could be given to the boy, with no leniency for his age.

In that first jail and then the prison, there was always the harsh banging of utensils against the bars, with constant yelling by men, not just during the day, but at night too. The echo of heavy doors opening and closing added to the assault on Dudley's ears. Other older boys were crude and surly toward Dudley. They often discussed him between themselves. They had a name for him too—pambi boy.

Understanding everything that was happening was impossible because Dudley was still in a continual daze and not able to think with the constant conflict surrounding him. He obeyed the strict rules, but still refused to respond to the daily interrogations. They came at different times, even at night. The warden wanted a full confession and tried every means—including threats—to get Dudley to tell them where the weapon was. Dudley wondered why, since the trial was over and he had been found guilty.

CHAPTER FIFTEEN

Thomas Bealer remembered Barry Tierney, a classmate from the one-room grammar school in Mayetteville. They both became lawyers but Barry had stretched further than Thomas during the last fifteen years. He went on to become a very prominent man in the United States Senate and was always busy with serious issues for the state. Even so, he still arranged time for his wife, who contracted Polio after her first and only pregnancy. She spent twelve years of their marriage in an iron lung and was then bedridden for three more years at home.

The people in his district held their senator in high esteem because of his sparkling character and tireless work for the state and his own community. When he and Thomas met, quite by accident in Indianapolis, at a State Lawyers Conference, Thomas spilled his deep concern for his nephew over lunch where they were seated next to each other.

Barry seemed very interested in the matter, since he had known the whole Bealer family from his boyhood.

"Didn't you have an older brother by the name of John?"

"Yes, he's the pastor at St. Gregory's in Mayette and head of the orphanage there too."

"And a little sister by the name of Louise?"

"Yes, she had Dudley out of wedlock. Louise was married at the time, but her husband Michael was overseas during the war. I guess she was lonely. She met someone—a charming man at a friend's house and he was married too. Who knows what happened? They fell in love and had an affair. It almost broke up the man's marriage when Louise had their child."

"That had to have been hard for her and your family, too."

"It was the hardest for Johnny. He had a devil of a time talking her out of an abortion."

"Oh, so many young women think abortion is the solution, don't they?" Barry said, not asking, but stating a known fact.

"Well, Johnny promised he would help find a family for the child, and he did."

"How did your parents take it?"

"She wouldn't tell my folks. Not until after her husband Michael died. It took a little nerve for her to do it, though," Thomas explained. "But then—it was an unexpected opportunity to have Dudley back with her and her other two children, Paddy and Annie."

"Then who raised the boy all those years?"

"He was with a nice family for several years, but then the man died and left the woman without any funds. She reluctantly let the boy go back to Louise. That's when Johnny stepped in and took him into the orphanage so that he could look after him, along with the other children."

"Is Dudley a hardened boy, I mean has he been in a lot of trouble over the years?"

"No, he's never had a problem until he went to live with his mother and two siblings. That's when he started running with a gang of boys from school and that's why he got into trouble."

"What did you say the boy's last name is?"

"It's Best—Dudley Best. Louise had a boyfriend at one time who had that name, and my mother cornered him once, right on Main street in Mayette."

"She did…in public?"

"Yes, and he curtly informed her that he had been living in another state for several years at the time in question, so the child couldn't have been his. He also told her that he hardly knew Louise and only dated her a couple of times. I think Mom learned a lesson. It was most embarrassing for her."

"I wonder how he got that name? I mean...how many people with that name live nearby?" Barry questioned.

"I don't know. Only Louise knows and she prefers not to reveal it to anyone. Maybe when Dudley gets older she'll tell him, but who knows?"

"You said he plays the piano?"

"Yes, he's a virtuoso at the piano and attended the Chicago Conservatory on a full scholarship when he was only ten years old. He had his piano debut—the featured pianist playing with a full orchestra, *Tchaikovsky's Dance of the Sugar Plum Fairy,* for all the little ballerinas."

"Oh, he does sound talented." Tierney continued to ask questions, first this and then that, right up to the time they had to leave the capital building. And then, without being asked, he said, "I will personally look into the reason Dudley Best had to take the rap when other boys were also involved, and I promise you, Tom, I'll get the real facts as to why your nephew is being railroaded. Here's my card with my address and phone number, and I would like to have yours so I can let you know what I find."

CHAPTER SIXTEEN

It was four o'clock early morning, too early for all the glaring lights in the prison facility to be turned on. Dudley was awakened from a sound sleep when two officers unlocked Dudley's cell door, slid it open and stepped in. The heavy rain storm, with lightning bouncing through the small window and a flashlight helped the officers see while they gathered his belongings into a pillow case. Dudley jumped up, still in his shorts and t-shirt.

"Put your pants and shirt on, kid," one guard ordered. Dudley quickly did as he was told—slipped his feet into his untied shoes—then had the cuffs clamped on his wrists before they led him out of the building.

The three of them ran fast on the sidewalk to keep from getting too wet. Shoving him into the back of a waiting police car, Dudley fell into the seat, shaking with fear. His knees were knocking and his lips were trembling as he remembered all the horror stories of what could happen to someone taken away during the night.

In the patrol car, the officers didn't speak to him, but carried on a conversation between themselves as they drove through the storm. Thoughts of where they could be taking him went through Dudley's head as they zipped along the highway, passing fields and small towns, only slowing as they drove through them. The rain kept beating down hard and the wipers struggled to keep up.

Hours seemed to have passed when they abruptly made a right turn and entered a long drive with grass and flower beds in large circles. At the end of the drive was a two-story, red brick building and several smaller concrete ones. The sign at the front of the drive read, An American Reformatory, and then the next line, A Modern Correctional Facility For Incorrigible Boys. Compared to the prison, Dudley thought the grounds looked like a picture postcard.

The cold drizzle was still coming down. After stopping as close to the building as they could—one of the officers yelled at Dudley to hurry and run for it! Dudley's feet got tangled from stepping on his untied laces and he slipped on the wet pavement. The officer pulled hard against the cuff on his wrist as he struggled to get up, and then they both ran until the steel door slammed shut behind them and the wind and rain became silent. All Dudley could hear was his own heart beating wildly.

The guards led him into the induction room. They handed a woman Dudley's papers, undid the cuffs and left. Dudley rubbed his burning wrists, which were stinging, and then brushed the wet off his face and arms with sweeping, downward motions.

"I'm Mrs. Helen Thompson. Please follow me into the dressing room. Shower and change into the clean clothing and throw all the clothes you take off into that bin."

There were five sets of neatly stacked clothing on a bench. Along with them were handkerchiefs, a small comb, a tube of toothpaste, a toothbrush, and a bar of soap in a small holder. There were also towels, large and small ones including washcloths. Dudley closed the door, removed his clothes and dropped them into the bin. When he turned on the shower, he was surprised by very hot water and stayed longer than the usual minute. He tried to wash off the prison using the soap and by holding his face up into the spray, turning, first one way and then the other, getting his hair and scalp squeaky clean. He put on one set of the clothing: underwear, khaki colored pants, matching shirt, tie, dark socks, and black shoes.

Brushing his teeth with the supplied toothpaste thoroughly made his mouth feel clean. For some reason at the prison, they wouldn't give him all the toiletries his uncle sent and he brushed only with plain water and his finger. Carefully now, he examined every tooth he could see in the metal mirror above the sink, making sure he didn't have any cavities, although he didn't know if anything could be done even if he had found one. He opened the door and stepped out.

"I'm finished, ma'am."

Mrs. Thompson was sitting outside the room, writing in a notebook while waiting. She looked up.

"I see that you are, young man, Dudley Best. You look very nice. Do the shoes fit?"

"No, ma'am. They're a little big." He walked a little so she could see them flopping.

"I'll have a guard get you a better fitting pair and you'll need a haircut. Please bring the other sets of clothing with you and follow me to the barber and then to your room," she said, very kindly. Dudley thought she looked a little like his grandmother, only much younger. She seemed nice.

"What's in the pillow case?" she asked, as she glanced into the shower room where it was still on the bench.

"Oh, they threw my street clothes and underwear in it before we left."

"Throw it all into the bin, you've already been issued everything you'll need."

"Yes, ma'am."

"Dudley—Mr. Best?"

"Yes, ma'am?"

"I see you have a red spot on your wrist—the skin is broken. Does it hurt?" She knew it did.

"It's just a little scrape, ma'am."

"Later I'll get you some salve. You can rub it on when you go to bed. It'll heal faster."

She waited while the barber shaved Dudley, and he became bald for the third time since he was incarcerated. Then, they walked down several long halls before they got to the room that was to be his. The first thing he saw when the door swung open, was the brightness of the room. It was a pale green and had a window without bars overlooking the outdoor lawn and flower beds. Next to the twin bed was one wooden chair and a desk. The chest of drawers was across the room, and the toilet was behind a half wall with a sink, a shelf above, and a metal would-be-mirror above the shelf.

"Put socks, ties and handkerchiefs in the top drawer, underwear in the second, and folded trousers and shirts below," Mrs Thompson explained.

"Yes, ma'am," Dudley said as he listened closely.

"They'll issue you a winter jacket and a warm cap later—it goes on that hook on the back of your door. Now, when you hear the bell, which should be in a few minutes, go to the lunchroom for the noon meal. You may sit anywhere you feel most comfortable.

"But, ma'am, where is the lunchroom?"

"When the bell rings, just follow some of the boys down the hall, turn right, down a flight of stairs, and walk through the double doors into the cafeteria. After lunch, there will be a guard who will give you a class schedule. Follow it to the letter and you'll be okay."

"Yes, ma'am."

"Oh, one other thing about your room—sitting on your bed or having any other inmate in your room is a serious infraction. Do you think you can remember that?"

"Yes, ma'am, I'll remember."

She could already tell that Dudley wasn't one of those smart-alecky, juvenile boys who were usually sent to this facility. She continued...

"Showers are at the end of the hall, but use it only once a week. On days that you have gym or calisthenics, you should shower in the gym's adjoining shower room; otherwise, sponge bathe in your room when you need to."

"Yes, ma'am. I'll remember everything. Thank you very much." For the first time in months, Dudley felt fully alive.

After the lady left, he looked at himself in the mirror hanging above the sink, and then ran his hands over his uniform to straighten any creases on his shirt and trousers. When his hand brushed over his shirt, he felt something in the left pocket—at the very bottom against the seam. Unbuttoning it to see what was stuck in there, he felt around the bottom with his finger and found a very tiny gold metal cross. Holding it in his hand, he wondered how it could have gotten there, since all the suits were folded and seemingly brand-new. At that moment, the bell rang. He shoved it back into his pocket, buttoned it, and followed the others going to the cafeteria. While he ate his lunch, he wondered if he should dare to keep it and every once in a while would touch his pocket to feel if it was still there. He could hardly feel it through the cloth, and thought that it was good because no one else could see it, either. That night, after the lights were out, he got up—set the tiny cross on the edge of the bed and knelt down. It was dark, except for the light trickling in from the parking lot.

"Thank you, God for bringing me here," he whispered into the dark with his little boy voice. It was the first time he felt like praying since this whirlwind of trouble entered his life. Before, he felt it was useless, but now he knew God was with him the whole time.

* * *

The reform school was different from any school Dudley had ever attended. Different from the public school where he began his education, the orphanage, and lastly his high school in Blenning where he lived with his mother and siblings. They were all lenient by comparison. This school's main focus was on academics and behavior. Residents were to rise at five sharp, with thirty minutes of military exercise outdoors or in the gymnasium including Sundays. That meant the boys had to be in the cafeteria no later than five-forty because classes began at six sharp and the students were required to be in their seats, and not one minute later, or demerits were given. If an inmate had more than three, there could be solitary confinement and according to the guys, demerits were not hard to stack up, and solitary was not a place to sleep.

The school was regulated by bells. Each day and each class started and ended with a shrill bell. The boys were expected to go to the next class without any talking. Silence was to be observed all day, except for the one hour of recreation where they were allowed to let out their frustrations by playing basketball and other team games at the sole discretion of the outside hired coach. Everyone was required to play on a team.

In this brick and concrete building, every aspect of living was regimented. Late afternoons and before dinner, the young men had assigned chores such as kitchen duty, floor cleaning and trash collection. After dinner, all unfinished homework and recreational reading was completed in the study hall. Assignments and books were kept in small individual lockers stacked at the back of the room. Every boy was responsible for his assigned locker and key.

Even the lights were controlled by a main switch in the central part of the building. At exactly nine o'clock, everyone was required to be in his own room and in his own bed when the switch was pulled.

Dudley's first morning class was Algebra, then English, Reading and Science with Gym or Basketball before lunch. Afternoons were Writing to be Understood followed by a two-hour Woodworking class.

After three weeks, Dudley became accustomed to the routine and began to excel in his classes. Algebra was his favorite subject, but he also enjoyed reading the classics and any current reading assignments. The silence worked a remarkable miracle on Dudley. Now, he could think very clearly about why he found himself in this place—this reform school for incorrigible boys—and why the authorities believed he was one.

After being there one month, Dudley felt settled in. One morning after breakfast, one of the senior guards handed Dudley a note telling him he was to meet with the headmaster at ten o'clock in the morning the following day. Dudley mentioned it to Ron and Joey during gym class. They were on the same basketball team and the only ones who acted somewhat civil toward him. They were also the ones happy to fill him in with juicy bits and pieces about the school, warning him about solitary confinement with beatings and deviant behavior. It was to be expected if he ever committed an infraction that was serious enough. He was also told the guards sometimes made up infractions if they didn't like you. And sometimes demerits stacked up if they liked you, a little too much!

Dudley was glad they told him but he spent a sleepless night trying to think of what he did wrong to be summoned to the principal's office. All kinds of nightmares crowded in, mainly about solitary confinement. When he awoke, thoughts about the meeting crowded out everything else. *Could someone make up something about me? What could it have been when I don't know anyone?*

CHAPTER SEVENTEEN

Dudley knocked on the principal's door at ten o'clock sharp. He smoothed his hair with the small comb kept in his pants pocket and straightened his tie. Then he lightly touched his shirt pocket where he kept the tiny cross.

"Come in, Mr. Best," the man called from his desk, knowing exactly which boy would be knocking. No one else would dare without a directive, except under grave circumstances.

Dudley opened the door, stepped inside, then closed it. He stood there silently.

"Come in and take a seat," the man directed.

Dudley took the chair directly in front of the desk, on which sat a picture of three laughing children, standing close to each other.

Thoughts began running through his mind. *Probably his children,* Dudley thought. *The boy appears to be my age, and the girls are a little older than, Annie.*

"Are you well, Mr. Best?" the man asked, observing every move Dudley made.

"May I answer aloud, sir?"

"Yes, when I ask you a question directly, you may answer," the man said, annoyed. It seemed so obvious to him.

"Yes, sir. I am well," Dudley replied, but would have liked to tell him he was hungry. *I wonder if his children are ever hungry?*

Then the man stood and walked over to where Dudley was sitting and stretched out his hand. "I'm Jonathan Dennison. You may call me Mr. Dennison. I'm the director or the principal here, whichever you prefer."

When Mr. Dennison stretched out his hand, Dudley immediately stood up and shook it and didn't sit down until he was told. Dennison liked that this boy seemed courteous and careful to obey the rules. He also noticed that this boy had four stripes on his sleeve. *Must be a new classification*, he thought. *Why do they keep changing things?*

"Now, Mr. Best, I would like to ask you some questions. Do you think you could answer them truthfully?"

"Yes, sir, I can." Dudley answered, not saying anything more than necessary.

"Are you happy here?"

Dudley had to think for a moment, because it never occurred to him that he should or would be happy in a reform school. And he never thought he would be asked that kind of question. He had to reach down inside to see whether he was, but there were too many conflicting thoughts swirling through his mind. *Which were the true ones?* he silently asked himself.

"Well sir, I...I like the silence."

"You like not being able to talk to the other boys between classes?" Dennison asked, a little surprised.

"Yes, sir." He made eye contact with the director at that moment. "It's better than in that prison with all those men yelling, screaming and swearing."

"Why? Why is it better, Mr. Best?"

"Well, sir...I can think my own thoughts and concentrate on my studies," he explained, hoping his answer would be enough for this man with the piercing eyes and strange questions.

"Just what kinds of things do you think about, Mr. Best?"

"Now, I think mostly about algebra, and how the numbers work. I like the books we read too, but mostly I think about the songs that play in my head."

"Songs? What do you mean 'songs?'" he asked for clarification.

"I can hear the notes on the piano as clear as day, that is, if I concentrate on the melody. It's better than talking."

Mr. Dennison had never heard a boy in this institution speak this way and he was taken by surprise.

"Can you play an instrument or the piano, Mr. Best?"

"I played the piano a few years ago, sir." He didn't volunteer anything about the conservatory he attended when he was ten years old.

"Well, Mr. Best—Dudley—when I sent for you, I didn't have any idea that you might be interested in a class we are going to begin. We have been instructed by the state to implement some music lessons with the possibility of a small band or orchestra for the school. We have a music teacher who will be interviewing a few boys who may be interested. Would you be a candidate?"

"If you think he would want me, I would be interested, sir." Again he was being careful not to say more than this man may wish to hear, or to appear too eager. But in his heart, he began to feel a slow timbre of hope.

"Okay, Mr. Best. I'll give him your name. You will be asked to meet with him when he comes to our school. Here's a pass for the class you missed while meeting with me," Mr. Dennison said as he wrote on a slip of paper and handed it to Dudley.

Dudley stood, as he believed that he was finished with the meeting.

"One other thing, Mr. Best. Exactly what brought you here?"

"I...I don't know, sir," was all Dudley could get out.

"That will be all...you may go."

Dudley walked to the door, opened it, and walked through, closing it softly.

He was only an hour late for his reading class. The book for their new assignment was called *Cast About on the Sea,* by Chandler. As the bell rang and he received his copy, he thought, *I guess that's the way I'm feeling...cast about on the sea.*

CHAPTER EIGHTEEN

Mathilda set up another meeting with Father John Bealer, Thomas Bealer, and the two members of the board from the St. Gregory's Orphanage. Everyone was surprised and elated when she proposed that she would donate most of Crow's corn acres for the new larger orphan home including a certain amount of money for a separate library. She had some conditions.

"I think I would like the school to be named St. Gregory's Orphanage, Wheatlander Addition, donated by Mathilda Barlow Millering, with signage in front of the building. Would that be possible?"

"Mattie, yes, I don't see any reason why this couldn't be done, and this is more than generous—are you sure?" Father John asked. He and Thomas knew she had something on her mind but never imagined that she would or could be so benevolent. The other gentlemen nodded in agreement as Mathilda continued.

"I haven't told Henry yet—he's been too depressed about the crops and all that's happened to Dudley—but I've decided to sell a good amount of my wheat acres too. In this way, he won't have that heavy burden and maybe he could go into the seminary now, before his dream of training for the ministry will die. That is, if he is still interested."

The board members all looked at Mathilda intently, listening closely to her plan.

"We did very well with the crops over the years, but now with the war over and the need for housing so acute, I believe I can do as well selling and investing than worrying over things like black fungal rust and sooty molds on so many acres of wheat."

"That is a worry, isn't it, when you lose a crop that big? It's a huge loss. Also, I believe housing is important for a lot of our GIs," Father John said as he mulled over her reasons.

"It sounds as though you've thought this out for some time, but it's a big step—and remember, there are a lot of charlatans out there. They'll take you for everything you have, Mattie, and then some!" Thomas said, rubbing his chin nervously.

"Well, there's this man who builds little communities—he's been doing this for the last eight years. I went to see him and the houses he's completed. They're beautiful, but most important, they're affordable for an ordinary working man. The developer's name is Marcus Marrianett. I would like you to go over all the details including the contracts so as you say, I wouldn't be taken advantage of."

"Yes, Mattie. I'll be happy to look out for your interests as though they were my own. You can be sure of that."

"Mrs. Millering, we certainly weren't prepared for such a generous offer. You can be sure we'll give all the particulars to the Bishop, and then be in touch with Father John and Mr. Bealer." Mr. Johnson said this with a huge smile, already visualizing the new facility that would take care of the overcrowding. He and the other board member stood, shaking hands with everyone and thanking Mathilda profusely as they left.

CHAPTER NINETEEN

The well-trained staff at the reformatory were never informed of past behavior, so there wouldn't be any preconceived ideas of what a boy might or might not do. It was a new non-investigational way of training. Observing the boys immediate behavior was the determining factor for merits and demerits. The teachers and staff met at seven every morning to give their ideas about any intervention techniques that may be needed and administered that day. It was in this way that it was known immediately if a boy was a truant or continued to act out his aggressiveness toward others.

Each morning, Mr. Dennison listened and observed those reports in detail, and it suddenly struck him that there were no demerits or other offending behavior ever reported for Dudley Best. In fact, ordinary helpful acts were observed by some of the teachers and staff who carefully recorded them. Finally, Dennison decided to do some of his own investigating

Why did he feel so conflicted after meeting and speaking with Dudley Best? There was something more going on here and he wanted to know exactly what it was.

* * *

Jonathan Dennison went to the induction office to meet with the lady in charge of admissions. He explained that he would like to see all the trial records and any other gathered information for Dudley Best, a fifteen-year old sophomore. He also requested parentage, siblings, place of birth, everything and anything in his file.

"I'm sorry, Mr. Dennison, but those records are sealed and that includes the trial records. No one can get them except through a Mr. Marlow—the District Attorney in Blenning. Why do you want them?"

"Oh, I'm just curious, that's all."

"And I'm curious too, sir. As to what's happening with this boy that a senator would be asking for the same records, and only yesterday?"

"Someone else asking about Dudley Best?" Did he get anything? I mean any pertinent information about what had happened and why the boy is here?"

"No, sir. As I told you, everything is sealed. No one is permitted to see them, but that senator seemed determined. Maybe he'll have some luck." She said this with concern in her voice. "He knows people that know people."

"What's the senator's name? I mean if you don't mind telling me."

"His name is Senator Barry Tierney."

"A senator checking on him? Hmm…"

"You know, Mr. Dennison, I met that boy, Dudley Best when he first came in. He was very polite and eager to obey whatever he was told. Seems like too nice a boy to be in here."

"Yes, well thank you. What did you say your name is?"

"I'm Helen Thompson—Mrs. Helen Thompson—and I have a boy about the same age as Dudley. It's hard for me to visualize my own son being in a place like this. Sometimes I want to cry for some of the boys when I hear how they're treated. Is it true what I'm hearing about the abuse in detention with solitary confi—"

But, she couldn't finish the question because she knew Mr. Dennison was a trained psychologist and would know infinitely more about the behavior of boys in a place like this. She had only one boy, Bailey.

Dennison seemed a little confused by her abrupt silence as she stifled the comment, but thought it better to drop the subject when he saw her embarrassment.

CHAPTER TWENTY

"Hello, Mr. Henry," Booker T. said as he and Mathilda got out of the car and greeted him. "I've missed seeing you, sir."

"I know, I've missed you too, Booker. How's Mrs. Mathilda been treating you?" he said, laughing as he grabbed Booker T. by the hand and shook it hard.

"Oh, you know, she's okay," Booker said winking at Aunt Mattie before remembering she hated any winking.

"So, why haven't you come to see me, Henry?" Mathilda asked pointedly. "I've waited as long as I could for you and today, Booker T. and I decided to come out and see you. We just had to go out for a drive on such a beautiful Autumn day. The colors of the trees are exquisite."

Henry quickly put the tea kettle on and made them comfortable in Crow's old living room until the water began to boil. Mathilda could almost see her old friend sitting across the room in his familiar chair, smiling at her. The home had been tastefully decorated, all it ever needed was a woman's touch and Mathilda had to admit that Catherine did a splendid job. When the tea was ready, they both sat at the kitchen table with Henry.

Booker T. was drinking a cup of tea too, and was enjoying sitting with the adults and not being told to go into another room or outdoors. He was listening and thinking, but held his tongue as Aunt

Mattie taught him to do, unless he had something important to contribute.

"Aunt Mattie, I'm so ashamed of how I managed the wheat and lost it. I just couldn't face you because I didn't know what to say," Henry confessed.

"But Henry, the loss would have happened no matter who was managing, don't you understand that?"

"I should have been more vigilant. It was my duty to be vigilant—so it was my fault," he said again more forcefully. "And—God always answered my prayers before, so I had to have done something wrong for Him to let this happen."

"Nonsense, Henry, that's utter nonsense. God didn't punish you, me, or the others. I thought that at first too. I thought that maybe it was some kind of curse. That old minister put things like that in our heads over the years and I almost believed it. Now, I see what happened as a stepping stone, one to force you to go forward with your dream. Do you remember it?"

"You mean learning about my gift of healing?"

"Exactly that."

"Yes, sometimes I do. I used to think I wanted to go to the seminary, but that was before. I have big responsibilities now to Kats and my boys. I can't be running from them to do my own thing."

"Well, what if you could? What if you had to because there were no more crops to take care of? What then, Henry?"

And then, Booker T. had to say what he had been thinking.

"I think your wrong, Mr. Henry, sir." He said this with a hush in his voice, as though a little apprehensive for interrupting.

"Booker, you're too young and don't know the whole of it yet," Henry said. He wasn't very willing to listen to a kid's advice.

"Oh, but I think I do, sir, at least in this case. Remember when my fingers were broken, and then, when those boys threw stones and made me fall? Well, if those things hadn't happened—and it was bad and real painful for me, well, I wouldn't be here right now with a job helping the good doctor."

"What do you mean, a job with the good doctor, Booker?" Henry asked.

"What Booker T. is trying to say is that when those boys were after him and he got hurt after they threw stones, along came a doctor who helped him. His name is Doctor James—Doctor 'Jimmy' James. He offered Booker T. a job of going on calls and preparing him for the medical entrance exams. He said something like…he was waiting for the right boy. You know…to pass it on."

Booker T. cut in again. "Doctor James' mentor was a Doctor Higgs. He made him promise that Doctor James would help another boy. He thinks I'm that boy, so you see how it works?"

"You're saying that sometimes when things happen and seem bad, they aren't, because they force us to go forward. Is that what you mean, Booker T?" Henry asked, while mulling over the idea internally.

"Yes, sir. I'm thinking of the wheat crop, and about what happened to my friend, Dudley, because he's in a real bad place—that reform school. But maybe there's something good out there for him, too, I mean when it's all over."

"Oh my, maybe you're right. I guess my eyes have been closed, and I'm only thinking of my own immediate pain."

"Have you asked whether you could visit Dudley?" Mathilda asked.

"I'd like to visit him, but they won't allow me, but so what… what good would it do if I could go to see him? I can't pray…it's all gone."

"Let me see," Booker T. said, as he put out his hand to touch Henry's hand. When their fingers met, nothing happened. The sting was gone. He should have realized this when they shook hands, earlier.

"See, I told you—nothing!"

"Never mind, Henry, just apply to the seminary that you want to attend, and be assured that the finances will be taken care of, that is, if you're still wanting to go?"

"But what about Catherine and my boys?"

"Catherine's mom and I will help, I promise. Anyway, I'm selling the land, all of it, except the eighty acres around your home and the eighty acres around my old house. You'll have to sign off the old deed before you leave and I'll have a new deed made completely in your name and Catherine's. You will own the house and land outright to do as you see fit."

"But if I'm in school, how will I work my eighty acres?"

"Same as always—the hands will continue to plant and harvest even though they'll be working primarily for the neighbors. You'll pay them for their work and you'll have a nice little profit at harvest time."

"Will you sell your old home and the acres to Jesse?"

"No, I'll continue to rent to Jesse. I love my first home and don't want to part with it, at least not now."

CHAPTER TWENTY-ONE

Good behavior during the previous month, with no demerits would allow a boy one visitor who was not on the family visiting list. Since Dudley's mother no longer came, the staff decided to allow a woman by the name of Mathilda Millering to visit since she was Dudley's aunt. The appointed day was a Sunday, early afternoon. The meeting would last forty-five minutes in the bright and cheerful lounge, set up with grouped chairs for the families.

Dudley ran over to hug Aunt Mattie and then led her to a group of chairs where it was a little less crowded with parents and other visitors. They sat facing each other. Mathilda thought Dudley had matured and she no longer saw that cute shaggy blond boy, his forehead and chin seemed broader, and his hair had darkened. He resembled someone, maybe still a bit of his Uncle Thomas, but someone else too. She tried to bring it up in her memory, but just couldn't recall who it could be. He looked much older now, more adult than child.

"Aunt Mattie, you look so good."

"You do too, Dudley. Are you well?"

"I think so, I've lost some weight though."

"I can see that you have, and you're as straight as an arrow. You look like you're in the army, so clean and sharp looking."

"Yes, we're required to wear this regulation clothing," he said as he pointed to his uniform. "We all look the same, except our ties are different shades of khaki. They can tell right away if a student is a freshman, sophomore, junior or a senior. Seniors are the only ones who wear black ties. A few seniors are trustees in the Senior Patrol. The arm stripes—everyone has them, are some sort of classification too. I don't know anything about it and none of the other guys seem to know for sure either. I guess it's only for the staff to know."

"Oh, you have four stripes on your shirt sleeve."

"Yes, but as I said, I don't know what they mean. The patrols carry leather billy clubs, just in case somebody gets out of line. I think we have the army supplying us with everything."

"I see that. All the boys look very neat and clean," she said, glancing around the room. "Dudley, I think about you all the time. I wish I could come more and write to you."

"I know, but maybe they'll let me have more mail when I've been here a year. That's what some of the guys say."

"It's November already and I don't want you to be here a whole year!" Mathilda's voice was pained.

Dudley changed the subject and asked,"How's Booker? Tell me everything, Aunt Mattie."

"Well, he's taller than I, but so are you. He still looks like Booker T., though he worries about you all the time. Did you know that he prays for you?"

"I didn't know he cared...that much?" Dudley said thoughtfully.

"If I can't find him, I usually walk over to St. Gregory's, and that's where he is. And, best of all, he has a new job with a local doctor and gets paid every week."

"What does he do?"

"He goes on calls and helps with everything, like sterilizing and packing the black bag. He's also studying so he can pass the entrance exams for medical school. Of course, that's in the future, but it's never too early to understand the terminology."

"How did that happen, I mean, I thought coloreds couldn't get into the good colleges?"

"Doctor James says Booker T. has the brains and it's a perfect answer during these few years that are so hard for teenagers...you know what I mean?"

"I know what you mean, Auntie. Can I tell you something real important?" His voice changed to a whisper as his eyes carefully observed first the whole room, and then the chairs close to where he and Aunt Mattie were sitting. But the people next to them seemed intent on their own conversation, not paying any attention to them.

"Yes, tell me, tell me everything I need to know."

"They threatened me, and not only me, they threatened you too, and my mother. One of the guys that I ran with, well, his father is the District Attorney in Blenning. He said he could do anything he wanted and would get off, so he never worried about getting caught. What he didn't say was that he would pin it on someone else, and I was that someone."

"Why didn't you tell...someone?"

"I just did."

Dudley started looking around the room again trying to see who was there that might be watching and listening.

"Uh oh...maybe I've said too much."

Dudley continued to turn this way and that searching the room with his eyes.

"But you could have told your Uncle Tommy. I think he could have done something."

"No, I couldn't tell anyone, and I shouldn't have told you even now. It's just that I'm so scared!"

"Dudley, I have to tell you that there is someone who has already pulled some strings to have you transferred from that awful prison to this institution."

"But who would do that for me? Do you know, Auntie?"

"Someone your Uncle Tommy knows, a senator I think…" and then as she was about to say more, the shrill bell rang and people began saying goodbye and walking toward the door. Loitering was not permitted.

Dudley and Mattie stood up, and as he hugged her, he spoke hurriedly into her ear.

"Auntie, I do own a pen knife. I never carry it and it's at home in my bedroom dresser. That day, I thought I heard a gunshot and ran to see why Rudy was on the ground with blood pouring out of his stomach. I touched him—that's why I had blood all over my shirt—I wiped my hands on it while Rudy cried, 'help me.' I ran away and so did the other guys but I keep hearing his voice, begging. Aunt Mattie, I wanted to help him but ran with the other guys…I'm a coward!"

Mathilda nodded, then glanced around the room.

"Nice grand piano over there," she said out loud, but listening closely and hearing every word he was whispering.

"We're not allowed to play it though. Bye Auntie, come again when you can," he said after their hug.

"Bye, Dudley." Mathilda found herself being carried along through the double glass doors by the other visitors.

Down the hall and just as she was about to exit through the heavy outside doors along with others, a song on the piano rang out. It was the familiar, *Fur Elise,* echoing throughout the building. She knew it was Dudley playing. For a minute, she stood there while people filed past. She wasn't sure what she should do. *Should I go back in*? Others were leaving completely oblivious to the message of danger Dudley was sending.

CHAPTER TWENTY-TWO

Visiting was over, but the fallout from that visit was just beginning. In Dudley's gym class later that morning, Joey told Dudley not to hit the showers because there was trouble brewing for him. Dudley heard enough gossip about what could happen when targeted, so he quickly decided to change from his gym clothes into his uniform and go see Mr. Dennison. Just inside the locker room door were two senior guards.

"We've been waiting for you, Duds. Get in the showers and do it now," Prinze yelled, in his stern, pulling rank voice.

"But I didn't play so I don't need a shower," Dudley said, trying to reason with him. "I'll get dressed and go."

"You heard the man," Stanton said as he slipped off his shoes and then his socks. Undoing his belt and unzipping his pants, he stepped out of them, kicking them to the side. "We're going to have a nice shower with you, Dudsie boy."

"No, I'm not taking a shower with you or anyone else."

Prinze pulled at Dudley's gym shorts while Stanton held him from the back, pining his arms tight. In a minute, they were off.

"We're serious, Duds," Prinze said. "We're going to teach you how to keep that yap of yours shut." Their voices bounced off the walls and reverberated back and forth.

"It's too noisy out here, lets get him in the showers where no one can hear," Stanton yelled to Prinze.

As the two pushed Dudley toward the shower room, he resisted by grabbing and holding tightly to the rail against a wall. There was so much commotion, they didn't immediately see Mr. Kracker, the gym instructor. He was hired for the gym sessions conducted every day. Exercise and keeping the boys fit while incarcerated was his main job but he enforced discipline as he saw fit as well as the other personnel.

"What's going on here?" Kracker yelled into the room as he held the swinging door open as far as it would go. The boys were now thoroughly surprised and frozen, standing perfectly still as the three searched for some sort of an explanation.

"Dudley wanted us to help him shower, sir," Stanton said. Kracker could see that Stanton was out of his uniform and almost naked along with Dudley.

"He said he was scared to be in there alone, sir," Prinze added while pointing toward the showers.

"Scared? What nonsense. Get your uniform on, Mr. Best, and get yourself over to Dennison's office immediately, you hear me?"

"Yes, sir. I'm on my way." Dudley didn't try to explain what happened and it took only a minute to change into his uniform and leave.

"And I'll be there as soon as I dismiss my class," Kracker added as Dudley was leaving. "Please inform Mr. Dennison. You two, Prinze and Stanton, isn't it?"

"Yes, sir," Prinze answered.

"You Prinze, you're up for parole in December, aren't you?"

"Yes, sir."

"Well, this isn't the way to teach anyone a lesson before you leave this school. We can teach him a better lesson a little later tonight in solitary and it's all legit, understand?" Kracker was sizing up the situation and smiling at his own wit and expectations.

"Yes, sir." Prinze placed the billy club he was holding, back into its holder.

"Are you forgetting who has seniority here?"

"No, sir. Sorry, sir." Prinze and Stanton answered with one voice.

"Both of you meet me in solitary after the bell for lights out. But it'll cost you."

"Oh, yes sir," they both responded. "Will Dudley be there?" Prinze wanted to know. "I'll only pay if Duds will be there."

"If I have anything to say about it, he will."

"Sir, does this mean that the directive we received to leave him out of the loop has been rescinded?" Stanton asked.

"Just bring the cash and I'll do all the rescinding," Kracker said laughing crudely. Their voices echoed against the stark white glazed tile walls.

CHAPTER TWENTY-THREE

Dudley knocked timidly on Mr. Dennison's office door and entered when he was told.

"Good afternoon, sir." Dudley stood at the door.

"Oh, good afternoon, Mr. Best—you had better have a good reason for coming without a pass."

"Yes, sir, I think I have a good reason, sir."

"Then out with it. Come and sit."

"Yes, sir." Dudley took the same seat as the last time he was there, only now he sat on the very edge of the chair.

"So, what is it?" Dennison seemed annoyed that a boy would come, knowing there could be consequences.

Dudley didn't know where to start. "My aunt came to visit today."

"So your aunt came, so what!"

"Someone here thinks I squealed and told her things I wasn't supposed to."

"Go on."

"Well, just now in the gym, some of the guys warned me not to hit the showers. All kinds of things happen in the showers, sir." Dudley's lips were trembling as he spoke. He was embarrassed and didn't want to spell it out. After all, this man should know what goes on here.

"I think those are rumors, probably to scare you. Why not go back and I'll not put this visit on your record. I can see that you're rather anxious, so I'll make an allowance for you this one time. Is that understood?"

"No, sir. I mean yes, sir. I understand…but I'm afraid to go back."

"Well, let me remind you: you have no other choice. Now get going or you'll go to solitary. Is that what you want?"

"I don't know, sir. Is solitary better than what they can do to me in the showers?"

Dennison suddenly felt he should listen further.

"Okay, tell me what happened—all of it."

"Today, for the first time, I told my Aunt Mattie what happened when Rudy got hurt—was killed—and I was blamed for it."

"Suppose you tell me too?" Dennison remembered that Dudley had nothing to say about why he was here when asked at his last visit.

Dudley went into detail and told everything exactly the way it happened the day Rudy was supposed to have been stabbed, but was really shot, except he didn't reveal who did the shooting. Even so, it was hard to tell. But he felt that he could trust this man. He had to trust someone.

"When my aunt was leaving, I whispered in her ear, about my knife still being in my room at home and about the shot I heard. I thought I was only whispering but someone must have heard me because all of a sudden, two upper class guys showed up, one on each side of me. They were going to escort me…somewhere, but I backed up and walked over to the piano, sat down and began to play as loudly as I could, hoping I would get in trouble and maybe the patrol would bring me here."

"That was definitely an infraction. They should have brought you here."

"Yes, sir, but they didn't. They left. They disappeared out of the meeting room. No one said anything until I got to the gymnasium. That's when a couple of the guys told me about the showers. I wanted to change and get out of there real fast, but two senior patrols were waiting for me and started pushing and pulling at me trying to get me into the shower room. No one can hear when you're in the showers, sir."

"That's right, they constructed that room so the noise wouldn't carry through the corridors."

"Yes, sir. They said they had ways to teach me to keep my mouth shut. Then Mr. Kracker walked in and told me to get dressed and report to you, sir. He said he would be here shortly, along with the patrol, I guess."

"Mr. Kracker, ah yes, he's the gym coach, isn't he?"

"Yes, sir. I'm telling you the truth, sir. I wouldn't lie about something so important."

* * *

Mathilda knew she had to tell Thomas immediately about what had happened at the school, and it couldn't wait until she got home because Dudley was in physical danger. She had to get to a phone immediately. The little restaurant had one—she had seen it on the wall near the door when she stopped earlier for a cup a tea before her visit with Dudley.

"Dudley told me some things that you should know about, Thomas. Things that are important."

"What do you mean, did you see him today?"

"Yes, and we had a good visit, but when I was leaving the building, he started to play the piano that's in the meeting room. It echoed through the whole building. You probably saw it when you visited. Do you remember?"

"Yes, it sits in the corner by the big windows."

"As I was leaving, I mentioned that it was a nice grand piano. Dudley said students weren't aloud to play, so I think he was trying to let me know something happened. Can you do anything?" she asked, panic in her voice.

"Maybe someone asked him to play?"

"Thomas Bealer! You know better! In a place like that?"

"Exactly what kinds of things did he tell you, Mattie?" He was trying hard to understand her anxiety.

"Dudley said he did own a pen knife but kept it at home in the dresser of his bedroom. He never had it on him that day. He said he heard a shot and that's when he ran over and touched Rudy's bloody chest—that's how he got blood on his hands. He wiped them off on the front of his shirt. Thomas, a shot! It means Rudy died of a gunshot wound! It's so different from the evidence presented at his juvenile hearing…Dudley's being framed!"

CHAPTER TWENTY-FOUR

After the children were in bed, Henry told Catherine about Aunt Mattie's plan for the farm.

"It's the end of everything, Kats," Henry said with a heavy heart.

"It seems so, but remember how hard it was for you with the crops. I don't think you're cut out to be a farmer, like Crow or your father," Catherine said thoughtfully.

"It's hard work, and I don't mind it one bit, but it's the unknowing that's the hardest…not knowing what the year will bring for Aunt Mattie. I feel very appreciative for all she's done for me, and I do try to give back, but…"

"Listen, you decided to stay because it would have been a good place to raise your boys, right?"

"Yes, a great place for Hank and little Doug…I thought they were my boys, but they were Douglas Winthrow's sons. I don't know how I could have been so dumb—completely ignoring all the little signs. I believed Lauren was my wife, and was utterly duped by them both."

"That certainly was strange how they deceived you, for the land or for who knows what?"

"It was strange, and I could never figure out Douglas' logic. I guess I'll never know why he pretended to be her grandfather when he was really her husband. I…"

"Stop, Henry, that's all a part of the past and now it's time to move on and do what your heart asked of you years ago."

"You wouldn't be mad, Kats? And you would support me if I were accepted at a seminary, maybe the one in Chicago?" he asked hesitantly, hope rising in his heart.

"Yes, look, I have my mother to help me with the twins, and I know we can manage while you get your degree. So yes, you can have your dream…because I love you Henry Millering."

"And I love you, Kats, more than you can ever imagine," Henry said as he gathered her into his arms, smothering her face with grateful kisses.

CHAPTER TWENTY-FIVE

All the legal work for the selling of the land was progressing. Thomas checked the contracts with others who were experts in land purchases for development, including the implications to the surrounding areas. He studied the division and the placement of the future homes, the streets, and even the backyards. The Elm trees along the streets and in front of each residence received attention as well, placing them in the little park with benches. The location of all the little things was as important to Mattie as the four-room grammar school. Every aspect seemed ready, except for signatures.

The land for the orphanage and the architectural layout was also complete. The Bishop was touched by Mattie's generous offer and by her willingness to help a church that wasn't even her own and he readily agreed to all her terms. Building would start in early spring.

The town was a-buzz with the prospect of new people and new businesses. They formed a new town council and began the planning of the roads. Complete strangers came in to buy up property alongside the established businesses. They bought the property right next to the barbershop, the small restaurant, and the mercantile. Even the minister at the little Methodist church had dreams of a bigger church with a separate building for the town meetings. They would definitely need a funeral home, more land for a larger cemetery, a small police station, and lastly, a post office with an American flag flying proudly.

The businessmen were sure this little town would begin to grow and someday be as large and prosperous as Mayette, but the old-time farmers like Maxine's Mister didn't see any value in the kind of changes that were being planned. *Why not just drive the eight miles?*

CHAPTER TWENTY-SIX

While Dudley Best was talking, Dennison felt a chill in his gut, when he realized that there may be some validity to other claims about the showers and solitary confinement. He always thought they were only stories made up by some to get out of punishment. Anyway, the type of boys here did consistently lie. Who could believe them? But then again, Helen Thompson said something too. *What was it that embarrassed her?*

There was a quick double knock at his door which interrupted his train of thought.

"Who is it?" he shouted across the room.

"Sir, it's Alex Stanton and Marvin Prinze. We're with the senior patrol and have orders to speak with you immediately," Prinze shouted.

Dennison stood and walked over toward Dudley.

"Come quickly. Go into the room over there while the boys are here. It's my inner office for private meetings with parents and staff. I don't want them to find you here…so lock the door."

Dudley did as he was told while Dennison took his seat behind the desk and shuffled some papers.

"Come in." Dennison was peering into a folder, looking occupied.

The door opened and the two boys stepped into the room but remained standing by the door, according to protocol.

"Sir, may we speak?" Prinze asked.

"Yes, please speak. That's why you're here, isn't it?" Dennison said, always annoyed at this stupid rule.

"Sir, there is a sophomore missing."

"What's the boy's name?" Dennison asked, acting as though he knew nothing about the incident.

"Dudley Best is the culprit, sir. He had a visitor today and was playing the piano in the lounge, skipped gym class, and was misbehaving in the showers, and…that is all, sir," Prinze replied.

"What did you say your names are?"

"This is Alex Stanton, sir, and I'm Marvin Prinze," was the prompt reply as he pointed to the other boy first and then himself.

"Shall we take this infraction to the office and have an all-alert sounded, sir?" asked Prinze, as Stanton's hand was nervously fingering the billy club that hung sheathed at his side.

"Thank you, no. My secretary, Mr. Lenton, or myself are fully capable of taking care of that procedure. Do you think he left the grounds?"

"We don't know, sir, but we can spread out. I mean with the other senior patrol and comb the area in and around the school if you like, sir."

"No boys, you may go to your next post. Thank you for your quick response." Dennison opened the door, showing them the way out. As he did so, Mr. Kracker was about to knock.

"Oh, Mr. Kracker, please come in."

After they both sat down, the coach began. "I believe that the boy, Dudley Best, is unquestionably incorrigible. I found him in the locker room with the two senior patrols. He was naked and trying to get them to go into the showers with him. They immediately put him on report."

"I'm glad they acted so fast, and as you know, the school always encourages the staff to recommend the punishment when they find a situation like that."

"Yes, and I believe a little time out in solitary confinement would teach that boy a lesson."

"Where is he?" Dennison asked, continuing the charade.

"I explicitly told him to report to you, sir. I don't know where he could have gone—maybe his dorm room—unless he is trying to escape, which I wouldn't put past him."

"I'll take it from here, Mr. Kracker. And when I find him, he will definitely be down in solitary, you can be sure of that."

The minute Kracker left, Dennison dialed the internal number to the office. He hoped that Helen Thompson would still be there as it was very close to quitting time for the day staff.

"Good afternoon, Helen Thompson speaking. May I help you?"

"Helen, this is Jonathan Dennison. Would you—could you—please come to my office before you leave the building for the day? It's very important that I speak with you as soon as possible."

"Why yes, sir. I'll be there right away," she said, as quick fear drained her face. *Perhaps I misspoke when I told him about the senator. Now I could be in trouble and lose my job.*

Dennison walked over to the room where Dudley was waiting and knocked. Dudley unlocked the door.

"Come and sit down. I have to figure a way to get you out of here for the night."

It was only a few minutes before Helen was at his door. After entering, she was surprised to see Dudley sitting there. She gave him a brief nod.

"Mrs. Thompson—Helen—I'm up against it here and I don't know whom I can trust. Everything is getting a little muddled, so I'm asking you, do you think you could help me? I wouldn't ask, but you said you had a youngster about the same age as Dudley and that you have a heart for some of the boys here."

"Yes, I did say that. I'll help you any way I can, but wouldn't your private secretary, Mr. Lenton be more able to help?"

"No, no. I need someone else, someone not connected to me directly."

Then Mr. Dennison explained the incident about Dudley and the senior patrol. "I would like to smuggle the boy out. I could take him home and call that senator you told me about. But I can't call from here. Something is going on here that I don't like."

"How—but how can I get him out?" she asked, and as she looked at Dudley, felt a little shiver of fear.

"You could walk out of here with your son. You did say your boy was about the same age, didn't you?"

"He is...but..."

"He needs different clothing...I may have to go home and get some of my son's clothing. I live nearby. And then he could walk out with you!"

"Oh, wait, in my office, I have a bag with my son's pants and jacket. I was to drop them off at the cleaners after work. They'll be a little crushed from the bag but I can shake them out. I think they would fit him."

"And I have my son's cap sitting right there with his baseball. That would cover your hair, Dudley, wouldn't it? Here, try it on."

Dudley put the cap on. He was now in a bit of a fog with everything happening so fast.

"What do you think, Helen?"

"It looks casual enough. Pull the brim down so your eyes don't show, Dudley."

"Like this?" Dudley asked as he pulled the cap forward and down.

"Yes, that looks good. I'll get the suit. It won't take me but a few minutes since it's dinner time. The senior patrol won't be a problem at this time," she added.

"And as the next shift starts coming in, it'll look like you're leaving with your son," Dennison said. "Here's my address. Bring the boy there just as fast as you can. You know, Helen, I may get fired for this, and you too."

"I'm aware of that," she said as she hurried out.

During the ride to Dennison's home, Dudley felt hollow inside, like an empty container, doing whatever he was told and hoping it could save him. Helen knew he was worried but didn't say anything even when his head tilted back, resting, probably trying to calm himself.

She walked Dudley up the stairs to the front door. It was a beautiful home, much nicer than the house she lived in. When they stepped in, they smelled the unmistakable scent of pot roast. Dudley immediately removed his cap, nervously twisting it around and around while filling his lungs with the delicious smell.

Mrs. Dennison invited them to sit in the living room to wait for her husband. She went back to the kitchen while the three children stood at the doorway, watching Helen and Dudley closely and wondering if maybe they were coming to dinner.

"Wow, what are you doing with my cap?" Richard, the oldest of the three, asked. "It's the one my dad had in his office."

"Well," Mrs. Thompson explained, "there was a little problem. I think your father will explain everything when he gets here, okay?"

The children watched as Dudley twirled Richard's baseball cap in his hands. It was only five minutes but to Dudley it seemed like an hour before the school principal arrived home. Both Helen and Dudley felt ill at ease, and since they had no explanation to give for their appearance, they wore slightly pinched smiles as they waited.

When Dennison finally arrived, he introduced Helen and Dudley formally to his wife and children. Then he spoke to Helen.

"Helen, I have good news. One of the people in your office must have seen you leaving with Dudley. She mentioned that you were probably going to a school game or something with your son. I think we pulled it off, Helen. Thank you for all your help."

"I'm glad I could help, sir. Here is the bag with Dudley's uniform."

"Oh, I almost forgot about it. What a mistake that would have been, finding the uniform in my office. Thank you for remembering to bring it," he said as he took the bag from her. "Do you need Bailey's suit back right away?"

"I'm sorry, I do because he needs to have it back from the cleaners before tomorrow evening, and if I hurry, I still have time to drop it off."

"Dudley, please go up with my wife. She'll find you some jeans and a shirt. Hurry so Mrs. Thompson can leave."

"Yes sir, I'll hurry, but can I please take something out of my uniform pocket?"

"Yes, here's the bag."

Dudley quickly pulled his shirt out of the bag with everyone watching. With shaking fingers he opened the pocket and retrieved the little gold cross, placed the shirt back into the bag and flew upstairs, following Mrs. Dennison. Looking back, he said, "Thank you, Mrs. Thompson," and with a grin, threw the cap to Richard.

Mr. Dennison headed to his downstairs office to place a call to Senator Tierney. He explained to the secretary that he was the Director of the Reform school and it was urgent he immediately talk with him about an important matter. He gave his number and hurried back upstairs for dinner with his family and the boy, Dudley Best.

CHAPTER TWENTY-SEVEN

Mathilda didn't waste any time after she got back to Mayette. She went directly to Thomas' office and hoped he would be there and not on an errand or in a meeting.

"I would like to see Mr. Bealer, please," she said, offering her best smile to the new receptionist. She was a pretty young thing, about seventeen, and the only staff member in the office. She had long dark hair with a swooping wave that fell over her right eye, just like the movie star, Veronica Lake.

"Do you have an appointment, ma'am?" the girl asked. She was chewing gum and to Mathilda it looked like a large wad by the way she moved it around in her mouth—kind of slow because of its mass.

"No, I hurried to see him before he left. Is he still here?" she asked this mere snip of a girl trying to act as a competent receptionist.

"Yes, ma'am, he is. But he left sp-sp-specific orders not to be interrupted," the girl explained, while the gum was vying for first place in her mouth, but she did manage to speak after pushing it into her cheek, creating a bulge.

"But I have to see him. It's very important."

"I'm so sorry, ma'am. Mr. Bealer said abso-abso-absolutely not to disturb him unless someone was dying or the place was burning down."

After relaying this important information, the young thing chewed even faster. Mattie didn't think it was cute or funny.

"Look here, I'm Mathilda Millering and Mr. Bealer is a good friend of mine. You had better go in and tell him I'm here or I'll walk in anyway. I'm telling you that it's important I see him immediately!"

"But, ma'am, I don't know what to do. He said no one and I could get fired. I need the work experience for my credits at school."

"Oh, I'm so sorry, dear. I'm sure it'll be okay. I'll take complete responsibility."

"Well, if you say so. Everyone else has left and I just don't know what to do."

Mathilda had enough talk. She walked over to the door that had his name engraved on a brass plate. It said, "Thomas Bealer, Attorney at Law." She opened the door and slipped in.

Looking back before closing the door, Mathilda saw the young girl chewing even faster while unwrapping another stick, taking small bites and adding them to the wad already in her mouth. Mathilda thought she might unintentionally swallow the whole wad, or even worse, choke, but the girl was still able to crack it, which caused Mathilda's brows to scrunch up, wrinkling her forehead.

"My dear, what is your name?"

"It's Gladice, ma'am, Gladice Flitt."

"Gladice, you're such a beautiful girl. Do you know that it's better not to chew gum when you work in a professional office? It's much harder to talk to clients and be understood, but most of all it spoils your smile." Mathilda shook her head as she said this, emphasizing her point. She wanted to tell her that it made her face and mouth look contorted and unbecoming, but she held her tongue, not wanting to be rude to the child.

"Thank you, ma'am. No one's ever told me that I was beautiful before, except of course my mother."

After Mathilda closed the door, Thomas stood up and walked over to her, leading her to a chair.

"Thanks for that good advice for our newest hire." Thomas said. "Mattie I'm so glad you're here, because after talking with you earlier, I called Senator Tierney. He just called me back after looking into the situation since he also received a call from Mr. Dennison, the principal at the reformatory."

"I just knew he was in trouble."

"You were right, because Tierney said that Dudley was smuggled out of the building a little while ago. He was in real physical danger. Mattie…it means he's out of that place! He's really out of there!"

"I can hardly believe it. Thank God!"

At that moment, the young girl knocked on the door, opened it, and blew a bubble, cracking her gum again. As she stepped in, she said, "I straightened the files in that closet. Is there anything else I can do before I leave, sir? And I'm sorry about the lady coming in, but she said it was important and I didn't know what to do."

"You did fine, Miss Flitt. Go ahead and go home and we'll see you tomorrow after school." Thomas spoke very kindly, and then added, "and it would be better to leave all the gum at home tomorrow."

"Yes, Mr. Bealer. Goodbye, Mr. Bealer," she said, as she turned and waltzed away—swaying her body like some movie actress she was trying to imitate. As soon as she closed the door, Thomas and Mattie laughed at her antics.

"Her first day?"

"Yes, her first day." Then as their eyes met, he returned to the matter at hand. "Let's go out to dinner, Mattie. I have something more to tell you about Dudley and about your property. Do you have the time?"

"I'll have to call home and tell them that I'll be late and not to hold dinner."

"Sure, I'll dial it for you."

"Oh…I see you still know my number by heart."

Mathilda felt a small sting poke at her heart, whenever she remembered Thomas' words to his brother. Mentally, she tried to forget those words…but her broken heart couldn't.

* * *

"Hello, Mathilda Millering's residence. To whom do you wish to speak?" Booker T. asked.

"Hello, is that you, Booker?"

"Yes, ma'am. Guess what I did today?" he asked when he recognized Aunt Mattie's voice.

"I don't know. What did you do?" She nodded at Thomas who was standing right next to her and could hear the excited boy shouting very plainly.

"This lady was having a baby and I helped Doctor James. Oh, Aunt Mattie, it was…it was scary and…the baby cried and I got to wrap him in a blanket and hand him to his mother. It was a boy. I'll tell you all about it when you get home," Booker T. said, almost crying with emotion.

"Booker T. that's wonderful. You're like a real doctor, already."

"Doctor James said I did swell. Gotta go, Auntie. I gotta memorize another list and do my regular homework."

"Tell Miss Sadie and Miss Angela that I'll be late and not to hold dinner for me, okay?"

"Yes, ma'am, I'll tell them. Oh Auntie, It was like…like a miracle!"

"Booker T., I'm so very proud of you. Goodbye, Doctor Fraze."

"Goodbye, ma'am," he said as he hung the phone up, smiling from ear to ear.

CHAPTER TWENTY-EIGHT

Thomas decided to take Mattie to a small hidden away restaurant where they served the best filet mignon in Mayette and featured an accomplished pianist playing soft dinner music.

As they were seated, Mathilda was reminded of that first time he had picked her up at the Chicago train station. They were on the way to see Dudley at the Conservatory and stopped at a similar place where they danced to romantic stringed music before eating a delightful dinner. *But why now? He isn't interested in marriage,* she thought, *and I'm not interested in only bits and pieces of him!*

"Let's just relax for a while. You've been under so much tension lately, and now there's a good chance that Dudley will be exonerated and I have good news about the contracts for the sale of your land."

"I could use some good news, Thomas."

"Must you continually call me Thomas? You used to call me Tommy...all the time...don't you remember?" Tommy wasn't scolding, just reminding as he smiled and lightly touched her hand across the table.

"Oh, I just thought that maybe it was too...too forward and a little cozy?"

"Well, I prefer it, Mattie. And I do like cozy...very much."

"Well, yes...okay...Tommy," she said as she her heart felt a familiar pang.

"Anyway, Marcus Marrianett seems to be on the up and up. I couldn't find anything wrong with the way he's been doing business."

"See, I told you he was legitimate."

"And so you did, but the lawyer in me had to make totally sure. I looked at some of his work and the people working for him. It all looks good. They say that they can start early in March of next year if the weather cooperates, or April at the latest."

"That's splendid! I'll let Henry and Catherine know right away."

"But as far as the orphanage goes, they aren't interested in having horses and stables. They thought that the upkeep might make it prohibitive. Mostly donations would be funding an operation like that and it can't be counted on."

"I understand. But the children would develop much better with some responsibility, don't you think?"

"I agree, but I'm not on the board and don't have any authority to push it through. But they did propose growing vegetables and the like since there would be room on some of the acres. They could have them for the table, canning and for sale if there were an excess."

"That sounds good too, with all kinds of possibilities. But tell me the most important thing…about Dudley?" Mathilda wanted to hear all the details. "Could he really be cleared of all the charges against him?"

"Yes, if Senator Tierney's investigation can prove Rudy was shot and Dudley was railroaded—and I definitely believe he can. You know, Mattie, the Juvenile Court hearing only talked about a knife being used. This information about a gun can break the case wide open since someone purposely concealed the evidence."

"I would think the coroner would have had that knowledge…and he would have had to put it in his report…unless…"

"I'm sure there are more people who knew. It's a conspiracy, that's what it is," Tommy answered, getting angrier as he thought about it.

"I guess Dudley being freed and exonerated would be the best thing that could happen," Mathilda said as they sipped sherry from tiny crystal glasses and ate soft hot rolls and butter while waiting for dinner to be served.

"The thing is, Mattie, this Senator Tierney is very interested in the boy. I guess he wants to help because we were old friends and went to school together."

"What do you mean, 'interested?'"

"Well, he asked me to tell him everything about our family. You know, about Dudley's birth and where he's been living. He wanted to hear about his attending the Academy of music when he was so young, and well, just about everything, even about Louise. He asked a lot of questions about her."

"When was this?"

"We were both at that State Lawyer's Conference. We met by accident just after Dudley was sent to prison. I was so disturbed that day that I told him all about it. You did know it was Barry that got Dudley transferred from the prison to the reform school, didn't you?"

"I did, and I mentioned it to Dudley when I visited."

"Was he surprised?"

"A little…he wondered who would want to help him. Thomas—Tommy, did you tell him about Louise's husband dying?"

"Yes, he sounded as though he was glad that the man was dead! His exact words were, 'oh, he's *really* dead,' and then he said that what he had meant to say was he was sorry to hear about her loss."

"What do you think?"

"I don't know, but this was the clinker today. He said that under-cover police had been investigating the school for the last six months. Parents were already complaining, and, I guess since it's a state reform school, they're afraid the people will get riled up if this isn't cleaned up quickly."

"I know I'm upset that something like that happened to Dudley and the other boys, even if they were guilty of serious offenses," Mathilda said.

"The police said that Dudley couldn't go back to his own home till the investigation was finished, because there would be repercussions. Because of this, Tierney offered to take him to a place he knows would be safe. It's in the suburbs—almost in the country."

"He'd like to take him to where?" Mattie asked surprised.

"I did some checking. He lives in Cranston. It's about an hour's drive from the reform school, so it would probably be somewhere around there, but who knows, he wouldn't tell exactly where. According to him, Dennison could get in some deep trouble if Dudley stays at his home any longer. He says he has a perfect place to hide him and he's willing to take him there."

"But...that makes sense, doesn't it?"

"Well, Tierney has all kinds of options that I don't have. He knows people that know people that know people, and I only know that I was lucky to run into him when I did."

"I don't think we could have done anything more."

"Our hands were tied. I tried so many ways and couldn't get any information. I think Dudley would never have seen the outside of that reform school until he turned eighteen, and then he would have been transferred to another prison."

"What did you say the man's name is?"

"We always called him Barry at school but his name is Barrett Evan Shannon Tierney."

"Oh my, that is a long name for a boy. I can see why they just called him Barry during his school years."

"I guess it would be the best thing for Dudley. When I told Louise that Dudley was okay, and where he was going, she was very relieved that he would be in a safe place."

"I'm glad you told her. She's been quite worried."

"You know, Dudley didn't want her to come to see him at all. He's been feeling pretty bad about her giving him away at birth. There's so much pain on both sides."

"Dudley's still too young to understand how love makes people do things…things they wouldn't normally do." Mathilda was thinking about how that suave Douglas Winthrow had talked her into a trip with him only a few years ago.

"He needs to grow up a little more. Only a few more years and… Mattie, let's change the subject for a little while. Could we?"

"Yes."

"Let's dance. And by the way, how are your new dishes doing?" he asked as he led her onto the dance floor and pulled her close, snuggling his cheek against hers. As they began dancing, she felt as though she belonged right there in his arms.

"You know…at first I felt guilty that I stopped for those dishes, and then I thought—"

Mathilda quickly cut in and said, "It would have been us—you and me—that would have had to turn him in, and I don't know whether we could have…could we?"

Tommy's cheek was now caressing the side of Mattie's cheek and before Mattie knew what was happening, he slid his face so that their lips met for a wonderful moment.

CHAPTER TWENTY-NINE

Mrs. Dennison came into the living room where the children were now talking to their unexpected guest to say that dinner was ready. After taking their places at the table, Dudley observed the three children and the father and mother sitting down together. A family eating together was something he never experienced. Mr. Dennison bowed his head and the children quickly followed as he said a blessing over their food. Dudley did too, he lightly touched the pocket of his borrowed shirt.

No sooner was the platter in Mr. Dennison's hands, when the maid came in to tell him there was an urgent call, so he passed the platter of roast beef to Dudley. Dudley knew he couldn't pile the meat on his plate the way he would like; he had been hungry for so long that it looked like a magnificent feast. He took a small helping and passed the plate to Sarah, holding it for her as she helped herself, because it was too heavy for an eight-year old. Then he passed the platter to Mrs. Dennison.

When Mr. Dennison came back to the table, he mentioned something to his wife about probable corruption from the top at the school and that the senator already had a call from a lawyer—a Mr. Bealer telling him about the prosecutor in Blenning possibly hiding the facts in this case.

"Sir, Mr. Bealer is my uncle. Aunt Mattie must have called him when she heard me playing the piano in the meeting room. I think I told you about it," Dudley offered though he didn't know whether he should interrupt. After he spoke, he dropped his head and said he was sorry.

"Dudley, you did tell me and it explains a lot of things. For instance, why Mr. Tierney would want to see the transcripts of the hearing. I hope they can get to the bottom because this school was thought to be one of the best rehabilitation schools in this part of the country. I for one thought that with the teachers meeting and reporting every morning, we had a good grasp on everything going on."

The children were all eating silently and taking in every word of the conversation. Richard looked at Dudley with keen interest since he couldn't remember his father ever bringing a boy home or even talking about one at the dinner table before. And he liked this guy. He seemed…okay.

"Dad, if Dudley will be staying the night, he could bunk in my room," Richard offered.

"That's a very kind offer," Mr. Dennison said. "I believe he will be staying."

"Thank you, Richard," Dudley replied, a little surprised at the offer.

"Daddy," Betty said, "may we show Dudley our tree house after dinner? I think he would like it." She was a year younger than her brother, Richard.

"A tree house?" Dudley asked. "Right in your back yard?" He could hardly believe such enthusiasm about a simple pleasure, and some of the weight he carried all day was starting to dissipate as the children talked and included him. He felt welcomed and wanted.

"Yeah, we have a ladder going up," Sandy, the eight-year old, said, excited at the idea of showing it to Dudley. "We can have snacks up there and even sleep up there if we want too."

"Okay, kids," Mr. Dennison said, "right after dinner you can show Dudley the tree house, but you can't stay up too late because you have school tomorrow, and besides, it's getting pretty chilly out there."

"Oh Dad, it's not that cold," Richard said, embarrassed at being told about it in front of Dudley.

"One other thing: I don't want any of you talking about our guest at school. Do you understand?"

They all said, "yes daddy," and continued eating so they could go outside before it got too dark.

During that telephone call, Tierney informed Dennison that there would be a surprise lockdown, happening even as they spoke. All the inmates at the reformatory would be ordered to take their books from the study hall lockers to their own rooms. They would be allowed to read and study until lights out but, no-one would be allowed out of their rooms until the investigation was complete with questions answered and depositions taken from everyone: teachers, staff, and inmates alike.

Another undercover unit would be picking up the Blenning District Attorney and his son for questioning, and then processing the release of every paper pertaining to Dudley Best, sealed and unsealed.

Lastly, Senator Tierney mentioned that he wanted to meet the boy the next day. He said he would take him to a place outside the city until things settled down. But he didn't say where that would be.

CHAPTER THIRTY

"Hello, dear," Angela said as she and Mattie entered Catherine's kitchen, "How's my favorite daughter?"

"Hello mom, hello, Aunt Mattie. I just put the water on for tea," Catherine said as she put out three pretty tea cups, and a large platter of cookies. "Henry and the boys should be back in a short while. They're over at the farm with Jesse and Donnie giving rides with Lil Peaches pulling the cart up and down one of the lanes."

"Oh, I used to do that, and I made pretty sunbonnets for my own, Lil Peaches."

"You did!" Angela said, not knowing that her sister could even handle a horse, let alone give children rides.

"Yes, the bonnets didn't do much of anything for the horse, but the children loved all the ruffles and bows and Lil Peaches liked the attention."

"Will we have to sell our Lil Peaches, Auntie?" Catherine asked.

"Not at all, dear. Jesse said he can still take care of her even though he'll be working for Mrs. Maxine and the Mister. The sale won't disturb your homes at all. By the way, that's why we came. I want to let you and Henry know that they plan to start building early in the spring, and I need him to sign off on the original deed."

"I'll tell him, Auntie. I'm glad that all the building won't affect us. We love this old house because it's our first home, and you know, it reminds me of Crow and the wonderful man he was. He would have been proud of how nice everything looks, except that last rusty crop," Catherine said as she scrunched up her nose.

"He certainly would have been proud of the way you and Henry take care of everything. Not to change the subject, but did Henry ever make a decision as far as the seminary is concerned?"

"Yes, he's been accepted into a theological school in Chicago for the January term, and the best part is that he can live right on campus and won't have to find a flat or a rooming house."

"I'm glad that it'll be so convenient for him, and I could move in with you and the boys, couldn't I, Catherine?" Angela asked. "So you and the children wouldn't be all alone out here."

"Oh mom, I didn't want to ask because I didn't want you to feel obligated, but as long as you did, I can't think of anything any better," Catherine cried. "I don't think I want to be out here all alone with just the children."

"Will it be all right with you?" Angela asked Mattie, looking directly at her, wondering how her sister would feel about her idea.

Angela had been living with Mathilda for almost four years, and didn't want to distress her elder sister, since they were separated as children after their mother had died. The many good times during the last years flew through Mathilda's mind, and now she realized that the house would seem empty without her dear sister. They were still catching up on all the lost years.

"Of course I'd like to keep you with me and I'll miss you, but I want what's best for Catherine, too."

"Oh, Mattie, I just knew you'd understand," Angela said.

"It'll be a good time for both of you to be together, so no; I don't mind. I'll be visiting often, though, if that's all right?"

"Not only all right, Auntie, we'd feel slighted if you didn't come as often as you can," Catherine said, reassuring her further.

"If Dudley is released, and I hope and pray that he is, let's have the Christmas party here again before Henry goes away to school," Mathilda suggested.

"I remember that was the first party we had and Mom, you couldn't come that year," Catherine said. "We'll have a wonderful time this year and I know Dudley and Booker T. will love it!"

"And Jesse and Mary Beth and little Donny," Mathilda added.

"And we can invite the neighbors to say goodbye to Henry," Catherine said enthusiastically. "He has so many good friends from the church and from town. That's a grand idea, Auntie."

"It's a splendid idea, and I'll be looking forward to it," Angela said after taking the last sip of tea. "We must go now, but tell Henry and the boys that we'll see them at church on Sunday."

"And tell them we're sorry we missed them," Aunt Mattie added. "And don't forget, he'll have to meet with Tommy and get those papers signed as soon as possible."

"I'll remember to tell him. Bye-bye, and thanks for coming."

CHAPTER THIRTY-ONE

"Off to bed, everyone," Mr. Dennison said as the clock struck eight-thirty.

"I'll take Dudley up, Dad," Richard said, "I have some pajamas that he can use."

"How did you like the tree house, Dudley?" Dennison asked.

"Really nice, sir. It's up so high and when it started to get dark, we could see the stars in every direction. I've never been in a real tree house before."

"Hey, Dad, Dudley showed us where Draco and the Big Dipper was, and the Great Bear's Tail and the North Star and the…"

"So you all got a little astronomy lesson," Dennison said, rather pleased.

"Yeah, I guess we all did," Richard said, as they headed for the stairs, still a little awed that Dudley knew so much about the constellations.

I probably should get a book for them to take up there, Dennison mused. He also wanted to speak with Dudley privately, but decided to wait until morning so the boy could get some much needed sleep.

That evening, Dennison sat with his wife in his study, trying to relax a little, but began worrying.

"I'm wondering what's happening at the school tonight?" he said so softly that Mary could hardly hear him. "The boys must be going through a tough time," he said a little louder.

"They'll get through it, dear. And things will be one-hundred-percent better for them too. So don't fret. You'll know soon enough," she assured him.

"I wouldn't even tell you the kinds of things that were probably going on. I should have taken them seriously when some of the boys reported them. I was a dumb-ox."

"I'm sure you did your best. Anyway, it'll be taken care of now."

"Maybe, but there are powerful people out there that will do anything to dodge what they've been involved in. They could still end up doing the same things and maybe more if it's not handled right."

"I'm so sorry this happened on your watch, Jonathan," Mary answered, but she couldn't voice the real worry going around and around in her own mind. "And all I can say is let's be very careful that our children do not end up in a place like that!"

CHAPTER THIRTY-TWO

Dudley was accustomed to that five o'clock bell and awoke with a start until he remembered he was at the Dennison house. He began thinking about yesterday and wondered if Aunt Mattie knew where he was and what was happening to him.

Richard stirred and looked across the room. Seeing Dudley awake, he rolled his legs over the side of his twin bed and sat up.

"You're awake, Dudley?"

"Yep, I woke up early and couldn't go back to sleep."

"Oh, probably thinking about that reform school, right?" Richard asked.

"Yeah, I'm hoping and praying that I'll be cleared of all those charges against me, and I guess I miss my Aunt Mattie and best friend Booker T."

"Booker T., that's some name. We touched on that name in our history class. It wasn't in our book but the teacher wanted us to know about the man, Booker T. Washington."

"Then you know he was a Negro?" Dudley asked.

"Yeah, we knew. Only in class they didn't say that he was Negro, colored or black. They just said he was a n...." Richard stopped short when Dudley interrupted.

"Yeah, well Booker T. is a Negro. I met him when I was studying at the conservatory in Chicago"

"And you're friends with him? That's weird."

"Maybe, but we can play an arm and leg on a piano together and it's a lot of fun, at least to me. He lives with my Aunt Mattie now."

"Wow, your aunt is a…is black too?"

"Na, she's white, but it's a long story and it's not anything I want to talk about now. By the way, thanks for everything. Ya know, your clothes and stuff."

"No problem man, we guys have to stick together, don't we? Sometimes I wish I had a brother…instead I got two sisters."

"Oh, they're not so bad, are they? I mean Betty and Sandy seem okay for girls."

"Yeah, well, they're nothing like a brother, but that's the way it is. Guys can do so many things together…and girls, like my sisters, they don't know nothin' and they're not interested, either."

"Oh yeah? Don't kid yourself. Most can do pretty much what we can do…that's what I hear, anyway."

"But dad said I'll change my mind about girls pretty soon, and I think I know what he means. There's this cute girl in my math class. Sometimes she'll look at me with a little grin. I think about her a lot," Richard said, "and at night, I wonder if she would say yes if I asked her to one of our sock hops?"

"I've never had that happen, I mean with a girl actually interested and looking at me. I don't even know any girls to talk to, except your sisters and my younger sister."

"Well, I'm not allowed to date. Dad says I have to be sixteen. Hey, how come you're in that reform school, anyway?" Richard asked.

"I've been running with a gang, and got in trouble."

"Wow, what's that like?"

"Nothing you'd wanna do. It was dumb and I was set up, taking the blame for what they did."

"They didn't like you?"

"They used me."

"But why did you let them?"

"Once you join them, they let you know that you're like family, and now you know too much about each other. But we had some fun times too and I felt like I belonged. One of the guys, played the violin. That interested me so he invited me to his house to play it. No one was ever home at his place. He could do anything he wanted. He and I would hang out there, and we also stashed the stuff the gang stole in his basement."

"We have a few gangs at our school too. They act pretty tough."

"Yeah, just don't get involved with them…for any reason," Dudley cautioned.

"I don't intend to. I just wondered how it was with you."

"Ya know that guy, Simpson, the one who played the violin? He only acted tough when we were with the other guys," Dudley said, "otherwise he was okay and he was interested in music, like me."

"Hey, what was it that you had to take out of your pocket yesterday?"

Though Dudley didn't want to tell anyone, and felt his face grow hot, he decided to be truthful to this guy who had shared his room and clothes.

"Oh, it's just a tiny little cross that I found when I first got to the reform school. I would kinda like to keep it."

"I just wondered what was so important," Richard answered thoughtfully.

After breakfast, there were fast goodbyes as the Dennison children left for school and then Mary and Jonathan Dennison were left alone with Dudley.

"I see Richard's clothes fit you pretty well," Mr. Dennison said.

"Yes, sir. We're about the same size. Thanks for helping me, yesterday, sir."

"Yes, Dudley, it was a quick hard decision. Let's go into the library and have a little talk."

"Yes, sir," Dudley said as he got up from the table. "And thank you, Mrs. Dennison, for everything. The breakfast was really good."

"I guessed that you liked it with all those helpings of pancakes," she said as she picked up his dishes.

"Yes, ma'am. I guess I was hungry," Dudley said as he followed her husband into his study.

Dudley took a seat in a wing-back chair and Dennison sat down across from him. He was trying to see deeper into this boy who caused the school to go to a lockdown.

"Mr. Best—Dudley—you had a lot of courage yesterday in refusing to go back to the showers."

"Yes, sir. I was scared."

"But you stood your ground. If you hadn't, I think you would have been in solitary confinement today."

"Yes, sir," Dudley answered. What else could he say? He was still reluctant to say too much to any adult he didn't know very well. But he did know that maybe with a different director, he *would* be in solitary.

"Okay, a man by the name of Barry Tierney will be picking you up shortly. He's a senator in our state and he'll be taking you to a place in the country for a few days, or however long it takes to get this case straightened out."

"Yes, sir. Why would he want me…I mean, does he know me?"

"I don't have answers to that either, except I was advised that if you stayed here, I could get fired from my job. Maybe I will anyway because I deliberately removed you from the State's jurisdiction. Anyway, Senator Tierney probably had to pull some strings just to let you stay on the outside so you have to be on your very best behavior wherever he takes you."

"Yes, sir, I will."

"It's a touchy situation and will take time to get to the bottom of things—things going on at the school that I wasn't aware of."

"Yes, sir." Dudley was listening closely.

"This is for the safety of your family too," Mr. Dennison explained further.

"I know sir. That's why I couldn't talk about what happened. The guys threatened me. They said they would hurt my family if I talked, and I've got a younger brother and sister."

"I guess that was pretty scary for you," Mr. Dennison said, softening his voice, thinking about how his own son would have felt under those circumstances.

"I've been scared for a long time."

"Even now?"

"Yes, sir. Especially now."

"Why…especially now?"

"Because I may have to go back to that place, sir."

"Oh, I understand."

"Do you want to know more about the school, sir? I mean, about how hungry we were…all the time?"

"I didn't know…what else?" Mr. Dennison began taking notes on a pad of paper he pulled from his back pocket.

"The guards were always looking for something, anything to get us demerits so we would end up in solitary."

Then Dudley told about how he was somehow ignored and overlooked until that last day when Aunt Mattie visited. It had something to do with the four stripes on the arm of his uniform—he noticed that only one other inmate had them.

Next he told Mr. Dennison about all the good things that impressed him, like some of the teachers, the library with all the adventure books, current reading materials, algebra assignments, and the silence that helped him think and understand his dreadful behavior. The silence helped him the most.

CHAPTER THIRTY-THREE

Dudley liked Mr. Tierney's home, but he noticed a clinging sadness, hanging like a forever damp, rainy night. He could feel it in every room of the house. Maybe it was because Tierney's wife died last year from the complications of Polio. She had been ill a long time, since 1940, but in spite of the sadness, Dudley was happy he was there and not in prison or that reform school.

He had permission to use the indoor pool, the music room, and the huge library where he was allowed to look through dozens of shoe boxes full of postcards and pictures, or to read any of Tierney's law books. In the center of the room were two long library tables that Dudley guessed were used to do research on particular cases. On the end of one of the tables there were two typewriters: one with a normal carriage and the other, an IBM Electric that had an extra wide one, probably for legal work.

Dudley usually devoured adventure books that could carry him away to new places. He read at least fifteen while in the reform school, but in Mr. Tierney's library, only law books filled the shelves. They were piled high with stacks on the floor too, sorted together for some particular reason, so he began reading about juvenile law.

One day, Dudley was standing at the window holding one of the books, thinking hard about something he had read while watching the gardener. Mr. Blanchard always pushed a squeaky wheelbarrow around with rakes, hoes, and other yard tools. It was old and rusty as though it had seen better days, and as Dudley watched, the hoe fell to the ground. Blanchard stooped to pick it up, but he also picked up a flower that had fallen and was lying red against the greenish-brown grass—the rake handle must have clipped it as it hit the flower bed. Blanchard stood holding it, looking at it's brokenness, maybe counting the petals. Finally, he gently placed it in his pocket and adjusted the garden tools in that trojan horse. Suddenly, Dudley felt as though he were intruding on something very private, and walked back to the table where he had been sitting with the piles of books.

The staff at Tierney's house was small: Manny, the cook, and Oren Blanchard, the gardener. They were both very nice. Manny fixed all the meals but she liked baking sweet desserts better than anything else, and made all the pies and cakes Dudley and Blanchard could eat. She was a tall, thin lady with unruly, tight curly hair, like the healthy corn stalks Dudley saw growing on Mr. Crow's farm when he was little. She said she never worried about gaining weight and could eat anything she liked. This lady could light up the room like sunshine when she smiled but she was tough too, directing the cleaning people that came in on Fridays, telling them everything they needed to do from a list, checking off each item as it was completed. And at Mr. Tierney's dinners with important guests, Manny made sure the maids came in wearing crisp, white-collared uniforms with caps and aprons to match. It was their job to serve the many-course meal, after which there would be a thorough cleaning of the kitchen and dining room to set things back in order—without a speck anywhere—before they were paid and allowed to leave.

After lunch one day, Oren Blanchard invited Dudley to help rake the grounds that were piled high with autumn carpet-colored mounds of leaves, forced by the wind between and under all the shrubbery and completely covering the lawn. It was exactly the exercise Dudley needed to make him feel worth all the trouble he created for Mr. Tierney. After that first day, Dudley began spending more time with the gardener, tagging along and watching as the man worked. After a few days, Blanchard and Dudley began putting the garden to sleep before winter set in. Blanchard welcomed the two extra strong arms and it was good for Dudley too because he finally slept through the night without continually waking and worrying. Old Blanchard reminded Dudley a little of Mr. Crow who cared for his Aunt Mattie's grounds and was the overseer at the Wheatlander farm four years ago. He was easy to talk and be with because he always explained the why of everything he did.

During their daily lunches, Dudley found himself telling Blanchard and Manny about the yellow painted sled Mr. Crow had made for him when he was only ten, and about the other one, the bright red one he made for Mr. Henry's son. They talked a lot during their lunch breaks, just sitting at the kitchen table while Dudley spilled his life story in little pieces.

Blanchard liked to hear this boy talk and figured Dudley couldn't have been involved in any kind of killing like the papers said. He knew he could spot a phony. He always had previously.

CHAPTER THIRTY-FOUR

"How are you, Dudley," Mr. Tierney asked one Friday evening after returning home with his fifteen-year old daughter.

"I'm okay, sir."

"Dudley, this is my daughter, Elise. Elise, this is Dudley Best." The two teens looked at each other without any emotion or interest.

"Hello, Dudley Best," Elise said sarcastically with a feigned smile and questioning eyes, before quickly running upstairs. She was home from boarding school, only for the weekend and today, she was decidedly uninterested in Dudley Best, for whatever reason her father invited him.

Dudley nodded but avoided looking directly at her. Surprised by the curt way she spoke to him, he unconsciously pulled his shoulders together and blinked his eyes, wondering why she was annoyed with him. As usual around girls, he felt shy and awkward, but he did notice that she wore a maroon school uniform: pleated skirt with matching sweater. The light blue blouse made the blueness of her eyes sparkle, and the dot-of-a-dimple on each cheek was very pronounced with that quick, pretend smile she gave him.

"Come and sit in the study with me," Mr. Tierney said to Dudley.

Taking seats across from each other, Tierney began, "Are you doing okay here, Dudley?"

"Yes, sir. And thank you for letting me stay, but could I please go home or to my aunt Mattie's house?"

"Well, that's not possible because you're still in danger. You see, son, the people who will be prosecuted and put in prison have many friends out there and it wouldn't take long for them to find you, your mother and siblings, and maybe your aunt too."

"How is my mother?"

"She moved to a town west of Mayette with your brother and sister. No one is saying where she is, and so she's safe for now, but she may have to move again, maybe even further away."

"And what about me?" Dudley asked, wondering if he would have to move again.

As they were speaking, Dudley heard a violin sigh a sad, haunting song come from the music room, and his attention to Mr. Tierney was broken.

"That's Elise playing—she plays in the Junior Orchestra. It's only by invitation and tryouts, so it's quite an honor."

Dudley could hear the pride in Dennison's voice and remembered that same tone when his Aunt Mattie spoke of his own playing.

"How old do you have to be, I mean, to be invited?"

"Well, they take applicants as young as fourteen, maybe even thirteen. Elise is fifteen and was a kind of Christmas present to us when she was born because my wife, Susan, was in one of those iron lungs, having contracted paralytic polio. But Susan played the piano too. I bought it for her when we moved here. Did you see it in the music room?"

"Yes sir, I glanced through the doorway and saw it but I didn't go in. Do you live here all alone?"

"Yes, it's just Elise and I, except for the help. Elise's mother passed away in May last year and we're still trying to get accustomed to her being gone. We're not doing very well," he said, his voice dropping. "Elise seems depressed when she's home, just mopes around and plays nothing but the songs her mother loved."

"I'm sorry, sir," Dudley said, not knowing what else he should say.

"Well, time will work it's magic, I'm sure. My wife wouldn't want Elise to feel so sad. It's been too long and I'm hoping things will change soon."

"What kind of violin does she play?"

"I'm not sure, but Elise said she would like to get one similar to the one at school. I don't know too much about violins."

"I think it sounds excellent, that is, from what I can hear."

"Would you like to go into the music room and listen?"

"Yes, sir. Would it be all right, I mean, with Elise?"

As they stepped through the threshold, the girl stopped playing.

"Hello, Daddy. Hello, Dudley Best," she said, turning her head and squinting at them as she removed the violin from her shoulder. "Did I disturb your talk with my father?"

"No, I don't think so. We weren't talking about anything that important," Dudley said.

"Well, my daddy doesn't talk to anyone about anything he considers unimportant. So how are you *important* to my daddy?" she asked suspiciously. "And why are you here?"

CHAPTER THIRTY-FIVE

"Elise, please don't put Dudley on the spot like that. It's most embarrassing and that's why I pay to send you to that private school—so you would learn some proper manners. Dudley will be staying here for a few months, regardless of how you feel. So get used to it!"

"Oh, Mr. Tierney, she doesn't mean anything by it. She's probably just tired. And we did interrupt her playing, sir." Dudley said this to ease the situation.

"Yes, that's true," Tierney said, looking directly at Elise. He was ready to speak when Manny came to the doorway.

"Sir, there's a phone call for you in your study."

"Okay, excuse me for a moment," Mr. Tierney said and he hurriedly left the room.

"I'm sorry to have interrupted you," Dudley said to Elise, hoping it would help.

"It's nothing—I'll just start over. It's only an old song and I'm supposed to be practicing scales."

"Oh, I know about scales."

"Do you play the violin?" Elise had a certain hope in her voice.

"No, I play the piano."

"Oh, then you could accompany me when I play mom's old songs?" Her pursed lips formed a most beautiful question.

She's...so pretty, Dudley thought, and felt his heart push upward, beating rapidly. He was completely unprepared for her change of mood.

"There's some sheet music in the piano bench. Why not see whether there's anything you can play," she said, still smiling at him.

"I don't need sheet music," Dudley said. "I can play anything you can play."

"Oh, yeah, sure," she laughed.

Placing her violin under her chin, she decided to play something that would embarrass him because of his silly overconfident remark. She began playing *Sweet Leilani*, a song her mother loved, and the one he most certainly wouldn't know.

Dudley listened to the end of the song and then asked her to begin again.

"Let me give you a little intro," he said, and proceeded to give her an improvised grand arpeggio, after which he stopped and waited for Elise to begin.

They played the song over and over with different timing as though trying to trip each other up. And then Elise transitioned into, *I'll Be Seeing You*, another of her mom's favorites.

After his call, Mr. Tierney stood in the doorway, listening to the youngsters play. He hadn't heard the piano in this house ever give such a splendid performance. Elise's face looked angelic as she pulled the bow back and forth, becoming one with the instrument as her fingers danced along the neck of the violin. Finally they stopped and looked at each other, smiling. It was as though Elise were seeing Dudley for the first time.

Tierney cleared his throat. "It sounds as though you've been playing together for much longer than the last ten minutes."

"Oh Daddy, it was just wonderful," Elise said happily, and then she turned toward Dudley. "Where do you go to school, Dudley?" she asked, expecting him to tell her that he studied at some famous music school, perhaps in New York at Juilliard, or in Paris, France, or maybe with the Berlin Philharmonic Orchestra.

She had stars in her eyes when Dudley blurted out the truth. "Well, at present I…I live at a reform school, but…"

As he spoke, his face turned beet red and Elise didn't want to hear anything further. "Daddy! You brought someone from a reform school to live here—with us?" she cried.

"That's right dear, I—"

The rush of Dudley's heart that he felt a few minutes earlier, now dropped, like a blow from a bowling ball, hitting him in his already aching stomach.

"Excuse me sir, if it would be all right with you, I'll go up to my room now. Goodnight, sir. Goodnight, Elise—I'll see you in the morning."

"Go ahead if you wish, but what about your dinner, Dudley?" Mr. Tierney asked. "Manny has it almost ready."

"I'm not very hungry, sir. We had a huge late lunch this afternoon."

"Well, okay then. We'll see you at breakfast. Good night, son," he added feeling caught between Elise and Dudley. It now crossed his mind that maybe this wasn't such a good idea.

Elise just glared at her father—her face now completely changed in the course of only a moment. Dudley turned and left the room.

"Why, Daddy, why did you bring him here?" she shouted at her father.

"It's part of my work dear," Tierney answered calmly.

Dudley could hear the conversation clearly as it echoed up the stairs he was ascending.

"But you never did this before. Has your work changed, Daddy?" she asked, trying hard to understand his motive.

Those words were the last ones Dudley could hear because he quickly closed his door and threw himself face down on the bed. His stomach suddenly hurt more than the usual on and off pain he'd been experiencing during his imprisonment.

CHAPTER THIRTY-SIX

The weekend passed slowly. Elise avoided Dudley and wouldn't eat at the same table unless her father threatened her. But during the evening, Dudley cracked his bedroom door so he could listen as Elise played the haunting melodies late into the night. He felt helpless with his circumstances and the hope he was hanging onto was diminishing more each day. His own despair was now becoming one with the sadness of Tierney's home.

For sure, I'll end up in that reform school again. After all, how long can this man put himself out for me, a perfect stranger, causing his daughter to be disgusted with her own daddy!

* * *

Monday morning began with a rain so cold it was almost snow, pouncing against the library window panes. Dudley watched it stick and create slow dams that broke and ran like tears; like his own and Aunt Mattie's, but maybe his mother was crying too.

He decided to spend the entire dreary day in that room because winter was beginning to show its face. There would be no garden work with Mr. Blanchard today.

Dudley was missing his Aunt Mattie, wondering if maybe he could call her. He hated to be whiney and troublesome, but maybe he could get rid of the hurt rumbling around inside of him. That would be the next best thing. Next time Mr. Tierney came home, Dudley would ask, but today, he would continue to read the books in the library and shuffle through the stuffed boxes, full of letters, snapshots, and picture postcards from all over the world.

Tierney traveled extensively during his years as senator, and always collected the prettiest ones for his wife and daughter. They always intended to make a scrapbook but Susan Tierney's death made it seem unimportant.

Sitting at the library table with several law books open, Dudley noticed that every volume had a decorative label glued on the first page. It read, "This Book Belongs to Barrett Evan Shannon Tierney," with a date. It seemed like a very distinguished name for the man he knew as Mr. Barry Tierney. There were also a few labeled, "With all my love, from Susan."

Oren Blanchard knocked softly and opened the door, breaking Dudley's concentration.

"Looks like the rain will turn into snow later," he said as he walked across the room to the fireplace. He carried a large pail of wood. After adjusting the damper and crumbling newspaper, he stacked the wood on top and lit the paper underneath. The roaring flames burst forth, catching the dry wood and throwing expected heat. Blanchard stood there for a moment, rubbing and warming his hands.

"Thank you, it is pretty cold in here. Doesn't the heat work for this room?"

"Manny tells me that sometimes it doesn't, and Mr. Tierney says it's temperamental like a woman," Blanchard said, laughing. "Though they say that after a few days, the boiler finally adjusts, but for today, a little fire will make it nice and toasty for you. I'll throw a few logs on and you won't have to wear your coat."

"Thank you. Did you happen to know Mrs. Tierney before she died?"

"No Dudley, I'm pretty new here. They hired me when the other gentleman—I think it was Mrs. Tierney's father—had to leave. He was having a hard time after his daughter's death, and the work—which he enjoyed—was getting too much for him."

"Oh, I just wondered."

"He stops in now and again to see the girl, though, you know, his granddaughter, Elise," Blanchard explained, and then left the room as quickly as he entered.

Dudley had hoped Blanchard would have stayed to talk, but knew work had to be done, so he returned to reading some interesting cases about juveniles much younger than himself caught in the system.

The room warmed up nicely, and Dudley settled in for the rest of the afternoon, making extensive notes. He then tucked his own notes into the appropriate pages next to the ones the senator had made.

CHAPTER THIRTY-SEVEN

Booker T. was lying on the davenport reading and studying his medical terms. Ever since he fell off his bike, he'd been having spasms, a kind of a catch that a little heat would relieve. Dr. James was sure it was only temporary and would clear up, but Sadie wasn't so sure.

"You'd better just stay right where you are and rest. I'll get breakfast started and bring you a nice hot water bottle."

"Thank you, Miss Sadie," Booker T. said. "I don't like to be a bother to you or Aunt Mattie."

"You're no bother at all. Like I said just rest, and I'll take care of your chores this morning. You know, Booker, Mrs. Mathilda should get you an appointment with another doctor since Dr. James doesn't figure that the pain is anything serious. We should find out for sure."

* * *

Booker wanted to go to church with Sadie and Aunt Mattie that Sunday morning. The services were in Mayetteville at the Methodist church where he always felt welcome, and this week Booker T. had it on his mind to talk to that new minister about what you had to know to become a good Methodist, and if they would have him. Being black, he wasn't sure the Methodists would want him. But today, he probably wouldn't be able to go because the pain wouldn't stop as it usually had before, though the hot water bottle did feel good when Miss Sadie placed it on his side. He still had on his pajamas and housecoat and was sitting propped up, balancing his textbook, using the time to study when the angry pounding at the inner front door started. It sounded as though something was plenty wrong. Booker T. set the water bottle down and limped over to answer the door, holding his side tightly so the pain wouldn't radiate down his leg. When he opened the inside glass door, he was surprised to see an officer wearing a badge, though it was a different colored uniform than Sheriff Bordon wore. The officer had entered the porch area without knocking on the outer door and without anyone inviting him to do so. Booker T. couldn't remember anyone ever doing that before and Aunt Mattie would say the officer was taking liberties and was rude.

"Yes, sir. May I help you?" Booker T. asked the officer, who pushed his way in, bumping and almost knocking Booker T. over as he closed the door behind. Booker T. steadied himself by gripping the three-legged table, almost tipping it and the decorative fruit bowl sitting on it.

"I'm looking for a Mathilda Millering and a young boy by the name of Booker," he said, in a very crusty voice while reading from the piece of paper he held in his hand.

"Yes, sir. I'm Booker and Mrs. Mathilda is still upstairs getting ready for church. She'll be down soon."

Booker's knees began knocking against each other and he felt a little faint. The fear had intensified the pain in his side. He never had an occasion with the law before, and in his mind he quickly reviewed all the happenings since he first came to live with Mathilda Millering. Everything that had happened during the four years he lived in Mayette, Indiana crossed his mind and he couldn't think of a single thing he might have done wrong to anyone, except those boys who always called him names on his way to the orphanage. But he only waved his fist and told them to stay away.

"What have I done? Have I done something wrong?" Booker T. asked, not once but several times. The officer ignored his questions.

Sadie heard the furious knocking too, and the voices coming from the front hall. *Who would be calling on a Sunday church morning?* she asked herself as she entered the room.

"Who is it?" she shouted toward Booker T. and then saw the officer standing there with his face scrunched up, looking like dreadful trouble was brewing.

"Are you Mathilda Millering?" the officer asked.

"No, she's upstairs," Sadie answered.

"I'll go up and get her, Miss Sadie," Booker T. offered. He was still standing near the door, afraid to move, even to go back into the living room.

"No boy, you just stay right here. You there, you go up and get her," the officer said, pointing at Sadie. "I want to speak to her— now! Tell her so."

Sadie was never one to argue with the law. She turned and ran upstairs immediately, but she was so flustered, Mathilda could hardly understand what she was trying to say. She thought she heard that a cop was going to take Booker T. away. Mathilda thought it a mistake and it must be something about Dudley. She hurried down, only to be yelled at the minute she entered the front hall.

"Are you Mathilda Millering?" the officer barked.

"Yes, I am. What can I do for you?" she answered courteously.

"Do you know you can be arrested for kidnapping?"

"Yes, I know that a person can be arrested for kidnapping, but what has that to do with me?"

"You are under arrest, madam, Mathilda Millering."

"Under arrest...for what?" Mathilda gasped, thoroughly surprised by those words.

"You kidnapped this boy from Chicago, and he must be returned immediately to his mother. She's preparing to press charges against you."

Booker T. was standing there, spellbound, trying to understand everything this policeman was saying, and when he heard that his mother wanted him, a large lump rose up into his throat. Booker T. thought it must be his heart.

"My Mother!" Booker T. said, unbelieving but excited that he might see the woman he hadn't seen for over eleven years—the woman who used to hold him and rock him and sing to him and tell him about walking in the footsteps of the man he was named after.

"Where is she? When can I see her?"

Again, the officer ignored his question. "I'll be taking him back to Chicago, unless there's going to be a problem," the officer said, as he directed his comment toward Mathilda.

Everything that Booker T. had accomplished flew through his mind. Go back to Chicago! He had his work with the doctor, with the families he had come to know and with the little ones who looked up to him. But now he also wanted to see his mother. He needed to see his mother and he would have to choose. He looked at Aunt Mattie with pleading eyes, not knowing what to do or say.

In all Mathilda's years, she had never been talked to in such a surly manner as by this officer. And not once did anyone ever come to her door accusing her of anything as serious as kidnapping. She was confused at that moment too. *I just can't lose Booker T. now. I can't lose them both.*

"Where is Booker's mother exactly?" Mathilda wanted to know.

"I'm not answering any of your questions. If the boy won't come, we'll all go down to the station."

Mathilda was never one to meekly submit to what she thought was wrong and she began to explain.

"I didn't kidnap Booker T. His father gave permission to bring him here when the boy was hurt and Mr. Fraze couldn't care for him."

Sadie could see things were not going well for Mattie. She slowly backed up toward the kitchen while they were talking and promptly called Attorney Thomas Bealer.

"What should I do, Aunt Mattie?" Booker T. asked again. The thought of seeing his mother was like hot coals burning inside of him.

"Auntie? What a joke! This woman isn't your auntie you dumb kid." The officer said this as he laughed, screeching at the top of his voice, all the while twirling the handcuffs as though he could hardly wait to use them.

"But she...she..." Booker T. didn't know how to answer this rude man. "She is my auntie. Just ask her."

"Here lady, let's forget all this crazy talk. I'll just put these cuffs on you and we'll all go down to the station to get this sorted out."

Mathilda obediently turned around while he clipped the cuffs over her wrists. It was at that moment that Thomas Bealer walked in. He took in the situation and became angry when he saw Mattie in handcuffs like a common criminal.

"You'd better take those cuffs off the lady and then show me your credentials." Thomas said, handing the police officer his card. The officer took out his identification and promptly handed it to the attorney.

"These do seem to be in order but I'll have to call Sheriff Bordon. He can be here in just a few minutes."

"Okay, I'll remove the cuffs for now, but I don't care if you do have your sheriff—whatever his name is—come or not. It's the law," he said adamantly. "A mother has a right to her child even if it'd been years ago that he's been kidnapped."

"Well, that's true about a mother's rights," Thomas said. "But this mother abandoned her home and the boy when he was still a little guy. I think the court will have something to say about that."

"Please, everyone," Mathilda said while rubbing her wrists and looking at the officer. "Why not come back after dinner and if Booker T. wants to go with you, it'll save us all a lot of trouble.

The police officer thought for a few minutes. "Okay, but don't try to run away or anything like that. And have your stuff all packed, ya hear, boy!" he said, looking at Booker T. with his face all puckered up again.

"Yes, sir. I hear you. Where did you say my mother is?" he asked again.

"I'll tell you when I come back."

"If Booker T. decides to go with you, he'll be ready. He just needs time to pack his things," Thomas said to the officer, latching onto Mattie's idea to stall for time.

CHAPTER THIRTY-EIGHT

The minute the officer walked out of the house Booker T. tried hard to stifle his cry of confusing feelings.

"Aunt Mattie, I do want to see my mother—I have to see her. Should I get my things together?"

"Well, Booker T., there isn't anything as important as your mother, but maybe she would want you to continue your work with the doctor and finish high school. Mothers are like that. They want what's best for their children and your mother is no exception. Remember, she gave you a name to grow into."

"That's right," Tommy added, "if I had a son doing as well as you, I would want him to continue his studies right here. Maybe when you see her, you can ask whether or not you could stay?"

"Yes, I know, but I want to be with her—wherever she is," Booker T. said. "Even if it means going back to Chicago."

"Excuse me, breakfast has been ready for some time. You all need to eat something before you make any big decisions, and you too, Mr. Bealer," Sadie said as she heard the front door slam, believing the officer had left. "Are we still going to church?"

"I think we should go," Mathilda said.

"I just can't go with you today, ma'am," Booker T. said. "I have some deep thinking to do, and some packing too."

"Mattie, I'll come over later today when that officer comes back," Tommy added. "Meanwhile, just have your breakfast and go to church. Pray and try not to worry."

* * *

That Sunday turned out to be warm and sunny, almost springlike. From the parlor window, Booker T. could see people walking and laughing together in the park across the street, probably without any of the heartache he was experiencing. He tried and tried to come to a decision but couldn't, because no matter what he chose, he knew he would lose something important. Finally, he went to his room, pulled out the luggage Aunt Mattie had given him last Christmas and packed the two suitcases he never had an occasion to use before. Folding each piece of clothing slowly and neatly, as he had seen Aunt Mattie do many times, he forced them down into the suitcase so they would all fit: shirts, sweaters, suit jackets with matching slacks, ties, and socks. He also put his better work clothes in a paper bag, just in case he had to do chores. He would also have to write a note for Doctor James so the doctor would know why he wouldn't be working for him any longer. Booker T. thought he should call him, but the doctor might be out on a call, and he didn't want to leave a message with anyone else. He practiced what he could say in a note…

I think my mother found me, and I want to live with her again. Thanks for helping me all you did. Aw—that sounds too stupid? I really should go see him, but there just isn't any time.

Carrying the bags downstairs he placed them near the front door, and in that moment, decided to take a walk, even though he'd been warned again and again never to do so. He remembered what happened last time but this was different. It was stuffy in the house and he was tired of pacing from one room to the next. He had to get away so he could think more clearly, and walking would help him do that.

Out the back door he went and took the familiar two-block walk toward the orphanage. He began remembering all the good times he had at the home when he stayed there with Dudley. *Poor Dudley,* he thought, *if I go to Chicago, I'll probably never see him again.* Then his imagination took over and he could hear them yelling to each other with their voices echoing in his ears as though it were happening all over again:

"Hey, Duds, let's make a jump for the sleds," Booker T. *yelled.*

"Yeah, man. We can find a board over in the shed."

"And pack it with snow," Booker T. *added.*

"And when we go down, we'll...fly," they said together and *began laughing.*

Then the time at the grocery store, while walking with their arms around each other's shoulders. People's faces were aghast, but the boys laughed and giggled all the way home about the looks they received and the cries of shame on you!

Another time, Booker tied their shoestrings together causing them to fall with Booker landing right on top of Dudley. They began tickling each other until they couldn't laugh one more laugh because they were so exhausted...so many good times.

Without any thought as to what he was doing, he slipped through the double doors of St. Gregory's Church—again.

He found himself in the vestibule. Usually, there was a hubbub of people coming and going, but today it was silent. Opening one of the tall wooden doors into the church, he saw daylight filtering through the stained glass windows and took a seat in a middle pew—his pew. He recognized the familiar feeling of anguish, his worry about leaving Aunt Mattie forever and never seeing Dudley again. Today, there was no hurry, so he sat still, his hands folded on his lap, and watched the colors come through the windows, pulsing, touching him just like a kaleidoscope, first this way and then that. His emotions wouldn't allow coherent words to be formed, but his skipping, jumping, leaping anxiety slowly fell silent as he remembered his mama. She told him he would be a fine man when he grew up. A man who would help people, just like his namesake.

Am I supposed to be a doctor? Was that what mama meant? And how could she have known? If I decide to go now, will there be another Dr. James and Aunt Mattie to help me in Chicago?

CHAPTER THIRTY-NINE

Catherine and Henry were busy gathering the necessary things Henry would need while away, placing them on the table in Catherine's painting room. He was happy now, every day, singing and humming as they worked. He would finally be doing what he believed God had been leading him to do during the last five years. During those years, he thought that his dream was an impossibility because of the endless work on the farm, and Mathilda Millering, the wife of his dead father, needed him. In his heart, he always felt obligated, mostly because his father had deceived her and their marriage vows and he was born out of wedlock. Ever since he met this gracious lady, he had tried to make up for that sin—somehow. It was his main goal in life.

After Crow had died, the entire burden for the growth of the wheat fell to Henry and to him alone. He felt a constant, heavy responsibility during the year, but when those crops came in, ripe and full, his heart burst with pride.

This last year, when all the golden crops, Aunt Mattie's as well as the surrounding farms, were destroyed by the fungus, he felt that he had failed. Whatever made him think he could be the farmer his father sent him to school to be? He never did have leanings in that direction. But after his mother died at the hands of that deranged minister and after high school, it was easier to go along with his father's wishes. Anyway, he had no other choice. His aunt with whom he had lived couldn't care for him and his maternal grandparents didn't want him.

Catherine interrupted his thoughts. "Don't forget, to wipe down those sleds," Catherine reminded Henry. "I'm sure they're full of grimy dust and all the kids will want to use them if there's enough snow this Christmas."

"I know, and Dudley might be home by then, only a month or so left before the end of the year," Henry said. "I'll have to look over that hill they'll be using, too, just to make sure new saplings aren't growing in the way of a swift run."

Suddenly Catherine stood still and stared at Henry. "What if they don't let Dudley go free?" Every word was catching in her throat.

"I don't know, but I do know they're trying to get all the people responsible. Some are very clever at hiding behind others, but all the big fish will be caught, hopefully soon. Come on, it's time to go to church. Call the boys and let's go or we'll be late."

* * *

After the service, standing outside, Henry and Catherine and the boys waited for Aunt Mattie and Sadie to join them.

"Where's Booker T. today?" Henry asked when the ladies finally came out and started hugging the boys.

"Booker's real mother wants him to come home," Sadie cried. She had a hard time being silent all during the service, with her thoughts jumping around, visualizing the house without Booker T. or Dudley.

"Yes and I'm afraid he'll have to go with her," Mathilda added, "unless the woman would have a change of heart."

"Does he have a choice?" Catherine asked as the boys jumped around impatient to go home.

"In a way, he does," Mathilda said.

"But if he refuses to go with his mother," Sadie said, "your auntie will be arrested for kidnapping. That's what that officer said, and he's coming after dinner today to pick up Booker. First Dudley and now Booker T.," she continued with a fretful voice.

"But that's ridiculous. His father wanted him to come with you. Booker T. can attest to that. Do you want us to be there when he comes?" Henry asked.

"No, Tommy is coming and Angela will probably be home by then too, along with Sadie and me. I don't think we need anyone else," Mathilda said.

"Not to change the subject, Aunt Mattie, but just where is *my* mother?" Catherine asked, wondering when Angela would get home.

"She should be back this afternoon and I'm sure she's having a good time with her friends."

"Ask her to call me about Thanksgiving dinner when she gets home. Please Auntie," Catherine begged.

"I will. But she'd call you even if I forgot to mention it, you know that, dear."

"I have to get these boys home before they wear out the remaining congregation with their antics," Henry said as he grabbed the two by their hands, leading them to the car. "Bye, Auntie."

"Oh, I almost forgot. Do you have any idea where Dudley could be?" Mathilda asked with her most innocent voice.

"No, Auntie. No one seems to know or they won't let that information out," Henry replied.

"Just thought I'd ask. Bye everyone."

Mathilda didn't want to say a word to Henry or Catherine about trying to find Dudley. And she didn't say anything to Sadie or Angela. But she had her mind made up to find where he was staying. No matter what anyone said, she would find a way to see him.

* * *

That same evening, after supper, Booker T. insisted he would do all the dishes. He washed, dried, and put the white dishes away in the pantry, straightening each shelf, and stacking everything neatly, the same as his auntie would do. As he worked he thought the new ones were much nicer than the ones that were broken, and now he hoped that she wouldn't be so upset with his decision that she would break these, too.

Later, Mathilda, Angela, Sadie, Booker T. and Thomas Bealer all sat in the parlor waiting. No one spoke; each was absorbed in their own thoughts. Booker T. sat stiffly on one of the wing-back chairs. He wore his best clothes as he waited to be taken to his mother, only now he was calm without any of the earlier anxiety. When the grandfather clock struck the half-hour at nine-thirty, Thomas left for the night. Booker T. stood up, kissed his Aunt Mattie lightly on her cheek, said goodnight to Miss Angela and Miss Sadie, then carried both suitcases upstairs. He unpacked his pajamas, changed and crawled into bed. Tomorrow, after school, he'd work with Doctor James. *Maybe another baby would be born.*

CHAPTER FORTY

The following Saturday morning, Mathilda decided to go see Mr. Dennison, principal of the American Reformatory. Knowing he lived in the same town where the reform school was located, she decided to go to the little restaurant where she had stopped for tea before visiting Dudley. They had a telephone near the door and most likely a telephone book with the listings for everyone in the town. At least she hoped so.

On the floor, beneath the telephone and the listing book was a stack of newspapers with Dennison's picture on the front page. Before leaving, she read the entire article stating he was removed from his position because of the corruption coming to light during the investigation. Now, she was sure he would certainly know where the boy was staying and he could probably tell her the truth about how the case against Dudley was progressing.

* * *

Mathilda pulled up to a red brick home with spacious grounds in the affluent part of town. Evergreen shrubs and almost bare trees surrounded the house. It had a wrought iron fence, red brick pillars and an open gate across the wide driveway where she parked. A brass knocker was centered on the door and she struck it two times.

After a few moments, a lady wearing an apron over her dark uniform and little white cap framing her head, opened the door.

"May I help you?"

"I would like to see Mr. Dennison, please."

"Is he expecting you?" she asked in a very businesslike manner.

"Well no, I'm Mathilda Millering. I'm Aunt Mattie to Dudley Best, and I need to speak with him." The maid was a little hesitant for a moment, as though deciding whether to invite her in.

"Please come in. I'll see whether he can be disturbed."

"Thank you," Mathilda said as she followed the lady and took a seat in the library. She could hear children's voices echoing from somewhere in the house and after a few minutes a man's deep voice welcomed her as he entered the room.

"Hello," the gentleman said as he stretched out his hand. "It's good to meet you—I'm Jonathan Dennison." Mathilda stood up and extended her hand for his gracious handshake. Then, Dennison turned and quickly closed the door before taking a seat in the chair across from where Mathilda was sitting. She sat very straight with her large black purse nestled on her lap.

"Mr. Dennison, I hope you don't mind my stopping like this. I've been very concerned about Dudley and decided to just take a chance that you would be home and maybe have some news for me."

"I do understand how you must be feeling. Dudley has told me a little bit about your visit at the school."

"I'm glad he did, I didn't know whether you would know who I was, but I had to try. No one seems to know or is willing to tell me where the boy is." Mathilda nervously ran her index finger back and forth over the silver clasp at the top of her purse as she spoke.

"I could tell you...but it would be dangerous for you and the boy's mother because we aren't sure who they all are. They may even now have my house watched, or the place where he's staying."

"But why? Why would they be so concerned with me or his mother? We can't identify them."

"They would very much like to know where all his family lives so they could continue to threaten Dudley, and that's it. But they're smart and ruthless and especially don't want the true details about that Blenning case to resurface again. That case seems to be tied together with the reform school in some way."

"Then the investigation would stop and nothing would change!"

"That's right, and they're looking for any little clues. This is serious business, madam, more serious than anything I've ever been involved in. You shouldn't have come here under any circumstances."

"I'm so sorry," Mathilda said apologetically. "But I read in the newspaper that you're not at the school any more, and I thought—"

"Well, it seems that I've been terminated," Dennison said as he took off his glasses and wiped each lens with his handkerchief pulled from his pants pocket, then he placed them back on his nose, peering through them as though looking for tiny specks.

"Can't seem to keep them clean," he said, feeling uneasy because people read all about his dismissal.

"Because of Dudley? You were terminated because of Dudley!"

"Yes, because of Dudley."

"But why?" Mathilda was trying to understand.

"Because the investigators have to use their own people to get to the very bottom of every reprehensible crime committed at the school. So you see, there isn't any way I can tell you what you want to know."

"Then you do know?"

"Yes, and he's okay." He was now thoroughly exhausted with this woman's endless questions.

"Does he go to school?" Mathilda asked further.

"No, he can't go out alone."

"Not at all, oh my...is he..."

"Listen, he's a strong boy so don't worry because all this should be over soon."

"Thank you, I won't trouble you again." Mathilda dropped her eyes, feeling as embarrassed as the gentleman. She opened her purse and reached to the bottom where she found what she was looking for.

"Here is my friend's card. Thomas Bealer is Dudley's uncle—he's an attorney. And he has another uncle who is the pastor of St. Gregory's in Mayette. They're…well…we're all concerned about him."

"Yes, the boy did tell me about his uncle, the attorney. If something happens, I'll call him, I promise. Now, you must go so as not to endanger my family any further."

"Oh my, yes. I'll leave immediately. Goodbye, Mr. Dennison, and thank you for everything." Mathilda stood and quickly placed her purse under her arm.

"Goodbye, Madam. Is this your number on the back of the card?" he asked as they were walking to the door.

"Yes, I put it there, just in case."

CHAPTER FORY-ONE

It was after five o'clock when Mathilda opened her door and walked into the front hall. She was completely surprised when she was greeted by the same policeman that was there the previous week.

"It's about time you got here," he said arrogantly. "I'm taking the boy to his mother."

Booker T. was sitting in the parlor—waiting with the officer for his Aunt Mattie to come home. He packed his two suitcases again and was neatly dressed for the two and a half hour trip.

"Did you bring my mother this time?" he asked, finally getting up the courage to speak now that Aunt Mattie walked in.

"You'll know about that very soon," the officer said.

"Don't worry, Auntie. I'll do whatever my mother wants me to do. I thought it all out during the week, and I don't want you to get in any trouble on account of me."

"That's perfectly okay Booker T.," Mathilda said, as his foot tapped against the floor, almost as fast as the woodpecker she spotted on the side of her house last year.

"I can hardly wait to see her again, and I know everything will work out, no matter where I live. Here or there makes no difference as long as I'm with her."

"Yes, Booker T. I know it'll work out."

Then she shouted to Sadie who was still in the kitchen. "Sadie, please call our lawyer, and tell him we're going to the station."

"Does this lawyer happen to be Thomas Bealer, the man who was here last week?" the officer asked.

"Yes, he's our attorney."

"That's what I thought. Don't bother to call him," he said sarcastically to Sadie as she popped her head into the vestibule to hear better. "He and that Reverend Bealer are already at the station. Come on boy, we can't waste any more time as we have a long drive ahead of us."

"Should I bring my suitcases?"

"Yes, I'll put them in my trunk and we'll be on our way," the officer said, a little more kindly than before.

"Okay, I'm ready," Mathilda said, as she walked over to the buffet in the dining room. Pulling out the top drawer, she grabbed a fat envelope and slipped it into her purse.

"I don't think you'll have to go with us, and I won't have to use the handcuffs since the boy is ready to go."

When the cop said that, there was a big sigh of relief because Booker T. hated the way Aunt Mattie was treated last week.

"But we gotta hurry," he added. "I've been waiting for you for the past hour." He didn't like Mathilda's nonchalant attitude.

"Well, anything of value is worth waiting for," Mathilda whispered to Booker T., but not loud enough for the officer to hear. For the moment, it made Booker T. smile broadly and release a little giggle. Then she addressed the officer.

"I'm sorry you had to wait so long, but I didn't think you would ever come back when you didn't show up after dinner last week." Mathilda suddenly understood that he didn't have any intention of going to the station with her and Booker. He wanted to leave directly for Chicago alone with the boy, and there wasn't any way that Mathilda would ever let him take Booker T. alone. She would pretend she didn't understand what he was saying and simply get into the car and go with them.

As the three of them walked toward the door, carrying all of Dudley's things, there was a quick light tapping on the glass. Booker T. turned and opened the door wide. A young colored girl was glaring at them.

"What are you doing here?" the officer asked crossly. "You were supposed to wait in the car!"

"I thought something was wrong, 'cause you were taking so long."

"Well, I had to wait for the lady. The boy wouldn't leave without her knowing he was going. She just got back."

"Yeah, I know. I saw."

"Who's the young lady?" Mathilda asked.

"Booker should know," the officer said. "You should know, boy," he said, now addressing Booker T. directly.

They all backed into the foyer and closed the door.

"No, sir. I don't know her. Who is she?" Booker T. asked.

"This is your mother, boy. You should know your own mother!"

Booker's eyes almost popped right out of the sockets—turning big and round while staring, trying to see his mother in her.

"She's what? She's not my mother," Booker T. shouted. "She's not! Aunt Mattie, I can't go with her!"

"I am too your mother! Your daddy and me was married right after you went away, and he told me that I should raise you up if anything ever happened to him."

"What's your name?" Mathilda asked, as she began sizing up what was happening here.

"My name is…they call me Missy. Fraze and me was married four years ago, just before he was in that accident. He said his son, Booker would be a good worker and would help me if I needed him."

"I see," Mathilda said, giving a nod of knowing assent.

"Listen, that's enough talk, Lets go 'cause Bubba's waiting for us," the officer said. He was pacing back and forth, not expecting this to be played out the way it was going.

"I'm not going with her, no matter who says I have to," Booker T. said in a calm rational voice. "I ain't never—I've never seen this lady before today."

Now, everyone had been standing in the foyer for some time and Booker T. started to walk toward the inner doorway.

"Where do you think you're going?" the officer asked.

"I gotta go to the bathroom."

As he started across the room, his hip and leg gave out and he slipped to the floor. The officer helped him up but Booker T. could only limp back into the living room and plop himself down on the davenport. His side was hurting worse than before and he wished he could stay home and put a little heat on it.

"May I talk with you for a few minutes before we go?" Mathilda asked the girl who was looking at Booker T. with wide, dumbfounded eyes.

"Sure, talk away. I'm listening," Missy said.

"I mean a little private talk, maybe in the kitchen?"

"Yeah, I can talk in the kitchen. I ain't afraid of what you kin say to me 'cause I know my rights," she said as she followed Mathilda into the kitchen.

The officer sat down across from Booker T. to keep an eye on him but found himself placing a pillow under Booker's leg to prop it up and make him more comfortable.

Missy was a pretty girl, with short black curly hair that gently framed her petite face. She was young—very young. Mathilda would guess that she was all of eighteen or nineteen at the most—much too young to be raising a boy only a few years younger than herself. She wore a peasant blouse gathered softly around her neck with full sleeves. It was white but looked a little dingy, like it had weathered too many washings. She had it tucked into her long, almost-to-her-ankle broomstick skirt, with tiny red rick-rack along the bottom—very popular with the young girls. She also wore black mid-heeled shoes.

"Let's sit here at the table," Mathilda said as they entered the kitchen.

"Sure got a nice place here," Missy said, as she took a seat across from Mathilda.

"You know, Missy, it's not easy raising a young boy. He could run away or get involved with street gangs, and how could you keep him in school and have him work at the same time?"

"Well, my boyfriend, Bubba, has two sons, and he's real good with them too. He knows how to make them toe the mark, so it ain't no problem 'cause he's got his ways," she explained. "He's teaching them to be real men."

"I'm sure he is, but Booker T. has a bad hip. You saw how he fell earlier. He's under a doctor's care, and I'm wondering if you and Bubba are prepared to pay for a doctor in Chicago, or for the surgery if he needs it?"

"You're saying he might need surgery? How long would he be laid up?" Missy asked, completely startled by this unexpected information.

"We don't know yet, but the doctor is watching him carefully."

"We don't have money for doctors, or for any surgery," she said quietly as her furrowed brow revealed this new worry. "Do you think he'd be able to work, I mean, after?"

"Listen, I'm thinking that your boyfriend had this idea because he thought it would be a way to get some extra money—or you would've been here four years ago, right?"

"Well, we talked about it, and I mentioned that I promised Booker's father to see about him. I just wanted to make good on my promise, that's all."

"The other boys, his sons, do they work, too?"

"Yeah, they got jobs, but they're not little. Both are in their teens like Booker. I'm not sure what they do, but they always got money to give Bubba. He takes care of that and I just want Booker to come home and help out, too. Kinda doing my part for the household."

While she talked, she pulled and twirled strands of her curly hair between her fingers while her elbow rested on the table.

"I'm thinking, my dear, that maybe you got yourself into something that might not be the best for you, and I stress 'for you.' You seem like a very nice girl, who is being used by someone much older for his own gain." Mathilda spoke very softly, trying to help her see the truth.

"I ain't got myself into nothin' that I don't want," was her immediate response.

"But where are your parents, Missy? I mean do they know what you're doing?"

"I only got my mother, and younger brothers, but she ain't got no time for me."

"Oh, I see and I'm so sorry, but do you think that if you had some money to get away from this—Bubba—you would do it?" Mathilda asked this very bluntly, the thought having just occurred to her that very moment.

"I don't see how I could."

Missy said that aloud but Mathilda could tell she was mulling it around in her mind by the look on her face, a kind of a question with her eyes.

"You know, Missy, he's too old for a young girl like you. Maybe you could go back to school for more education, maybe learn a trade," Mathilda explained. "How did you meet Booker's father?"

"Well, I was already out of high school when me and Fraze met. It was on a street car and I tripped over his feet. We laughed and sat together and then we both got off at the same stop on Racine Street. I was applying for a job at a drug store. He said he was thirsty so he sat down at the counter, bought a coke and waited for me."

"Did you get the job?"

"No, it was already filled. But then Fraze bought me a strawberry sundae and we sat and talked for a long time. I liked him 'cause he was interested in me and what I liked. After, sometimes I visited at his flat."

"Did you know Booker T. at that time?"

"No, Fraze said his son had to go away so his fingers could heal, or something like that. Anyway, he said he was lonely when he got home from work. The house was too quiet…so I moved in."

"Then you didn't have to find a job, did you?"

"No, I took care of his house and was there when he came home every single night."

"And you got married?"

"Yeah, but after Fraze got in that accident, I couldn't pay the rent, so Bubba, he was my mother's boyfriend at the time, he offered to pay my rent and everything, all free!"

"Free? There isn't anything free, Missy. And you know that he expects something—like using you and Booker T. for his own gain, not yours." Mathilda wasn't sure she was getting through.

"But he loves me and I love him. He'd do anything for me. He buys me stuff, just like a real husband."

"He probably told your mother that he loved her too."

"Maybe he did, but he said that I was prettier, and she still had the little boys at home. He didn't much like kids you know—I mean that little. Said they're always yelling and fighting. He always paid attention to me, though, sorta like Fraze. Sometimes he would give me a little kiss when he was leaving mama's house when she wasn't looking."

"Oh?" Mathilda said.

"Yeah, mama didn't like his talking to me all the time, so I left and moved in with Bubba and won't ever go back, no matter what happens. He doesn't go there anymore, either."

"But you're not married to Bubba and you could start over."

"How? I have nowhere to go, and he did so much for me already!"

"What if—what if I would give you some money to get your own place? A place he wouldn't know about. Where you could take some classes in clerical or secretarial skills or maybe a hair stylist, or something that you would be interested in doing? Wouldn't you like to get on your own and away from Bubba?"

"I might. You think I could get into a beauty school? I always liked to do people's hair. I do my own."

"I like the way you have it cut. And you do have a diploma—that's a real plus. I think you could do well for yourself."

"But…"

"Listen, Missy," Mathilda said as she opened her purse and pulled out the envelope she had placed there when she came home. "I can give you what's in this envelope, but you would have to promise to stop this nonsense with Booker T. and get on with your own life."

"But how—I don't know how?"

"Well, you could go to one of the suburbs, toward South Chicago, Evergreen Park, Blue Island, or even Harvey. Rent a furnished place—find one in the classifieds. But only take the bare essentials—clothes, and whatever else you can put in a cab. After you have a place to live, get a part time job and enroll in some classes."

"I do have a friend that lives in Beverly Hills, it's on the South side. She's a maid for some rich folks and lives with them. She has her own room and everything. Maybe she can help me find a place," Missy said, becoming more interested in Mathilda's plan. "How much are you planning on giving me?" she asked getting down to business and whether she could do this thing that Mathilda told her about.

"In this envelope is seven hundred and fifty dollars. It's enough for you to do everything I told you to do, with a little left over for some clothing and good used furniture, if needed."

"You would give me that much money? You would help me that much?" she asked really surprised.

"Yes, but you have to promise that you will never come here again. And that you will get away from that man, Bubba. And tell me, Missy, you were never married to Fraze, were you?"

"Well, he was still married to that woman who couldn't be found, but Fraze knew someone who was studying to be a minister through the mail. He married us and even gave us a certificate. Fraze said I'd feel better after the ceremony and I'm sure it was kinda legitimate, so I *am* Booker's mama…sorta."

"That's what I thought. Just how old are you, Missy?"

"I'm twenty-two, ma'am."

"I guessed entirely wrong, I thought you were much younger. But because you are older, you *can* do better, if you would just decide that you're not going to be bossed around by any man who wants to use you. That's all you have to do."

"Yes, ma'am. But he says he loves me…do you really think a girl like me can do better, better than my mama?"

"I know you can. Now, do you want the money?"

"Yes, but, how…?"

"Here is what you should do. Tell the officer who came with you that you want to go home right away so you can check with Bubba because Booker may need surgery. Don't say any more then that. After you get home, while Bubba's at work, call your friend and see what she can do for you. She may even know of a job, or she can ask the people where she works if they know of one. It's worth a try, isn't it?"

"Yes, ma'am. I'll do exactly like you say."

Mathilda handed her the envelope and she immediately put it inside the top of her full-gathered blouse. It hid the envelope very well.

They both walked out to the living room, where Booker T. and the officer were waiting.

"I have to go home before we can do anything more here," she said to the officer.

"We're going home…without the kid?" the officer asked so that he would be absolutely sure that's what she meant. "Are you nuts? What's Bubba gonna say? He'll kill me!"

"Well, I think we'll have to talk over this surgery stuff before we can go any further," Missy explained to him. "I'm not gonna babysit and wait on any kid having surgery."

"I don't know," the officer said, clearly agitated. "I had a deal to get paid for doing a certain job, and now I probably won't get the dough from him." He scrunched his face and put it right in front of hers. "You got money to pay me for all my time and gas, and all the extra dinners including last week?"

"We're going," Missy said, simply and defiantly. "Goodbye, Booker. Goodbye, Ma'am. And thank you for the information," she said, as she walked out with the officer reluctantly following and still murmuring about money under his breath.

Booker T. was exhausted. He quickly got the water bottle, filled it with hot water, took two aspirins and went up to bed.

Another hour had passed before Thomas showed up.

"Mattie, I thought for sure that officer would bring you and Booker T. in," he said as he sat down next to her on the davenport.

"Yes, that's exactly what I thought, but then he said that he would take Booker T. without even going to the station."

"That's crazy! What did you do?"

"I acted like I didn't understand. I would have gone with them but the girl showed up saying she was Booker's mother and it changed everything. After talking to her, I got the drift of the situation real quick.

"Seems like he didn't want us walking in on him, here, that way he could skip town with the boy, without Johnny or me knowing about it."

"That's what I thought too."

"While we were waiting, Sheriff Bordon called the Chicago Precinct with the cop's badge number. They informed him that he had been suspended over five months ago. He doesn't have the authority to arrest anyone or do anything on a criminal or civil matter."

"Well, no use worrying any longer, I don't think they'll ever be back," Mathilda said, knowing full well that she settled everything, but was reluctant to tell how she did it.

"I'm sorry Booker T. had to go through all that, and for his sake I hope it's all over," Thomas said.

"Like I said, I don't think they'll be back."

"Mattie Millering, did you have something to do with them leaving without him?"

"So what if I did? I'm nobody's fool," she added, just to make sure he knew very well that she could do without him too. She was sure he would get the drift of exactly what she meant.

Mathilda had a good reason why she would never tell Thomas about the money she gave the girl. Mainly because he would probably say it was against the law and call it a bribe. And she was all right with not knowing for sure because she had never broken the law before. Well, not on purpose anyway.

CHAPTER FORTY-TWO

The days were dragging and Dudley was still being held captive, only in a much nicer place than the reform school. To pass the time, he filled the empty house with different renditions of the songs he knew by heart. As he played, old memories would come.

He remembered when he was going on eleven years-old, how he brought tears to Grandmother Bealer's eyes as he played the rainbow song. He knew she was his grandmother right from the start, however, she had no idea that Dudley was her grandson. He couldn't say why he felt she was his grandmother. Maybe it was because she used Lemon Verbena like Aunt Mattie, whom he loved. When he thought about it, Aunt Mattie was the only one he could really say he loved, because she loved him with no strings attached. As far as Grandmother Bealer was concerned, she loved him because he was musically talented like her grandfather—a violin virtuoso. And Dudley could play the piano like a virtuoso too, but then again, maybe that was enough…maybe?

Mr. Tierney's library held a lot of interest for Dudley. When he read the books on juvenile law, he enjoyed thinking about the young people who found themselves it situations like his, and in which every one of them said they were innocent. He was consumed by how a defense lawyer could ever prove his client's claim against the so called real or stacked evidence? The more he thought about it, the more he was beginning to understand how some of the prosecuting attorneys presented their cases, purposely trying to misinterpret the evidence to the judge and sometimes a jury in order to get a swift conviction. He gleaned this from the extensive notes placed between particular pages. They were the explanations with the results of the cases and why Mr. Tierney agreed or disagreed with them. They were always noted as solely belonging to Barry Tierney and initialed, B. T. The more Dudley thought about how the books in the room were stacked and sorted, he realized Tierney was doing some extensive research about money kickbacks for boys being swiftly locked up. Dudley didn't know if he should ask about it. He would like to, but it wasn't any of his business as Aunt Mattie would say, and he didn't want to intrude on the man who opened his home to him.

The following week, when Tierney came home for the weekend, Dudley got up the nerve to ask whether he could call his Aunt Mattie. The senator's response was that Dudley should stop thinking about it because it was out of the question. He explained again so there would be no misunderstanding.

"I don't think you know how serious your position is, Dudley. For some reason the other side knows exactly where you are and what you're doing all the time. We can't take chances that would implicate another person and then have to protect that person too."

"How would they know, sir? I don't talk to anyone other than the gardener and the maid. Does Manny know who I am?"

"No, I've never told her or anyone else why you're here or who you are."

"Except your daughter sir. I told her when she asked what school I went to."

"Yes, you did, but we were alone, and I don't think anyone overheard us. Even so, someone is informing about you."

"I'm sorry sir, I won't mention calling again," Dudley distractedly said, because now mulling around in his mind were his daily talks with Blanchard. "When I think of it, the only conversations I've ever had were with the gardener...but he's so nice to talk to. You know, he's a lot like my old friend, Mr. Crow."

"Crow, my what an interesting name. Where is he?"

"Oh, he died a few years ago, but he left me all his money in a trust so I would have a start when I get out of school. Aunt Mattie keeps it for me in a savings account at the bank."

"Be careful to whom you're telling things like that, young man," Tierney cautioned.

"Yes, sir I will. And I'll never mention it to another person."

Tierney didn't say anything aloud but thought, *I'll have to get that man checked out. The idea that someone could have been planted in my own home never occurred to me.*

"I have a couple of things planned for this weekend, Dudley, if you're interested?"

"Yes, whatever you say, sir." Dudley was happy to get out of the house for a few hours and was in no position to say no to anything.

CHAPTER FORTY-THREE

Thanksgiving morning brought an unusual winter storm—a big surprise to everyone. That much early snow and ice was unusual and Mathilda couldn't recall another time that weather conditions had spoiled their plans for a delicious turkey dinner. Mathilda, Angela, Booker T. and Sadie were supposed to go to a festive feast at Henry and Catherine's home, but they had to call it off. With slippery roads even eight miles would not be considered a restful, happy day for any of the ladies.

Angela missed being with Catherine and her grandchildren and Mathilda missed Dudley, but she was grateful that at least Booker T. and her sister were with her. They put together a very tasty dinner even though they didn't have a turkey. Sadie already had apple pies baked and ready to take to the farm and Mathilda had her famous cranberry relish with oranges and apples—it would be a perfect side for the pork chops Sadie found in the freezer. Angela had baked banana bread in four empty cans and they were ready too.

Playing board games with Booker T. helped pass the time and kept up their spirits. The usual list of words and medical definitions to be studied for the day were set aside while the boy helped Aunt Mattie and the ladies cook and set a festive dinning room table. He had neglected playing the piano since he began work with Doctor James, so after dinner, he mentally made a list of all the songs the ladies liked and then played them to their enthusiastic singing. After, he added his own intricate renditions of the Jazz and Blues he always played with Dudley. Mathilda, Angela, and Sadie sat on the davenport, loving it all and clapping after every song. Usually there was never enough time for Booker T.'s studies and playing, too, so today, he sunk down into the music, letting it enter his soul. There were probably calls for the day, but Doctor James said for Booker T. to stay home and rest his sore hip.

Booker T. didn't know if it was the right time or not because he didn't want to spoil the day for Aunt Mattie, but he figured he'd better tell her about what the doctor proposed.

They had just finished an evening snack with sandwiches and more dessert. Dudley was the main topic—where he was and what he probably had for Thanksgiving dinner. But now, Booker T. knew he had to present the question looming in his mind. He had to tell them while they were all together.

"Aunt Mattie," he said hesitantly, with a quiver in his voice. "I need to talk to you about something Doctor James approached me about."

"My, Booker T., your vocabulary certainly is getting polished," Angela said.

"Yes, ma'am. Dr. James insists that I speak articulately."

"What is it, Booker?" Mathilda asked as she and the ladies looked closely at Booker, waiting for him to say what was on his mind.

"Well, yesterday after I sterilized all the instruments and also cleaned Dr. James' office, as I always do, well, when he dropped me off he asked me if I would be interested in living at his place next semester."

"Oh, Booker, that would mean that I wouldn't see you every morning and evening!" Mathilda said, a little startled at the proposal.

"I know, and I told him I didn't know how you would feel about it."

"How do *you* feel about staying there?"

Before he could answer, Sadie interrupted and put her two cents in right from the start.

"Listen, Booker, Mrs. Mathilda would be missing you somethin' bad now that Dudley's away." She made it sound as though Dudley was on a holiday trip or something.

"I know, but maybe he'll be coming home. What do you think, ma'am?" Booker T. was now speaking directly to Mathilda's sister, Angela, for her opinion.

"You know, I won't be here either, but perhaps weekends and Sundays we could get together if you do decide to go." Angela suddenly felt sad for her sister because this huge house would be so quiet.

"Booker T.," Mathilda said, "this is your decision and you should base it on your willingness to help the doctor. You know he's doing his best to help you and he wouldn't have asked if there weren't a need."

"Yes, ma'am. I think he does need me there?"

"Now don't go worrying about me. This is about you, and you need to decide if it's something you want to do."

"Yes, ma'am," was all he could say, feeling the enormity of this decision falling entirely on himself. He finished eating and went straight to bed after saying goodnight to the ladies.

CHAPTER FORTY-FOUR

On that same Thanksgiving morning, Tierney woke early hearing the sound of wind and wet snow pelting against the windows. His plan to take Dudley and Elise to his parent's home for his mother's turkey dinner was crushed. Barry wanted to surprise Dudley and Elise by whisking them both away on that special day. As far as Tierney was concerned, no one would have to know but as it turned out, they remained home because of the ice-covered roads.

Old Blanchard had already left, having taken several days off to spend with his own family, and Manny was supposed to go away too with her three fresh chickens, but didn't leave the day before and now she had to stay. Manny informed Mr. Tierney that this would be their Thanksgiving dinner. Nothing fancy like turkey, but better than anything else sitting in the refrigerator.

When Dudley saw the weather that morning, his thoughts went out to his Aunt Mattie, wondering if she and Booker T. would be going to Mr. Henry's house for dinner or if the snow and ice would stop them. He wished he could be with them, but being here was so much better than being in that reform school. He had no reason to complain, not even a little.

Elise was home. So Dudley quickly ate his breakfast of cornflakes and milk and then went into the library to spend time alone. He didn't want to get in Elise's way, because she hated him with a passion. She wouldn't speak, even when they passed each other in the hallway with not even an 'excuse me.' Even so, Dudley thought she was the sweetest and most beautiful girl he ever knew. And even though she acted distant, he thought that his feelings for her must be true love. He only knew that when she was around, he felt a little queasy on the inside, and very awkward on the outside.

What would it be like to hold her hand or even kiss her soft sweet lips, the same ones that pout and pucker whenever I'm near?

Richard told him about the girls he and his friends knew and wondered if those guys who always bragged about necking and making out ever felt this kind of awe for a girl. Dudley felt he would only want to protect Elise and not do anything that would hurt her or make her feel bad.

When lunch was ready, Dudley ate quickly and in silence while Elise read from a book at the same kitchen table, never looking up to acknowledge him. Dudley ate his sandwich and drank his milk with one or two gulps, then hurried back to the library. Elise must have eaten fast too because in a few minutes, he could hear her playing scales on her violin, followed by the songs that her mother had loved.

She's probably feeling lonely today, thinking about her mother's absence, Dudley reasoned. *Her actions probably have nothing to do with me at all.*

On one of the long tables, Dudley placed two newer looking books about Juvenile law, but then he spotted another bulging shoe-box on the top shelf and pulled it down. It was packed with post-cards, pictures, and letters. Getting as comfortable as he could in the cold room, he looked through the picture postcards that were from places as far away as Japan, Brazil, and Argentina—places he would like to visit someday. He also came across a group of letters tied with light blue ribbon and tucked in the center of the box. They seemed to be private, and maybe Mr. Tierney forgot that they were there so Dudley didn't attempt to read them. Instead he placed them at the back of the box. Dudley then pulled out six or seven black and white photographs and looked closely at the people. One picture was of a very little boy, dressed in short pants. He had very light hair, maybe blond, and Dudley guessed he looked a little like Mr. Tierney, maybe when he was just three or four years old. The boy was standing on a sidewalk in front of a house with pealing paint and a shutter that was hanging, about to fall, but the photo didn't have any notation about whom it was or where it had been taken.

The house caught his attention, and even after he picked up a few other photographs, he kept going back to the picture of the boy and the house. *Where had he seen that house before?* And then he came across another one with the same boy sitting on the front steps of the same house. He turned it over and saw a notation; it said, *"from L., three years old."*

There was another picture of a baby in a buggy with a hood. The baby was laughing and had its hands outstretched, as though wanting to be picked up. No one else was in the picture, but it seemed as though it had been taken in a park because Dudley could see trees, grass, and a bed filled with flowers. Another was marked, "Elise and Mommy," with a baby girl being held by a lady who was smiling and sitting in a stuffed chair next to a large tube. There were objects hanging on the wall next to her chair. Dudley guessed it was Elise and her mother in a hospital room and it made him feel sad for her. Maybe she felt like he did all his growing up years, missing his own mother.

After Dudley had rifled through the box several times and while he was still deep in thought about Elise's childhood, he became startled when Tierney came in carrying a bucket of wood. He worked at crumpling newspapers and stacking kindling in the fireplace, placing the split logs on top and poking until roaring flames began to heat the room. Mr. Blanchard usually did the same thing, but the fire lasted only a short time, and it soon became chilly again. It didn't matter to Dudley; he had become accustomed to the cold library and began wearing his outdoor coat whenever he spent time there.

"I'm sorry it's so cold in here," Tierney said. "I'll try to warm it up for you."

"Oh, it's okay, I'm used to it. Mr. Blanchard always tried to keep the fire going, but it usually fizzled out after an hour."

Dudley stood up and removed his coat now that he could feel the heat, knowing it wouldn't take long for the whole room to get toasty.

"You seem to be enjoying the books and things in this room. Have you come across anything interesting?" Tierney asked, as he sat down across from Dudley at the library table. He wiped his hands carefully on the cloth that was hanging on one of the buckets and then looked closely at Dudley's blue eyes.

"Yes, sir, I like your law books."

"I see you found some old pictures and cards, too," he said, as he began shuffling through the photographs that were now lying on the top of the box. "I'd forgotten all about these pictures."

"Yes sir, I didn't read the letters tied with the pretty ribbon, though, 'cause I thought they were probably personal, but I saw the pictures of Elise and her mother. She was beautiful…I'm sorry."

"Thank you, Dudley, you're very thoughtful. And yes, she was beautiful."

"I enjoyed the histories in your law books—they're interesting. And I like your notes about some of the cases too. I think I would agree with you on the ones you commented about."

Dudley wanted him to know that he wasn't just snooping through his things.

"Sounds as though you stumbled upon what could be your profession? What do you think?" Tierney asked jovially when he heard Dudley speak about the cases.

"Do you think I could become a lawyer? You know my uncle Tommy is, only I think he is more into business law."

"You seem interested in juvenile law, and that's a good field to help troubled youth."

"Yes, I think I'd like Juvenile law better than business. Then I could help other kids like me who are accused of something they didn't do," Dudley answered very seriously.

"Yes, my boy, I can see that you could do just that, and it's an honorable ambition and profession."

"Sir, I've been scouring your books looking for arguments in presenting evidence which should include living conditions. It could have an effect on why they joined gangs or stole things. Also if they had parents who didn't care much about them. Don't the judges take any of that into account when sending them away?"

"Yes, those things do have a negative impact on youngsters, but the courts say they aren't in a position to provide leniency in high profile cases because the public demands justice and people are only interested in getting incorrigibles out of their own neighborhoods. Most don't care where they end up, as long as they're not next door."

"But some of them never had a chance and they'll spend their early lives in the juvenile system and then in the adult penal prisons, just like Joey and Ron at the reformatory. They seemed okay...I mean they were nice enough."

"What were they in for?"

"Joey said he stole money for his mom and younger brothers. He said they were hungry and didn't even have electricity at home. He said they stole a large sum—over one thousand dollars from a man coming out of a bank. The guys caught him just before he got in his car and dragged him into the ally—stole his money and divvied it up. All the kids were charged and sent away."

"Well, I agree with you, Dudley. There should be someone who could stand up for boys like Joey so they wouldn't get caught in the system."

"I think that's what I'd like to do if I became an attorney."

"You know you wouldn't be that popular among your peers. Mostly the parents of the youngsters you defend are the ones that would be grateful, but they usually don't have big chunks of money to hire you. You would have to work for a lower salary than some of the prosecutors, that's for sure. Or you could be a court appointed defense lawyer. Hardly any money in that!"

"Why do some prosecutors do better, Mr. Tierney?"

"Well, most, though not all, are looking to further their careers. Maybe even becoming judges. They need convictions to show the public they're serious about putting crime behind bars. That's how they get their names out there and elected when they run for office. It's an angry world out there, son, and the sooner you know what you're up against, the better."

"Yes, sir."

It was at that moment, Elise opened the door, peeked in, and entered. She walked to the fireplace and rubbed her hands to warm them before heading over to the table where they were sitting.

"What unimportant things are you discussing with my father today, Dudley Best?"

Dudley noticed the dimple in her cheek when she spoke.

"Well," Dudley began—he knew he had to give her some sort of an answer since she had addressed him directly.

"Now, listen Elise, we were talking about Dudley's future as a defense attorney for juveniles. Nothing more, nothing less. Care to join us?" Tierney's voice was now revealing quiet annoyance.

"Well, dinner won't be ready anytime soon, Elise said, so I guess I'll sit in here. Have you looked out the window lately?"

"I did," Dudley said. "It's a blizzard out there."

"I know, and I think we'll be snowed in for a week. By the way, Daddy, you haven't talked to me one time about my future. Why are you holding back?"

"Do I detect a little jealousy?" Tierney asked even more sternly. He was becoming peeved with the way she'd been acting lately, toward Dudley and himself.

"Me? Why Daddy, you know I couldn't possibly be jealous after all the attention you pour out on me?" She was looking her daddy straight in the eye.

"Hey, do you have a Monopoly game that we could play until dinner? It would be fun and better than just talking about nothing, right?" Dudley asked.

"Yeah" Tierney said, "we have a stack of games in that cabinet over there, and we could set up the Monopoly game right here on the table."

"I'll clear the books and the boxes off the table so we'll have some room to spread out," Dudley said, glad to break Elise's hostile attitude.

"I'll get the game," Elise said, jumping up, knowing exactly where it was stored.

Dudley and her dad were both surprised when she offered, but neither said a word.

"Come and sit at the table with us, Manny. I don't want you eating all alone in the kitchen after all that work preparing our Thanksgiving dinner," Tierney said.

"Thank you sir, I'll do just that," she said, as she put out another place setting and removed her apron. Mr. Tierney had instructed Manny earlier to set the table in the dinning room the same way as when he entertained important guests. They used his wife's gold rimmed dishes, set on golden chargers along with the crystal glassware.

Elise said the table looked extra elegant and Dudley agreed, but his mind was mostly on the chicken which was every bit as tasty as any turkey he ever ate. The huge baked potatoes with dripping butter, glazed carrots, cranberry sauce and homemade rolls made it a grand dinner, and he could hear his Aunt Mattie say those very words. And now he could hardly remember those scrimpy meals at the reformatory.

Manny had worked for the family for the last twelve years and she was a delight to have dinner with that evening. Her black southern drawl made everyone laugh at the funny stories she told about when she first began to work in white folks' homes with new electric appliances she never had occasion to use before, like the mixmaster and the mess she created.

"I gotta tell you, Manny, I didn't do too well with that mixmaster thing the first time I used it. I was trying to make pancakes and the batter was everywhere, on the counter, on the wall, and even in my hair," Tierney said and they all laughed, thinking what a sight that was.

After dinner, Manny suggested that the three of them have their dessert in the library, so they could continue their game of Monopoly. They played until after nine that evening, but the game was not over.

The laughter, so long absent from that gloomy house, warmed Manny's heart. Tierney fetched more wood for the fire and they began teasing each other about who would get that fourth railroad or the coveted Boardwalk. After playing a while longer, Tierney became a lot more quiet and thoughtful. He had something on his mind, and he had to say it before the moment would be lost.

"I have something I want—need-to tell you, Dudley. It's important, and I think it's something that both you and Elise need to know about," Tierney said.

"Yeah, what is it, Daddy?" asked Elise. "You make it sound kinda crucial. Is it?" she asked, direct as usual.

Dudley raised his eyes from the game and looked closely at the gentlemen—a complete stranger who had opened his home to him. He felt content for the first time in a very long time and waited for whatever Mr. Tierney wanted to say.

"Yes sir," Dudley said, waiting and not wanting to move his red car to Park Place because Tierney wanted their attention.

There was a light knock, and Manny stuck her head in the doorway.

"I think you should know, sir, that Mr. Blanchard just pulled into the drive. I think he's stuck out there because he's rocking his car back and forth. Sakes alive, why would he come back on such a night?"

"Thank you, Manny, I guess I'll have to find out." And then to the kids, "I'll finish this conversation later, okay?"

"Okay, Daddy. It's close to my bedtime anyway, and I'm tired," Elise said. "Let's leave the game right where it is so that if the weather is bad tomorrow, we can just continue."

"Good idea, Elise. After all, I need some of those properties you practically stole from me, and I aim to get them back tomorrow," Dudley said smiling. He was happy Elise had tomorrow all planned out. He too was feeling tired and maybe a little too-full after that great meal.

The kids both ran upstairs. Their rooms were across the hall from each other, and as Dudley watched Elise go into her room, he wished he could invite her to a sock hop or a school dance like the ones they had at his old high school. He never went to one, but he was sure they would have fun together because she smiled at him and was easy to talk to now that they were starting to know each other better.

As Dudley got ready for bed, he watched the men from his bedroom window. Tierney was helping Blanchard, holding each other, arm and arm, heads down, trudging toward the house. Snow was already sticking to their winter coats and hats, but it was getting hard for Dudley to see as the window was getting caked with the sleet that blew hard, pelting and sticking like glue. Dudley couldn't watch any longer, as he suddenly became chilled and started to shake with sharp pains in his stomach. He hurried to get into bed to warm himself.

CHAPTER FORTY-FIVE

Elise could hear strange sounds coming from across the hall. The clock on her bedside table said three-thirty. She quickly got up, put on her robe and opened her door. Then, she heard it again, and realized that it was some sort of moaning coming from Dudley's room. She knocked softly.

"Can I be of some help?" she asked.

"Elise…my stomach hurts something awful."

Elise opened the door and walked over to the bed where Dudley was tossing back and forth in pain.

"I think I'm gonna throw up, ooh…"

Elise thought quickly, and dumped the trash from Dudley's metal waste basket on the floor and held it while Dudley puked, emptying his dessert and then his dinner, all the while crying with pain. When he stopped for a few minutes, Elise took the container into the bathroom, emptied it into the toilet, rinsed it and put a little fresh water into the bottom. Then she just stood next to the bed, looking at him as he whimpered in pain.

"Dudley, I'm going to get daddy. I'll be right back."

While she was gone, the cramps started again, much worse than before. Dudley tried to reach for the basket but fell to the cold floor, perspiring profusely, trying to puke again and again, hanging his head into the container.

"My goodness, boy," Tierney said as he followed Elise into Dudley's room to see the boy on the floor.

"Here, let's get you back into bed."

Tierney quickly picked Dudley up and set him back into bed tucking the blankets tight around him.

"I'm sooo cooold," Dudley said through chattering teeth.

Elise found two extra wool blankets on the closet top shelf and placed them over the other blankets, hoping they would help.

"I can't stand the pain, please call someone that can help me, please," he cried.

"I will, Dudley. I will. Hold on now, while I call for an ambulance," Tierney said as he tenderly wiped the perspiration from the boy's head, face, and neck.

Picking up the phone in the hall, he found no dial tone. It was completely dead. *Thank God we still have electric*, he thought.

"What can we do, Daddy? I've been watching out the window and there aren't any cars getting through. How can we get him to the hospital?"

"Wake Manny and ask her to get Mr. Blanchard. We'll have to try, or…"

Elise ran down the stairs to the kitchen and knocked hard on Manny's door. Meanwhile, Dudley started moaning again and holding his stomach with his hot hands.

Manny put her coat on over her housecoat, pulled a shawl over her head and started out the back door. On the porch was the boot box. She had to find hers quickly.

We never gets snow this early, why do these things always happen in the middle of the night? As she stepped into the snow drifts to cross the drive, she kind of jumped—finding spots that weren't so deep. Finally, she was at Blanchard's door. She pounded until he opened it. His eyes forced wide open but not quite awake.

"You gotta come right along 'cause Mr. Tierney needs us all. That Dudley boy is real bad sick."

Then she turned and tried to step into her just made footsteps, but the wind was blowing hard gusting at her back and pushing her. She slipped but caught herself, hands hitting the ground and snow forcing itself up the sleeves of her coat. She was on all fours and tried to get up, only to slip and slide down again and again. Blanchard, following a little ways behind, helped pull her up. Holding onto each other, they walked with heads down to the back porch, pushed the door open, and stomped hard to shake the snow off.

"What a night," Tierney said as he met them on the back porch. "I don't know what we'll do because the phone is dead and we can't call an ambulance."

Elise came into the kitchen. "He's thirsty, Daddy. Can he have some cold water?"

"No, honey, he probably should only suck on a few pieces of ice in case they have to do surgery." Tierney was already thinking appendicitis—he knew the symptoms.

"Oh, my land," Manny said. "There's some ice cubes in the freezer. Let's crush 'em first and put 'em in a glass." And that's what they did. Manny had a hammer in the kitchen, wrapped the ice in a clean towel and started to pound, filling a glass, then a water bottle.

"Manny, you're wet from head to toe! You'd better get changed," Tierney said when he saw her teeth chattering while she worked.

"Yes, sir. I better...afore I gets my death," she said, immediately going to her room to change.

"What can I do?" Blanchard asked, brushing off the wet snow from his trousers. "How can I help?"

"We need an ambulance and I don't think we can wait till morning."

"But how? With that wind we could hardly get into the house, and my car is blocking the driveway."

"We have to try to push it over to the side."

"Maybe we could push it back toward the road, since we can't go forward, maybe we can go backwards?" Blanchard offered.

"How were the roads coming in?"

"They were getting plugged in different places with big drifts."

Tierney put his coat and hat on as they both hurried out. "Why did you come back?" Barry yelled over the wind as they were walking toward the car to the end of the drive. "You knew it was a rotten night for driving."

"Yes, sir. But I did, and now we have to use all our efforts to get the boy to the hospital."

Elise went back into Dudley's room with the glass of ice and spoon fed a few pieces into his barely-open mouth as she sat next to him on the edge of the bed. He placed the iced water bottle on the right side of his stomach.

"The pain feels a little better, thanks, Elise," he said, with a weak voice as he laid one of his hot hands on the cold red bottle.

The two men pushed the car back almost to the road where it got stuck again, but at least it wasn't in the center of the drive. They didn't know what else to do except to go back into the house. Then Blanchard had an idea. "As long as the electric's still on, why don't I blink the outside lights at the front of the house—maybe someone will see it as a distress signal."

"It's worth a try," Tierney said. "If that doesn't work, I'm going to begin walking toward town until I find help. We can't wait much longer."

They both went to the front door when Elise came bounding down the stairs, all out of breath.

"Daddy, with the phone dead, what'll we do?" Elise asked, now starting to panic.

"I know, honey. How's Dudley doing?" Tierney asked, pulling his daughter close and giving her a quick hug.

"I gave him a few slivers of ice and then he fell asleep. He said he felt a little better."

Blanchard started flipping the lights on and off. When he flipped the front porch lights, the lights that were on top of the four pillars at the end of the drive also blinked.

"Look, honey, that's quite a display. Surely it'll attract some-one's attention."

"I hope so, Daddy," Elise said as she turned and hurried back upstairs.

Dear God, I hope so, Tierney silently prayed.

CHAPTER FORTY-SIX

Tierney followed Elise back upstairs, felt Dudley's forehead and realized the boy was burning up with fever. He began bathing Dudley's face and neck with cool cloths over and over, as fast as Elise could run them under cold water, wring them out and bring them to him. Dudley began to talk incoherently under his breath hardly audible. Tierney placed his ear close so he could hear.

"Auntie, I'm feeling so sick, and I'm so tired."

"Here, Dudley, hush, you'll feel better as soon as the doctor gets here. Hold on, now, ya hear?" Tierney wanted to give him hope, as he continued to bathe him with the cold cloths.

"Auntie, I didn't kill Rudy. It was Beemer and he used his dad's gun—got 'em right in the stomach. Beemer, you shouldn't have done it...Rudy...Rudy, are you okay? Come on, Rudy, open your eyes, let me help you up. Aunt Mattie, you look so nice and smell good, like le-lemon ver...let me rest my head on your shoulder... please make it feel better. Did you hear the applause? Auntie, you're crying. Please don't cry. I'll get better I promise. I promise I won't die. I don't wanna die, Aunt Mattie, please help me."

As he cried those words, he continually tossed his body from side to side while Tierney kept re-covering him with the blankets.

"What's he saying, Daddy? Is he dying?" Elise cried.

"He thinks I'm his Aunt Mattie. I just don't know what else to do." His voice was soft and almost inaudible.

Time was moving strangely and becoming hypnotic as the lights glared on and off through the bedroom window. The constant bathing of Dudley with the cool cloths reminded Tierney of his own Susan's death in this very room. He could taste that same bitterness of time as it moved, sometimes galloping as a racing steed and sometimes waning as a turtle crossing a road. With a shudder, Tierney recognized his deep feelings of helplessness.

* * *

The clock on the night stand showed it was six-o'clock when they heard the vehicles pull into the drive. The first one had a snow plow on the front, clearing a path for an ambulance that pulled in right behind. Tierney and Blanchard ran out to meet them.

"Thank God you got here. A young boy is seriously ill, I think he is having an appendicitis attack," Tierney explained to the medic in the ambulance. Meanwhile, Blanchard walked over to the snow plow driver.

"How did you know to stop?"

"We picked up the lady and I decided to come back down this road because the lights were constantly blinking and it wasn't much farther to go."

"You suspected something, then?" Blanchard asked.

"Yep, like something had to be wrong."

"I don't know Morse code, but I had to try, hoping someone would see the lights going on and off."

* * *

The Medic didn't know what he should do. "I don't think we can fit him in. I already have a lady in labor."

"Oh, but you must. He'll die if you don't take him right now," Tierney pleaded, "and he's only fifteen."

The women who was lying on the gurney in the back of the ambulance could hear the conversation.

"Listen, my labor pains aren't that close together and I can sit in front, can't I? The boy needs help right away."

"Well, I guess you could, if you're sure," the Medic said, surprised at the offer, but thankful that he would be able to help the boy.

The lady, with the help of Blanchard, moved into the front seat while the medic and attendant went in to get Dudley. They carried the boy out on a stretcher, completely wrapped in blankets, including one over his head. Tierney jumped in back for a tight ride, crouching next to the boy, giving Dudley's hand a reassuring squeeze every few minutes all the way to the hospital.

Elise, Manny, and Blanchard were standing at the back door, watching as they left—each silently hoping it wasn't too late. The snow plow opened a wider path and sped out of the drive ahead of the ambulance with the siren telling everyone that mercy was on the way.

* * *

At the hospital they didn't waste a moment since the resident surgeon was on duty that morning. Dr. Bentley and staff quickly prepped themselves and Dudley for surgery, but the appendix had already burst, sending poison into every part of Dudley's body. He survived the operation, but he would have to fight to live. They began giving him massive doses of antibiotics.

Barry Tierney knew that he couldn't do anything more for Dudley—he was now completely in the hands of God and the doctors—but he did notice the wall phones on the first floor. The family had to be notified so he immediately called his old friend, Thomas Bealer.

"Hello, Tom, this is Barry Tierney and I'm here at the Templeton Hospital. Dudley's condition is critical with a burst appendicitis. He's in surgery right now and I think you and your sister, Louise, should come. If you can, bring Dudley's Aunt Mattie too. He's been asking for her for some time."

The next call he made was to the other senator who was working on the case. It was still very early and Tierney was counting on him still being home.

"Thornton, this is Barry Tierney. Hey, you'd better get your people to close up all the loopholes on this reformatory case. Dudley Best is in critical condition with appendicitis. This time I heard it right from the boy's mouth who killed Rudy Mullens. Round up everyone on the list and don't let anyone get away, book them all. And don't forget a kid that goes by the name of Beemer. He's the one who pulled the trigger, killing Rudy with his father's own gun. I believe he's the son of Baxter Marlow, the district attorney there in Blenning. This is important...round them up all at the same time. They all have blood on their hands, including the coroner, so don't forget him. His name is Adkins, Mark Adkins."

CHAPTER FORTY-SEVEN

After those two calls, Tierney left the hospital in a cab. He had reasons why he didn't want to be there when the family arrived.

The roads were already being plowed and scraped so the cab driver had no trouble getting to his home. The man who did the snow plowing during the winter season came in and cleared the drifts, knowing his drive needed to be kept open. Tierney wished the plowman would have come last night—when he desperately needed him.

When he entered the music room, he could see Elise was asleep on the sofa but he didn't want to wake her so he fell into one of the chairs thoroughly exhausted from the long night. His head fell forward almost immediately with eyes closed.

"Daddy, how's Dudley?" Elise was instantly awake upon hearing him walk across the room and plop into the chair.

"Oh, I'm sorry…I didn't want to wake you," Tierney whispered.

"Is he okay, daddy?"

"He's…well…he's pretty sick, honey. His appendix burst and the poison is—"

"What does that mean? I mean…the poison…could he die from that?"

"Some people do, but the doctors are doing everything they can. He has to want to live, dear. He has to fight for life."

"We had so much fun last night, even though we couldn't go to Grams for dinner. Why did this have to happen, Daddy, when I just started to like Dudley?"

"I don't know, honey, I—" and suddenly Manny was at the door all excited and out of breath.

"The po-lice is here. They on the back porch with Mr. Blanchard, and they want *you*—right away."

"I'm coming," he said as he quickly left the music room and rushed out to the back porch. When he opened the door, he saw two officers, one was handcuffed to the wrist of Oren Blanchard. They were ready to leave for the station.

"We had orders to pick up everyone connected," the officer said. "We wanted you to know."

"You—you're involved?" Tierney asked Blanchard, hardly believing he was harboring a person who could harm Dudley and maybe even Elise. The man lowered his eyes.

"But you helped me get help for Dudley. You helped me push your car out of the way and then blinked the lights for hours… and…"

"Yes, sir. I got to know the youngster quite well when he volunteered to help with the garden work. He's a good boy, sir." As he spoke, his eyes dropped with shame. "I'm sorry I took the job, but once I said I'd do it they wouldn't let me quit. I had my family to think about too," he explained. "My wife and me…we needed the money."

"Then you weren't anything more then a snoop at my house?"

"Yes, they would meet me in the lunch room at the restaurant and I would tell them what they wanted to know. Mostly if Dudley went anywhere or if anyone came here to see him, and I would give them the license number. I guess I'm a spy."

"Please, just take him away," Tierney said to the police sergeant as he threw his arm, pointing toward the door. He was feeling too disgusted and tired to comment any further.

"Don't act too surprised, Tierney. I hear that some of those who thought they were safe are now being plucked, and you can be sure they'll get every last one."

Blanchard said this as he was leaving with the officer. Because of this ugly sneer, Tierney felt some internal consternation at the words. He considered them a personal threat directed at him.

CHAPTER FORTY-EIGHT

Thomas' idea was to pick up Louise and then Mathilda for the trip to the hospital, but Mathilda thought it would be better to drive herself so she could stay as long as she thought necessary. Quickly she threw a few clothes into a valise, just in case the weather turned wretched again. As it was, the roads were now looking better, except a few icy spots. She was sure she could manage alone.

Thomas Bealer and Louise were anxiously waiting to meet with the doctor when Mathilda walked into the waiting room. It was eleven in the morning. Louise's tears were anguished and hot and Thomas looked glum too, like he could break out crying just like his sister who was constantly dabbing her eyes. After hugging and saying hello to both, Mathilda sat down on a chair across from the brother and sister. She had her own thoughts to deal with. Dudley had been an important part of her life during the last few years and it would be devastating if anything happened to the boy. Even as Dudley got older, he was still the little boy she befriended on that park bench when she was so distraught with her own illness. She believed she owed her happiness to him and wished she could do something—anything for him.

"Who is Aunt Mattie? Is she here?" the doctor asked as he entered the waiting room.

"I'm here, doctor," Mathilda said, rising from her chair along with Louise and Thomas.

"Normally the parents go in first, but the boy keeps calling for you, so I think you should go in and see him, but only for five minutes."

"Doctor, tell us—how is he doing?" Thomas asked.

"If he could have come in sooner, we wouldn't have had to deal with a life threatening situation. We just don't know. Some people make it, and others—well we're doing everything we can. Are you the boy's mother?" he asked looking closely at Louise.

"Yes, I'm his mother," Louise said quite loud, as though affirming this fact to herself as well as to the doctor. "I'm his mother and I would like to see him…I need to see him!"

"And you are his father?" he asked, looking at Thomas.

"No, I'm his uncle. I brought Louise and was hoping I could see the boy, too."

"You both can see Dudley, but for only five minutes, right after his Aunt Mattie," the doctor said. "By the way, my name is Philip Bentley. We're doing everything we can to save the boy. Remember, he's strong, and he's fighting hard."

"Thank you, Doctor Bentley. Can you please keep us informed as to his progress?" Thomas asked, knowing he was helpless and that there wasn't anything he or Louise could do. Everything about Dudley's care during the past months slipped out of his hands. *And I'm supposed to be a good lawyer!*

Thomas took a seat next to his sister who continued her silent weep.

Mathilda, feeling their pain as well as her own, stopped at the waiting room to let them know she was leaving after staying the allotted five minutes with Dudley, then she hurried to find a telephone.

* * *

"He's not responding, Henry, please come as fast as you can… will you?" she pleaded.

"Aunt Mattie, I don't think anything I do will make any difference at all. I haven't been able to pray...you know that."

"But you have to try, Henry—we have to try. I don't want Dudley to die, Henry. You can understand that, can't you?"

"I do understand, and I want Dudley to live, too, Aunt Mattie."

"Then come and pray, please Henry. Come as fast as you can!"

Mathilda could hear the hesitation in his voice and then he finally spoke. "Aunt Mattie, I—I'll come because you're asking me."

"If you can, bring Booker T. with you."

"Oh," Henry said, as his voice dropped, understanding what she meant.

CHAPTER FORTY-NINE

Dudley had slipped into a restless, unconscious sleep with events and people slithering around in his mind. He found himself standing at the front of a huge theater-like room with seats that slanted up toward the ceiling as they reached back into the dark. Strange looking men with stiff, pallid faces and dark cavities for eyes sat on those seats. They wore long grey robes with matching hoods covering their heads. Dudley felt scared. He couldn't see the person who began asking the questions but he could hear him plainly. He wished Aunt Mattie was here with him, he knew she could protect him.

"Please state your full name and tell us about your life. Start from the beginning," a deep voice growled, sounding low and guttural.

"Are...are you God?" Dudley asked.

"You are only to answer the questions. You are not allowed to ask any, do you understand?" the voice uttered. Dudley sucked in his breath. The pain in his head worsened and he wished for some cold water for his dry mouth.

"We're waiting."

Dudley swallowed hard, he had to try. "My name is Dudley Best, and I...I was born near the beginning of the second world war. I spent time in jail and then in a reform school for something I didn't do."

"They always say that, no matter how guilty," the voice bellowed in a sing-song fashion, casting doubt on Dudley's explanation. The men in the seats began shifting around as though they expected something more. When they moved, it sounded like the rustling of sheets of crisp paper being crumbled. The sound was magnified directly into Dudley's ears.

"Yes sir, and no matter how much I pleaded my innocence, the authorities wouldn't believe me. One of the guys in our gang killed Rudy Mullens, and he and others set me up to take the blame."

"But you're lying! You killed Rudy, didn't you, Dudley Best?"

"No God, please, I wouldn't—couldn't kill anyone."

"You had the knife, and you killed him. That's a mortal sin, you know that."

"No. I didn't do it. One of the other guys did it."

"Write that in the book," the deep voice directed someone Dudley couldn't see.

"What else did you do?"

"Before that, we took stuff from stores, cheap stuff we didn't want or need. We did it just to do it."

"You robbed stores—so you're a thief!"

"Yes, sir. May I please have a drink of water now?" Dudley asked as he wiped the sweat forming on his forehead with the back of his hand.

"What about your thoughts, are they as pure as when you were ten?"

"I...I...have thoughts about girls, God, but.."

"Do you have a girlfriend?"

"No."

"But you would like to have one and make out like the others... and you think about them, don't you?"

"Yes. No...I don't know."

"You were flunking your classes, weren't you?"

"My daily class grades weren't so good, but I easily caught up when it was time for a test."

Dudley thought his voice sounded odd, kind of hollow in his ears as he began to shake with the frigid cold and then intense heat—so hot he thought he would pass out and crumple to the floor. He wished he could so this questioning would be over.

"But I asked for you to begin at the beginning of your life. Did you not understand?"

"Oh, I was thinking you wanted to know why I was here, in this h—"

"You are not in hell yet, Dudley Best. You are simply being asked to tell about your life. Is that understood?"

The chorus of dry crumpled paper rustled and crackled in Dudley's ears even more loudly as the hooded men began fidgeting again, leaning forward as though they were waiting for something—some important revelation.

It's odd that those sounds could hurt so bad!

"Oh, I thought I was." Dudley was trying to keep his mind on God, who was asking the questions, and not on how he thought and felt about the hooded men.

"Well, please start at the beginning and continue."

"I was born in 1940. When I was ten years old—that was probably the year I began putting two and two together to figure why I didn't have a mother and father like other boys. I remember crying after going to bed every night, but during the day, I tried to act as though I didn't care much. The person who came even close to being my mother was an old lady I met sitting on a park bench. That's where I went to listen to someone playing the piano—a lady playing so loud that I could hear the notes across the street in the park."

"What a waste of time, sitting, listening, and not obeying your elders, just a big waste of time!"

"Yes, sir. But I when she played, blocks of notes, like little cubes, attached somehow to my mind. They jumped around, moving like stepping stones. They had different bright colors—real bright, florescent even—falling on the piano keys. And after, if I could sit down at a piano, those colored cubes appeared and I could finger the keys with colored sounds coming out—not just one hand, but both."

"You went there without anyone knowing, didn't you?"

"Yes, God. I was living at the St. Gregory School for Orphans and I wanted my friend Arthur to go with me but he was afraid of the punishment for leaving the grounds without permission. I wasn't a bit afraid because my uncle was the priest-principal of the school. Arthur and I sang in the school choir and we played marbles and other games together."

Dudley stopped, as he tried to remember something—anything else he could tell.

"What else, what else?" the voice bellowed, stressing each word—urgent and demanding.

"Ugh, sometimes newer boys came to the orphanage and told us stuff, like the facts of life which were hardly believable to my friend and me. We were ten, and I was only interested in playing and getting adopted, only I found out I could never be adopted!"

"That's because no one wanted a liar, thief and a killer. But again boy, I asked for you to start at the beginning. This will count against you, do you understand?" The voice sounded harsh.

"Yes sir, God, I'll try again. How will it count against me?" Dudley asked, still shivering with the sharp pain in his stomach. He wanted to double over but tried to hide it from God.

"Please continue, Dudley Best. We are waiting so please stop the sniveling and stick to the facts."

"Can I please sit? I'm so tired."

"No, just remain standing where you are and continue—and hurry. We don't have all day and it's already getting dark."

"Yes, sir. The lady from the house across the street would come and sit on the bench during the time I was there. Sometimes her friend would come and talk to her. She was too loud, maybe thinking the other lady couldn't hear, and I would leave because I couldn't hear the notes and the cubes got all mixed up. One day, she told me who she was and asked for my name too. I had to be polite, but I also wanted to be obedient to what we had been taught about not talking to strangers. She said she understood, but because we shared the bench so many days, we couldn't remain strangers any longer and at the time, I believed she was right. After all she was the adult and would know about such things."

"Are you sure she was a real person, or are you making up a story? A mighty good one, I might add."

"No, sir. I wouldn't make up a story for you. The songs I heard would always play in my head. By the time I got home, the cubes would jump and slide around, making grand beginnings to the songs, but they were trapped inside. The school piano was in the basement music room. It was locked. Arthur told me to just sing and forget about listening to the piano on the park bench. Father John— that's my uncle's name—he didn't know where I went and I didn't tell him about the little cubes dancing around in my head and neither did my friend."

"Go on, don't stall."

"Sister Ruth was really nice and was always mending our trousers. Our knees always had holes in them and mine were the worst of all the boys. But she told me not to worry about it, just to keep playing marbles and ball if that's what I liked to do, cause that's what boys are supposed to do. I liked sister Ruth."

"Well, that's better, anything else? It seems as though you were a most disobedient boy and also an extremely good liar. Now go on."

"One day the old lady told me to call her Mrs. Mathilda, and she would call me by my name. She seemed sick and didn't come to the bench every day, and then she didn't come at all. Once though, she invited me over to have some cookies and milk. I was hungry so I said yes. After I ate in the kitchen, I walked into her parlor and saw the big piano by the window. I could hear the cubes jumping in my head and I asked if I could please play. Mrs. Mathilda said I could if I promised I wouldn't pound. I promised and sat down. The last song that Miss Sally played was the song I heard in my head. She played *Fur Elise*, and it just popped right off the tips of my fingers. I never played it before and was surprised that I could do it. It was so pretty, but then the clock struck five and I had to run. I would probably miss my dinner again and I knew I'd get in trouble for sure."

"Just as I thought. You were deliberately late and broke the school rules again."

"No, sir. I didn't do it on purpose. It just happened. Anyway, I couldn't leave the school grounds anymore. Then the lady—I call her Aunt Mattie now—she came to see me. She thought I was ill and talked to my uncle, who I was supposed to call Father John and not Uncle John. Anyway, they somehow worked it out so I could go to the conservatory in Chicago. I didn't want to go, but they said it was an opportunity so I went with the lady. Mister Crow was nice to me and he was the lady's very good friend. I thought they would get married and adopt me, but it never happened because he died after the best Christmas party I ever went to."

"You killed this Crow-man, didn't you?"

"No, sir. I never killed anyone. I loved Mr. Crow."

"If you didn't want to go to this school of music, as you say, you wasted the money and the lady's time as well. That was very sneaky of you."

"Yes, sir. I guess so…but I was only ten years old. I didn't know anything about wasting anything or being sneaky. But while I was at the conservatory, I played with an orchestra on the largest grand piano I'd ever seen. Uncle Tommy and Aunt Mattie took me to the zoo too. Ziggy was there. He was a huge elephant they kept tied up. They said he was mean but I thought he was just sad…like me. I would be mean too if they tied me up like that. Aunt Mattie and I became good friends, almost like mother and son…I was the son.

She seemed to love me and she had a real nice house and everything."

"Well, that's enough. We already know about the reform school so we'll let you know what we decide if we get to keep you. If we do, we'll have a special place for you." The voice started laughing a horrible croaking. "For now you'd better not try to run away, but just to make sure, we'll put a tether around your ankle."

It was a long, wide black belt that one of the hooded men quickly ran up and secured around Dudley's ankle. That man had a stench that rose up into Dudley's nostrils, making him feel like puking, but Dudley had to hold it 'cause puking in front of God would be disrespectful.

"One more thing, Dudley Best…"

"Yes, God?"

"You have a friend who is not your kind."

"You mean, Booker T?" Dudley questioned, because he heard it many times from his buddies.

"Exactly. He's not someone you should be friends with. He's different and not like you."

"But God, Aunt Mattie never told me that and I didn't know that it was wrong to be friends with him. Are you sure? I mean, I'm sorry if I did something wrong."

"You know you're not sorry. You never confessed it!"

The session was over. The hooded men who were seated, now stood and began to walk slowly and stiffly toward Dudley with the crackle of paper becoming louder and louder as they approached him. Each had their gnarled index fingers pointing at him. Finally he fainted—fell over as dead before the first one could lay a hand on him.

CHAPTER FIFTY

Henry decided to go directly to the hospital—alone. The waiting room was empty now and a snippy nurse informed Henry that because he wasn't an immediate family member, he couldn't go in to see the patient. She said there was someone with Dudley at that very moment and that it was enough company for someone that ill.

Surely I didn't come for nothing, so I may as well wait for the person who's with him to come out. Henry sat down. He didn't know what else he could do since it was a long drive back.

It was Father John Bealer who was sitting beside Dudley's bed, waiting for him to awaken, even for a few minutes. When the nurse came in to adjust the intravenous tubes, Dudley finally opened his eyes—kind of squinting as though he couldn't see clearly who was talking to him.

"Hi, Dudley," Father John whispered when the nurse was satisfied that Dudley was comfortable for the moment and left the room.

"Uncle John," Dudley whispered. "How come you're here?" He said with a croaky, hard to understand voice.

"You're pretty sick, Dudley. I wanted to come and pray for you, and tell you I'm sorry too. You know, I could have done much better for you...we all could have."

"Not Aunt Mattie though...she did everything for me, just like my real mother—the one I always wanted."

"I know. It's hard to understand now, but adults do make mistakes and things get complicated. As you get older, you'll see what a sacrifice your mother made and then you'll know the truth."

"I thought I hated her. But I guess I'm jealous of Annie and Paddy. They always had her with them, and I…you said you wanna pray for me?" Dudley abruptly understood why his uncle was there. "You mean the prayers 'cause I'm dying." It wasn't a question. Dudley's eyes closed when he asked, "what's heaven like, Uncle John?"

"It's the most beautiful place there ever could be, a beauty that we can't even imagine. But it's not only a place, it's who will make it heaven…who will be there."

"Uhh, oh, you mean Jesus? Do you think I could go there? I mean even if I sinned, you know, a mortal sin?" Dudley whispered with his eyes still closed. "I don't think God wants me. He didn't even know whether he could keep me, and I didn't get to tell him I'm sorry."

"I know that you could go there…but not now. Now, you have to fight to live. And Dudley, he knows you're sorry."

And then the priest understood Dudley's words.

"God told you he didn't want you?" he asked, trying to get it straight.

"I want to sleep now, and not wake up." His voice was now much more gravelly than before. Father John had to put his ear close to Dudley's mouth so he could hear every word. "I'm like Ziggy… can't you see how I'm tied to the bed?"

"Dudley, you have so much to live for. Your whole life is ahead of you. Who's Ziggy and what makes you think God doesn't want you?"

"They're fighting over me…asking me questions and pulling me away from the door and they tied me up like Ziggy…can't you see?"

"What door? Who's Ziggy?" Father John asked again, looking around, particularly at the door and then pulling back the sheet slightly to look at Dudley's feet.

"The one over there—see the bright light? I wanna go there, but God's mad at me," he said, his voice trailing off.

"What do you mean? Tell me so I can understand!" There wasn't anything unusual about the door or his feet when Father John looked, trying to see something—anything.

"Sometimes I would think about girls. I know I shouldn't have… and Father Augustus at our teen retreat said it was a sin, a real bad sin." Dudley's voice was only a whisper now. "And now they want me."

"Yes, but Dudley, God will forgive you for anything, if you're sorry, don't you know that? And besides, he wouldn't give you appendicitis just because your thoughts were impure. He doesn't do that."

"Yeah, but he did…but I would never think like that about Elise. She's so…just go, please, the pain is starting again," he said, repeating himself as he began twisting, first one way and then another.

"Make them stop, please, Uncle John, make them stop! They're taking me…I have to go…"

"You're not going back to that reformatory. God will help you. I know he will."

"But, I can't fight any mo…"

Father John called the nurse. As soon as she looked at Dudley, asked Father John to leave, nodding towards the door. Then there was a lot of scuffling around as the nurses sent for Doctor Bentley. Father John slowly walked toward the waiting room. It was late, already eleven o'clock.

CHAPTER FIFTY-ONE

Henry was still there, waiting. At night the waiting room took on a depressing gloomy aura. There was the water cooler, six hard back chairs, and a table with a small lamp burning a sixty-watt bulb under a gray shade. A faded green sofa faced the chairs on the opposite wall and the large windows were covered by matching green drapes that fluttered with every gust of cold air.

When Father John entered, he saw Henry nodding, eyes closed and coat pulled tightly around him.

"Henry, is that you? Are you okay? How long have you been waiting?"

"I don't know...how is he?" Henry asked, getting up and grabbing Father John's hands in a warm clasp.

"He seems to be getting weaker and says he doesn't want to live. He's so tired. I have to go back as soon as the doctors leave his room. I have to pray, even if he doesn't want me to. He seems scared—scared of things I couldn't see and says that God is mad at him."

"Please, John, I have to go in with you. Aunt Mattie asked me to come and pray for him but the nurse said no."

"I'll get you in somehow. You know Dudley believes you have healing power in your hands. It'll give him hope. Thanks for coming, Henry."

"But it's Aunt Mattie who has the hope, and the faith. I haven't been able to pray since I lost her crops."

Father John and Henry entered Dudley's room to find the boy in an uncomfortable, agitated type of sleep, tossing every few minutes. "I wonder if they gave him something more for the pain?" Father John said, not really expecting Henry to answer. And then he began to administer Extreme Unction—the last rites of the church.

"Have mercy upon Dudley, O God, after thy great goodness…" The prayers took the next twenty minutes, ending with the anointing of Dudley's forehead with sacred sweet smelling oil. Dudley seemed to begin to rest in that prayer, but as soon as Father John said the last amen, Henry walked over to the other side of the bed. Suddenly, he fell down on his knees and cried out.

"Please Lord, when we touch Dudley, fill him with your life giving spirit and raise him up, even as you raised Lazarus and as you raised me. Surely this boy and his family have been through enough. Surely Lord, you'll have compassion for him as you did for me that fateful night when you heard my feeble prayer and raised me up."

Then Henry, on one side of his bed and Father John on the other side, held hands across the bed and each held one of Dudley's hands. Henry had no more to say. He was sure that God had heard both him and Father John, because he felt the old tingle in his fingers. Something like an electric current filled his arms and traveled all through his body, almost as if he had his finger in a socket. Even the bed began vibrating while Dudley squeezed the men's hands hard, as though he were hanging on for dear life. After a few minutes, Dudley's grip fell away. His eyes were still closed and he sank down into a peaceful, deep sleep. Exhausted, Father John and Henry went back into the waiting room.

Henry fell onto the sofa and Father John sat down on one of the chairs. They were both shaken from what appeared to have been electricity that coursed through them as well as Dudley. They knew

Dudley felt that power, but they would have to wait for morning to find out how God answered their prayer.

CHAPTER FIFTY-TWO

That same day, the day after Thanksgiving, when Doctor James was driving home from the last call, Booker T. felt a new kind of anger. Why did those old memories about his father have to suddenly pop up, memories that turned the love he had for him into hate?

Long lost words that slipped into his subconscious when he was very little, rose like angry ocean waves. He could hear them clearly now, and he was reluctant to tell the doctor what he was thinking, but Doctor James was no fool. He knew how Booker T. was affected by that last sick call, because it had affected him, too.

Booker T. could actually hear the words spoken by his father the night before his mother left.

"You gotta give me more money for food," mama shouted, "the kids are always hungry, and so am I."

"Why? I want that money for things I need, not for kids that don't do nuthin' around here. And those kids are gonna have to start listening to me, ya hear me, lady?" Fraze yelled. "Ya need to teach 'em better."

"But they don't even know you. You're always gone. So what... what do you want from them? They're growing fast and are skinny as a rail, can't hardly see them when they stand sideways."

"I want peace and quiet after a hard day of work, and I want them to respect me without all that yelling and screaming in this house."

"Oh, they learn that real good from us, in case you hadn't noticed—you're always yelling at me. And you know what, you earn respect when you give it, and you get it by being a father instead of a boarder," she shouted back.

"You stick up for dem little hoodlums—that's all they are, hoodlums—probably not even mine."

"Oh, they're yours, but how would you know, you never came to the hospital with me when they were born. All you know is how to yell, and they're only being kids. The only place Elroy, Ruby, and Booker T. get anything decent to eat is at my mama's."

"I told you, stop coddling them. I guess I'll have to show 'em how to listen to me—them making all that noise, I can't stand it. The neighbors will complain and we'll have to move. I'll show 'em right now," he said as he took off his belt and walked into their bedroom.

"No, please stop*!"*

Where are they, my brother, Elroy and sister, Ruby? And where is my mama? Booker was startled by the thoughts and feelings that suddenly surfaced.

"What did you say, Booker T?" Dr. James asked as he looked at his young passenger who was shaking his head back and forth. His eyes were closed and was kind of mumbling under his breath. "I can't stop right here."

"Oh, nothing. I guess I was talking to myself. I'm sorry."

"I think you're as upset as I am by that last call. I'm sorry that we can't do more when we find situations like that."

"Yes sir, I'm sorry too," Booker T. said aloud but didn't understand why they couldn't.

"It was very nice of you to give the children the little car and doll. Did you see their eyes light up?"

"I did, sir. Those toys don't cost very much at the dime store, and the kids were so happy but then they got a little noisy and..."

"I know..."

"Dr. James, why are some of the papas always angry or always gone? Either out or out for good, and always barking at their families? Don't they love them?"

"They do, but in their own way. And because they never had anything themselves, they want what they want. They're like little children themselves."

"That papa was yelling at the lady who was awfully sick. At the kids too, and they were just playing. They couldn't help it if they made noise and it was unfair they got whipped so hard. "

"I know Booker…I know."

CHAPTER FIFTY-THREE

It was almost five-thirty the next morning, when Mathilda found two exhausted men sleeping in the hospital waiting room.

"Have you been here all night?"

Henry and Father John both woke with a start when she spoke.

"I guess we kind of fell asleep," Henry said.

"How was Dudley last night?" she asked, anxious to know whether he was any better.

"Mattie, it started to be a real rough night, but I prayed over him and gave him the sacraments, and then Henry called out to God. We felt His power when Henry touched Dudley, but haven't heard anything yet. Excuse me, I have to wake up. I'll go and wash my face," Father John said, "and then I'm going home. I have some appointments and things that have to be taken care of this morning. Call me...with any news."

"Bye Johnny, thanks for everything," Mathilda said as he left and then she looked closely at Henry. "Are you okay?"

"Just tired, Auntie."

"Let's try to talk to a nurse or the doctor," Mathilda said, as she turned and walked toward the nurse's station, Henry following behind.

Several doctors including Dr. Bentley were making their rounds and were talking intently outside Dudley's room. They were looking over the chart one of the interns was holding. When he saw Mattie and Henry, Bentley walked over to them smiling.

"We were just talking about the change in the boy."

"What change is that?" Henry asked.

"Well, he seems to have turned a corner. It's highly unusual for a patient to change so significantly in so short a time. If I didn't know better, and only looked at his vitals, I would say he never had a burst appendix. He's sleeping a deep, normal sleep, and I don't think he'll awaken for a while."

"Dr. Bentley?"

"Yes?"

"Father John and I prayed for him last night, and I believe that God heard and answered our prayers."

"Uh…well…the thing is, he's better and that's what counts," Dr. Bentley said as he cleared his throat and turned to leave.

"Thank you, Doctor. Thank you for all of your fine care," Mathilda said feeling a great surge of relief.

"I do believe he's on his way to a full recovery. He's a strong boy," Bentley said, then he and the other doctors walked away, continuing their rounds and already talking amongst themselves about another patient.

"I knew God would hear your prayers, Henry."

"Not only my prayers, but Father Johns powerful church prayers. And now I'm so tired, I guess I'll go home and get some rest." Henry gave her a much needed hug and turned to leave.

"Okay, Henry, please let everyone know that Dudley will be okay and don't forget Father John."

"I won't forget and thanks for calling me. I needed that nudge to start praying again. You know, Auntie, it wasn't God who couldn't hear me, it was I that couldn't hear Him. He was there all the time, waiting for me!"

CHAPTER FIFTY-FOUR

Mathilda sat down in the waiting room, determined to see Dudley the minute he awakened. After a few minutes, she heard a man's deep voice echo down the hall, asking about Dudley Best.

Someone's checking at the nurse's station as to his condition, she thought, but didn't recognize the man's voice and wondered who would come so early in the morning.

Then the gentleman walked into the waiting room, placed his hat and overcoat on an empty chair and took a seat. Mathilda noticed right away that he was well dressed—dark business suit, white shirt, and blue striped tie. His shoes were polished to a high sheen. No one else was in the room so she addressed him from where she was sitting.

"Hello, I'm Mathilda Millering. Dudley calls me Aunt Mattie and I've been waiting to see him too. Did they tell you at the desk that he's sleeping normally and is much better?"

"Yes, they did. Oh excuse me, my name is Barry—Barry Tierney. I'm glad to meet you, ma'am. Dudley has mentioned you many times."

"He has? And you know him from where?"

She was surprised, and wondered when Dudley would've mentioned her to this complete stranger.

"I guess you may as well know that he's been staying at my home."

"Then it's been you, hiding and caring for him! I've been quite worried. In fact, I became very determined to find him, but couldn't…and now suddenly, here you are."

"Yes, I can imagine how you must have felt."

"But what happened to him? I mean to land here in the hospital?"

"Well, that Thanksgiving Day storm snowed us in. We—my daughter Elise, Dudley and I—had dinner together, played monopoly, and then Dudley went to bed, only to awaken with severe stomach pain. We got here as fast as we could."

"Thank you so much for helping him, Mr. Tierney. I mean that from the bottom of my heart. He means the world to me."

"I kind of guessed that, the way the boy spoke about you. Did they say he would recover fully?"

"Well, Doctor Bentley said he was a strong boy and that he had turned a corner, so I think that it means that he'll get completely well. They never say too much."

"Did you drive over this morning?"

"No, I drove over early yesterday, but last night I stayed at the motel down the street. I wanted to be close."

"I hope you were comfortable."

"It was adequate. The hot water was cold and there wasn't an extra blanket but other than that, it was as I said—adequate."

"My goodness, my dear lady, if you decide to stay longer, you must come to my home. I have plenty of room and it's not that far from here."

"You would allow me to be where Dudley is? I thought it was a secret?"

"Not after today, I think from now on it'll be safe."

"I guess I would like that. Could you write down your address with a little map of how to get there from here?"

"Of course." Quickly, he scribbled on a pad of paper he kept in his back pocket. After he finished, he looked closely at Mathilda and asked, "Why not let me take you to breakfast since we'll be here for a while and Dudley is still sleeping. You know it's been over an hour already?"

"How kind of you. I would like that very much."

Mathilda walked over to the nurse's station and left word that she and Mr. Tierney would be back shortly.

Barry and Mathilda talked a lot while eating at the coffee shop around the corner from the hospital. He filled her in on all that had happened since Dudley came to his house, and how much he enjoyed having him. He also told her about his daughter Elise and about his wife's death the previous year.

After another hour or more they returned to the hospital and found an officer guarding the door to Dudley's room. Mathilda thought something was terribly wrong when the head nurse started mumbling that a boy so ill shouldn't be disturbed by anyone, especially by the police. She seemed abrupt and stated that if they decided to stay, to please wait in the waiting room until the officers left.

"Please excuse me, ma'am, I have a few calls to make," Tierney said, as he quickly turned, practically running to the downstairs phone he had used yesterday. Mathilda decided to speak again to the nurse working at the desk.

"Is someone else in the room with Dudley? Is he awake?"

"I'm not at liberty to say," was the nurse's curt reply, as though someone had warned her about saying anything about the situation.

"Did he wake up yet? I mean since we were gone?"

"I'm sorry, this is entirely out of my hands. You'll have to ask that officer over there about that. But I can assure you, that he isn't in any mood to answer questions."

Mathilda scrutinized the officer standing at the door, but decided not to cross him. She walked back to the waiting room, but could hardly wait for Tierney to get back so she could tell him about the continuous odd behavior of the head nurse. Fifteen long impatient minutes passed before he entered the room with a grim look on his face.

"Mattie, something strange is going on here so I called the local police. They'll be here…oh, there they are," he said as two very husky police officers entered through the glass doors. Their hands were straddling the revolvers strapped around their hips. They walked to the station where the head nurse sat and after the officers had a few words with her, she led them to the officer guarding Dudley's room. Barry and Mathilda followed and watched from a short distance.

The officers asked to see the credentials of the burly man at the door who wore police attire, but he had none.

"Open the door," they demanded, ready to take action if they weren't immediately obeyed.

The police officer opened the door quickly, and made a hand motion for the other man to come out. He was holding a filled syringe with a yellow colored substance. Since there was nowhere to hide the hypo, he threw it into the waste basket before he exited the room. They were both handcuffed and led away but not before the arresting officer took out his handkerchief and carefully used it to confiscate the hypo from the trash. Very deftly, he placed it into his coat pocket.

Mathilda ran over to Dudley's bed. He was already trying to sit up when he saw them come in.

"Hi, Aunt Mattie," he whispered. "Hi, Mr. Tierney."

"Wow, Dudley, you gave us a terrible scare." Tierney said.

"Aunt Mattie, Mr. Tierney…the fighting stopped last night and I fell asleep in the brightest light I ever saw. I was surrounded by it and they couldn't come near me any more," he said excitedly.

Mathilda and Tierney looked at each other with questioning eyes, wondering what he was talking about.

"I'm glad, Dudley. You know Father John and Mr. Henry were here praying for you." Mattie wanted him to know it was God who helped him.

"Oh I don't remember that. I only know the fighting stopped and God changed his mind about keeping me."

Tierney had tears in his eyes. "I'm so sorry you had to go through all this, Dudley. I'm sorry, and it's all my fault."

Mathilda looked at this man whom she had just met and was surprised that he had such deep feelings for the boy.

"Mr. Tierney...Barry, I think you've got it all wrong. It was you who *saved* Dudley by getting him here in time for the doctor to do the surgery. Thank you!" She said this while touching his arm lightly in gratitude.

Tierney wiped his face and eyes with his handkerchief.

"I'll say goodbye for now, Dudley. And...Mattie, please come, I would love to have you stay at my house."

"Goodbye, Mr. Tierney, and thanks for everything," Dudley said, as he left. "Aunt Mattie, are you thinking of going to his house?"

"Yes, he invited me so I wouldn't have too drive so far to visit you."

"He's really swell and treated me like...like I was his...like a part of his family," Dudley said. "I thought he would be an old, stuffy man when Mr. Dennison told me he was a senator and very important."

"My goodness, he didn't mention that he was a senator and I didn't realize it until now when you said it. I should have recognized the man's name from the newspapers."

As they talked, the nurse brought in a tray with a small bowl of hot oatmeal, a piece of buttered toast and a small glass of milk. She said that if he kept it down she would bring something more substantial for lunch.

"Maybe a hamburger?" Dudley asked teasingly.

"Maybe not a hamburger. Maybe some soup, and something else, whatever they have down there for someone who was as sick as you," the nurse said, laughing along with him. She too was relieved to see his quick improvement.

"Yes, ma'am, maybe some ice cream?"

"We'll just wait and see," she said as she left the room.

Mathilda made herself comfortable on the chair and watched Dudley eat while he talked between bites.

Different doctors streamed in, looking at the latest blood reports on Dudley's chart. Every one of them raised their eye-brows and seemed surprised after such a difficult night. But they didn't say much aloud and Mathilda couldn't tell what they were thinking.

"You know, Auntie, I felt scared like something was wrong when that policeman was in my room. I pretended to be asleep but I was watching him with one eye slightly open. I thought he was going to take me back to the reform school."

"It was a good thing you were so alert, Dudley."

"I could see him mixing something over there by the window. He pulled a little bag from his pocket, and I saw him squeeze the hypodermic needle until some liquid shot up. Then, the door opened and he left. I was ready to holler real loud if he came near me though."

Noticing that Dudley was getting excited while talking about it, Mathilda thought she should change the subject. "By the way, how was your stay at Mr. Tierney's house?"

"Okay, but he wasn't home much except for the weekends. I kept busy working with Mr. Blanchard, the gardener—he reminds me of Mr. Crow—a lot," Dudley explained after finishing the hot cereal and chewing the last piece of toast.

"Like Crow? My goodness, I'd like to meet that man."

"You probably will if you're going over there. And Aunt Mattie, Mr. Tierney has a music room with a baby grand just like yours, and his daughter plays the violin."

"Oh, sounds as though you had something in common to talk about."

"When Elise—that's his daughter's name—when she was away at school, she left it sitting on the piano so I picked it up and figured how to get the different notes with the fingering. I tried to imitate how Elise moved her fingers so easily, up and down on the neck, just like Mr. Graham. You remember, he was the old, stuffy man hired by my grandmother to play her grandfather's Stradivarius for Mary Beth's wedding. He was staying at her house the day we were there. One of the guys in the gang had one. He showed me a little, too."

"Oh, he did?" Mattie said, very surprised.

"Aunt Mattie, why did I stay with them? They were mean and not my friends at all."

"Maybe you just needed somebody—anybody," Mathilda said as she thought about it. "Sometimes, we're just that needy, Dudley."

"I guess I didn't have any other friends, except Booker T., and he became a problem with the guys, if you know what I mean."

"Well, you said they would rub you out…would they?"

"Yeah, I think I would've had an accident of some kind."

"One way to look at it, Dudley, is that because of you, they're able to finally prosecute the people responsible for covering up Rudy's death in Blenning, and to clean up that reform school. I'd say that it's quite a feat for someone so young."

"I was scared in that school all the time, because those guys were worse than the guys in the gang. I mean they were really tough." And then another thought occurred to him, "Aunt Mattie, could I go home to your house if the doctor says I can get out of here?"

"That would be wonderful. Sadie could fix meals that would get you up and on your feet again in no time."

"No one's looking for me anymore, are they?"

"Mr. Tierney would know that. We'll have to wait and ask him."

CHAPTER FIFTY-FIVE

Senator Tierney hired a private nurse to care for Dudley after he was released from the hospital. She was to keep track of his temperature, and make sure he received nutritious meals while the Senator was away on state business—everything Mattie could have done while she was there for the week, but Tierney had to have his way. After all, it was his home.

On the last day of Mattie's stay, she obliged Dudley by looking through all the old pictures in the library and finishing their long game of Monopoly. They had a fun bet that he could get Boardwalk, Park Place and all the railroads before Mathilda would leave for home, but changed his mind when it didn't happen.

"Oh Auntie, you're right, we need a lot more time for a game like this," Dudley said, when the game continued with no end in sight. So on the day she was leaving, Dudley began stacking the property cards and all the little houses into the game box and put it away in the cabinet.

"Couldn't you stay just a few more days?" he asked with his ten-year-old winsome voice.

"I'm so sorry, you know there are only a few more weeks before Christmas and I have a lot to take care of, including checking on Booker T." she explained. A light knock sounded at the library door, and in walked Mr. Tierney.

"How are my favorite people today?" he asked, looking fondly at Dudley and then Mathilda. He took a seat across from them, folding his hands on top of the table.

"I'm feeling good, sir, but Aunt Mattie is talking about going home today."

"Yes, Mr. Tierney—Barry, there are things that need to be taken care of, and Dudley is doing so well, there's no reason for me to stay any longer."

"Except to keep this fine gentleman company."

"It was good, but now it's time to go. I saw most of the pictures in the boxes. I must say, they're most interesting."

"Oh, you did? You saw my wife and little Elise when she visited her mother in the hospital?"

"Yes, your wife was a very beautiful woman. I'm sorry she was ill for so long."

"I guess some things just happen, and nothing can be done about it." He felt a little uneasy. He hoped it didn't show too much. He quickly reached into his pants pocket for his handkerchief and dabbed at the perspiration building on his forehead. His eyes diverted across the room, not wanting to make contact with Mathilda's.

"Do you think I could go back to your house, Aunt Mattie, now that I'm well?"

"Well, Barry, what do you think? You're the person who would know whether Dudley was still in any danger from those thugs."

"I believe it's okay to get on with your life now, but it's been the best weeks of my life. I wish I could keep you here, Dudley, but I know it's time. I think that right after the new year, you could leave. Of course, the doctor has to say if you're up to going to school."

"I feel good and I'm especially happy that you got my record wiped clean so I don't have to go back to the reform school. What a relief!"

"That's the greatest miracle of all," Mathilda added, "and you're probably the only person who could've done it." She smiled at Senator Tierney as she spoke.

"I'm glad it all turned around, and it was my pleasure to be a part of it."

"You certainly have been kind to Dudley and myself. You must know how much I appreciate it."

"I assure you, I was happy to do whatever I could. As you know, Dudley, Elise will be home in a few days and maybe you both could play some of those songs together. I'd love to hear them again, before you—"

"And then I can go home...for good?" Dudley interrupted.

"You mean, to your mother's house?"

"No, I'd like to, but..."

"Maybe you first have to get to know her better, because she's a kind, loving lady."

"But how would you know that, I mean, do you know her, sir?"

"I can just tell. When you get to be my age, there are some things you just know."

"I guess I'd like to be at your house, Aunt Mattie. Then I won't have to go back to the high school in Blenning. They know all about me there, and it would be embarrassing."

"But if you live at my house, you'll be going to school with Booker T." Mathilda reminded him.

"Oh," is all Dudley said, his thoughts already running wild about having to fight because a black kid lived in the same house. Tierney picked up on Dudley's hesitation and tried to soften his worry about the situation.

"You still have time to decide what you should do. Why not think about your options so that you make the right choice. I also want to talk to you and Elise as soon as possible. It seems that whenever I start, something makes me put it off."

"Okay, sir. Will I like what you're going to tell me—us?" he questioned.

Mathilda wondered why Tierney brought up the subject, if he had to wait to tell it. *And he's supposed to be an educated man!*

"Why not just wait till the man is ready, Dudley," Mathilda suggested, "since it must be important or he wouldn't have brought it up."

"I'm sorry sir, I guess I can wait for you and Elise. It's just that it sounds so mysterious and you mentioned it before."

"So I did, my boy, but we'll get on with it soon." As he left the room, Tierney tousled Dudley's hair in good humor.

Mattie had to leave too. "Goodbye for now, Dudley, maybe you and Mr. Tierney can come to the Christmas party at Henry and Catherine's…I'll mention it to him on my way out."

"That would be swell," Dudley said, as he remembered that first Christmas at the farm. "Will Booker T. be there?"

"Yes, we've all been invited including Booker T. and some of the neighbors. It'll be a little going away party for Mr. Henry, too, because he's been accepted at a seminary in Chicago."

"He's finally going to the seminary?" Dudley said, mulling around in his mind the idea of Henry leaving the little boys and Catherine.

"Yes, he's waited for an opportunity like this for quite some time," Mathilda said, but she was now picking up on something, the way Dudley said the words. *Was he remembering how it was without a father?*

"I hope Mr. Tierney can take me. Do you think the sleds are still hanging out back?"

"I'm sure they are but they're probably a little dusty."

* * *

Elise arrived home from school for Christmas break very early the next morning. She stayed for few hours, only while she packed for her grandparents on her mother's side. They were planning a trip to visit grandmama's sister in North Carolina and were looking forward to taking Elise with them while showering her with all sorts of gifts she didn't need. She loved it and loved being with them because they reminded her of her mother. Even their voices were similar.

Dudley and Elise hadn't seen each other since his hospital ordeal, but she remembered how nasty she had been when he first came. And now she had a plan to make up for it before leaving for her grandparent's home—a daring plan she and her friends at school discussed thoroughly.

It was barely seven o'clock, and Dudley hadn't been awake for more than five minutes when Elise knocked softly on his bedroom door.

"Can I come in, Dudley?" she asked when she was sure that her dad and the nurse were downstairs in the kitchen and they would be alone.

"Sure, Elise, come on in," he said, surprised but pleased to hear her voice.

"I'm so glad you're okay, are you?" she asked hesitantly, as she crossed the floor to his bed and sat down beside him, the same as she did when she put cold cloths on his forehead. "You don't feel like puking again, do you?" she asked, laughing.

"No, but thanks for helping me when I was," he said. He felt embarrassed about the ordeal he put her through.

Dudley pushed himself higher on his pillow, still a little groggy with sleep.

"I'm ready to leave for Grandmama's, but I've been wanting to tell you that I'm sorry for the way I treated you when you first came. I'm sorry I woke you just now too."

"No, I've been awake, just too lazy to get up."

"Well, I am sorry, Dudley. I don't know why I was so angry at you when you first came, and I know daddy was embarrassed by how I acted too."

"But we had fun that last night, playing Monopoly together." Dudley didn't want to think about those first days.

"Yes, and when you played the piano for me it was…you play so well, I would like to do it again when I get back…that is, if you're still here."

"I'd like that Elise," Dudley said. "Your daddy says I'll be here until the new year."

"Good, and I'll be back right after Christmas. By the way, what's it like in a reform school?"

"Elise, you don't want to know. A girl like you…"

"But I wondered…are girls…in the same reform school?"

"They probably have their own. This one was for boys only— tough guys they were trying to rehabilitate."

"Did it work?"

"I wasn't there long enough, but I would say no, not the way they were treated."

"What was that like?"

"Elise, don't ask, it's not anything you should know about."

"Oh, okay, but I'm glad you're out."

"Me too."

"You know, since you came, Daddy does seem happier than he's been in a long time."

"I didn't know. He always seems very nice."

"And I'm glad you'll be here while I'm away with my grandparents because I won't feel guilty about him being here all alone during the holidays, I mean, without me."

"I'm glad I'm here too, so don't worry."

"Well, anyway, I'll see you after Christmas, but I have a little Christmas present for you."

"Oh, no. I don't have anything for you, Elise," Dudley said, embarrassed again, his face turning raspberry as he pushed himself up even higher on his pillow to see whatever it was that she would give him. Elise suddenly bent forward and placed a kiss on his lips, lingering a little longer than she thought she would or should, more than a moment, and then she whispered, "Merry Christmas, Dudley Best. You have received my very first kiss to a boy, and it's my gift to you."

Dudley tried to grab her hand and pull her toward him, but she was too quick and he lost hold, only brushing against it. He was so stunned, he could only mummer a weak, "Merry Christmas," as she ran out and the nurse came in through the opened door.

"Well, Mr. Best, it's time to vacate that bed and get your shower. Breakfast is almost ready"

"Yes, ma'am. I'll be down in a few minutes."

"My goodness, you look...starry eyed. Are you okay?" she asked in a very businesslike voice.

"Yes, I am, ma'am."

But all he could think of was that Elise kissed him. He could still feel her tender, sweet girl lips lingering on his. She didn't know it, but it was the very first kiss his lips ever tasted.

Later that same afternoon, with too much energy and nothing to do, Dudley was on all fours with a dust cloth hanging out of his back pocket. He straightened and dusted thoroughly all the game cupboards and bookshelves in the library. He was wearing one of the warm sweaters Mattie bought for him after he left the hospital, but today a stout fire warmed the room nicely. After he cleaned, he sat down at the table and began reading more interesting case histories from a book he found on top of a stack sitting on the floor. Even though it held his attention, he found himself thinking about his response to Elise about rehabilitation. *What kind of system could have a better outcome with boys? There had to be a way for them to see themselves as better than what caused them to land in that school.* He remembered that he felt, "less than and not wanted," and that's why acceptance of the gang members was so important.

A knock at the door startled Dudley as Tierney and two deputies entered the library. They explained that it was time for Dudley to give his deposition under oath to the court reporter. An officer and the Senator were present as witnesses. Doing so, he wouldn't need to appear at any of the trials that were now beginning. Being a minor, he would be shielded from that kind of trauma, even so, the newspapers were full of accusations. Arrests of people in high places were reported daily. Dudley found that out quite by accident when he had picked up a newspaper that was forgotten a few days earlier, left carelessly on a chair in the kitchen. It was the biggest thing to have happened in Blenning, with fallout stretching into surrounding states. Now, he knew for sure; he couldn't live in Blenning with his mother. He had to attend school somewhere else. But where?

CHAPTER FIFTY-SIX

It was only three more weeks before Christmas, and Booker T. was smiling every day, happy that Aunt Mattie was finally home. He always felt secure when she was in the house, making sure everything was running smoothly. On this particular evening, it was later than usual, almost seven, when Dr. James dropped him off after a particular busy afternoon. The doctor parked in back by the carriage house but left the motor running as he spoke in a soft gentle voice to the young man.

"Booker T, it's getting inconvenient for me to be dropping you off after a long day like this."

"I know, Doctor James. I'm sorry, but do you want me not to go on those calls with you?"

"You didn't give me an answer about moving in with me and Ethel for the next semester. It would help me. And remember, you could still go to the same high school. The only thing that would change is that I wouldn't have to drive you back and forth."

"I don't know how Mrs. Mathilda would like that," he replied, careful not to call her Auntie. He liked Doctor James' family, but Booker T. wasn't sure that he wanted to live with them, especially when Dudley might be coming home.

"Will Mrs. James want me there all the time?"

"I spoke with her and she said yes, but you will need to give it some thought, and if you agree, I'll speak to your aunt, myself."

"I will, sir. I'll think about it."

"Something else, Booker T. You've been constantly sheltered from what has been going on with our people."

"What do you mean, sir? I don't think I've been sheltered, not with Nate Marsh and his friends at school always trying to do me in."

"Well, it's a lot more than that. Things are happening, so many injustices, we can't put up with them much longer. It's just not right."

"No sir, but what—"

"There's talk. A lot of talk about a man named King—Martin Luther King, Jr. There's going to be marches and things like that."

"What are marches? Do you want me to march?" Booker T. couldn't even imagine what the Doctor's words meant.

"No, that's what I want to explain to you. It would be better to only concentrate on what we have to do, because people depend on us. We have to be available, not marching on the streets or rotting away in some jail when we're needed for sick folks and babies."

"Oh, I didn't know, sir."

"Your main purpose is to prepare for medical school and nothing else. Just keep that in mind if people at church try to get you involved. Don't get involved, you understand?"

"No sir, I mean, yes sir, I understand. I won't get involved unless you tell me."

* * *

"Good morning, ma'am. May I have a word with you?" Doctor James asked when Mathilda answered the light knock at the back door.

"Oh, Doctor James, please come in. Let's sit in the parlor. It's much more comfortable in there."

After they chatted for a few minutes, Doctor James brought up the burning question he had on his mind.

"Do you suppose Booker T. could move in with my wife and me after the new year? It would free me up from all the driving, and it also occurred to me that the boy needs to have a better grasp of our culture and rub shoulders with his own race a little more before he goes off to college."

"Do you think it's important that he move when he has been doing so well here?" Mathilda asked.

"Yes, he is doing well. But I think he is missing the reality of how it is with us. He sees everything though rosy glasses. Your rosy glasses I might add."

"Well, he's aware of danger almost every day, but in your opinion, what else?"

"He needs to understand how hard it is for a man to make a living when he's discriminated against. He has to see it every day."

"Oh, I see. Yes, I believe he has a lot to learn about that and so do I."

"He could still spend time here when he can, but it would help me to have him at my place. You know, ma'am, he's become my right hand. I'm not sure I can do without him now that I have learned to depend on him. There's another reason I came...I understand his father signed a permission slip of sorts. I'll need to have that in my possession."

"This means that you believe he can make it, that he is absolutely capable of becoming a doctor!"

"That is certainly what I mean, and I'm glad you understand that."

"Then Booker T. can ask Father John for that little slip of paper but I always thought that once you were sixteen, you could even quit school and such without getting permission."

"I think that may be true, but I have to make absolutely sure that I won't get in trouble, but I also want to thank you, ma'am, for all you did for this boy. He won't truly understand any of it until he becomes a man himself, but I know. And I do thank you from the bottom of my heart."

"You're very welcome, Dr. James. But you see, I've grown to love Booker T. and that's why I want the very best for him."

CHAPTER FIFTY-SEVEN

"What a surprise. I'm so glad to see you," Father John said as Booker T. stepped into his office. "Are you well?"

"Hello, Father John. I'm well, but I thought I should ask you if it would be alright if I stayed with Doctor James for a few months? Aunt Mattie wanted to come and talk with you, but I said I should do it since it involves me."

"Of course you may, if that's what you need to do. He's invited you to stay at his house?"

"Yes, and he said that it would be better for him—saves him driving—but he also thinks it's safer for me too. What do you think?"

"Tell me more, Booker T."

"Well, he says he wants to teach me about so many things he thinks I should know. Like about the black lady, Henrietta Lacks."

"Who's Henrietta Lacks? I don't think I know her."

"Doctor James said she was a lady who died a couple of years ago, and they found that she had genes that everybody is wantin' to study. He said I need to know about her because her contribution to medicine will be more important than any old gold mine, and not just for our race, but for everyone."

"A contribution to medicine? I definitely would be interested in knowing more about a lady like that. Tell me whatever you know, Booker T."

"Well, Doctor James said she died in 1951, but her genes are reproducing at a staggering rate. The whole medical community is interested in them. He said it's very unusual and it's never happened before."

"I never heard about that, but it sounds like a wonderful break-through for medicine."

"It is. And he told me about another black man by the name of Dr. King who wants freedom for our people."

"Dr. Martin Luther King, Jr. Yes, I've read about him…his name has been in the newspapers."

"You know, Doctor James says that Dr. King may be the man who can help us break the barriers. Do you know that down south we have to sit in the back of buses, and give our seats to white people? Even old people have to stand, even if they're sick, makes no difference at all."

"I know that, Booker T. and I certainly hope that things will change so that everyone can live peacefully with respect, regardless of their color or heritage."

"But he made me promise not to get involved so I don't get distracted from my real goal of studying to become a doctor."

"He said that?"

"Yes, he said there are plenty others who can do the work, without me. I don't understand everything he's talking about most of the time."

"You just need a little time and you will. But what about school, if you move in with his family?"

"Doctor James says he lives on the border of my school district, so I could still go to my school. He also said I can go to church with him and his wife and kids, too. They have a real good preacher at their church."

"You've been there?"

"Yeah, I mean yes, sir. I go sometimes on Wednesday night and Sunday mornings too. Mrs. James takes me and the kids if the doctor can't take us."

"Well, I'm glad you're going. Church is very important and it was what your father asked you to do."

"Yes, sir. I like your church too. Miss Sadie says I have to pick only one church, is that true?"

"Well, that's usually the way it is, because each denomination has a different doctrine, you know—things they believe—and each denomination believes they have the whole truth."

"Oh, but here too? I mean, you don't want me to come here if I'm going somewhere else—or can I still come here even if I'm going to Doctor James' Pentecostal church or Aunt Mattie's Methodist church?" Booker T. wanted a straight and direct answer to his burning question.

"Booker T., this is entirely your decision and whatever you decide, it's okay with me. As you study each one, you'll understand better. I'd love to see you here whenever you choose to come."

"Thank you, Father John, I think I might like maybe to become a Catholic. You could teach me, couldn't you?" Booker's ears turned red as he said those words because he said it to the Baptist minister and also to the Methodist minister.

"Yes, I still have Sunday afternoons free."

"Could we start next Sunday like we used to when I was waiting for my papa to call? Do you remember how we played chess?"

"Do I ever! You took me to the cleaners quite a few times and you were only ten years old. I won't be playing with you any time soon," Father John said, laughing loud and hearty.

"Okay, then we'll stick to the catechism," Booker said. "But I know all the answers in that little green book already."

"How is that, you weren't required to memorize those lessons while in St. Gregory's school, were you?"

"No, but I heard them being recited and I just memorized them. Did I do something wrong?"

"No Booker, you didn't do anything wrong, nothing at all." But Father John couldn't help thinking what an amazing young fellow Booker T. was.

"Father John, the main reason I came today was because you have the paper my papa signed. You know, a kind of permission paper. Doctor James doesn't want to get in trouble."

"I'll get it from my files and take it to Doctor James. Just how legal that paper is, I don't know, Booker T. Your daddy wrote it when he was under a lot of pressure at the time."

"He never called me, so I'm thinking I was just in his way and he didn't want me anymore. He hated all of us kids, including my mother. That's why she left us."

"Don't even think that. No, he didn't call you but there was probably a good reason at the time. Anyway, I'll make sure Doctor James has the signed note in his possession while you're staying there. You know I'm very proud of all your hard work so keep doing your best and don't forget, I'll see you Sunday afternoons." Father John squeezed Booker's shoulders affectionately.

"Yes sir, thank you sir, I am trying. I promised Aunt Mattie I would."

CHAPTER FIFTY-EIGHT

The Balsam Christmas tree reached from the floor to the nine foot ceiling and Tierney placed it in the corner of the huge living room. Tierney, Dudley and Manny began unpacking the string lights and different sized ornaments brought up in dusty boxes from the storage area in the basement.

"They look as though they hadn't been opened in some time," Dudley said.

"Well, this year we'll have it all ready for Elise, when she comes home after her Christmas holiday with her grandparents," Tierney said to Manny and Dudley, who was now on the stepladder putting up the star. Tierney insisted that he put it up first—even before the lights that took the longest to attach. He wanted as many colored ones on each and every branch that would fit.

"Sakes alive, it's nice putting a tree up again. I think we missed a few years when Miss Suzy was so sick, and it smells real fresh and nice, too," Manny said as she handed out the colored glass balls one by one to Dudley and Mr. Tierney. They hung so many ornaments, there wasn't a single bare spot showing.

"And don't forget the silver tinsel," Tierney reminded Manny. "We have lots of it somewhere because Susan loved the way it glowed with the lights on."

Manny searched the bottom of that last box till she found some folded newspaper at the bottom dated January 1950. The tinsel was wrapped around it.

"See, they look just like icicles," Manny said as she unwound and held the long silver strands up for Dudley to see. They each took a bunch and hung them on almost all of the branches with the light bouncing and glittering. They stood back and admired their work.

"And now we're finished!" Dudley said as he picked up the cord and plugged it into the socket.

"It looks like a wonderland," Tierney said, eyes shining.

"It's beautiful…and I think Elise will like it too," Dudley said. At the moment, he could almost see the awe reflected in Elise's eyes.

"You and Elise seem to be friends now and I'm glad about that, son."

"I wanted to be her friend when we first met, sir. But I don't think I made a very good impression. I thought she hated me for being in that reform school."

"Well, I'm glad she got over that."

"She like you fine, Mr. Dudley. Her eyes make stars when she see you," Manny added as she gathered the empty boxes to be taken back to the basement.

Dudley's ears were starting to turn red when Manny said that with Mr. Tierney standing right there. He wanted to change the subject—fast.

"I hope we can go to Mr. Henry's party and spend Christmas at the farm," he said out loud, but his mind was still clinging to the words Manny had just spoken, savoring each like a delicious meal, full and satisfying.

"Yes," Tierney said, "I think it would be a nice change to visit the farm and meet everyone."

"My uncles and mother would probably like to meet you, although I think you already talked to my Uncle Tommy—he's the lawyer."

"Yes, yes my boy, I do know your Uncle Tommy, and of course your Aunt Mattie. She's a very nice lady."

"Yes, she is. I have to remember to tell her how nice you were to take me fishing."

"I declare, that Blanchard near had a fit when you two went tramping off on that fishing trip. I thought he would plain blow up." Manny rattled on and on as she remembered when Tierney snuck Dudley away for the day.

"And you fixed us fried chicken and that angel cake to take with us, just in case we didn't catch anything," Dudley said. "But, we caught some largemouth bass and ate them first—and were they ever good!"

"I didn't know he was that angry," Tierney said, paying sudden rapt attention to what Manny was saying.

"Well, he was. He say, 'not a word to no-body' so I didn't tell," Manny added. "But he was a-threatenin' you somethin' bad."

"Exactly what did he say, Manny?" Tierney asked. "Do you remember?"

"He say he found out some things and, 'you'll get yours too, cause you ain't no saint and you ain't got everything sewed up, yet.'"

"That does sound like a threat, sir...all because of me," Dudley said, a hint of worry in his voice.

"Now listen, because of him, you're alive, Dudley. Never forget that! And everybody has a little bad in them, but that doesn't cancel out the good that they do." Tierney suddenly became very serious and the lighthearted mood vanished.

"Now that we're finished with the tree, I'll put the gifts under it," he added.

"You mean you aren't waiting for Santa Claus?" Dudley asked.

"My goodness, Mr. Dudley, you still believe in that roly-poly man in the red suit?" Manny was laughing as she stared at Dudley to see if he was serious. Dudley just shrugged his shoulders, raised his eyebrows and grinned a silly grin back at her.

Just as the weather ruined the Thanksgiving Day trip to the farm, the same unusual weather pattern—high winds and drifting snow—made the roads treacherous for the Christmas party. Dudley had hoped they could go until the last minute, but Tierney didn't want to get stuck somewhere, especially after Dudley's bout with appendicitis. They would have a long drive compared to Mattie's eight miles. However, if it had been better weather, Tierney had been looking forward to that day at the farm. Even Elise wanted to go, but she had to be with Grandmother and Grandfather Steavens.

Good wishes and goodbyes for Henry brought only his close friends and neighbors from the nearby farms, and after that send-off, Henry was ready to leave for the seminary. Now that the time was finally here, Catherine was dreading his departure, even though she had said he could go during her better moments. When she said it, she had meant every word. But that was before she knew that she was pregnant. To tell Henry and shatter his happiness would be cruel, and she hated to renege on her word. She would have to swallow her constant dread and not think of it, at least, not during the day.

CHAPTER FIFTY-NINE

Monday after Christmas, the nasty weather still kept everyone at home. Dudley and Mr. Tierney were discussing some of the juvenile cases that Dudley was particularly interested in when suddenly, Dudley's heart flew into his throat. Elise entered the library and it was as though someone turned on a bright light. As she removed her winter coat and hat, Dudley couldn't help but notice how pretty she looked in her plaid skirt and dark blue sweater. She had on matching knee socks and those forever black and white saddle shoes that most of the girls wore. Her silken blond hair was falling softly to her shoulders accentuating her blue eyes, and cute pouty lips.

"Hi, Elise," Dudley said shyly as she waltzed into the room.

"Hi Dudley. Hi Daddy, I'll take my stuff upstairs and then come down."

"Okay dear, we'll be waiting for you," Mr. Tierney said as she kissed him lightly. As her lips touched her daddy's cheek, Elise's eyes met Dudley's for only an instant, leaving him with a wondrous feeling pulsing through him, as though heaven dropped down. It happened before, when her sweet lips kissed him and her essence lingered. Since then, she was the one he thought of during the day and before sleep every night. *The next few days will be good, because Elise was home.*

* * *

Booker T. was bustling around, gathering all the containers and boxes he could find to pack the things he would need while living at Doctor James' home. Angela too, was just as busy packing her things to take to the farm where she would be staying with Catherine and her grandchildren while Henry was studying in Chicago.

This holiday break turned out to be a treasured time for Booker T. since he needed the long relaxing days with Miss Sadie, Miss Angela, and Aunt Mattie, talking about his concerns and his future. He could always count on all of their skillful, bright encouragement, which built him up and made him feel as though everything would work out for him.

It was three o'clock in the afternoon when the ladies and Booker T. were sitting at the kitchen table having hot tea and leftover slices of the cherry and apple pie. Their mood was light and happy because they were excited that Dudley would be coming home in just a few days to attend high school.

"I wish Dudley could taste this pie, Miss Sadie. He would absolutely love it," Booker T. drawled as he placed piece after piece into his waiting mouth.

"He does love cherry pie," Sadie said, smiling as she thought about all the pies Dudley had eaten in the past. "I'd say that it ranks right after oatmeal-raisin cookies."

"Well, I'm sure you'll find some time to bake more cherry pies when he comes home," Angela said, smiling as she and Mattie slowly sipped their tea.

"And I happen to know there are about eleven more quarts of those cherries down in the basement," Mattie added.

"I'll not only bake a cherry pie, but I'll make those oatmeal-raisin cookies too," Sadie said. As she stood to rinse her plate in the sink she glanced out the back window just in time to see a beat-up old gray car drive around the back of the house. The front fender was bashed in and the motor was running loud. *Maybe without a muffler,* she thought. Two high school age boys got out and ran to the back door while another fellow kept the motor running. They all heard the loud, crisp knock.

"I'll get it," Sadie said. "A couple of boys are coming to the back door."

Booker's face turned ghostly pale when he heard Sadie. *Maybe they're looking for me*, he thought.

"Just one minute, Sadie." And then Mathilda looked directly at Booker. "Please take your pie into the other room until they leave."

Mathilda was always careful when young white boys were around. She had warned Booker T. to stay clear at other times so he didn't have to be told twice. He picked up his cup and pie plate and left. After he was out of sight, Mathilda answered the back door with Sadie and Angela standing behind her, listening. Booker had his ear pressed close to the kitchen door so he could hear everything that was said.

"Yes, may I help you?" Mathilda asked. As she opened the door, a blast of frigid air hit her face like a slap. She touched and rubbed the side of her cheek and hair, as though trying to push the frosty draft aside.

"We're Dudley's friends from school. Is he home?" one of the boys asked as the wind whipped their hair and turned their bare ears bright red. To Mathilda, they looked almost frozen as they stood on the top step.

"You're friends from Dudley's school?" she asked again.

"Yeah, school starts back in a few of days and we just wanted to check out our class schedules to see if he'll be in any of our classes this semester. We're also going for a drive in Dan's car and wondered if he would wanna come. We're just gonna knock around a bit, ma'am."

"I see. But Dudley's not here right now and I'm not sure when he'll be back."

"Is he still over at the senator's house? We thought he was comin' back here." The boy quickly put his hand over his mouth when he realized he said something he wasn't supposed to. "I mean, we all hoped he'd come back this semester...we miss 'em." Both, Sadie and Angela put their hands over their own mouths and looked at each other with wide questioning eyes.

"Oh, my, now how would you know that?" Mathilda asked, alarmed but still trying to keep a calm outward appearance.

"Ah, never mind, we'll see him at school next week," the other boy said. "I told ya we shouldn't have stopped," the one boy said, turning to punch the other's arm as they jumped down the stairs.

"What are your names?" Mathilda shouted as they ran toward the car, "so when he comes home, I can tell him you were here looking for him?"

"It's okay, we just thought he'd be here, but we'll see him at school," one of the boys shouted back. Then the two boys fell into the back seat while the driver gunned the motor and spun out of the drive. Old snow and dirt flew up, but Sadie still saw the license plate number and wrote it down.

"I don't know what to think," Mathilda said, the alarm audible in her voice. "Do you think I should call Mr. Tierney?" She was already searching for her small address book, answering her own question.

"Ma'am, I think you should call Mr. Tommy too. It's funny with those guys just dropping in, don't you think?" Booker T. said, with a worried look on his face as he sat down at the table again.

"I think the boy is right, call them both," Angela advised.

"Did you recognize them, Booker, I mean their voices?" Mattie asked

"No, and I don't think they're from around here."

"Well, I'll try calling, but if his phone is still dead, I'm driving out to Tierney's house." The distinct taste of fear flooded her mouth, replacing the sweet cherry pie she had almost finished eating.

"You weren't able to call Dudley the last two days?" Angela asked.

"No, and I don't think I should wait." She ran upstairs, grabbed her valise, threw a few things in it that she would need and then hurried back down.

"Goodbye, Sadie, Booker, and dear sister, Angela" Mathilda said as she hugged each one. "Sadie please call Thomas and tell him what happened here and also please keep trying to call Mr. Tierney and tell him I'll be there as fast as I can. Tell him some boys are looking for Dudley, and they knew he's been at his house and that he'll be going to school here the next semester. Oh, just tell him they knew everything about him!"

After Mathilda left, Angela excused herself and went back to packing her things since nothing more could be done. All she could do is pray her sister would be careful. Sadie immediately called Thomas Bealer and explained everything those boys had said and done, and then she tried the Senator's number again but couldn't get through. Looking closely at Booker, she recognized that certain look in his eye.

"I don't want you disappearing and going off to that church. Things don't feel good here, you hear me, Booker? Stay right here at home and be safe."

"Yesum," Booker T. said, feeling disappointed and surprised that she could read his mind so easily.

"And cut out that word, you hear me, or I'll have to tell Mrs. Mathilda."

"Sorry, I hear you, ma'am. I guess I'll pack my stuff too."

"And what are you doing over in that Catholic Church anyway when you're a good Baptist boy? Or are you a Methodist? I declare, you go to more churches then I can count."

"Yes, ma'am. But why do I have to choose only one?"

"You just do. That's the way it is."

"Yes, ma'am," he said aloud, but thought to himself, *Aunt Mattie never told me I couldn't go to all of them, and Father John didn't say that either.*

CHAPTER SIXTY

Thomas Bealer tried to reach Senator Tierney by telephone several times after Sadie's call. He just couldn't understand how someone as important as a senator could have his phone out-of-order for so many days. Something didn't sound right about those boys and he also knew that Mattie must have had the same feeling. A woman's sixth sense shouldn't be ignored!

It took only a minute for Thomas to decide to drive immediately to the Senator's house. As he sped down the hi-way, he thought, *now the immediate challenge* was, *not getting stopped by some eager young cop!* And then, the old guilt started, *I don't know why I didn't take Dudley to live with me in Chicago in the first place. None of this would've happened if I hadn't been so selfish. None of it!* They were the same thoughts he punished himself with when Dudley had his appendicitis attack.

* * *

On arriving at the Senator Tierney's house, Thomas pulled through the open double iron gates, unto the curved drive. The lights on each pillar were turned on. He parked right behind Mattie's green sedan and saw that she was already at the top of the front steps, her hand reaching for the brass knocker.

Thomas was directly behind her when Dudley opened the door. Tierney was there too, standing behind Dudley with his hands on his shoulders. They both laughed when they saw the two had driven in separate cars.

"What a wonderful surprise! Hello, Aunt Mattie. Hi, Uncle Tommy," Dudley shouted. Mathilda, now completely out of breath, acknowledged Thomas, beside her, and then Dudley and Tierney with a nod and a slight smile.

"You drove in separate cars!" Tierney teased.

"Come on in," Dudley said. As he swung the door wide open, a cold blast of winter whipped into the front hall.

"We saw you coming up the drive. You were sure driving fast, Aunt Mattie. I'm glad you decided to use the brakes and stop," he teased, joining in on Tierney's fun.

Mathilda didn't have a chance to answer, for at that very moment, a pounding at the back door echoed through the long hallway from the back to the front of the house. Manny was gone so Tierney waved at his guests and disappeared to the rear.

"Be right back," he said, "I have to answer the back door."

Then they heard yelling. It was so loud that Mathilda, Dudley and Thomas could hear every word.

"Where's that Dudley Best? We came to see the squealer," the voice echoed through the hall.

"Hey, you can't just push your way in here. I won't allow it," Tierney said, but fell against the wall when he was shoved to the side.

"We want to see Dudley now, old man," one boy said and they both began to walk through the hall toward the front foyer where Dudley, Mathilda and Thomas still stood at the front door. The voice registered in Dudley's head as Dukie's, one of his old gang buddies. Then the other boy yelled, "we'll get 'em no matter how long it takes, ya hear!"

Aunt Mattie's voice was low and stern and Dudley knew she would not take no for an answer.

"Come with me this very instant," she said as she grabbed Dudley's wrist and pulled him out the still open door with Uncle Tommy following them. A shot went off and the bullet buried itself in the door Thomas had just slammed shut. He ran down the same steps they had just come up, trying to keep up with Mattie and Dudley. Aunt Mattie opened the back door and shoved the stunned boy into the back seat.

"Get down on the floor," she shouted. Dudley couldn't grasp with his mind what was happening. Everything was so fast, but he obeyed. They could all hear Tierney yelling clearly through the door.

"You're gonna kill my boy, you idiots!"

The gun went off again and Tierney yelled, "Oh my God—Elise—don't come down!"

"Coming or not?" Mathilda screamed at Thomas as she ran around to the driver's side. He jumped into the front seat as she took off and could hardly close the door before they were speeding out the drive, heading to the main road.

"Lock your doors," she yelled again without looking back.

"Why are they shooting at us?" Dudley asked, his voice quivering with fear and cold as he reached up and pushed the lock down on both back doors. He was too scared to sit up on the seat.

"My dear lord, what should we do?" Mathilda asked. "Where can we go?" She was speeding, foot pressed down hard on the gas pedal while her head was reeling with fright. The words she had heard were echoing in her head, but she could hardly believe what she heard.

"I don't know, give me a minute to think," Thomas said.

CHAPTER SIXTY-ONE

"Who are they?" Dudley shouted toward Aunt Mattie and Uncle Tommy.

"Some boys from your school. They said they were in several of your classes and wanted to talk to you about your schedule." Uncle Tommy turned toward the back so Dudley could hear. "That's what Sadie said when she called me."

"But I don't have any friends at school...except for the ones that were in my gang in Blenning and it almost sounded like Dukie." Dudley was crouched on the floor, shivering while he talked through chattering teeth.

"They came to our house," Aunt Mattie said. "They were questioning me about your whereabouts. Something seemed really strange—thank God I got here in time."

"After you pulled up, Auntie, we heard what sounded like an old jalopy go around the back. I think Mr. Tierney forgot to close the gate across the drive. It sure made a lot of noise."

"I know, they peeled out of our drive too, but Sadie got their license plate number. We can report it, but who knows, they could have borrowed the car."

"Or stole it," Dudley piped in.

"Listen," Uncle Tommy said, "I don't know of any place around here that's safe for you, Dudley, unless we drive clear to Chicago.

I'm pretty sure we could stay with some friends until we figure this out. Are you warm enough back there?"

"I'm pretty cold."

"I think there's a blanket on the floor on the other side. Grab it and sit up on the seat now," Aunt Mattie said. "I just hope this heater keeps working since I've been having a few issues with it lately."

As they left the residential area and turned onto the main highway, two police cars and an ambulance with flashing lights and sirens were traveling fast in the direction they just departed.

"Do you think Mr. Tierney is okay?" Dudley asked, almost crying the question. "Maybe they killed him and Elise…how will we know if they're okay?"

"Well, Dudley, I'm hoping they're okay but I don't think we can take any more chances. You'll just have to hide again for a while." And then turning her head toward Thomas, Mathilda said, "I'm so glad you got here. How did you know to come?"

"Sadie told me where you were going. I thought I could catch up to you, but you were going too fast. Listen, Dudley, I'll try to find out how Tierney and Elise are as soon as I can…so try not to worry."

"You know, Uncle Tommy, Mr. Blanchard, the gardener, was arrested. He knew everything I did and reported it to somebody. Mr. Tierney found out about it and the police took him away."

* * *

After driving for more than an hour, Mathilda was so exhausted and stressed from the ordeal that her shoulders and neck were completely immobile, stiff as a board. Thomas took the wheel for the last part of the trip since he knew the way to the address he had in mind.

"You know," Mathilda said, rubbing her neck and turning it from side to side to loosen it, "we could bump into Henry in Chicago, or if I knew what seminary he was going to, we could visit, that is, if we are here any length of time."

"First of all, Chicago is pretty big. There's not much chance of just bumping into someone. And secondly, I don't think you should have any communication with anyone from back home for a while."

"Yes, I do believe you're right," Mathilda answered thoughtfully.

During the whole trip Dudley slept, wrapped in the wool blanket. He dreamt about Oren Blanchard liking him so much that he made cream puffs for him. Blanchard said they were better than any Manny could ever make, so he forced Dudley to eat every last one while he watched, tapping his foot loudly under the table. And then Elise kissed his sweet lips over and over again.

* * *

"Whose house is this?" Mathilda asked when Thomas stopped in front of an elegant brick home in Beverly Hills, a suburb on the south side of Chicago.

"This is Colette's house. She and her husband live here. Remember, you met her at Mary Beth's wedding?"

"Oh yes, she had to leave early that afternoon. Seemed very nice...but very businesslike."

It was already midnight when they all got out of the car. As they did, Mathilda used her fingers to straighten her hair, and then her coat, getting the wrinkles out after sitting on it for so long. Dudley stretched too, but left the wool blanket on the back seat of the car. All three hurried toward the front door where the porch light was still on. Suddenly, a car pulled up behind Mathilda's and a girl jumped out, yelling and waving bye to the people who dropped her off. Mathilda stopped short of ringing the doorbell as the girl ran up the walk.

"Hello, what a dandy time to be visiting?" the young girl said sarcastically while laughing. "We always love to get visitors at midnight."

"I'm sorry, we don't usually visit this late, but seem to be having a little emergency. This is where Colette Larson lives, isn't it?"

Thomas asked. He knew it was but was trying to let the young lady know he wasn't a client, but a friend.

"Who wants to know," she asked even more rudely.

"I'm Attorney Thomas Bealer, a friend of Colette and Alexander…and this is Mattie Millering and Dudley Best."

"Oh, sorry, come on in, Mr. Bealer. I'll wake my sister. My name is Binkie," she said as she slid her key into the lock and opened the door.

As they stepped through the threshold, Dudley, Mathilda and Thomas were glad to feel the warmth of the entry hall.

"I'll run up and get her. Please make yourselves comfortable in here," she said as she pushed the switch that lit all the lamps in the living room.

A few minutes later, Colette and her husband came down and greeted them.

"What a nice surprise to see you, Thomas. You remember my husband, Alexander?"

"Of course, hello Mr. Larson," Thomas said as he shook his hand.

"Hello, Thomas, just call me, Alex." Alex was still pushing his shirt into his trousers.

After all the introductions, Colette led everyone into the kitchen to make some coffee. They sat around the table while Thomas explained what had happened and why they were there.

"So do you think you could put three vagabonds up for the night until we can figure what to do," Thomas asked, laughing as though it were a joke.

"I don't think it's a bit funny," Mathilda said. "I was scared to death."

"Yeah, Uncle Tommy, it's not one bit funny. Aunt Mattie grabbed me, shoved me in the car, and drove all the way here without a stop. For a few minutes there, I felt as though I was being taken hostage."

"Well, don't complain, Dudley. At least you got some sleep and don't forget, you're alive!"

"Hey, we have plenty of room," Alex said. "And you're more than welcome. I've read all about your case in the newspapers. Funny you should show up."

"Yeah, funny," Binkie said. She was leaning against the doorway, watching and taking in the situation. "How old are you, Dudley," she asked.

"I'm almost sixteen, ma'am," he replied at which everyone laughed.

"This is my sister, Cynthia," Colette said. "She's staying with us until graduation, We call her Binkie…don't ask me why, we just always have."

Dudley felt he had to say something, so he said, "It's a nice name, ma'am," at which everyone laughed again.

"Not to change the subject, Thomas, but just how are you doing now, I mean, after those two heart attacks you had before you moved?" Colette was anxious to know and stared at Thomas until she got an answer.

"Oh, it wasn't anything at all," he said even as red crept up his neck and filled his cheeks.

Mathilda was surprised and startled, but didn't say anything aloud about the remark.

"See you guys in the morning," Binkie called out as she winked at Dudley and left the room.

The morning couldn't come quick enough as far as Mathilda was concerned. She had a hard time sleeping. Her thoughts raced because of Colette's unintentional words about Thomas' heart trouble.

CHAPTER SIXTY-TWO

Colette and her husband, Alex, were deeply interested in Dudley's dilemma. As friends, they wanted to help in any way they could. Alex presented an idea to Thomas and Mathilda the next morning at breakfast.

"Last night, I thought a lot about Dudley and how you could hide the boy by changing his name, and sending him to a public high school here in Chicago. Those thugs who are after him would probably think he would go to a good private school, so the public school Binkie goes to would be ideal."

"Where does Binkie go?" Mathilda asked.

"Calumet High, it's on May Street and not far from here. Binkie could coach him until he got the hang of the new school."

"We could get him a new name," Mathilda said. "Maybe just a different last name would do, don't you think?"

"Johnny—Father John should be able to get new records with a date of birth and such with a new last name," Thomas said.

"Then we probably should wait until you send them before we try to register him at the school."

"Yes, I can take care of that when I go back and also find out about Tierney and Elise. I'll let you know somehow. At this point, I don't know exactly how."

"You know, you can send the papers to our office downtown. You've been doing a lot of that anyway so it wouldn't look unusual if they're watching the mail," Alex offered.

"Or better yet, don't put a return address on the letters and drop them at a post office outside of Mayette," Colette added.

"Yes...that might work," Thomas said, "but I'll have to take your car, Mattie, because mine is still parked at Barry's house."

"Oh, you can take my other car," Colette suggested. "I hardly ever use it since I got my new one and I was thinking of selling it. But you're welcome to borrow it for as long as you need it."

"That's a great idea. Thanks Colette, and you too Alex."

"Hey, Dudley, were you able to get some rest last night?" Uncle Tommy asked as the boy came into the kitchen where the discussion about him was taking place.

"Yes, I had a little trouble falling asleep but once I did, I slept really good," Dudley said as he took a seat at the table with the others.

"I'm glad you got some rest after all the trouble yesterday. I'm ready to head back to Tierney's place and then home. Mr. Larson will fill you in on a plan he has for a new school, so try to fit in and don't make any waves, okay?"

"I won't, Uncle. But...will you let us know if Mr. Tierney and Elise are okay? I'm kind of worried about them."

"I'll let you know as soon as I find out," Uncle Tommy answered. He was already at the door, ready to leave.

"Could you please get your coat, Mattie, and walk out to the car with me?" Thomas asked.

Mathilda was surprised, but got her coat from the front hall closet, put it on and followed him out.

Alex pulled Colette's car out of the garage and handed Thomas the keys while Mathilda stood next to him on the sidewalk.

"Goodbye, Tom, I'll do my best for the boy," Alex said, as he shook his hand, then turned and left them alone.

"Goodbye, Alex, thanks for everything."

"Get in, Mattie, I want to tell you something before I leave," Thomas said as he opened the passenger door for her.

Mathilda got in pulling her coat tight around her. It was cold—zero degree weather with a Chicago wind that reached into her bones. Thomas turned the heater on to it's highest setting.

"Mattie?" he said, taking her hands, cupping them with his own and blowing on them with his warm breath.

Her questioning eyes met his.

"I've never had a chance to tell you why I said those things to Johnny that morning you overheard us, and it's bothered me ever since. I mean, I've had a good many chances, but it didn't seem like the appropriate time."

"I didn't expect an explanation, Tommy. It was how you felt at the time and I respect that."

"But I want you to know that I made a mistake in not believing in you enough to tell you about my heart. I didn't want your sympathy and I wanted to spare you any indecision about marrying me, but now I realize that when you love someone, you have to take the good with the bad. I also know that the love we share is too deep to let something like that come between us. Can you accept my apology?"

Mathilda could see how sincere Tommy was and answered, "I do accept your apology, and I do understand."

"And will you let me kiss you…goodbye? I've wanted to for a long time and I'm so very sorry I acted stupid all these months by actually pushing you away."

Tommy now pulled her two hands close to him, then quickly releasing them, wrapped his arms around her and whispered into her ear, "I do love you, more than you could ever know." His lips now brushed against her lips and wisps of their warm breath washed about them.

Mathilda felt wondrously warm and didn't think she could ever be cold again, not with Tommy's love finally surrounding her.

"I think I'll just drive back here in a couple of days and bring news about everything that's happened. I'll also bring the papers for Dudley with me rather than mailing them...I think it would be better."

"That sounds good, but please be careful."

"Mattie...maybe Dudley could live here with Colette and Alex, then you could just come home after you get him situated and...we could get..."

"Oh, I'm sure they would offer, but that's a lot of responsibility to saddle them with and they already have Binkie. I'll just stay for now and get Dudley settled in...so he can be a regular teenager again."

"Listen, I think if you rented a place, there wouldn't be any legal papers filed for buying a house under your name."

"Okay, renting will work for now. Goodbye, Tommy, please check on Booker T. He's supposed to move in with Dr. James in a couple of days. Tell him I'll call him at the doctor's home some time in the late evening and please tell Sadie and my sister everything that happened."

"Okay, I will...and I'll fill Louise in on where Dudley is so she won't worry. Don't you worry either!"

"And please make sure Booker T. doesn't need anything and tell him to be patient until we can be together."

"Okay, I will...Mattie, quit...I'll take care of everything!"

"One last thing, if you're able, try to get Dudley's clothes from Tierney's house and bring them and my new white dishes the next time you come. And tell Sadie to pick up some others, maybe some inexpensive ones for every day."

After another lingering kiss, Mathilda jumped out of the car with a new spring in her step. She pulled her wrap tightly around her, ran to the front door and waved goodbye again throwing another kiss as he drove away.

True to his word, the following week Thomas brought the new birth certificate and school transcripts with a new surname for Dudley. He would now be called Dudley Bates at his new school. Thomas also surprised Mathilda with an expensive strand of cultured pearls renewing his deep love for her. During the long weeks and months that followed, whenever she would start to miss him, because his practice kept him away, she would hold them in her hands, caressing their round softness, against her face, remembering that each pearl was formed not in a day, but matured over the span of years, just as their own love continued to mature. His letters, arriving two and three times a week, always smelled of Tommy's sweet aftershave with promises of a new future that would unfold as soon as Dudley's trouble had finished. And it was then that she wanted to be with him—more than anything else. Sometimes, a feeling of urgency washed over her—like they must seize this love before it would be too late and something would cause it to fly away, again. And sometimes she wore those beads, that he so lovingly placed around her neck, to bed, so she could close her eyes and feel his closeness.

The house was for sale for the last eight months. Alex passed it as he drove to the train station every morning and made a mental note to tell Mattie about it.

CHAPTER SIXTY-THREE

Mathilda didn't know too much about the lady who befriended her at the Methodist Church, but she did know that her name was Harriet Barns and that she was gracious and outgoing. Mathilda liked her right from the start, mainly because she reminded Mathilda of her dear friend, Maxine, who was very honest and forthright with her opinions.

Harriet and Mathilda started going to lunch after church each week, sometimes at their homes, and sometimes they went out to a nice restaurant. Neither of the ladies knew it, but they both had a hidden past, a past that they were reluctant to talk to anyone about. One Sunday Harriet confessed to that fact.

"I'm so glad I've met you, Mattie. I've been going to that church for almost a year but I haven't made any friends. I guess I'm just not into joining any of the ladies groups."

"Well, I'm not into the ladies guilds and such either. They always want to know way too much. The very first thing they ask is where your from and if you're married, and do you work outside the home? That's way too many questions for me. I guess I'm a kind of a private person."

"I am too," Harriet said, "but I've been needing a friend like you, a kind of older sister to talk and do things with."

"I know exactly what you mean." Mathilda knew all too well what could happen if anyone tracked Dudley here. Harriet never asked any personal questions, and Mathilda didn't pry into Harriet's business either. They complimented one another perfectly.

Harriet began showing Mathilda everything about Chicago: movies, live theatrical performances, and fancy places to eat. Mathilda mostly went to pass the time and to be with a friend since Dudley was settled in and busy with school and social activities and even attending church with Binkie and her family.

After a while, Harriet began taking her to pawn and antique shops. It was the one thing she liked to do best, or it seemed so. Harriet's main interest was buying silver pieces. She wanted tea and coffee sets, trays, candy dishes, anything made from good quality silver and with the right stamps on the bottom of the pieces. Those silver items lined all the shelves she had made for that purpose and still she bought more, storing them in boxes piled in the corners of her basement. At different times, she sold all the pieces at once. Mathilda assumed it was a kind of hobby or lucrative business, buying and selling, probably for a very good profit, because Harriet always had money. Mathilda never asked. Everything she knew about Harriet she learned by observation because it was none of her business.

Harriet was instrumental in taking Mathilda to the shop that destroyed any good thoughts she ever had about her late husband, Henry. And she did have many good thoughts of him, in spite of his indiscretion. After all, she couldn't discard all the happy and tranquil times with him on the farm!

It was a Saturday afternoon that Harriet invited Mathilda to lunch, after which they would go see a Mr. Kempler, the owner of a pawn shop, who dealt in quality silver pieces.

On this particular day, while they enjoyed lunch, they talked about a new potato soup recipe and then about some of the books that Harriet loaned Mathilda from her own library. Steinbeck seemed to be Harriet's favorite author and became Mathilda's favorite too—

after all, he was born at the turn of the century, just as she was. Mathilda had just finished *The Pearl* when Harriet asked her to read *The Moon is Down,* and brought it with her to lunch that day but left it in the back seat of the car. Steinbeck wrote the book in nineteen hundred and forty-two—about the German occupation in a Scandinavian country though he didn't mention the identity of the country. Harriet was interested in any books written about the second world war and before. At the time, Mathilda didn't understand why Harriet was so interested in that time period, but later everything became clear.

The book they discussed during lunch *that* day was *East of Eden.* Harriet thought the book was worth reading again and asked Mathilda for her opinion and whether she would enjoy reading it twice.

Before meeting Harriet, Mathilda hadn't read many current books but now, books opened up a whole new world with thoughts about how other people lived and fared in different parts of the world. She had been an avid reader while still in grammar school. Her teacher had rows of books students could borrow, but when she had to quit school—all reading stopped. First, her mother's death and then her early marriage to a farmer at age sixteen crowded out that type of reading. Even the mercantile in Mayetteville didn't carry any books for the pure pleasure of reading. And her elocution teacher, the dear lady that tried to help Mathilda with voice and vocabulary, didn't mention that reading was the best way to learn to speak properly.

The next time Mathilda was shopping downtown, she bought a self help book that she stumbled upon in the book department at Marshall Fields. She would never tell anyone that she was reading *Wake Up and Live, by Dorothea Brande.* She didn't even tell Harriet. That book gave her much information about being a happy, fulfilled women, but as far as *East of Eden*, Mathilda thought reading it again would be a waste of her time and she explained to

Harriet that if you read about Cain and Abel in Genesis, you have a good grasp of the story and didn't need to read it again. Harriet said she wasn't the least interested in Cain and Abel but they had a good debate during lunch that afternoon, going over the many conflicts in the Hamilton family.

Afterwords, they headed for the pawn shop Harriet loved. She parked her car three blocks away in a parking lot because the parking spaces on the street were full. A couple of blocks away from the shop was a little cafe, and directly across the street from the shop was a large theatre-like building, with a marquee announcing; "Healing Service, Today at 4pm," with huge, yellow, blinking words. Two men walked back and forth carrying signs that read, "*A work of the devil!*"

It was Mathilda's first trip to the shop. As they stepped up onto the stoop, she was surprised that a little bell had to be rung before they were allowed to enter. There were no windows and the black door had a sign that read, *Pawn and Jewelry.* Above the sign were three golden balls—*an emblem for pawnbrokers?* Mathilda thought that's what it meant, but didn't ask. A man opened the door; he was short and a little stooped, with thin gray hair and thick spectacles on his crooked nose.

"My, my, Mrs. Barns, how are you, already?" the man said, shaking her hand and welcoming her into his shop.

"Mattie, I would like you to meet, Mr. Benjamin Kempler. Mr. Kempler, this is my friend, Mattie Millering. We're going to snoop around your shop today. Is that okay?"

"Of course it is, ladies. My shop is your shop, snoop away and have fun," he said as he locked the door behind them. "I have some work in my books, but let me know if I can help, or if someone wants to come in and I don't hear. My hearing is getting a little *vey iz mir*…woe is me. I don't hear too good and it's making me a little *meshuga*—it's making me crazy!" he said again, trying to explain further.

"You're far from crazy, Mr. Kempler, I can attest to that," Harriet shouted.

"Thank you," Mathilda added, speaking more loudly, "We'll let you know if someone comes. Meanwhile, I'd just love to browse a little." The whole shop reeked of cigar smoke, the tobacco fumes now stinging her eyes.

"Browse a little, browse a lot," Mr. Kempler offered. "Take your time, ladies. Take the rest of the day!"

After walking around the isles and while Harriet went downstairs to see whether any new silver pieces had arrived, Mathilda lingered over many of the glass cases. Exquisite jewelry, diamond rings and necklaces were in several along the wall, but the case right in front of the door drew her attention; Atop the highest glass shelf sat a decorative box that looked exactly like the one she had buried in her basement. The box was cradled on some black velvet, half-hidden as the end of the cloth flipped up against it. Many other valuable items such as gold watches and different kinds of faceted jeweled brooches were crowded on the other two shelves.

Seeing only the one side, Mathilda's heart began beating hard as a scene from her past played out in her mind. Suddenly, she could see herself sitting at the kitchen table, mending, while Henry labored over a small, wooden flower, carving the petals just right using his sharp tools with precision. She remembered how comfortable it was and how she believed those evenings together would continue forever. She and Henry were mostly silent; there was no need for words.

Why now? she silently questioned. *Why, when I buried those unanswered questions so long ago?* Her complete interest in the boys, Dudley and Booker T., had consumed her thoughts recently, but now she would have to face the same disturbing questions all over again. She knew she still had to come to terms with the letters Henry wrote, the ones in which he vowed he loved only her, and was sorry he had committed the little misdeed for a good reason!

Mathilda walked back to where Mr. Kempler sat—working on his books. He was solely intent on pulling the handle of that old Victor Adding Machine and jotting numbers into a book, never looking right or left, almost as though he was a part of the machine, producing totals that meant profit or loss. She stood watching, hesitant to interrupt him as he pushed away a strand of gray hair that fell over his eyes while he sucked on his stubby cigar, slowly turning the wet thing over and over in his mouth as he worked. He and that machine *were* one!

"May I disturb you for a moment?" she finally asked, raising her voice so he would be sure to hear.

Being so close to the smoke, Mathilda found her throat burning. It reminded her of Henry's smelly old pipe and the smelly old green chair he loved. That upholstered armchair held a brownish, smoky odor that wouldn't let go even after repeated cleanings. *Why do men smoke?* she asked herself.

"Of course, it's no problem at all. I can do numbers any ole time, but to help a lady, that is my delight," the busy man said as he placed his cigar down on the ashtray after taking one last puff.

Mathilda led him to the glass counter at the front of the store. "May I see that little box…that one," she said as she pointed into the case.

"Of course." He used a small key he had on a chain along with other keys hanging from his pants pocket and then carefully set the box on top of the glass case.

CHAPTER SIXTY-FOUR

When Mathilda looked at the box closely, she sucked in her breath and almost said aloud, *where did you get this box?* But she caught herself, and only rubbed her index finger haltingly over the tiny rose petals and scrolling leaves. They were still polished with a strikingly soft patina, like lustrous taffeta. She recognized the lacy detail that the rich, dark wood brought out and could almost see Henry rubbing it over and over, until he was completely satisfied with the smoothness.

"Do you like the box, Missus?" the man asked, breaking into her thoughts.

"Yes, is it for sale?"

"Not yet, but if the little woman doesn't come back, I'll have to sell it."

"How much will you be asking for it?"

"Twenty-five dollars—it's a work of art."

"May I ask who brought it in?"

"A very soft-spoken woman. I could hardly hear her—she spoke so softly. She said she would come back sometime in the late afternoon."

"Will she come today since it's Saturday afternoon?"

"I doubt if she'll be here today. Maybe some afternoon next week."

Mathilda turned the box over and saw the initials, H.M. on the bottom. She was stunned for a moment, seeing and understanding that her Henry had carved them lovingly...for some other woman!

"Just look at the inside." Kempler urged.

He turned it back over and ran his jacket sleeve over the scrolls of the little petals she had touched with her fingers, then quickly snapped back the tiny gold hinges, allowing the top to open.

"Oh my," Mathilda cried as she saw the perfectly carved horse on the inside lid.

"Beauti-ful, eh?"

"Oh yes, I see." She pulled a little tab attached to the red velvet bottom panel, bringing it up. The tab was the same as in her own box, hard to see because it blended in perfectly with the velvet folds.

"Ah, I didn't know it came up...you got good eyes, Missus. Look, there's a paper or something!"

"Yes, I see it," Mathilda said as she pulled up the plain white envelope and held it in her hand. On the front of the sealed envelope, written in Henry's script, was the name Elaine. Kempler gently removed it from Mathilda's hands and placed it and the panel back into the box.

"I'm sure it's private and the little woman will be surprised to see it," he said as he placed the box back into the glass case, locking it. He started to walk back to where he had been working when Mathilda asked him another question.

"Have you ever seen a similar box before?" She didn't know why she asked. *What would it matter anyway,* she thought?

"Maybe once before. Not exactly, but like it. Only not here in my shop," he quickly added.

"Do you remember where?"

"No, I buy from so many places, I can't remember them all. But it was here in Chicago, I know that much."

Harriet had come upstairs and walked over to the counter and saw the pallid look on her friend's face. "Are you okay? You're looking a little peaked."

"I—could we please go?"

"Oh my goodness, of course! We'll leave immediately." Then turning to the shopkeeper, she said, "I'll have to come back for the pieces you've set aside for me at a later time. They're absolutely perfect for my collection."

"I hope your friend will be alright, Mrs. Barns. Here, let me get a chair for her to sit."

"Oh no, thank you, Mr. Kempler. I just have to get some air," Mathilda said, patting her hair here and there—a nervous gesture. "Thank you for letting me look."

"Yes, alright and don't worry, Mrs. Barns, I'll save the pieces for you. And I think I'll need you for a few hours next week. I'll give you a call. Goodbye, ladies." He followed them to the door and after they walked out, they heard the dead bolt engage.

* * *

"You look as though you need to sit down and catch your breath before we walk over to get the car," Harriet said, concerned for her friend.

"Thank you, Harriet, I feel so much better now in the cool fresh air."

"Look, Kempler says they're always having some kind of public meetings across the street…let's go and take a seat until you feel up to walking those long blocks to the car."

"Yes, I think you're right. I could sit a few minutes, and maybe they'll have a drinking fountain there too."

"I'm sure they do. All public places have them."

"You know, my husband's son was interested in things like that, healing I mean. He has healing hands you know."

Mathilda told this to Harriet very casually, just an offhand remark as they were entering the building along with crowds of
people. It was almost four o'clock.

"Healing hands? I don't think I've ever heard of that," Harriet
said, "or read about it."

"I know, I didn't either, except when my husband's son, Henry
prayed for me…I was healed. He said it happens quite often."

"Oh, you're going to have to tell me about that, okay?"

"I will. I wouldn't mind at all."

When they entered, they thought they could find a drinking
fountain but were swept into the auditorium by the crowd. Harriet
managed to maneuver to the two seats in the back row while everyone else headed toward the front. They slipped in and sat down.
Harriet immediately went after the water, dodging between people
and going against the tide.

The huge room's sound system was much too loud. When different people spoke into the microphones, their voices reverberated,
causing a blare in Mathilda's ears. Suddenly, the people stilled as the
sweet organ music began playing. The air became electric with
anticipation. Most people were intent on the moment, experiencing
something within, and Mathilda was no exception. She felt some
sort of high energy radiating around her.

Harriet finally returned with the water in a little paper cup and
Mathilda immediately drank most of it down in one gulp, now
completely forgetting the box, the letter, and her previous weakness.

"We should leave as soon as you've caught your breath," Harriet
said very kindly.

"Okay, thank you, Harriet," she whispered.

Harriet's hand gently touched Mathilda's arm. Reluctantly
Mathilda rose, then the pair made their way into the aisle and
through the double door exit.

CHAPTER SIXTY-FIVE

Mathilda's dilemma spilled forth as Harriet drove home. It was almost as though she were talking to her friend, Maxine, so close a friendship had these two ladies developed.

Harriet wasn't surprised by what Mathilda told her about her husband, Henry, and about the box with the hidden letter—the letter Mathilda desperately wanted to read. Harriet said she had read about men like that, who all too often took advantage of the very person who loved and trusted them.

"Mattie, can I ask you a personal question? I know I shouldn't, maybe it's too personal, but I'm wondering if a person can ever get over being rejected, you know like by your husband? Have...have you..."

"I don't mind your asking. You know, Harriet, I loved Henry with my whole heart. There wasn't room for anyone else because he was the sunshine in my life. Papa told me that to love someone is the most wonderful thing that can happen to a person. He said my mama was everything to him and he would've walked to the moon to gain her love if he had to, so he knew what I was talking about when I told him I wanted to marry. I was only sixteen but Henry was my knight. Papa liked him too, and believed Henry loved his little girl the same as he loved my mama. I guess we were both mistaken...or else I couldn't hold his love for me. I still have doubts about that, always asking myself why and what could I have done better?"

"I guess I felt that way about my husband too. I mean, it seemed like a dream that he loved me and I loved him, and we were so happy. I don't know why he loved me. I wasn't as beautiful as some of his friends that I met at the parties we attended."

"I'm sure it was your loveliness, Harriet. You're a beautiful lady, and you have a wonderful mind. Why, I've learned so much from you in the little time we spent together. But to answer your question truthfully, I don't know whether other people ever get over it. I can only speak of myself, because I've not met anyone else who was hurt the same way."

"But Mattie, to have your love maliciously destroyed…do you think you could ever love someone else again…just as much?"

"I do love someone. It's different though—it's deeper and quieter, and I think maybe it's better," Mathilda said as she ran her fingers lovingly over the pearls she always wore. "But I still carry some of the that old hurt, and doubt about myself. Why do you ask, Harriet?"

Haltingly, Harriet began telling her own story, about falling desperately in love with a man who so drastically changed in a short time that she no longer knew him.

"What caused him to change?"

"Well, we married before I could tell him I was Jewish. He hated me for it and said I tried to trick him."

"Did you?" Mathilda asked, with her forever frankness.

"I wouldn't say trick, but I wanted to leave behind all the old ways in order to start fresh. I always thought I would tell him, but I never got up the nerve."

"Oh?"

"My real name was Smilansky. He said he always thought that I was Polish, and whenever he wanted to tease me, he called me his Sweet Polak."

"Smilansky, yes that sounds Polish to me, too. But then again, I don't know much about ethnic names."

"One day, after spending time helping the people who raised me as their own, who incidentally were Polish, well, when he came home that day he just came out with it and said he didn't want to father any little Jews. One day he was here, and the next day he was gone. Oh, if you only knew how his leaving hurt me."

"I'm so sorry...but...how did he find out?"

"While he was helping my family paint their house, they probably talked and the information was spilled. They must have told how a little Jewish girl came to live with them. I don't know, maybe he pumped them for it."

"We didn't know that much about what was going on during the war and before, I mean, Henry and me. Oh, the newspapers were full of the terrible things that were happening with the bombings and our boys getting killed, some right from our little town, and every day the radio had news about the war. It was almost always bad. All we knew was to produce the finest wheat, and I might add, we did! The Department of Agriculture told us that feeding the troops was as important as working in any defense plant. Our whole farming community believed we were involved in the war effort, and we all pulled together. Even the people in the cities had victory gardens in their back yards. How...what happened to you, Harriet, I mean when you were a little girl?"

"Well, I was hidden away by some Polish Christian people when my parents and grandparents were all sent to concentration camps. I had a sister and a brother, too, but I never saw them again. Later we heard they were all herded away like cattle in boxcars and I just wanted to forget all of that pain, put it all behind if I could."

Harriet began crying and wiping the flood of tears that began running down her face so she could continue to drive.

"I'm so sorry, Harriet. Believe me, I'm so very sorry."

"Since I was raised in a Christian family from such a young age, I didn't think of myself as Jewish—I didn't *want* to think I was Jewish. Mattie, we all had to wear a yellow star on our clothes indicating we were Jews. I remember my mother sewing one on my winter coat.

"How did you get away, I mean…"

"That wonderful couple took a chance and smuggled me out with their own children. I remember the lady cutting the star off my coat and burying it in their back yard before we got on a train the next day. They were so good to me…just like my own family. When we got here, they treated me exactly as one of their own children, but they never adopted me and I continued to use my own name. They thought if they did anything else, they would be robbing me of my heritage."

"I guess your husband was what they call anti-semitic. Is that the right word?"

"Yes, that's the word, alright. By the way, how do *you* feel about my being, Jewish?"

Harriet was suddenly thinking that Mathilda would think less of her and maybe not want to be friends any longer.

"Harriet! I'm so sorry you asked. I thought you knew me better by now. You're my dear friend and I don't care what nationality you are!"

"Thank you, Mattie, but some people can't see past my birth origin. If they find out, it's like I'm always being scrutinized. I hate it!"

"I know you don't have any reason to believe me, but I do understand. And it's probably because of a little Negro boy that I took under my wing. I love him and every time he's rebuffed or belittled by folks, it hurts me deeply. It's like they're doing it to me. Like they're punching me right in the stomach."

"I'm sorry, Mattie, please forget that I asked you that question. Can we still remain friends?"

"Not only friends, but best friends." Mathilda reached over and touched Harriet's hand ever so lightly as she was dropped off at her house.

"Don't forget the book, Mattie," Harriet said as she reached into the back seat to grab the one she wanted her to read next. "And thank you, thank you so much."

"For what? I didn't do anything."

"Just for being you, and for being my friend."

"Don't you know that I do it for myself too? I need you to be my friend," Mathilda replied as she got out of the car and waved.

CHAPTER SIXTY-SIX

Mathilda was grateful that Binkie had become the older sister during this waiting period of Dudley's life and he seemed happier than he's been in a long, long while. Ever since he had learned to roller skate, according to Binkie, he had become somewhat of a dancer on wheels. They always went to the Swank Roller Rink, further south on Western Avenue, which wasn't that far from where they were living. It was where the best live organ music was played for skating.

Patsy Conner was at the rink on most Saturday evenings. So were Dudley, Binkie and Binkie's younger brother, Stanley. Dudley would watch Patsy do twirls in the center of the floor during the free-for-all skate, and to him, she seemed like a Gazelle—flying through the air—graceful as a mythical goddess he read about.

The first time Dudley noticed Patsy was when she sat next to him in the school library doing homework and school assignments. Then when he joined the school orchestra playing the piano accompaniment, he saw she played first chair clarinet. He snuck peeks at her whenever he could, but Dudley was too shy to speak anything meaningful to her, either in the music class or in the library. Patsy always seemed happy, with that little upward turn of her lips. She reminded him of Elise back home. Sometimes, if he concentrated really hard, he could still feel Elise's tender lips touching his.

Binkie noticed Dudley watching Patsy every time they went to the rink and dared him to ask her to skate. After the third dare, and more dares from Stanley and his friends who got in on the teasing, he hesitantly asked her. He was surprised and pleased that she was so willing. From then on, they began skating together exclusively and even entered some of the skate contests in which they won free passes and free skate rentals.

At the Swank, an accomplished organist played all the Hit Parade tunes, but the ones Dudley liked best, were the slow waltzes. With the lights turned low, and the colored strobe lights flooding the floor any couple could skate, but usually the boy had to skate backwards and guide his partner around and around without bumping into the other skaters. With precision Dudley guided Patsy in the slow synchronized dance moves. He held her close, inhaling her light scented girl fragrance as they glided to the romantic music of *Mona Lisa, My Heart Cries for You, and The Tennessee Waltz.* The Hammond Organ sang—one song after another until the evening was complete. The last song played was, *Bewitched, Bothered and Bewildered*—it *was* the way Dudley felt while holding sweet Patsy in his arms.

When Mathilda arrived home that evening after finding the box, she found that Dudley had written a note saying he and Binkie had left early for the roller rink and they wouldn't be home until eleven-thirty—*another lonely evening*! Lately, whenever Dudley was busy with friends and she was alone, the house seemed to make all kinds of strange noises—snaps and creaks coming from different rooms— maybe normal household sounds but now that she began to feel homesick and with the added stress concerning that old box, it intensified her longing to be with Tommy.

After a light dinner there was nothing else to do but retire early and as usual the day played out before her. Now, she needed to consider the letter Henry had written to this, Elaine, and Mathilda's inability to hold his love. Questions she couldn't answer, wouldn't stop. *Could this failing of mine affect Tommy in the same way it pushed Henry to another woman? There's a letter in that box with Henry's handwriting on the envelope—what would it have revealed if I could have read it?*

As she dozed off, she made a firm resolution. She would drive to Kempler's pawn shop every day next week. She would go alone and spend the afternoons waiting in her parked car until the woman who owned the box showed up. She would go early to get a good parking spot on the street where the door would be plainly visible—with enough dimes to feed the meter for the whole day. To pass the time, she would read the book, *The Moon is Down.*

CHAPTER SIXTY-SEVEN

Mathilda found the perfect parking spot but after waiting all morning and afternoon, no one, lady or man had entered the shop, so she decided to get a bite to eat at the little cafe a couple of blocks away and then go to the auditorium across from the pawn shop. Her interest was piqued last week by the people packing the theater. *There must be something grand happening there, or people wouldn't go,* she reasoned.

A few blocks away was the well-lit parking lot Harriet always used, so Mathilda decided to move her car there. It was true that she would have to pay and walk, but it was better than the dark underground garages.

The same bright blinking signs on the building advertised what God was doing inside—saving and healing people—but on the sidewalk, a man approached her, warning her to stay away. Mathilda remembered seeing several last Saturday, but chose to ignore him just as the others did.

It was early, well before the music started. Crowds of people milled around, trying to find seats where they would be comfortable. Taking a seat in the back row again, she remembered the last time she was there with Harriet—that day the atmosphere became almost electric. *Was that God?* she wondered. *Could He be called on that easily to answer people's needs?*

Mathilda continued to think about the woman whose name was on the envelope. That woman had to have been a big part of Henry's life, and that made her a part of Mathilda's life, whether she wanted it or not! She would continue to go to that shop every day, even if it took weeks—tomorrow and the next day and the next—and then her compulsive thinking broke when people started to give what they called their testimonies into the echoing microphone.

A man told how God healed his five year old boy who had been paralyzed for two years. The child ran across the stage, back and forth, showing all he could do, while his mother stood on the side of the stage crying tears of happiness. The people became ecstatic with expectancy, that maybe, just maybe, they would receive what they needed too. They clapped and raised their hands in thanksgiving. Mathilda had never seen anything like it before. Maybe something would happen right now while she was here. She too began to feel expectant. A quick prayer came from her lips. Please Lord, I need to read the letter in the box. And then her heart sank because she realized she was self-seeking—absolutely selfish. These people needed healing or other serious requests and here she was thinking only of a little wooden box with a letter.

Mathilda forced herself to concentrate on what was happening on the stage and around the auditorium. People would go up and present a card. Then the minister would say what they were praying for, and he would pray for them aloud. A few of them would fall over backwards onto the floor, right there in front of everyone, as though dead. *I wouldn't want that to happen to me,* Mathilda thought. *So embarrassing for a lady!*

An hour went by quickly, when suddenly Harriet was making her way to the empty seat next to hers. At that very moment, Mathilda caught a glimpse of a couple walking up the aisle right behind Harriet. The man had his arm around the woman's waist, guiding her to a seat several rows in front. After helping her take her wrap off, he placed his arm around her shoulder and continued to hold her as though she belonged to him.

Mathilda froze as a sick feeling spread over her. She remembered that when Henry left for the seminary, he wrote home weekly, telling Catherine how his classes were going and wishing she and the children were with him, but he assured her that the time would pass quickly and they would be together again. After six or seven months, his letters came further and further apart, and soon stopped altogether. The last letter Mathilda received was from her sister last week. She remembered the words very clearly.

Dear sister,

My heart is heavy as I write to you today. The last time Henry called home, he said he had quit school quite a while ago. Catherine is very upset and so am I because that was the reason he left his family. He said he joined a ministry that set up tents in various parts of the city and sometimes he travels to other towns further away. Ministering directly to the people, getting them saved and healed went together. Mattie, he said he is being well taken care of by the donations of the people because they give generously, thankful for their healing or that of their loved ones. He also said he loves his children, but God's work must come first.

Catherine is utterly distraught, dear sister, and there is nothing I can do, but maybe you can think of something. The children don't understand why he can't come home, and little Angie doesn't even know her own daddy!

How have you and Dudley been, dear sister? The new orphanage is grand as well as the many homes in the subdivision, you will be pleased. I love you and take care,
 Angela

"Mattie, Mattie, what's wrong? I'm sorry if I disturbed you," Harriet said, after she sat down and saw Mattie's startled face.

"Oh my, Harriet, it's not you. It's that man over there. See right there, several rows in front of us, the one with his arm around that woman? He's my late husband's son. He has a wife and three children waiting for him at home." Mattie realized at that very moment, that her old suspicions about Henry, not really being her dead husband's son, were probably true. She was shocked by his resemblance to his two half brothers and their father, Bruno Baggs. *Now that he's older, he looks exactly like them!* she thought, but couldn't voice her opinion aloud—at least not yet.

"I see them, Mattie. Maybe they're just friends?"

"Yes, I guess they're awfully *close* friends."

"Mattie…I have something for you."

"For me? What do you have, Harriet?"

"I was minding the shop, you know across the street, and I want to give you this," she said, as she pulled the white envelope out of her purse. Mathilda stared at it, almost afraid to touch it.

"You mean you were there while I was sitting outside in my car?"

"I came in the back door so I didn't know you were waiting outside—not until I spotted your car later in the parking lot where I usually park. I couldn't think of anyplace else around here that you could be, so I took a chance and walked over here."

"I was waiting for that woman, Elaine, to come. I didn't know you were there."

"I'm sorry, Mr. Kempler called and asked me to mind the shop today so he could go to an important auction. I didn't have time to tell you."

"Oh my," is all Mathilda could say. "It's the letter from the box, isn't it?"

"Yes, and please don't even ask how I got it."

By now several people sitting directly in front turned around and said, "shush please, ladies!"

"Sorry," Mathilda whispered. Then, to her friend she said, "Harriet, if I had the chance, I would have done the same thing. Thank you, but I have to leave right away. I can't stay here another minute with him—right in front of my face. I'll have to read it later."

Mathilda placed the envelope into her purse and they both left the auditorium. Even though they were both silent and deep in thought as they walked to the car lot, Harriet could feel her friend's heart running wild.

"See you tomorrow, Mattie," Harriet said as she got into her own vehicle.

"Okay, I'll stop at your house in the morning. Thanks again."

CHAPTER SIXTY-EIGHT

The letter was like fire in Mathilda's purse. She wanted to tear it open and read what Henry had written to this woman, Elaine. But then she struggled with a new question: whether she had a right to read it since it was addressed to someone, who was probably as cheated and deceived as she. Before getting into bed, Mathilda stood the letter against the mirror on her dresser, where she could look, imagining hundreds of different hurtful scenarios before falling into a fitful sleep.

* * *

"I don't know what to do about the letter," Mathilda said the next morning to Harriet. "You...borrowed it from the shop and that man trusted you...and I would have done the same if I would have had the opportunity, so that makes us both thieves, me as well as you."

"I know, but the letter was there and old Kempler was out. I just thought I was helping you, that's all. I realize now that I was some-what rash. I'm sorry, Mattie."

"I hope you won't get in trouble."

"I guess I could if she comes in, and Kempler tells her about it and then finds the envelope missing."

"I have it right here." Mathilda removed it from of the bottom of her purse. "Maybe you'd better take it back today, before anything happens to it?"

"So what did you think when you read it?"

"I didn't read it."

"But don't you want to know?" Harriet looked shocked that Mattie could wait so long without opening it.

"Yes, I'm aching to know what a scoundrel my Henry was."

"Well, we can steam it open and then reseal it. That way no one would know."

"But I'd know, and it's dishonest."

"Is it? Is it more dishonest than Henry was?" Harriet asked, angry with this man Henry for making her friend so distraught.

"Well…no." Mathilda didn't tell Harriet that she had prayed about that letter yesterday. Was it God's way of answering that prayer? She intuitively knew that God would never tell someone to steal.

"Okay, then I'll do it myself. Here let me have it," Harriet said as she took the envelope out of Mattie's hand.

Harriet knew exactly how to open it without tearing it one little bit.

Mathilda followed Harriet into the kitchen where Harriet boiled water and then held the envelope over the spout of the teapot, gently pulling until the flap came up. She passed it to her friend and poured two cups of tea, then sat down across from her. It was only one single page and it was written on looseleaf paper.

"Read it and get it over with…and you'll be done with it forever! You know, Mattie, I've had to let go of many things too. Life goes on whether we want it to or not, and we can't change the past, we can only go forward."

Holding the sheet of paper in shaking hands, Mathilda began to read aloud.

My dearest love, Elaine,

I'm so sorry that I wasn't able to be there with you for your birthday last week, but you know how difficult it is while I'm traveling. I want you to know that you and our lovely little girl, Janie, are always on my mind. Surely, you know that you fill my life with a pleasure that I've never known before and can hardly believe—I don't deserve someone as fine as you, with such tender love for me.

I only wish that I could give you something that would mean more than the little trinkets I sell. I've been thinking and believe the little box I carved while we sat together so many evenings is just such a memento. Please always keep it as a memory of me and our love.

If you are reading this, it probably means that I went on to my just re-ward and you found the package wrapped on the top shelf in our bed-room closet. Please be at peace about everything. Things will work out. I have been and will always remain …
Your loving, Henny"

"He signed it Henny? What kind of name is that—Henny?" Mathilda asked as she folded it and handed it back to Harriet. "I think you were right, Harriet. I needed to read it so I would know exactly what was in it. He said he loved her and she filled his life with a pleasure he'd never known before, and…and they shared a bedroom!

"I think knowing what that letter said will eventually work wonders within you, my friend. I'll reseal it and put it back tomorrow, exactly where I found it. I'll go early." But Harriet didn't comment on what the letter said in any way.

"I think we're accomplices in crime," Mathilda whispered.

"No, I'm the one, but I appreciate your sharing the guilt, but now I have to find some glue to hide my misdeed." The ladies' sobering eyes met and held momentarily, at what would be their shared conspiracy.

"So you're going back tomorrow?"

"Yes, Kempler will be there but he'll be busy."

"No one must ever know about this," Mathilda whispered again as though someone was listening.

"Not another living soul," Harriet whispered back.

It was true. The letter in the little carved box revealed who Mathilda's Henry really was—a man who thought only of himself, deceiving others for his own gain. It wasn't Mattie at all who fell short in their marriage, and she was finally freed once and for all, of all the guilt that plagued her during the last eight years.

CHAPTER SIXTY-NINE

Dudley's graduation was a dream come true—an accomplishment he could hardly believe. Sitting around Aunt Mattie's table eating the last slice of chocolate cake she had made for that evening meant everything—a feeling of pride deep inside. Mathilda, Louise, Thomas, Barry Tierney, and Elise were watching as he flipped through the pages of the Juvenile Law books that Tierney had just given him. They were the very ones from Tierney's own library, and Dudley found that his own small paper notes were still stuffed between the pages along with Tierney's notes. Dudley also liked that each book had the little label indicating to whom they belonged: Barrett Evan Shannon Tierney. Now he had his very own set from someone he admired.

"I feel privileged to have these particular books for my own, sir. Thank you so much…thank you…all of you for coming." As he said this, he looked at each one sitting there, joining in his special day.

"I hoped you would like them, Dudley," Mr. Tierney said, as he observed what he thought was real pleasure in receiving his old books rather than new ones. "I couldn't bring all the volumes, but I picked out several that had the most notes. You'll have to pack the others when you come home."

When he said the words, "come home" he glanced at Tierney a little questioning, but only replied, "I couldn't ask for anything better. Can we continue to talk about the different cases in them before you leave?" Dudley asked. "I'd like to go over my notes and see if they make any sense to you, that is, if you have some time?"

"Why certainly, that's why I brought them, but right now, even though it's getting late, I have something else very important to tell you, and not only you, but also Elise, and I've been told that I put it off for too long already." As he spoke he glanced slowly at everyone around the table.

Dudley and Elise looked at each other, smiling because they thought it was a silly, unimportant little thing, a talk that would fizzle just like the other times.

"Is it the same something you were going to tell us when I had my appendicitis attack, and then again when Aunt Mattie dragged me away from those guys wanting to get me?"

"And if it weren't for your Aunt Mattie, who knows what would have happened," Tierney said. "Maybe you wouldn't be here today."

"What did happen?" Dudley asked. "Uncle Tommy didn't want to tell all the details, except little bits and pieces, and just that you and Elise were okay."

"You remember some of it. Two boys forced their way into the house and pushed me toward the front door where you and Mattie were standing. Mattie, you and Thomas ran out. It looked like Mattie was dragging you when the kid with the gun shot toward the door where you were last standing. When he heard someone coming down the stairs, he was so nervous that he shot upward toward Elise, not realizing his buddy was already about to grab her arm and pull her down the last four or five steps. His friend caught the shot and almost died."

"Then that guy saved your life, Elise!" Dudley remarked, awe in his voice.

"Yep, I was saved, but when I saw all that blood, I practically passed out right on the stairs. Daddy made me sit while he grabbed the kid with the gun and held his arm in back of him. It was a strange thing, because the phone wasn't working, but someone called the police. Turned out it was the neighbor. They heard those first shots, saw a car speed out of the drive and called them thinking there was a break in. Later they found another kid hiding outside in the bushes. He was the driver of the car."

"We heard them," Mathilda said. "As we turned onto the highway, the ambulance and police were going to your house, we were sure of it. But we didn't know what happened and couldn't turn around. Thank God you were okay, Elise."

"Mattie, I owe you everything for saving Dudley that night," Louise said. "And for hiding him here in Chicago. I know I couldn't have done that. It was all I could do to care for Paddy and Annie."

"At the time I just knew something was wrong and did what anyone else would've done," Mathilda said, looking at Louise with a gentle smile.

"We had to get new carpeting for the stairs, though," Elise added.

"Uncle Tommy only said that you and Mr. Tierney were okay. I didn't know any of those details. So what do you want to tell us, sir?" Dudley asked, changing the subject abruptly.

"Come on, Daddy, tell us now before something else happens and you put it off again."

CHAPTER SEVENTY

"Okay, I'll not put it off any longer because it's too important."

"Yes, sir," Dudley said, looking directly at Mr. Tierney. "It has something to do with me and Elise?"

Mathilda and Thomas looked at Dudley first and then at Tierney, their ears and eyes perked up at the exchange. Thomas wondered what Tierney had to say that was so important, and yet put it off so many times. Louise slowly lowered her eyes, looking down at the table. Elise stared at her father who was stalling. His lips wording without any sound. Then he said, "Dudley, your mother and I made a promise long ago that when you turned eighteen and graduated from high school, you had a right to know the truth about exactly who you are and your real parentage."

"My mother…and you? What do you mean? Are you saying you knew my mom eighteen years ago?" Dudley glanced at his mother for confirmation, but her eyes refused to meet his.

"Daddy, you didn't, did you?" Elise voiced. "You couldn't have known Dudley's mother then." Elise moved her sitting position way-back on her chair as though distancing herself from her father as they talked.

"Yes, we knew each other. You see, Dudley, I'm—I am your father." Everyone except Louise let out a little gasp. Tierney went on, "It'll take some time to explain what happened to us nineteen years ago, and we will, but for now, I want you to know how proud I am of you."

"But, Daddy, how can you be sure?" Elise asked, trying to digest this outlandish news.

"You're saying that you're my real...my biological father," Dudley interrupted, trying to understand what he thought he heard. "And that's why you—you helped me?"

Tierney dropped his eyes too, clearly realizing how awful this must sound to Dudley and Elise. Tommy was staring at Louise with a big question mark on his face. It was true, his little sister could keep big secrets, but he was watching for some sort of assent from her.

Suddenly what Tierney said, sunk into Dudley's understanding, just as Aunt Mattie promised years ago. She said he would have to grow up and then he would understand. He stood, turned and pulled his Mom up from her chair, hugging her while tears streamed down both his face and hers. Then Tierney stood up and walked over, encircling them both in his arms, his tears flowing easily. Elise, watching them, also understood that this person, this cute guy who could play any song she could play, the one to whom she gave her first tender kiss was her own brother!

Elise didn't want to hug them—she was speechless. Mathilda could sense Elise's shock and embarrassment, at her father's betrayal.

Dudley caught Elise's eye. "Hi sis," he said, winking at her. She was still sitting at the table, suddenly looking sullen.

"Hi Dud," Elise said. "I might have known...and you'll probably have to forget that kiss I gave you, ya hear me?"

"Yeah, no doubt about it, but now we're family." Dudley was caught up in the joy of the moment.

"Yeah...family." Elise's answered.

"But what's my real name?" Dudley asked Tierney pointing at himself.

"Listen son," Tierney said "your whole name is Dudley B.E.S.T., or Dudley Barrett Evan Shannon Tierney. How does that sound to you?"

"You mean you always planned for me to have your name?" Dudley asked as he stared at Tierney. "This is incredible...this is absolutely incredible," he mumbled aloud as he turned the words over and over in his mind.

"Yes, and that's the name you'll enter the university with. We'll have the high school correct your last name on your diploma and records if that's okay with you?" Tierney asked.

Dudley answered, trying out the "*dad*" word the only way he knew how.

"Yes, Dad, it's perfect. And can I study law too, like you?" He was watching Elise now, as she excused herself.

"You can study anything you choose, it's your decision. Music, law or both."

Still sitting around the table, while Mathilda was watching the happiness of Dudley unfold, Thomas was staring directly at Louise. She was smiling but crying tears of relief that her burden—that long held secret—was finally out.

"You surely can keep a secret, little sister. I never guessed for a moment!" Tommy said.

Tierney was surprised that Elise didn't turn her wrath on him and create a huge scene, but he knew it would come. He was sure of it because he knew his daughter, and he knew how much she loved her mother.

Abruptly, Dudley stood, excused himself, walked out the front door, and plopped himself on the top step of the porch. His head was reeling and he had to think, to get a grip because it all seemed like a dream, too much at one time. Sitting there in the dark, it felt good to watch the fireflies aimlessly flashing their lights here and there. He felt happy about Tierney being his father, he was sure of that, but now he had to think about something that had been on his mind for quite a while. And then, as his eyes got accustomed to the dark, Dudley saw Elise sitting on the bottom step. He couldn't say anything to her at first and neither did she speak. Sitting silently together, watching cars go by on the street and people walking on the sidewalk seemed to take on some important significance, something to pay attention to other than the dull pain starting deep inside.

Then Elise turned toward Dudley and said, "I'm thinking we've been fools. Do you know what Alexander Pope said about fools rushing in?

"Yes, and I also know that tonight was the night I wanted to tell you something that I had been thinking of for the last two years."

"No use telling me what I already know and can't have," she said with her usual sarcasm, but all the while, tears streamed down her face. And then reaching back, she touched his arm ever so lightly, and asked, "Dudley?"

"Yes?"

"How do you stop loving someone? Because I just don't know how."

"I don't know either," he said as he took her hand in his for a moment, forgetting that she was untouchable, as her exquisite beauty crept deeper into his inner being. It was all he could do to stop himself from kissing her on those soft lips—those lips that were still inviting him.

"Please, Elise, I have to go...please excuse me," he said as he jumped up and ran inside, taking the stairs to his room two at a time. The screen door slammed behind him.

It had been a long day, and now he wanted to cry. He hadn't cried since he had been in prison.

* * *

On Tierney's way to his room after everyone went to bed, he saw Mattie sitting alone in the living room, writing a letter.

My dear sister, Angela
I believe that I just might have a
solution to...

And then, Tierney paused at the threshold of the room, looking at her intently. "How did you know, Mattie?" he asked.

Mathilda looked up, "How could I not know. It was written in every book in your library, and I saw the pictures too. I just had to give you a little push, but you came through and that's what matters."

"Thanks for calling with the invitation and then giving me that ultimatum…maybe I would have put it off forever."

"Maybe, but I was tired of Dudley wanting a father all those years. And you know, when he told me you took him fishing and the other things you did with him while he was at your house, it made me realize that you love the boy dearly. The rest was easy."

"I do love him, and thank you, Mattie. I think you contributed to his life in a considerable way,"

"Contributed! Why, I only loved him, and that was all. And I'll tell you this now, Barry Evan Shannon Tierney, don't mess up the rest of his life, and don't you dare ignore Elise. She needs you as much as Dudley, and they'll both need an explanation as to what had happened. Please give it to them, and just hope you're not too late."

"I will. Louise and I are ready to share that with both of them," but he didn't catch what Mathilda was referring to when she said she hoped he wasn't too late.

"One other thing, Mr. Tierney—Barry…" Her voice softened.

"Yes?"

"Remember that senators come and go, but your family is forever, and they stick with you—with the good and the bad—all through life."

"Yes, ma'am, I agree. And you know what?"

"What?" she asked, looking at him intently with her large blue eyes.

"You're quite a lady." Barry was smiling as he bent over and gave her a soft kiss on her cheek. Mathilda blushed, her face turning a most beautiful pink as he left the room. Just then Tommy entered the living room to say goodbye. He had to leave and drive back to Mayette that same evening because of business the next day. He overheard Tierney and saw the kiss. Walking over to where Mathilda was sitting, he bent forward and gave her another kiss on her other cheek then took her hands and pulled her up, tightly encircling her in his arms. "Mattie, I love that you're wearing the pearls I gave you and I agree—you certainly are a special lady. I'll be waiting for you to come home...please let it be, soon.

* * *

Before Mathilda went back home to Mayette, she visited Mr. Kempler's shop. He was now willing to sell that exquisite wooden box since the woman who pawned it never came back. Mathilda neatly printed her name, Mattie, with her Mayette address and phone number on a little card. It was just in case the women would want to talk with her, and maybe want the box back. The truth was that Mathilda didn't know what she would do with it anyway, only that she felt compelled to buy it.

"Please tell that lady that she may call me or write to me at this address."

The shopkeeper understood, and said that he would be sure to give the card to her if she would come in.

When Mathilda got to her car, she opened the heartache box and removed the velvet bottom. The letter to Elaine was still there. Harriet did a good job in sealing it, but Mathilda promised herself that she would never open that letter again even if it did belong to her.

CHAPTER SEVENTY-ONE

The newspapers headlined the arrest of Baxter Marlow, the District Attorney in Blenning and his son, Beemer. Marlow got a prison term of fifteen years, and Beemer who killed Rudy Mullens with his father's gun was sent to reform school. His attitude and behavior would be reviewed when he attained the age of eighteen before being sent to an adult facility for life. Three boys in the gang received a three year probation sentence for their part in lying for the cover-up and three were sent to a juvenile detention home for the revenge attack on Dudley Best and Senator Tierney. Two Blenning police officers and the coroner, Mark Adkins, covered up the truth by rewriting the reports and depositions and having them sealed. They received long prison terms, also.

The investigation of the American Reformatory was also finished. The paper told of a ring, not of irrational mobsters, but men whom everyone believed to be upstanding role models in their communities. They silently controlled the school where abuses were being committed unless parents could pay for protection. Mr. Kracker, the gym instructor and a Mr. Lenton who worked as the private secretary to Jonathan Dennison including two other teachers, were convicted of getting periodic payoffs for keeping their mouths shut and even participating in the abuse. Prinze and Stanton, members of the senior patrol were charged and sent to another full security prison. Oren Blanchard who was not implicated in any way with the scandal, was only charged with a misdemeanor. It came out in the trial that Blanchard reported only the whereabouts of Dudley Best, but had nothing to do with the case.

The Attorney General's office had been biding time for the last six months after complaints of extortion. Two sets of brave parents ignoring the risk came forward with concern for their sons. The authorities were then waiting for a slip-up, but didn't have enough to go on until Dennison exposed the problem with Dudley Best by removing him from the institution for his own safety.

The paper also stated that Barrett Tierney, a senator from the state of Indiana for the last fifteen years, cleaned up the case almost single-handedly. He was a man with forthright courage and squeaky clean ethics who always got things done.

Thomas Bealer and Barry Tierney were informed that the violence and the fall-out from the town in Blenning and the reform school case was over. With all that good news, Dudley and Aunt Mattie set about packing all their personal things so they could leave as soon as they could close up the house. They were eager to attend the graduation of Booker T. and Mathilda was determined to have a party to celebrate both boys' graduation together. The house in Beverly Hills, which Mathilda rented first and then bought after living there a year, would have to be sold. But that would come later. Alex and Colette offered to keep an eye on it, as well as Harriet, who would pick up stray newspapers and flyers that might find their way onto the porch, sort the mail from the slot and forward anything that looked important.

Sadie stayed at the little mansion the whole time Mathilda was in Chicago. She kept everything humming and it worked very well for her, she had a home, and she and Father John kept tabs on Booker T., having him visit weekends and other days off.

Mathilda invited Harriet to the graduation party, hoping she could stay for a few weeks. She wanted to catch up on the books they were reading and also have her meet her dear friends, especially Maxine and her Mister. Since they were spoken about so often, Harriet felt that she already knew the lady, Maxine, even though they never met. The party was to be on a Saturday, during the first week of July. Harriet drew a big red circle around the date on her calendar.

CHAPTER SEVENTY-TWO

The day before Booker's graduation was hot and sticky, and he should've felt a wonderful freedom to finally be out of school, but he didn't really know what freedom would or should feel like. His destination on that day—a day without work or studies, was the eight miles out to the farm. He wanted to see Miss Catherine, Miss Angela, and the eight-year old twins, Henry and Andrew, and of course, baby Angela, named for her maternal grandmother and almost three years old.

Doctor James gave Booker T. several days off and permission to use his own bicycle for the trip. That day, on his way to the farm, Booker T. couldn't be his usual nostalgic self, turning things over in his mind to see how they played out, sometimes coming to new conclusions about happenings. But not today, because his black skin boiled and burned, not only under the hot sun, but under the unfairness of the school board's decision against his being the valedictorian. He rode hard and was happy to be out of school, but wondered what it would feel like to be truly free, like the birds flying anywhere they wanted, like the white folks.

Booker T. could see Aunt Mattie's farm house in the distance, and was admiring the acres of flowing wheat. Jesse had planted it for Mattie and they were completely golden again—that terrible day of rust forgotten. He planned on stopping at the old house first, where Mary Beth and Jesse lived with their son Donny, before continuing down the path to the farm.

The intense heat under the sweltering sun was taking it's toll. Sweat poured down the sides of Booker's face and neck. His handkerchief was now drenched from the constant wiping while pushing hard against the pedals.

Mary Beth could see Booker T. turning onto the old path, now a sturdier tar and gravel road built for the temporary convenience of the people working at the orphanage.

He's overheated, Mary Beth thought and waved him over to the side porch where she was standing.

"I have some freshly made lemonade, Booker T. Would you like a glassful with ice?" she shouted as he jumped off his bike and carefully leaned it against the side of the porch.

"Yes, ma'am. I surely would." Exhausted he plopped into one of the porch chairs. Just getting out of the sun and onto the shaded porch felt good. Mary Beth quickly brought out a pan of cold well water with a washcloth and towel. Booker took the pan to the bottom of the stairs and washed the sweat off his face and neck, then sloshed it over the tight black ringlets circling his head, letting the water fall to the ground. When he finished drying his face and sitting back down, she handed him a tall glass of lemonade filled with crushed ice cubes. Holding it in his hot hands, beady droplets quickly formed—sliding down the outside of the glass as he drank the sweet, tangy liquid, savoring each tiny piece of ice as it slipped down his parched throat.

After a few minutes and finally catching his breath, he explained that he was going over to see Miss Catherine and the kids and maybe Donny would like to come.

"How nice of you to ask, but Donny rode over about an hour ago to play and maybe go fishing with the boys, and Booker T., I'm so sorry about that school decision. It just isn't right since you won such high honors!"

Mary Beth knew about the unjust decision, because her husband Jesse told her about it a few days ago. He mentioned that someone needed to be notified, someone higher up than the school board, since Doctor James and Father John had both spoken on deaf ears.

"Yes, ma'am. Thank you, ma'am," was all Booker T. could say. If he said any more, he would cry and he was too big to do that with someone watching. And then he was off down the road.

"Tell Donny to be home by five," she shouted as he left.

"I will. Thanks again for the lemonade, ma'am."

* * *

"What're ya doing here, boy? Whose bike ya got there?" the indignant officer asked. He'd been watching the young black boy pedal down the road—following after him in the county's shiny blue police car.

"Oh, it belongs to Doctor James, sir," Booker T. said after he pulled to the side of the road. "He said I could use it today to visit friends."

"So ya think ya got friends here? I'm afraid not boy, and you'd better come to the station with me, folks here don't want to see the likes of you around here, lurking and looking for trouble."

"Oh...no, sir, I'm not looking for any trouble. Miss Mary Beth gave me a glass of cold lemonade and said Donny, that's her son, was at Mr. Henry's fishing with the boys. That's where I'm headed."

"I don't think ya heard me. You're not headed anywhere except to the station."

"You could ask Miss Mary Beth, sir. She lives right there in that house," Booker said, pointing back at Mathilda's old house that could still be seen from down the lane where he was stopped.

"Okay, we'll stop there first and speak with her."

After the officer knocked for about five minutes and stood around with his tense jaw chewing gum, working like a pump, the

310

man looked for someone in the barn. Finding no one about, he determined that the kid was lying.

"But maybe she went to town or somethin' because she said that Donny was over playing at Miss Catherine's house. Like I said, that's where I'm headed, sir."

"Well, that's enough of that. Let's go. You'd better put that bike in my trunk, and do it carefully so you don't dent it or scape the paint off, ya hear?"

"Yes, sir," Booker T. answered as he felt fear in the pit of his stomach. "I hear and I'll be careful. It belongs to Dr. James."

CHAPTER SEVENTY-THREE

The small brand-new building next to the mercantile, was the new satellite police station of Mayette. On entering, Booker T. could only think of Aunt Mattie for help and asked whether he could call her since she and Dudley arrived back from Chicago a few days ago, in time for his graduation tomorrow.

"Sure, you can call your Aunt Mattie. Tell her to get down here immediately because you're going to jail for suspected vagrancy."

He secretly hoped a parent would show up, someone he could harass and humiliate. He felt annoyed that some black kid wanted to put something over on him—he was a lot smarter than that! On the other hand, maybe there would be no parent or aunt, and in that case, he would put the kid in a cell—nice and new with clean cots, a chair and a sink. But they were only for holding one day or two, because the order was to bring any suspects into Mayette.

"Yes, sir. I'll tell her," Booker answered politely.

"First, I need some information. What's your full name?" the officer asked as the lady behind the desk typed his answers on a form.

"Booker T. Fraze, sir"

"How old are you, Fraze?"

"I just turned eighteen."

"Did you understand the charges?"

"Yes, sir. Sus...suspected of vagrancy, sir?"

"That's what I said. Suspected vagrancy."

"But I'm not a vagrant, sir, because I have a home. I live with Dr. James in Mayette."

"Yeah, sure, and what's your address, out there?"

"It's 426 155th place, Mayette, Indiana."

"Dumb kid, we know it's Indiana!" he quipped as he nervously tapped his pencil against the top of the desk, almost as fast as his jaw chewed his gum. *This boy is too well-spoken, and maybe he is telling the truth, but I have to be certain that his address isn't phony. One thing for sure, his kind shouldn't be tramping the streets out here.*

"Here's the phone, kid, make your call."

Booker T. dialed and reached Aunt Mattie's number.

"Miss Sadie, Aunt Mattie needs to come and get me out of jail because the officer said I wasn't supposed to be riding a bike down the lane, I mean, down the road to the farm. He says I'm a vag...he thinks I'm a drifter."

"Well, my land sakes, just a minute, Booker T., and I'll call her to the phone."

Sadie ran upstairs where Mathilda was putting her bedroom in order after unpacking more of her things. When she heard Booker say he was going to jail, she hurriedly straightened her hair, put on her hat, picked up her white gloves and purse and ran to her car. It was much hotter now than when Booker T. left, so she opened the small vent window on her side and also the passenger side, so a good breeze would blow right on her, helping to cool her now steaming hot-head.

* * *

Maxine had to pick up a few things at the Mercantile, so her Mister dropped her off while he took the time to look over to the new police station. It was built on the empty lot next door with a tall new flag pole, waving the stars and stripes proudly.

313

When the Mister walked in, he spotted a Negro boy sitting on a long bench in the anteroom, handcuffed. He could plainly see that the boy was very uncomfortable by the pained look on his face.

The secretary noticed the man looking around, got up from her desk and walked over to him. Before she spoke, she poked her head in the inner office and mentioned to the officer that a gentleman had walked in.

"Hello, may I help you?" she asked with a pleasant voice.

"Oh, hello, this is my first chance to look inside the new station and I had to check it out. It's very nice. I watched it being built."

"Yes, it is nice."

"And it didn't seem to take very long," he added.

"Hello, my name is Officer Duggan. We're always glad to have interested citizens stop in," the officer said as he extended his hand in greeting.

"I'm Humphrey Bauer, my wife just calls me 'the Mister,'" he said, shaking the officer's hand with gusto and a grin.

At that moment, Booker T. sneezed three times in a row.

"Who's the young Negro you got there?"

"Just a vagrant. I found him just hanging around on the road going toward the newly built orphanage."

"Oh, what's his name?" the Mister asked when it suddenly hit him that it just might be Mathilda's boy. He hadn't seen Booker T. in over a year, since he became so busy working with the doctor, and this kid was much taller, skinnier and older looking than the Mister remembered the boy to be.

"Says his name is Booker T. Fraze and that he knows the folks around here. I doubt that very much."

The Mister walked over to the bench and grabbed Booker's handcuffed hands, pulling him up.

"Hello, Booker T. I hear you're graduating tomorrow."

"Hello, yes sir, I finally made it with a fine scholarship too." Booker T. had a wide smile, his teeth showing pearly white against his dark shiny skin. "It's a medical scholarship!" he added.

"Wait a minute," Officer Duggan drawled. "You know this...this f...fellow?"

"You betcha, and I wouldn't be in your shoes for all the money in the world when Mathilda—Mattie Millering—finds out." He said, laughing so hard, he had tears seeping from his eyes and he had to blow his nose.

This has to be some kind of joke, the officer thought to himself.

"You mean his Aunt Mattie?" the secretary asked.

"That's exactly who I mean. You got her boy here—accusing him of being a vagrant?"

"She's supposed to be on her way," Officer Duggan said as his face began turning a bright red.

The Mister continued snickering. He just couldn't believe it and plunked down right next to Booker T. He had no intention of leaving until he heard and saw everything that would happen next.

CHAPTER SEVENTY-FOUR

"What seems to be the problem?" Mathilda demanded, as she flew through the glass door at the station, out of breath and out of sorts from the heat.

"Oh, Aunt Mattie," Booker T. said as he stood up when he saw her enter the station. "The officer said I couldn't be on the lane going back to the farm. He said I didn't belong there. I know I didn't do anything bad. I was only riding the doctor's bike. He said I could!"

"I'm so sorry this happened, Booker T.," she said as she placed her arm around his shoulder with a little squeeze. "I'll get it straightened out for you, you can be sure of that. Now stop worrying."

"Ma'am, please step into Officer Duggan's office, and you too, Bo...Booker Fraze," the lady at the desk said.

"Hello, Mathilda." The Mister quickly stood and acknowledged his wife's good friend. "I think an injustice has happened here."

"Hello, Mr. Bauer. Yes, I'm sure it has, but I'll get it straightened out promptly."

"I'm sure you will, no doubt about that!" He sat back down, confident that he would be able to hear everything from his vantage point.

The officer walked around his desk and sat down on the hard wooden chair.

"Please have a seat, ma'am, and you too, Booker. So you're the Aunt Mattie this boy talked about?" Officer Duggan asked, clearly surprised to see a well-dressed white woman, wearing a hat and white gloves. He was again tapping his pencil against the top of his desk to the rhythm of his nervous jaw, still chewing gum.

"Yes, I am. Just what is the problem here, and exactly why are you holding Booker?"

She wanted to shout, but held herself back considerably, only raising up her voice the smallest decibel.

"Well, what is your relationship to this here…fellow? I mean, he said you were his *aunt*?"

"Yes, Booker T. has always called me his aunt. Mathilda didn't want to say too much about their relationship because she was aware of not having any real legal authority over Booker.

"But ma'am, I just don't understand how you can be his aunt and besides, he doesn't live here and his kind shouldn't be around these parts. People get disturbed thinking someone like him is casing the place."

Mathilda ignored the question about being his aunt and said, "I'll have you know that this young man is entering the university in the fall, studying medicine, and here you are treating him like a common criminal, saying he's a vagrant, all because you saw him on a private road, and I might add, my private road! Please remove those handcuffs immediately."

"Your road, Ma'am?"

"Yes. Booker T. lives with Doctor James in Mayette. He is no more a vagrant then you are and by the way, why were you on my private road? Did someone call you? Was someone being threatened?"

"I'm sorry, ma'am, but I have orders to make sure there aren't any vagrants or no-gooders coming into this area that would be up to trouble. I saw him riding out there on the road."

"And how often do vagrants come here?"

"Well, none yet, but I have orders to be vigilant and check out every suspicion. It's my job."

"If you would have taken the time to speak with Booker T., he would tell you whatever you wanted to know." Mathilda's voice began to rise rather sharply, and Maxine's Mister could hear her very well indeed! "I'm telling you again, please remove the handcuffs, because you'll not put this young man into one of your cells unless you can prove to me that he did something wrong."

"Aunt Mattie, I did tell the officer that the bike belonged to Dr. James, and I did tell him that I had a glass of lemonade at Miss Mary Beth's house, but he just wouldn't believe me, so I did whatever he told me to do. Then I called you."

"Did Booker T. tell you he was visiting friends he knew?"

"Well yes, but you can never be sure that a story like that was true," the officer answered, as though he was talking about someone else, someone not even present. Then he pulled some keys out of his pocket and unlocked the cuffs. Booker T. rubbed his wrists while remembering that it wasn't so long ago that Aunt Mattie had cuffs on, too.

"I'll not put up with that kind of treatment of Booker T. since he was on my own private property and doing nothing wrong. Who's your superior, young man? I want his name immediately—is he the sheriff in Mayette, Sheriff Bordon?"

"Yes, we're a subsidiary of that police station and I'm just doing my job."

"I don't ever, ever want to hear that this young man is harassed by you or anyone else when he is out here. Do you understand me? And your superior will definitely hear about this."

"As I said, I was just doing my job, lady…ma'am."

"Well, just for your information, the lane you so declared off limits to this young man is not a public road. It is deeded in my name and is used only for my ingress and egress and to whom I give permission to use it. You do not have any jurisdiction over who comes or goes on my road."

"I didn't know that, ma'am," Officer Duggan meekly said, now realizing he could be in trouble with Sheriff Bordon when he gets word of this.

"Well, whose responsibility is it to know where you may arrest people?"

"I guess it's mine."

"I suggest you get your thinking cap on and go through your manual again before arresting people. Now, please remove the bike from your trunk and put it in my trunk. I saw it there when I came in, and be careful with it, Dr. James won't appreciate any dents or scratches."

The officer, with Mathilda and Booker T. following, walked through the outer office, shocking his secretary because he readily accepted the scolding and obediently did as this woman demanded. She heard every word distinctly at her desk in the lobby, and so did the Mister who quickly stood and followed them out to the car. He was joined by Maxine who was coming out of the Mercantile with several parcels.

Mattie and Maxine gave each other quick hugs when they met, and Maxine and her Mister both shook Booker's hand with great enthusiasm and then left.

"See you at your party, Booker T.," Maxine shouted, as they got into their truck for their trip home.

After the officer carefully put the bike into Mattie's trunk, she took off down the lane to Catherine's house to see her sister, Angela and the children.

"Thanks, Aunt Mattie," Booker T. said. "I guess I would have been in jail if you hadn't come to help."

"You're welcome, Booker T. I'm just sorry that you have to continually endure this kind of treatment."

"Yes, ma'am," was all Booker T. could say.

When they pulled in, Catherine and Angela came running out of the house to greet Booker T. and Mathilda. It was a real surprise to see them, but neither told them about the nasty ordeal and the real reason for their visit. Booker T. spoke to everyone, telling them how happy he was that he would be graduating the next day, and how much he was looking forward to college. After a few minutes, he hiked down to the shallow pond where the children were fishing and wading to cool off.

"Look, Booker!" eight-year old Andrew shouted. "I caught a fish with only my hook—he just up and grabbed it when I threw my line in." Andrew held up the little minnow for everyone to see.

"Here, let's put a worm on your hook and maybe you'll get a bigger fish," Booker T. offered as he searched in the can for a fat one.

"Eh, I hate threading them on the hook," Andrew said, as he backed away. "They're so icky!"

"We hardly ever go fishing anymore since daddy doesn't come home very often," little Henry said as he watched Booker's deft fingers thread the worm. "He used to take us to the big lake all the time and would always bait the hook for us."

"Where is my daddy?" little Angie asked, as she looked up at tall Booker T. She thought for sure he would know. Booker stooped way down so he could see her eyes.

"Well listen, little lady, I really don't know, but I bet he would like to be here with all of you, because that's how daddies are."

"I wish he could be here," little Henry said very thoughtfully.

"My daddy is always home," nine-year old Donny said, while listening closely to the conversation. "My mom says he loves us too much to be away."

"By the way, Donny, your mama said to be home by five." Booker T. was glad he remembered to tell him, and he knew Donny didn't say that to be mean. It was just what he knew and had to tell.

On the way back to the house, Booker T. carried little Angie on his back. She squealed as she bumped along, as though she were riding Lil Peaches while the boys ran alongside to keep up. Booker forgot all about the road incident after being with the kids down at the pond, and he could see plainly that others had heartaches too. Even little kids have worries.

Mathilda was glad she came, since she brought Catherine and Angela all the news about Chicago and her new friend, Harriet. She even told them about the meetings at the large theater where people were healed, but she never mentioned seeing Henry there. Catherine asked numerous questions, telling her Aunt Mattie that her broken heart needed healing too.

Before driving back to Dr. James' house, Mathilda and Booker T. drove up and down the streets in the new development, looking at all the houses people were already living in. Men were mowing their lawns, and children were playing ball in the street, but they all turned their heads when Mathilda's car, with all the windows turned down, drove by.

Mathilda liked everything about the new community, but then Booker T. said something that she knew must have been bothering him for some time.

"You know, Aunt Mattie, you and I are living somewhere in-between, because it seems as though there's no way we can please the white folk, and there's no way we can please the black folk, either. You and me, we're living in a kind of limbo."

"Yes, Booker T.," she answered, "we most certainly are."

CHAPTER SEVENTY-FIVE

The auditorium was packed with the usual proud parents and friends of the graduating class. Mathilda, Tommy, Dudley, and Father John were intently reading the program as the school band played stirring music before the graduates walked into the auditorium in their caps and gowns. As Mathilda sat there, her heart swelled with pride, because Booker T. Fraze was her boy as much as Dudley Best. She was particularly thankful for all the help Doctor James gave during Booker's high school years, especially for getting him into university. The doctor had all the skills that Mathilda lacked since he crossed those same troubled waters himself, and knew all the pitfalls to avoid.

On the stage, to the right and facing the audience, were the members of the school board, one member of the Mayette Town Council, the Mayor, and eight teachers. On the left side of the stage were fifteen students in the National Honor Society. There was one empty chair in the front row next to the valedictorian. It was for the student who became ill and could not attend.

Mathilda and others noticed that the principal, Mr. Martin Barton, seemed to be in a subdued dispute with the president of the school board. Barton's face was red and his expression furious. He had a difficult time keeping the discussion muted. As a word here and there became louder or more audible, the faces of those sitting closest to the stage became strained. Barton was pointing his finger at some of the other board members for agreeing among themselves to give the award to Nathaniel to further his career instead of Booker T. According to the board, "no one of Booker's race should ever receive such a coveted honor!" Barton had heard of the decision by way of the grapevine, but it was too late for anymore to be said. The music director raised his baton.

The commencement began with the usual *Pomp and Circumstance March* by Elgar. Everyone stood and turned to see the smiling faces of one hundred twenty-five students marching up the center isle. Bringing up the rear were twelve Negro students. Booker T.'s face beamed when he spotted Dudley sitting with Aunt Mattie, Mr. Tommy and Father John Bealer. Aunt Mattie and Dudley waved, and Booker with a quick swipe of his hand, waved back.

After the welcoming address by the assistant principal, ten graduates who were in the band during the last four years rose to perform for the last time with their class. Next, the Mayor of Mayette gave the customary speech about the graduates going out into the world and making their mark. After the Mayor, the valedictorian, Nathanial Marsh, spoke. He did so with much pride in his school, because it was there that he studied and won a scholarship to an esteemed university. He had the coveted four point average and his overall extracurricular activities at school were outstanding.

When Nathanial finished speaking, there was a boisterous standing ovation for him, after which he took his seat with the other honor students. Then Principal Barton slowly walked to the microphone. He had an announcement before distributing the diplomas.

"Honored guests, teachers, parents, students, and friends…an egregious error has been made, and will need to be corrected before going any further. I profoundly regret not giving my undivided attention to the awards given to this graduating class. As you all know, my wife's sudden illness caused me to curtail many of my duties, and I am sorry and apologetic to a student who diligently studied and never tried to call attention to himself. His grade point was even higher than Nathanial's perfect four point. Nathanial is a hard working, studious young man and certainly did a splendid job during his studies here. He has excelled, and his four point average can attest to that, so I do apologize to him personally for any embarrassment he will no doubt feel as I reveal some important information."

The room became quiet as a sanctuary. Everyone hushed, anxious to hear more, while fanning themselves with the paper programs. Mr. Barton turned and smiled at the young Nathanial, and then continued to look, squinting as he searched past the lights toward the seats where the graduates were sitting, until he saw the individual he was looking for, sitting in the last row of the graduating class. Then, he began again.

"A young man by the name of Booker T. Fraze finished his studies at this high school while working and studying medicine with Doctor James, a well known and recognized physician in our community. And he accomplished this while doing all his regular school assignments. Booker T. excelled in all his classes, and I might add, has a grade point of four point two. He passed the university entrance exams with some of the highest scores a student entering that prestigious university has ever achieved, and was immediately accepted into the B.S./M.D. Bachelor of Science/Doctor of Medicine program—an accelerated course of study. His extensive twenty page paper about Henrietta Lacks' contribution to medicine earned him a second scholarship covering all his living expenses during the first two years. I would be derelict in my duties if I allowed his achievements to go unrecognized. Please come up here, Booker T Fraze."

Sporadic applause here and there from the Negro students rang through the auditorium. Mathilda, Dudley, Tommy, and Father John stood as they clapped enthusiastically as well as Dr. James and his group on the other side of the auditorium. More applause came from Angela, Catherine, and best of all, Henry, who had arrived that morning and was now seated next to Catherine near the back of the auditorium. Others seemed stunned that a person of color could achieve the coveted award and had question marks on their squinched-up faces.

Booker T. walked slowly to the stage where the principal was about to distribute the diplomas. His ears burned and his knees shook at all the attention. It was more usual for him to take a back seat to whatever went on. It was only yesterday that Booker T. had lamented Nathanial Marsh receiving all the honors, because the boy always mocked Booker and called him Nigger at every chance, which was almost every day. Booker T. had ignored it all, knowing it wouldn't do any good to complain and would only cause more trouble. Anyway, that's what Aunt Mattie had advised him.

When Booker reached the top step of the stage, he paused for a moment, still reeling in the unexpected glory, before slowly walking the last few steps across the stage to the principal holding the mike.

"I want to pin you with the National Honor Society pin and give you a cash scholarship for six hundred dollars. Wear the pin with pride. You, Booker T. Fraze, will go far in your university studies if you continue the diligence you have displayed at this school. Can you please say a few words for us?"

"Thank you sir, for this great honor. It's more than I ever expected, but…but I don't deserve it." The silence in the huge room hung with expectancy, though the ladies continued to exert extreme vigor fanning themselves, with fully opened programs while the men pulled their handkerchiefs from their pockets and wiped the perspiration from their faces and red necks.

Booker T. straightened his cap, trying to keep it from falling off; he was so very nervous, perspiration seeped down the sides of his face. He laughed lightly to himself, and then, so did his classmates. Finally he continued.

"You see, there is a woman in this auditorium…no, she's a lady, a fine lady, who walked with me and cared for me every day and night since I was ten years old. She was always there for me and Mrs. Millering didn't see that I was colored, black…a Negro. She saw past that and saw me as someone of worth, and she taught me that I was somebody, even if no one else thought so. She's the one who believed I could do anything. Everything I am or will be is because of her."

He smiled at her. "Thank you," he whispered, lipping his words toward where Mathilda was sitting.

At this, most of the people in the stifling hot auditorium stood and clapped as they turned toward her. Even his white classmates cheered. Then, wiping beads of perspiration from around his hat and face, first with his bare hand and then with the new white handkerchief Mathilda tucked in the pocket of his gown, he continued.

"And then there was a man who had the kindness and foresight to literally pick me up off the ground and give me an opportunity that couldn't have come from anyone else. I wish to thank Doctor 'Jim' James, my mentor, my confidante, my friend."

Again Booker T. mouthed a thank you toward Dr. James, and a light applause for him rang out from different sections of the auditorium.

"I also can never forget all my teachers who demanded nothing but the best I could do…in everything. Thank you," he said as he glanced back on the stage where so many were sitting.

Tears streamed down Mathilda's cheeks, openly crying while, Dudley's chest was expanding with pride for his friend. His arm was around Aunt Mattie, holding her tight on one side while Tommy had his arm around her on her other. Tommy put his lips close the her ear and whispered.

"I've been wondering…you're going to have to tell me what you said to that woman who almost took him away, you know, the one who said she was Booker's mother?"

"Someday I may tell you, Thomas," she whispered back.

Booker T. wasn't quite finished. He cleared his throat several more times, swallowing and catching his breath. After looking at the principal, he scanned the others on the stage when his eyes landed on Nathanial. Suddenly a thought occurred to him. He placed his hand over the mike and turned toward the right side of the stage, looking directly at Marsh.

"Thank you, Nathanial Marsh."

With this statement, Nathanial looked stunned, and the honor graduates had questioning eyes, all focused on Booker T., wondering what he would say.

"Because without your constant humiliating remarks and regular stone throwing, I wouldn't be the strong person I've become, one who can roll with the punches, always picking myself up and going forward." Then he looked at the principal who still stood next to him at the podium. "And thank you, sir, for an excellent education."

At this, there was a low muttering of voices, people talking between themselves, surprised at the discomfort of the honor students and particularly, Marsh. Because Booker had covered the mike with his hand, the audience couldn't hear what was being said on the stage, but the principal, shocked to hear what Booker T. said to Nathanael, didn't display any facial expression and dismissed the remarks to avoid any kind of disturbance. Quickly he handed Booker T. his diploma while shaking his hand. Booker T. slid the tassel on his cap to the other side and turned to leave the stage.

Nathanial's face became fire red. He stood and walked toward Booker T., who was preparing to walk down the steps and take a seat in the auditorium with his classmates. As Nathanial came near, Booker T. turned toward him and without a word of any kind, Marsh punched Booker T. with all his might—first on his chin and then to his stomach. Booker T. fell backward, bumping his head hard against the floor on the wooden stage. He was knocked out—stone cold!

CHAPTER SEVENY-SIX

Doctor James jumped up from his seat and ran up the isle, inching his way over to Booker T.

"I'm a doctor," he said to the people crowding around. He knelt down next to the boy using the smelling salts that he always kept in his pocket. Directly behind Doctor James was Dudley, following him up the isle and onto the stage. He was now a six-foot-two, strapping eighteen-year old with a broad jaw, light sandy hair and a smile that could turn a girl's head even a block away.

Dudley took several high and long strides across the stage until he was directly in front of Nathanial who was ready to sit down but was first brushing his hands together, indicating that he took care of the situation and was thoroughly satisfied with the result. Dudley lightly tapped him on the shoulder. Nathanial turned to see who it was just as Dudley brought his arm back and then forward, punching him the very same way he punched Booker T., first to his jaw and then to his stomach.

"Yeah, thanks Nathanial, you did a good job," Dudley added, before he turned and walked down the three steps and out the exit door. The students sitting with Marsh had their mouths open. Some were laughing and others could hardly believe their eyes as Nathanial fell back onto the metal chair, head pushed back, eyes rolled up.

Everything happened so fast that the well wishers were in complete disbelief and stunned silence. Doctor James quickly walked over to the chair that Marsh was sitting on and held the smelling salts under his nose too. Then, asked one of the teachers to bring each of the boys a cold glass of water, which they both drank as soon as they awoke. The doctor helped Booker T. sit down on the only empty chair—next to Nathanial along with the other honor students.

Mathilda turned, first to the right and then to the left, observing faces. She could see that people were questioning. Something had changed in this now silent auditorium, not even one person was fanning themselves as they waited, not knowing what to make of the crazy happenings. To Mathilda, it was as though a very small part of a common taboo was shattered.

After a few minutes, Nate and Booker T. seemed to recover, so Mr. Barton started to call the names of the other students to come up and receive their diplomas. Booker T. continued to sit next to Marsh on the stage through the rest of the commencement. Every once in a while, he rubbed his jaw, but there was a firm satisfaction pasted on his face, as though the cat caught the mouse and ate him.

Standing outside the auditorium, after all the excitement was over, Doctor James congratulated Booker T. along with the Baptist pastor from Calvary Temple, where Booker still attended services on Wednesday evenings.

"Good job, fella," the pastor said as he shook Booker's hand.

"Thank you sir," Booker T. said.

And then, the Reverend Hollester from the Methodist church in Mayetteville where he attended with Aunt Mattie came up to shake Booker's hand too. They all congratulated him on his fine, unre-hearsed speech and also for his unbelievable grades and scholarships. Father John caught sight of the pastors talking together and walked up to Booker T. putting his arm around his shoulder.

"You're a very intelligent young man and your mother would be so very proud. I do believe you found those footsteps that she wanted you to follow and you were always looking for."

"Yes, sir. Thank you, sir. I believe I have."

He was then called away by someone who wanted pictures of all the students that received awards, leaving the pastors standing together with Doctor James. They began exchanging notes about the boy.

"That boy will certainly make a good Baptist," the Baptist Minister proudly said. "He was quick to learn during our Friday night meetings and he'll probably want to be baptized before he goes off to college."

"Why, that's funny," the Reverend Hollester said, "he and I have been talking since I first came to Mayetteville. He expressed an interest in becoming a good Methodist."

The ministers and the priest looked at each other and suddenly began to laugh, just snickering to themselves at first, but then burst into a hearty, strong guffaw.

"He's quite a young man, isn't he?" Father John said. "Once he asked me a question, 'why do we have to choose only one religion?'"

"Maybe he understands something far greater than any of us have ever thought about," Doctor James said as he, too, laughed at the ministers' dismay. "I myself believed he would become a Pentecostal, since he was always talking to our minister after services, and I don't know whether any of you are aware of it, but that boy is a praying boy. He prays for our patients all the time."

When the post-graduation picture taking and visiting finally ended Booker T. hurried to his party. On his way, he felt waves of joy that he never experienced before. They came up from some unknown depth and settled in a new place, where he felt this happiness would never-ever rub off. Gratitude toward everyone, especially Aunt Mattie for telling him to study hard. He knew he did it for her at first, and then he did it for himself. But how could he have known to do anything at all if she hadn't told him in the first place?

Ethel James spent the whole morning and afternoon preparing the table for the grand buffet: Booker's name on a three layer chocolate cake, dainty sandwiches and other ethnic dishes brought in by thoughtful neighbors filled the table to overflowing.

Mathilda and Dudley were sitting in the living room along with a group of Booker's many black friends—new friends that he had made when he started working and living with the doctor. As Booker came through the door wearing a wide smile and nodding at everyone, they all started clapping. He walked directly over to Mathilda and gave her the first huge hug. She hugged him back, long and hard, rocking back and forth, not wanting to let go because she was so proud of her boy. "Thanks again," he whispered into her ear.

Then, he saw Dudley right next to Mattie and felt a little awkward, not wanting to embarrass him. But Dudley grabbed Booker's hand, shook it hard, and put an arm around his shoulder, squeezing it. "Good job, Booker T. Man, did you ever do a good job!"

"Thanks Duds, thanks for everything," was all Booker T. could say pushing past the huge lump in his throat.

Each person received a hug or a handshake as he went around the room. He then placed his arms around Doctor James and Ethel who were still fussing over the placement of the chitlins, pigs feet and the black-eyed peas with ham hocks the neighbors sent over. "Thanks for everything, you're the best!" he said. "I can't even begin to tell you how I feel about all your help."

CHAPTER SEVENTY-SEVEN

The day after Mathilda left for Mayette, Harriet noticed a black coupe in her friends's driveway. Harriet thought someone was just checking a map, because a man's head was bent forward, until she realized that the same car was there several other days too. The following Saturday, Harriet saw a gentleman coming down the front stoop of the house walking toward that same coupe. He held a folded newspaper that he must have picked up on the porch. Harriet hurried up the walk to the house; she thought she'd better see what he wanted. They nodded to each other slightly.

"Excuse me. I was wondering, do you live here?"

"Are you looking for someone particular?" Harriet asked, deliberately not answering his question.

"Yes, I'm looking for a lady by the name of Mathilda Millering."

"Oh, she's not home right now, but I can take your name and tell her you came by. That is, when I see her." Harriet was not willing to tell a complete stranger exactly where her friend was or what she was doing. It was Mathilda's business to let friends know her whereabouts if that was what she chose to do.

"No, please don't bother. I'll check again another time," he said as he got into his car and sped away without looking back.

* * *

Harriet was extremely busy with her work, but still missed Mattie and the discussions that challenged her thinking. Mattie was someone who always had a somewhat different approach to things than anyone else she had known; she was interesting with a sharp sense of humor. It had been an inspiring two years but now Harriet would have to adjust and immerse herself wholly in what she was doing—retrieving the silver that was confiscated and stolen during the World War II years.

It was the next Saturday, early evening, when Harriet was driving home from the downtown pawn shop. She still had to deliver a few pieces of silver for Kempler. Her destination was to see a gentleman who lived near the Coral Theater on 95th Street. And then she still had to pick up the papers and mail that might be accumulating at Mattie's house. Hunger got the better of her and she stopped at the White Mill to order a quick hamburger, fries and a coke. As she hurried toward a table, she noticed a man who had just taken the seat she was headed for. She felt like a complete klutz when she tripped over his foot; he hadn't had time to tuck it under the table after sitting down.

"Oh, my goodness, I'm so sorry," Harriet said to the gentleman, thoroughly embarrassed by the mess she created on the floor.

"No, I'm the one who should be sorry. I shouldn't have had my foot in the aisle." Then the man looked up to see her startled face.

"He smiled. Aren't you the lady I met at the house when I was looking for Tillie—Mathilda Millering?"

Harriet quickly smiled back "Oh, yes, I guess we did meet there." she said, quite surprised to see the same man.

"I'm so sorry," he said again, "here, please let me reorder and pay for your meal."

"You don't have to do that. It was just an accident. My accident I might add."

Harriet felt the man's embarrassment too, and sat down at the next table while a busboy picked up the tray and food that others were walking around. A quick mop-up tidied the small area on the floor.

The gentleman stood and walked over to the next table, sitting down across from Harriet. He continued to apologize as his own meal waited for him, now completely cold.

"May I join you? I'm afraid that Mathilda Millering wasn't home, so now after I finish eating, I'll head back to my motel room."

"You're looking for Mathilda again?" Harriet asked, surprised, the words just blurting out.

"I was...I am...did she move away? The house seems as though it hadn't had anyone around for a while."

Harriet still didn't want to say too much because she didn't know who he was and what he wanted.

The man continued, "she and I are old friends and I thought I would see whether she would have dinner with me...since I'm in town on some business."

"Oh, then you do know her personally?"

"Yes, we used to see each other quite often a few years ago. Is she well?"

"Yes, she is."

"Perhaps, since she's away...maybe you and I could have dinner together? I'll only be here for two more weeks and I'm kind of alone. You know how it is, eating alone. That's why I was looking for her."

"Yes, I do know. But what did you say your name was?" Harriet asked.

"It's Douglas, Douglas Winthrow. And yours?"

"I'm Harriet, Harriet Barns. I don't think she's ever mentioned your name, Mr. Winthrow."

"Probably not. We kind of lost touch. But what do you say about dinner, Mrs. Barns?"

"Not Mrs.—just Harriet Barns," she corrected him, "and I'm Jewish and divorced."

CHAPTER SEVENTY-EIGHT

Silently, Harriet laughed at herself because of the way the information came out. Previously, she decided never to have her heritage discovered without saying it boldly and up front. Now, she thought it sounded rather out of place, but what was done, was done. *A little more diplomacy would be called for in the future,* she thought.

"Well, Harriet Barns, my food is cold and I've managed to ruin your dinner too. Please, may I make amends by taking you to a nice restaurant near the Midway Airport? The sign I passed said they serve the best spaghetti and meatballs, or something else if you'd prefer. It would delight me to have some good company to share a meal with."

Harriet was a little puzzled about the situation. She didn't want to be rude, but she didn't know whether she should go with a perfect stranger, though he did look like a very nice stranger—gentleman. He wore a gray pinstriped, three piece suit along with a white starched shirt and a blue paisley necktie. Slightly graying hair made him look very distinguished, and he smelled really good, just like the expensive aftershave her ex-husband used.

Though the invitation took Harriet by surprise, she found herself accepting since they both knew Mathilda. Harriet was lonely too, and hungry, and he was *quite* debonair and seemed *top-hat*.

"That would be very nice. I don't know why I stopped here anyway, except I thought I was hungry and in a hurry, but I do have time for dinner."

"Harriet, if you would like to leave your car here in the parking lot, I'll drive you back to this very spot after dinner."

"Oh, I guess that would be helpful. I'll just stop in the restroom before we go. I'll only take a moment."

Harriet combed her hair and freshened her makeup to look more presentable. She wanted to look her very best for Mathilda's nice friend, this distinguished gentleman.

He must have meant Santucci's. I think I remember the large sign on sixty-second and Cicero. It read *"best spaghetti and meatballs you ever tasted."*

Harriet was suddenly very excited that this complete stranger would want to buy her dinner and share her company, but then remembered that he wanted Mathilda—Mattie. *I'm his second choice, oh well!*

Douglas was waiting for Harriet at the door. As she walked toward him, he placed his gray bowler hat on his head, held the door open and walked her to his car in the parking lot. There, she immediately recognized his vehicle as the black coupe that had been parked in Mathilda's driveway yesterday, and all the previous days too. *A person who doesn't give-up,* she thought, *a grand quality as Mattie would say*!

"You've been at Mathilda's house quite a few times, haven't you?" she asked when she saw the obvious.

"Yes, I kept thinking she'd finally come home."

During the twenty minute drive, and also during the entire evening, Mr. Winthrow—Douglas—asked endless questions. He wanted to know all about this divorced Jewish woman who revealed something so personal at their first meeting, during the first few words of their conversation, even. He wanted to know what she liked to do for fun, if she owned her own home, and if she had a job.

Harriet never liked to be asked those kind of questions, and whenever she could, she gave short, non-specific answers, but Douglas also continued to ask questions about Mathilda, and that's where Harriet drew the red line.

"I can't say that much about her. She's a very private person, and we only talked of women things, like fashion, books and recipes. I can't say I know that much about her."

"Mathilda certainly must have someone she's interested in marrying by now?" he persisted.

"Well, as I said, she and I hadn't discussed much of her personal life." Harriet hoped he would quit asking and be content with just having dinner.

Over the next few weeks, they did have wonderful days and evenings together, and Douglas continually found outrageous reasons to stay on and on, even though he should have left Chicago after the two weeks he mentioned at their first meeting. He asked whether Harriet would accompany him again and again to dinner, movies or other places of interest. Harriet loved every minute and Douglas began to fill that lonely place deep inside. Once, after they had dinner in an elegant and expensive restaurant, in the heart of Chicago, he needed to borrow the money to pay for the meal and the gratuity. Harriet was glad she had enough cash to cover the bill and after that, she began to carry just-in-case-cash.

CHAPTER SEVENTY-NINE

It was one of those delightful July days, sunny and warm with a light breeze, perfect for the open house. Mathilda invited everyone who knew her boys since they were ten-years-old, wanting them to share in her bursting pride at their growth and accomplishments.

Sadie, Angela and Tommy, helped with all the preparations busying themselves with setting up the tables and chairs in front of the carriage house.

Senator Tierney and his daughter, Elise, wouldn't miss that day for any reason. They were both looking forward to meeting everyone who knew Dudley during his growing-up years. That was the Senator's reason, but Elise had another reason for going, something she couldn't or wouldn't reveal to her father. Something she kept locked, refusing to admit even to herself.

Grandpa and Grandma Bealer, who were not able to go to Dudley's graduation in Chicago, were hoping to meet the boy's father, now that the concealed information had been revealed. Grandma Bealer was saving a few choice words for that man when she could get him alone, that is, if and when she could get him alone, because she wouldn't want anyone else to hear what she had to say to him.

* * *

Elise and Dudley were in the parlor and began playing the songs Elise loved best, including some of the most popular ones, while

Booker T. sang. His voice was rich and mellow and he could croon "Nature Boy" as well as any Nat King Cole. As the music spilled out into the backyard where family and friends were eating and visiting with each other, Grandma Bealer secretly hoped they would play the rainbow song, even though she knew it would bring tears to her eyes.

As Dudley sat at the piano, accompanying Elise's deft fingers dancing across the neck of her violin, he tried very hard not to look at her beautiful face and eyes because Elise's fingers would begin to tremble. Whenever their eyes met, they held like strong bonding glue without assent from either one. It was as though their eyes had a mind of their own and she finally put down her violin, claiming she was too tired. Booker T. then sat down at the piano with Dudley, and they played their own renditions of the Jazz they had played as ten-year-olds, delighting the younger guests who came into the house to listen and watch. Elise sat on one of the wingback chairs watching too, but making sure she didn't look at Dudley. Mathilda loved every minute and so did Louise, who was absolutely beaming while she sat with her mother and dad and the younger children.

Harriet called early that morning and said she would be there by three o'clock at the latest, and that she had some important news. She was bringing a friend who would be a special surprise. She could definitely stay for the two weeks and was looking forward to spending all their time together, visiting and discussing important trivial things.

Mathilda was working at the kitchen table, frosting the last of the chocolate cakes that she promised the boys, when Henry walked into the room. A bond of love flourished between them way back when Mathilda first met him and Henry couldn't have been loved more if he were her own son. She would always remember his deep concern for her and his healing hands—hands that healed her in her time of deep depression.

"You wanted to talk to me about something, Aunt Mattie?" He hugged her lightly, but was a little hesitant, feeling a distinct chill. *Why is Aunt Mattie acting so distant...or is it me?*

"Yes, I do. But I'm terribly busy now, Henry. Do you think you could stay a little later so we could talk, or maybe come back tonight after you take the children home?"

"Well, yes, I guess I could come back. It sounds serious. Are you unhappy about the building going on, Auntie?"

"No, not at all."

"Are you sorry that you sold all those acres then?" Henry asked, trying to get a sense of what she wanted to talk to him about, but hoping she wouldn't bring up his work in Chicago.

"No, it was a good decision for me and for all the folks who now have homes of their own. I just want to talk to you alone."

"The houses are wonderful," Sadie said, overhearing the words about the acres, as she swooped up the cake Mattie was working on and carried it outside.

"I'm sorry I've been so occupied lately that I've kind of neglected Kats and the kids," he said, lowering his eyes. "It seems that God's work keeps me pretty busy, but I'm glad you saved those acres around my home. They're beautiful, and the wheat looks healthy too. Sure is a difference!"

"Yes...and you'll have a nice little profit, but let's talk a little later. I'm terribly busy right now, Henry." Mathilda was putting him off because she needed at least an hour to talk about what was on her mind.

"Alright, Auntie, a little later then." He felt uncomfortable, and he knew the real reason. *She's disappointed in me for sure, but she doesn't understand the way God works. If she did, she wouldn't feel the need to talk to me about anything.*

Henry went back outside to sit with Catherine and the children. They were at a table next to Father John, Doctor James and his wife Ethel.

Barry walked around to all the tables, introducing himself to the friends of Dudley and Booker T. After he spoke to almost everyone, he went over to the table where Father John was sitting with Doctor James and his wife, who at that very moment excused themselves to get some of Mattie's chocolate cake the boys had been raving about. After nodding to the couple as they left, he said...

"Hello, I'm Barry Tierney. Dudley's spoken about you quite often."

"Yes, hello. He's spoken about you too," Father John said as he stood up to shake hands and then sat back down. Tierney took a seat across from the priest.

"In all the years that Dudley was growing up, did you ever wonder who his father was?" Tierney asked. He said this without thinking; it brought an immediate confrontation.

"Yes, I have to say that I did think about it almost every day. I was always interested in what happened to my little sister, and I'd say it took you an awful long time to let Dudley know you were his father."

"You sound annoyed with me, and I'm sorry I didn't do things exactly to your liking, but followed Louise's wishes. It's the way she wanted to do things."

"Not at first. There was something else she would have done if I hadn't stepped in...something very wrong. Maybe you didn't know—or maybe you did know—that she was planning an abortion!" Father John startled himself when he realized he was lecturing the man, as though he was some immature kid. He didn't mean to, but old frustration just flowed off his tongue. "Perhaps you should have asked for advice. I could have given you some."

"Yes, well, Louise and I did what we thought best in order to preserve our families."

"Sure you did but, as Mattie always said, Dudley paid the price. It was a long and expensive price that touched his innermost being. I guess I'm not very happy about that and there isn't any way to change the harm that's been done."

"I'm sorry about that," Tierney said. He didn't have an inkling that this uncle of Dudley's would be so unwelcoming.

"Senator?"

"Yes?"

"Do you see that man and women over at the next table sitting with Booker T. and Dudley?"

"Yes, the elderly couple?"

"Yes, they're Dudley's grandparents—Louise's parents. They missed all his growing-up years because at first they didn't know about him. And when they did, my mother couldn't get over the shame she felt because of her daughter, and it caused more hurt for the boy."

"All I can say is I'm sorry. What's done is done," Tierney said and stood up, ready to go back to the table he'd been sitting at, but now avoiding Dudley's grandparent's table altogether. As an afterthought, and as the Doctor and his wife returned to the table, he turned and said, "You know, he does have grandparents that accept him—my parents. They've loved him from the very first moment they met him—just because he is my son!"

Tierney almost sat down but caught sight of a couple who just turned the corner toward the carriage house. The woman was looking at a piece of paper as though searching for an address. They seemed a little lost. When he looked closely, he realized it was Mattie's friend, Harriet, whom he had met at Dudley's graduation in Chicago. She and the gentleman were holding hands, Harriet kind of pulling him along while walking toward the house. Harriet's eyes met Tierney's as he greeted her, grabbing her hands with a wide smile. He knew Mattie would be happy to see her.

"Hello, Harriet."

"Hi, Senator Tierney. I guess we found the right house."

When Mathilda finally finished icing the last of the cakes, Angela shooed her out of the kitchen. At the very moment she was stepping down from the porch to take a seat at Tommy's table, she caught sight of Harriet. They ran to each other and hugged.

"Oh, Mattie, we just had to come and see Dudley and meet all your friends."

"I'm so glad you could make it. My, you look wonderfully happy, almost radiant!"

"I am, Mattie. I'm terribly, terribly happy, and I want you to meet the man I'm going to marry. This is Douglas Winthrow, and Mattie…he says he knows you." She turned and pulled Douglas forward. "We're getting married next month and we would like you to come to the ceremony and our small dinner party."

CHAPTER EIGHTY

The minute Mathilda heard the name Douglas and looked up at Harriet's friend—a man whom at first she didn't recognize—her entire countenance changed. First, her heart leaped to see someone she once thought she loved, and then it filled with a quiet rage when she remembered his sweet talk, leaving her in Chicago while trying to get his hands on her land. Now he seemed aged, much older than his years.

"Douglas and you—married!" she cried, looking closely into Harriet's eyes. In that instant, Mathilda's shining eyes squenched up and her brow furrowed. It gave her away and Harriet knew she should have mentioned his name before bringing him with her.

"Hello, Tillie," Douglas said. As he stepped forward with his hand out, a boulder tightened in the pit of Mathilda's stomach. She folded her hands together and found she couldn't speak because her vocal chords were suddenly frozen. Backing up slowly, inch by inch, she landed right into Tierney's arms. He was directly behind and caught her before she tripped, setting her smoothly onto a folding chair. From across the drive, Henry saw Aunt Mattie almost lose her balance. He sprang forward to see what was happening, thinking she may have become ill.

During that split second, as she was backing up, she saw herself encircled in Douglas's arms, remembering the words he had spoken, words that had touched her heart with a heady rush of passion while his warm cheek brushed against hers. He was irresistible—kissing her and snuggling his face against hers, trying to get her consent to go with him. He said their first stop would be in Chicago, and then his hometown to meet his friends. And then she remembered the shame of waking in that hotel room practically naked, and the nasty wink from the manager, implying something she could never forgive that man for. Her thoughts came in slow motion as she tried to right herself now, with Henry and Barry Tierney straightening the chair so she could sit for a moment and catch her breath.

"Hey, what are you doing here?" Henry said to Winthrow when he realized who it was. Douglas Winthrow was much grayer and walked with a little snap of a limp, not much, but probably the aftermath of the accident, Henry thought.

"You have no right to be here, and I'm telling you to get going," and then he looked back at Aunt Mattie.

"You want him here, Auntie?" he asked.

Mathilda found her voice as her composure returned.

"No, he's not welcome here. I'm so sorry Harriet, but Douglas is not welcome here...ever."

"I didn't know, Mattie," Harriet said. "I thought you both were good friends. I'm so sorry. We'll leave immediately." She hugged her friend goodbye and whispered in her ear. "I'll have to call you. Would you mind very much?"

"Harriet, could you stay, please? I'd love to have you," Mathilda begged.

Douglas didn't expect Henry and Mathilda to be so angry. He acted as though he didn't know why they should be. His face showed silent alarm, because Harriet was now looking at him intently, in a distinctively different way, a questioning way. Maybe for the first time, her own questions crystallized and poured forth in her mind. Harriet knew Mattie to be truthful and trustworthy, and if Douglas were not a welcome guest, it was probably for a very good reason.

Thomas noticed the distraction. He instinctively walked over, put his arm around Mattie's shoulder to support her while staring at the man and wondering what he could have possibly said to make them so upset. Dudley and Booker T. quickly found themselves standing beside Aunt Mattie. Dudley's hands were on his hips, waiting, and Booker T.'s arms were folded in front of him. Both boys were ready to dispatch the man into the street if Auntie gave the word.

"Don't worry, my dear. I'll handle this," Tommy whispered to Mattie.

He walked up to Douglas very slowly, noticing that Henry was getting ready to punch or shove him back towards his car. Thomas never saw Henry so angry before and it was completely out of character. He could see that Henry was finding it difficult to contain his raging, ragged anger, hidden so deeply against this man.

"Where is my son?" Henry shouted at Douglas. "You stole my youth, my wife and children with lies and trickery."

Thomas quickly stepped in between Henry and Douglas. He spoke very softly, putting his face very close to Douglas' face and enunciating each word clearly, so the man would understand the absolute meaning of his words.

"I suggest you not speak, not even one more word, but turn around and go. Don't ever come back here. Mattie doesn't want you here. Henry doesn't want you here. And I don't want you here." Then he turned and spoke to Harriet who was still watching, mesmerized by the events happening before her, with her mind focused on the words Henry had just spoke, "*where is my son?*"

"Please Harriet, I think Mattie would like you to stay...she's been looking forward to your visit, and I could drive you back home whenever you choose."

She was quick to respond to Mr. Bealer's kind offer.

"Yes, Mattie invited me to stay and I believe I shall."

Then looking at Douglas, Harriet said, "Goodbye, Douglas. I'll see you after I get things sorted out."

"All lies. They'll tell you nothing but lies, Harriet. I can guarantee it." Before leaving, he placed Harriet's two suitcases on the pavement and sped off in his shiny black car.

* * *

When the terrible tension broke Dudley and Booker T. caught each other's eye and both ran into the house, up to the cupola, taking two steps at a time. It was their preferred place to talk in private.

"I've been wanting to talk to you about something kind of important," Booker T. said, as he closed the door behind him. "But no one else needs to know, not even Father John."

"Okay, I won't say a word unless you say."

"Yeah, well I got this thing going on in my head, as Aunt Mattie always says when she starts thinking about doing something."

"I know exactly what you mean," Dudley said as he became more serious. He fell into one of the wingback chairs and Booker T. took the other.

"You know this room holds a lot of secrets," Dudley added as he remembered telling Aunt Mattie about so many of his fears, anger and sadness, and then, that terrible day about his gang trouble. Now he was ready to listen and offer whatever assistance he could to his friend.

"What's up?"

"I guess I'm nuts or something, because after studying so hard for a medical degree, I find I'm seriously thinking about your uncle."

"Which one?"

"The priest."

"Yeah, so…what about him? What do you mean thinking about him?"

"Well, I'm thinking that I would like to be like him. You know, helping people know God. I've been reading about a Negro priest—Father Tolton. He was a former slave who became a priest."

"But a doctor helps people!"

"I know, but something is inside me...like a burning. I find myself wanting to pray...all the time. Do you think it's too late to study to become a..."

A knock at the door stopped Booker T. before he could say anything further. It was Elise opening the door.

"Is this a private conference?" she asked, "or am I invited?"

"Well, it's kind of private," Dudley answered.

"Is it about me," she asked, knowing very well it wasn't.

"No, Elise," Dudley assured her. "At least I don't think it's about you...is it, Booker T?" He was clearly teasing Elise.

"Hey, if you two need to talk, I'll catch ya a little later, okay?" Booker T. said as he stood up and began to move toward the door that Elise had just closed behind her.

"I just want to say, before I leave for home, Dudley Best, that I love you!" She said it unashamedly, staring at Dudley with tears in her eyes as she leaned against the closed door.

The silence hung...heavy. Dudley could hardly believe he heard her right, and it took a moment before it registered in his brain.

"Elise!" Dudley cried, as he got up from the chair and walked over, grabbing her hands and looking deep into her troubled face. Pulling her close and encircling her in his arms, he said, "I've wanted to say those exact words to you since the first day I met you, and after the first kiss you gave me, remember?" He caressed his face against her cheek, inhaling her young sweetness as he held her tight against him.

Booker T. inched his way behind Elise opened the door, and as he slipped out, said, "See you both later."

"Booker T. you're a real gentleman, ya know that," Elise said as he was leaving.

"I'm sorry, Booker," Dudley said, hardly able to say anything else.

"It's nothin' that can't wait. I know you'll be leaving with your daddy shortly, Miss Elise, and I can wait." And then he was gone, running down the two flights of stairs and out.

Elise began to cry. "I've waited so long to tell you, Dudley. I just can't stop loving you because Daddy says we're brother and sister... I've tried, you don't know how hard. And now we probably won't see each other, again—Daddy will see to that and I can't bear it, it hurts too much."

"If he had only told us right away, we wouldn't be in this awful mess," Dudley moaned now as his gentle kisses covered her face catching her teardrops flowing and mingling with his like a mighty river—and then his eager lips lingering on her cherry-red pouty lips.

"What can we do now?" Elise cried as they both hung onto each other, not wanting to let go, while their tears mingled and their bodies clung tightly together. It was as though they were starved and had to get as much holding, touching, and loving as they could before they would be denied.

"Maybe we should talk to my uncle?" Dudley whispered.

"You mean the priest? Do you think he could help us?"

"I don't know, I've never known about a brother and sister loving each other. He's downstairs right now...do we dare tell him?"

"But we're only half brother and sister," Elise reminded him.

"Maybe that'll make the difference?" Dudley offered. "I can only hope and pray it does, because I want to care for you and love you forever. Will you marry me, Elise? Please say yes."

"I want that more than anything and I mean it when I say I don't want to be away from you at some old college for another four years. All I can think about is you!"

Just then, they heard a quick knock at the door and Aunt Mattie walked in. She was wondering why Booker T. ran out of the house so quickly but didn't expect to see Dudley and Elise locked in each others arms with tears streaming down their anguished faces.

"Oh, my," she gasped—completely overwhelmed with a loss of words, turned, closed the door and hurried downstairs.

CHAPTER EIGHTY-ONE

Barry spoke loudly in his deep baritone voice as he entered the kitchen. He was in a hurry and thought Elise would have been through saying goodbye to the boys upstairs. Mathilda was at the sink doing a few dishes while trying to sort out her feelings. He could only see her back, but he spoke up.

"Mattie, it's been a perfectly wonderful party and I think the boys will remember it all their lives. Thank you for inviting Elise and I, but it's getting late and we need to be on our way."

"Yes, it's certainly been that. I went up a few minutes ago to speak with the kids, but…"

"Is Elise ready? I told her we had to leave as soon as possible."

"I don't know." Mathilda now turned around to face him as she spoke.

"I think you have to go up yourself, because I'm not sure of what to say, or how to say it," she confessed with blurry eyes that wanted to cry.

"Of course, I'll go up and tell her." Barry didn't know what Mattie was talking about and simply said, "show me the way."

Mathilda led him upstairs and then to the small stairwell leading up to the cupola. "Just go up these stairs and you'll be there."

"Thanks, Mattie," he said as he darted up, knocking hard at the door, and not seeing any reason to be invited in—turned the knob and entered.

When the kids saw their father, they broke their embrace. Elise was very vocal as always.

"I hate you, Father. I hate you…I hate you," is all she could get out between her tears. Dudley only stood there silently, realizing the enormity of their dilemma.

Barry couldn't say a word. He now understood what was happening and knew why Mattie seemed so distraught.

* * *

The desire that had been in Dudley's heart for so long, was now aroused into fever pitch by Elise's tidal wave declaration of love. He wanted to give in to his feelings of passionate love that finally seemed within reach. It was more important than any old father business which now seemed insignificant compared to this aroused desire for Elise.

Father John did give his advice; it was stern and to the point, "stop acting like a spoiled little kid who doesn't know right from wrong and prepare to leave for college. There are serious reasons why marriage between you can never be, and it would be a good thing for you to look into those reasons."

After Dudley spoke with his uncle, he was sure that he and Elise would never see each other again. Barry would see to that, and that was the biggest blow of all. After finally finding his father—the father he had always wanted and needed—this same father who protected him from harm all those months, was taking away the one thing he loved in all the world: Elise.

CHAPTER EIGHTY-TWO

The two weeks Harriet and Mathilda visited together flew by, and it was now time for Harriet to go back to Chicago, but not before seeing the housing development, farm and the almost completed orphanage that would open in September. They were ready to enter the little eatery in Mayetteville and Mathilda had her heart set on a nice hot cup of tea when out of the blue, Harriet posed a question.

"Mattie, would you mind if I take a walk alone down those beautiful tree lined streets? I have some serious thinking to do and a nice walk might help clear my vacillating thoughts."

"I wouldn't mind one bit, and don't forget to sit in the new park for awhile. I'm told that it's quite peaceful, like a little piece of heaven. You can do some mighty good thinking there."

"That's exactly what I have to do before I see Douglas again. I have to decide if he'll fit in with my life, and I in his. And I have to decide for sure before I get home and see him again. You know how persuasive he can be."

"Take all the time you need. I'll have my tea and when you get back we can spend some time talking about my new book or anything we have a mind to. I have it in the car and I can read while you're out walking."

"I guess we were just too busy for books with all the visiting we did. See you in a little bit," Harriet said, as she turned and took long strides toward the little community.

Mathilda grabbed her book from the car and entered the restaurant. Emma Dokins the waitress greeted her. She was an old employee having worked there ever since Mathilda could remember, and now for Mr. Ranson, the new owner. He had the building totally remodeled even with new windows and red and white checkered curtains that brightened the whole room. Everything was very light, airy and inviting. Mattie walked toward the back to take a seat in one of the new upholstered booths.

"Hello, ma'am," Officer Duggan said as she passed the booth where he was seated. His head was down and his left hand was on the table, clenched into a fist.

Mathilda was somewhat startled but immediately remembered his uniform, voice, and his nasty confrontation with Booker T. She responded without thinking.

"Oh, hello, Officer Duggan. Have you been patrolling my road for vagrants lately?"

"No, ma'am. I got specific orders from Sheriff Bordon to leave your boy alone. I was called on the carpet as one might say. And for your information, I do have the authority to check out any suspicious goings on, even on your private road."

He was looking at her as though accusing her of reporting the incident and getting him in trouble.

"Oh?" Mattie said, a little surprised. She knew she didn't report the transgression, but remembered the Mister heard everything.

"I see that you carry some weight in this little burg. I'm sorry I didn't know about it."

Mathilda thought he was way too young to be so angry and have such deep scorn in his voice. *To be that angry he must be very unhappy.*

"You really didn't need to know anything, except to treat people with dignity, and you seemed to think you could harass the boy. Did it make you feel big?"

The cop didn't respond, so Mathilda took a seat in the next booth, ordered hot tea from the waitress, opened her new book, and settled in to read until Harriet returned.

When Emma brought the tea bags and the little silver tea kettle full of hot water, she set the cup and saucer on the colorful red and white placemat. "Is this the cop that gave Booker T. a hard time?" she asked turning her head to glance in his direction. She deliberately spoke loud enough for him to hear.

"Yes, it is, but he made a very unfortunate judgement and it probably will never ever happen again."

"Yeah, I think he did. The old timers, including Mrs. Maxine and her Mister, were very bothered about it and after Sunday morning church, it was discussed thoroughly, right here."

As she spoke, the cop gulped down the last of his coffee and extinguished his cigarette. He stood and was ready to leave, his face flushed with more hot ire. After he paid his bill and left, Emma brought a freshly baked Danish from the kitchen. She knew Mathilda would enjoy it, but mainly wanted to continue her conversation and let her know how the community was reacting to all the changes.

"He comes in every day—thinks he's God's gift to this little town. The other day he was yelling at the little kids who were waiting for the rides Jesse was giving the children, just because they were excited and yelling about who was next. Things are a-changing here, and the old timers don't like it one bit!"

The wonderful odor of the Danish wafting up brought bittersweet memories to Mathilda. Looking around at all the tables, she remembered exactly where she and Crow sat when they had breakfast after church so long ago. It was after her Henry's passing. Now she could see clearly in her mind's eye how terribly disturbed Crow was when he saw Baggs sitting there, eyeing them across the room. *Poor Crow was being so careful of my feelings by not bringing up the subject of marriage too soon. But not that Bruno Baggs; he had the audacity to disrupt our breakfast, wanting an answer to his dumb proposal.*

Henry's familiar voice suddenly intruded upon her old memories as he greeted Emma. The waitress was now behind the cash register at the front door.

"Hi Henry," Mathilda called over as he was about to take a seat elsewhere.

"Oh my goodness, Aunt Mattie, is that you? How are you and what are you doing here?" He grabbed both her hands in greeting and sat down across from her.

"Just a cup of coffee with cream," he called over to Emma. Mathilda set her book face down so she could give her complete attention to Henry.

"I came to show Harriet the farms and as far as I can see, everything about the housing and roads look beautiful."

"They are, and I knew you'd be very pleased. So where is Harriet?"

"She's taking a walk. She'll be back in a little while."

"I'm so sorry I couldn't get over to see you after the party for the boys, but not having been home for so long, I had to help with my own brood. Kats has been out of sorts with me since I quit the seminary, and now I'm getting the cold shoulder—she's decidedly sore at me."

"I can understand that. Can't you?"

"Yeah, I've been gone for too long. And Aunt Mattie...I think I'm in serious trouble...more than you know."

"I wouldn't doubt it. My sister tells me that she can hear Catherine cry every night, but of course during the day,s she puts up a brave front for the children. By the way, Henry, thanks for standing up for me when Douglas showed up."

"You're welcome, Auntie, I just hope that your friend Harriet didn't fall for his smooth talk as I did, and you too."

"Yes, she did, but I couldn't break her heart by telling her how he deceived us all, trying to get his hands on your inheritance."

"Don't you think we...you should tell her?"

"I only cautioned her to be careful and check everything with a fine-tooth comb. Maybe he's changed after the car accident—he seemed confused...like his memory was affected."

"Do you think she will? She knows something is not right about him."

"She's young but very wise, having gone through other hurts. She'll do what is best for her without my telling her what that should be. Well, how is your ministry doing, Henry?"

"Oh, it's doing well. You know, Auntie, when I see people getting saved and healed, their joy is contagious. I get so high that many nights I just can't sleep."

"I can understand that, because I felt it when I was healed...but what about your schooling?"

"That seminary didn't want me to be involved with the healing ministry. They said I had to choose, school or healing. And they said it may not be of God and would divide my attention, taking me away from my studies. Aunt Mattie, how could God's healing people ever be wrong?"

Mathilda's brow wrinkled, with a trying-to-understand look.

"I don't know the answer to that question, Henry, but you left the school because of that?"

"Yes."

"But you could have put the ministry on hold until you got your degree—your training. What did Catherine say?"

"She was—is angry—really angry at me because that's why I went there and paid all that tuition. It wasn't my money and I'll have to pay it back to you."

"You know what?"

"What, Aunt Mattie?"

"Well, if you're bound and determined to continue there in Chicago, I may be able to help you and Catherine."

"How, Auntie? You always have great ideas, but this is so different."

"Well, I have this house in Beverly Hills and maybe, if Catherine would agree, she and the children could move there with you. It's a very nice, quiet neighborhood. You and she would be together, and you would have a place to stay every night, and the children would see their father. You could continue your work, and maybe at times, Catherine and the kids could go with you to the services and maybe she would become interested in what God is doing, too."

"Umm," Henry said under his breath.

"You know she and the children need Him as much as all those other people?"

"Uh," Henry continued mulling the thought over in his mind. "Do you think she would want to?" he asked, almost hesitantly, his voice dropping off to a whisper

"I think your family is starving while you're feeding strangers. Henry, don't let this—this confusion come between the two of you. That can't be what God wants and I believe it's absolutely wrong."

She could tell that Henry was thinking about her offer; it certainly seemed that way. And then, he finally responded with the truth.

CHAPTER EIGHTY-THREE

"Auntie...there's a girl...a woman who ministers with me. We hear the same things from God. We work together as a team. It seems we're meant to work together and I don't know how that would change if Catherine was there with us, maybe she would be a—a—uh—" Mathilda cut in.

"Henry, if what I'm hearing is correct about this girl—this woman—you must run away from such an entanglement. Run fast and save your marriage! There are three children needing you and that's where your loyalty should be. Remember your marriage vows and remember that sweet love you had for Catherine. It always showed in your eyes."

"I can't just drop her, can I? I can't just drop God's work?"

"Dropping your wife and family can't be what God wants, can't you see that? I don't know much about your ministry, but that much I do know!"

"I didn't think of it that way," Henry said as he dropped his head. "I'm so mixed up, I'll have to let you know about the house and Catherine, but thanks for your offer." Henry stood. He wanted to leave as fast as he could because the heat of his conscience was rushing to his head making him feel dizzy.

And then, a clear, concise thought came to Mathilda, an uncomfortable pain coursing toward her heart; she was so very sorry she made it possible for this young man to go to the seminary. She could see that she made it too easy for him by providing the time and money. *Maybe this is the time to tell him the truth about what she suspected when she met his brothers—about his real parentage. I have to tell him.* Quickly she seized the opportunity and said. "There is something else, Henry."

"What more is there? What else could there be?" he asked as he stood up, now feeling raw annoyance. He was impatient to leave because he said too much; his guilt was fully galvanized for Aunt Mattie to see. Worst of all, he didn't mean to tell anyone.

"Do you ever think about your brothers?" Mattie spoke softly and up until this moment, she didn't have any idea she would say a word to Henry about what she had been thinking.

"What do you mean, think about my brothers?"

"Just what I said. Do you ever think about your full brothers?"

"Full brothers? You mean that you think...I'm not the son of Henry Millering and that I'm not even illegitimate?"

"You must have thought of it. If you look in a mirror, you can't help but see the truth because to me you look more and more like Bruno Baggs and your brothers."

"Well, yes I do think of it, but always push it away, because I don't want to know. It can't be true, can it? My mother wouldn't have lied about something so important, would she?"

"I think it is true. I don't think she could stand the abuse any longer, so she took advantage of the situation. Now, I think you should try to find the aunt you had lived with as a youngster, and then, your grandparents on both sides. Don't you think it's time they meet you and their great-grandchildren?"

"But they didn't want me! They never wanted me and I don't know whether I want to go through all that hurt again."

"Now you're sounding like a spoiled child—like Dudley just a few years ago. Grow up, Henry! They were shocked and hurt when their daughter died at the hands of that lunatic minister. They must have felt as though they were abandoned by God when such a tragic thing happened to their daughter. You're their grandson and you don't have an illegitimate bone in your whole body. And you know, Henry, someday, there will be a way to prove that beyond any doubt."

"But, if I'm not a real flesh and blood Henry Millering, what about us? I love you, Aunt Mattie," Henry whispered, holding back his emotions so the other diners wouldn't see his distress. He slipped back into the booth, eyes cast downward.

"Nothing can change our feelings for each other, Henry. No one can take away the love I have for you or the joy you brought into my life and I can guarantee that nothing will change." Henry found himself immobile and speechless.

"Henry, in life we don't have many choices—for instance we can't say when we want to be born or when we want to die. But, we do have a choice in how we conduct ourselves while we live. Whether we are honest, true, and trustworthy in the things we do will determine what our life will be, now and hereafter."

After hearing Auntie's words and really understanding how he hurt Catherine, Henry's self-recrimination began with unintended tears forming while murmuring—barely audible across the table.

"I know. I know Auntie, but I can still..." He felt his throat constrict and couldn't finish. He rose quickly walking out in great haste, almost bumping into the lady who was heading for Mathilda's table. Shoulders humped, and so wrapped in emotion, he didn't notice it was Harriet.

"Thanks for lending me so many of your books," Mathilda said as a smiling Harriet took the seat Henry vacated.

"I've finished the ones you gave me by Steinbeck and my, there is so much that we can discuss, but I wondered if you ever read anything by Pearl Buck—*The Good Earth or Sons*?"

Even before Harriet answered, Mathilda could see by Harriet's new carefree attitude that her walk was productive. She had arrived at a decision she was comfortable with, one she could live with. Mathilda hoped she would share it.

"Yes, I have read many of Pearl Buck's books, but here, let's see what you're reading now," Harriet said when she turned the book over that was lying on the table, face down.

"It's by Steinbeck too. The lady at the bookstore said they made a movie about it."

"Oh my, Mattie, have you read any of this, yet?" she asked as she looked at the title, opened the book and thumbed through the pages.

"Not yet. Henry just left and I didn't get a chance to begin."

"Well, you may not want to read it. You know, in some places like California, that book is blacklisted and I believe it may be banned."

"Have you read it?" Mathilda asked, not knowing what a blacklisted and banned book meant.

"Yes I did, and I'll just say this; keep an open mind if and when you do read it, I don't think you'll like it. Mattie, you really should return it, get your money back."

Mathilda quickly changed the subject.

"How did you like the housing?"

"You know, Mattie, I wouldn't mind living in one of those little houses. But maybe I would be like Booker T. and the community wouldn't be very welcoming."

Mattie didn't know how to answer her friend, but understood the pain of rejection very well.

"I was thinking the same thing. I mean, about living here. In fact, I have three lots saved, those closest to the road going back toward the orphanage. My little mansion is much too big for me right now and I've been thinking of moving back home, here in Mayetteville, and, Harriet, I would certainly welcome you. You surely know that."

* * *

The next day, Thomas and Mathilda drove Harriet to Chicago, spending another whole day packing the last of Mathilda's personal things at her Beverly Hills house. She especially wanted to bring back those white dishes that Tommy had bought when they were searching for Dudley: twelve plates, twelve cups and saucers, twelve soup bowls, twelve salad plates, the salt and pepper shakers, a butter dish and a gravy boat!

"I'm impressed, Mattie. Not one dish has even the tiniest chip of any kind!" Thomas said. Silently he thought, *I hope it's the very last time I have to carry these dishes.* But he would never say it aloud.

CHAPTER EIGHTY-FOUR

Thomas Bealer was leisurely reading the Sunday paper in the living room, when someone struck Mathilda's front door knocker two times. She was still upstairs so he set his paper aside to answer the door.

"Yes, may I help you?" he asked as he opened the door to find a young lady and a little blond boy. She was probably in her late twenties with long dark hair, and was dressed in a muted pink suit with a matching hat and white gloves. The youngster was a thin, slight little guy, maybe six or seven years old. He wore a dark suit with a blue shirt and tie.

"Yes, I'm looking for a woman by the name of Mattie at this address. Does she still live here?"

"Yes, she does. Please come inside and I'll call her."

The lady and the boy entered the porch area and then followed through the inner glass doors and into the foyer of the house.

Mathilda heard her name as she was about to descend the stairs even before Thomas had a chance to call her.

"Hello, I'm Mattie," she said, as she swooshed into the room with electric energy and a wide smile, happiness emanating from her. "Did you wish to see me?" she asked, greeting the lady while the boy looked up at Mathilda with big saucer eyes.

"Yes, I have your name on this little card. I believe you left it at the shop in Chicago a few months ago."

Mathilda immediately recognized the card she had filled out for Mr. Kempler. A swift feeling of both—surprise and apprehension went through her at the same time.

"I'm Jane Winston, and this is my son, Billy."

"Hello Mrs. Winston. Hello Billy. Please come into the living room and have a seat," Mathilda said, trying hard to hide the mixed emotions sweeping over her.

"I'll let you ladies talk while I finish my reading," Thomas said, as he returned to his chair, hiding his head behind the Sunday news. He didn't want to disturb them but could hear everything.

Before taking a seat, Jane Winston's eyes made one grand sweep of the room, observing the baby grand sitting in front of the window along with the comfortable furniture that filled the room. The little boy walked over to the piano and placed his index finger on one of the keys. He did not strike it.

"My, what a lovely home you have."

"Thank you, my dear."

And then Jane looked directly into Mathilda's eyes. She was candid, having only one thing on her mind.

"I came because of the box. The man, a Mr. Kempler, said that maybe you would sell it back to me? Mother couldn't get back to the shop because of ill health, and I guess it was you who bought the box before she could retrieve it. She shouldn't have left it there to begin with."

"I'm so sorry. Is she all-right, now?"

"She's doing better. But you see, my father lovingly made it for her years ago and now we both feel that we lost our one tie to the man we loved dearly."

The boy then sat down close to his mother, folding his hands in his lap. Thomas was observing him all the while, even with his head behind the paper. *This little fellow would really like to play the piano,* he thought to himself.

"Ah, then the box was actually carved by your father?" Mathilda said, acting as though she didn't know a thing about it.

At this, Thomas looked up from his paper with a surprised expression and then glanced at Mattie, but he didn't utter a sound.

"Yes, it was a treasure for her. My father was very talented."

"Do you mind my asking what your father was like, because he must have been a wonderful man for you to have come so far to get the little memento."

"Well, he was mostly on the road, but when he did come home, he was so very happy. And we were happy, too. He'd take us to the movies, nice places to eat and long walks in the country. My mother and he would talk a lot—and laugh a lot too. She always called him her, Henny."

"She called him Henny?" Mattie repeated the name that sounded foreign to her ear.

"Yes, it was kind of endearing name for Henry, something that only the two of them knew about and laughed about. That was my father's real name. He knew so many people and had friends every-where, some living outside Joliet, just west of Chicago. One of the families had a huge farm and grew wheat and corn. They also grew vegetables for the surrounding grocery stores. Often, we would pack a huge lunch and eat by the little stream that went though their property. We stayed all day and would fish for dinner, but it was funny because we caught really small fish. Not big enough to fry, but it didn't matter. We threw them back and laughed about how we could starve depending only on our fishing skills."

"It sounds wonderful. Your daddy must have loved you both very much."

"He did, and then sometimes he would hook up my horse to a little cart he made from old wood they had at the farm. I could drive Lil Peaches anywhere I wanted on that farm, as long as I stayed on the paths they had marked."

"Did you go to the farm often. I mean even when your daddy wasn't home?"

"Oh yes, Mother would drive me and my best friend Becky out there during the hot summers. That farmer took real good care of Peaches and he liked when we came to visit. Anyway, then about eight years ago, my father didn't come home anymore. We tried... but just couldn't find out what happened to him."

"I'm so sorry, Jane," Mathilda said, while the little boy snuggled even closer to his mother. "What was the name of the farm that you visited?"

"You mean the one where they kept Lil Peaches?"

"Yes, the people who live in Joliet."

"Oh that was the Sullavan Farm. They were really nice and had a little girl, Mary, about the same age as I. We played together a lot when we were little. She's married now, too."

"That was so nice of your daddy. I mean to get you a horse and cart." Mathilda said this while suddenly thinking of how her own Lil Peaches died, giving her life to get help for the person she loved. It happened when that old Mr. Baggs wanted to have his way with Mathilda and chased Jesse and the hands away, driving that cart full speed. Lil Peaches' heart was already too old for such a trek. But, now for a split second Mathilda forgot that she promised herself she would never think of that episode in her life again. After all, she had forgiven Mr. Baggs, and that was the end of that!

And then the girl said quite abruptly, cutting into Mathilda's thoughts. "I must be going now. The reason I came is because I would like to buy back the box. I can pay you double if you like, because of all your trouble."

"I can see it means a lot to you."

"It means everything to me. I only wish we could find out what happened to my father," Jane said wistfully.

"I'll get it—it's in the other room. Please excuse me for just one minute."

Thomas continued reading, turning the pages every now and then with his head still hidden. He didn't want to talk or put his two cents into something he knew was breaking Mattie's heart.

It was true. Mathilda's insides were swimming and churning by all she heard, but she was also sad for this girl, who came so far for the box, the beautiful little box that exposed Henry's secret life to Mathilda.

Should I give her my old heartache too? Mathilda asked herself as she lingered in the kitchen, trying to decide if she should say something about her dead husband Henry—now Elaine's Henny! She placed the carved box on the table, staring at the thing that was so full of deceit—treasured years that she thought belonged to her, vanished forever now that she knew without a doubt, that her Henry had another he cherished even more. Mathilda knew she was deceiving this young woman too, by not telling that she—Jane and little Billy were the heirs Henry always wanted—but she couldn't bring herself to tell. In fact, she knew she would never-ever tell. Henry finally had his way—had what his selfish heart wanted at any cost to others. How many more were out there...crying? How many had an inherited right to his Wheatland wealth—her wealth?

She closed her eyes, and could see Henry after the minister pronounced them man and wife on her sixteenth birthday. As she lovingly looked up into his young smiling face, she could still hear his words as clear as if he were speaking them audibly into her ear at that very moment.

"You're so beautiful, Tillie, and you're a delight to my eyes. I'm a lucky man!" And then he kissed her waiting lips.

Splashing her face with cold water at the sink and gently drying her tears so no one could tell she had been crying, Mattie walked back into the living room with her head held high.

The little boy was standing before the piano, touching the different keys and making soft sounds.

"Can I play, please?" he asked. "I take lessons."

"Of course, play something for me," Mathilda said as she sat down holding the box on her lap while looking closely at the child's face, realizing that this boy—this little Billy was Henry's own grandson.

The boy sat down at the piano, adjusted the seat and played a piece written by Chopin. It was one that Dudley played, the simplified version of the, *Polonaise Waltz*. Billy played it splendidly and they all clapped...even Tommy set his paper aside and joined in.

"Thank you, ma'am. It plays real nice. We have a big piano at home, but it goes up, not long."

Dudley always described baby grands the very same way. It must be something children notice most, she thought. Aloud, she said, "It must be an upright, but they all play the same, don't they?" Mathilda said, remembering how Mr. Anthony explained it to Dudley at the Conservatory. "You play very nicely, Billy."

"I like the sound of your piano better."

Billy's mother beamed at her son's sharp observation.

"Come, sit here next to me," she said to the boy while patting the davenport.

Mathilda held the carved box in her hands.

"Here it is, my dear. Is this the box you're looking for?" she asked as she handed it to the lady.

"Oh, yes. It's the very one." Reaching out, Jane received it into her hands delicately, as though she received a gift worthy of adoration and reverence. As she slowly lifted the cover, she delightedly said, "see, it has a carving of my Lil Peaches!"

"Look, Mama," the boy said. "It is Peaches! Oh, mama, Grandma will be so happy."

"There's a little tab—right there," Mathilda said, as she pointed it out. The minute she spoke those words, Jane felt for it with her index finger and pulled it up, exposing the white envelope.

"Oh my!" she cried as she picked it up with her shaking hand. "Neither my mother nor I knew the bottom came up!"

Holding the envelope, she turned it over several times, noticing her mother's name and that it was still sealed.

"I dare not open it…how wonderful. I'll give it to mother as soon as I get home. Thank you so much. Now, how much do I owe you for all your trouble?" she asked, opening her purse.

"Take it…it's yours."

"You mean take it for nothing?"

"Yes, just take it and remember your daddy kindly. And Mrs. Winston—Jane—sometimes it's better to let the past go and just try to enjoy each moment with your family and wonderful memories."

"Thank you, but Mother and I will never stop searching for my father. Are you sure I can't pay you something?"

"No, nothing. By the way, what kind of work did your daddy do? I believe you mentioned that he was gone so much of the time."

"He was in import sales—selling china, clocks and little trinkets. He sold to shops all over the United States, but he imported from different countries—mostly from China. Sometimes he would bring me lots of wind-up toys. Little tin people and animals that danced around. We would sit at the table all evening, making them all go at once and laughing hilariously."

"Well, my dear, God bless you and you too, Billy."

Little Billy wanted to tell Mathilda something, so he softly touched her sleeve to get her attention.

"My whole name is William Henry Winston. The William is for my daddy and the Henry is for my grandpa but everybody calls me Billy and I know where I live too…in Palos Park, Illinois…and I go to school there. I'm in the second grade and I know how to read and play the piano."

"I see that you're a very bright boy, Billy Winston."

"I know. Grandma always tells me that."

Jane believed it was a good visit, better than she hoped for, but it was time to be on their way. Thomas, with his arm gently around Mattie's shoulder, led the way to the outside porch. And then, Jane turned and asked, "what did you say your last name was? On the card it didn't have one—it only said Mattie with this address."

Mattie cleared her throat. "It's Mattie Bealer, dear, and this is my husband, Thomas Bealer."

"Thank you, Mr. and Mrs. Bealer. I can't even begin to tell you how much I appreciate your kindness."

And then, Jane and little Billy crossed the street to their car and drove away as Tommy and Mattie watched from the porch windows. Tommy gently turned Mattie around, gathering her into his arms, hugging her close. When she looked up, she saw those deep blue eyes shining, reminding her again of times long ago—when they were only six and eight years old, spending long summer hours catching frogs, talking, chasing, and playing beside the pond, behind the old barn.

"Darling, let's go home, you know, really home. We can build a little house on those acres you saved and watch the golden wheat as we grow old together.

"Oh, Tommy...yes I would love to go back home to Wheatlander and have a pretty little garden with flowers and—"

Then as he still held her, he whispered, "and to think I almost lost you by my foolish actions!"

"But I could never lose you...because I carry you in my heart-room...ever since we were little kids."

"Please throw that key away so I can never-ever-leave," Tommy groaned as he placed little kisses here and there over her whole face.

"I already did," she whispered in Tommy's ear.

THE END

Dear Readers,

Mathilda—Mattie carried forward the love and values ingrained in her heart by helping those in need. Perhaps we all could gently touch other lives daily, and just as roots grow and spread, unseen and hardly noticed, the fruit is passed along as the years progress.

It's true Mattie had the means to bless others but if we don't have those means, forgiveness and love, are truly enough.

Glorianna
gloriannaserbin@gmail.com

This book is a continuation of Wheatlander the Secret. Order it today, and you will discover how the characters grew into their deep relationships with each other. I know you will enjoy the beginnings of this "family".

Discussion Questions
and a little soul-searching...

1. *Could you or would you pay the price that Mattie paid? Was it worth it for her?*
2. *Do you think giving to those in need so unselfishly would help them along in their future lives?*
3. *As a nation, have we grown since the 1950's in our treatment of Negroes, women and other minority groups?*
4. *How did you feel when I used historically accurate derogatory words for Booker T.?*
5. *What did you think of the scene in which Booker T. received his high school diploma and what did it reveal about the values Mathilda instilled in this young man?*
6. *In your opinion, what is family?*
7. *Is there really a cost for everything of value?*

I'd love to hear any thoughts about the book from you... please email me at

gloriannaserbin@gmail.com

Proof

Made in the USA
Charleston, SC
29 November 2016